"*My Roommate Is a Vampire* by Jenna Levine is like your favorite red wine—familiar, tasty, and will definitely have you kissing hot strange vampires by the end of the night. Bloody delightful!"

—Ashley Poston, *New York Times* bestselling author of
The Dead Romantics

"This debut romance by Jenna Levine is wonderfully weird and sexy as hell. The amount of care Frederick J. Fitzwilliam takes in figuring out what will get Cassie's blood pumping! (Not like *that*.) It's almost enough to make you want to scour Craigslist for your own potential boyfriend, who'll be head over fangs for you. *My Roommate Is a Vampire* is a whole vibe."

—Alicia Thompson, *USA Today* bestselling author of
Love in the Time of Serial Killers

"Jenna Levine's sensational debut has everything I want in a rom-com—delightfully wry humour, a warm heart, and an utterly adorable romance with the most dreamy hero ever to don a cravat. *My Roommate Is a Vampire* is altogether a kooky, sparkly piece of happiness."

—India Holton, national bestselling author of
The League of Gentlewomen Witches

"Sweet, cozy romance that isn't scary or spooky but just very charming." —*Town & Country*

"A wonderful and entertaining paranormal romance that begs for a sequel." —New York Journal of Books

"Levine clearly had fun writing this lighthearted and memorable addition to the paranormal-romance genre, and lucky us, she invites readers along for the ride." —Washington Independent Review of Books

"This humorous debut from Levine is perfect for readers who enjoy the roommates-to-romance trope and a dash of sexy vampire." —*Library Journal* (starred review)

"From the dryly witty notes Cassie and Frederick leave for each other to the cast of quirky and endearing secondary characters, everything about this sneaky, sweet, otherworldly rom-com is a delight." —*Booklist* (starred review)

"This adorable odd couple proves easy to root for, with Frederick's awkwardness navigating modern life adding both humor and pathos. . . . This one is good to the last drop." —*Publishers Weekly*

Berkley Romance titles by Jenna Levine

MY ROOMMATE IS A VAMPIRE

MY VAMPIRE PLUS-ONE

MY VAMPIRE

PLUS-ONE

JENNA LEVINE

BERKLEY ROMANCE
New York

BERKLEY ROMANCE
Published by Berkley
An imprint of Penguin Random House LLC
penguinrandomhouse.com

Library of Congress Cataloging-in-Publication Data

Names: Levine, Jenna, author.
Title: My vampire plus-one / Jenna Levine.
Description: First edition. | New York: Berkley Romance, 2024.
Identifiers: LCCN 2024014174 (print) | LCCN 2024014175 (ebook) |
ISBN 9780593548936 (trade paperback) | ISBN 9780593548943 (ebook)
Subjects: LCGFT: Romance fiction. | Fantasy fiction. | Novels.
Classification: LCC PS3612.E92389 M98 2024 (print) |
LCC PS3612.E92389 (ebook) | DDC 813/.6—dc23/20240329
LC record available at https://lccn.loc.gov/2024014174
LC ebook record available at https://lccn.loc.gov/2024014175

First Edition: September 2024

Printed in the United States of America
1st Printing

Book design by Daniel Brount

For the Chaos Muppets

ONE

*Bright red Comic Sans text found
on an old GeoCities website*

SHOULD ANY INFORMATION ABOUT THIS:

CRIMINAL
EVIL VAMPIRE MASTERMIND
TERRIBLE GUY
COME TO LIGHT

PLEASE EMAIL THE COLLECTIVE IMMEDIATELY AT
THECOLLECTIVE_1876@HOTMAIL.COM

AMELIA

MY FRIENDS AND FAMILY HAD ENJOYED TEASING ME WITH
the adage *the only sure things in life are death and taxes* ever since
I became an accountant.

After hearing it for the hundredth time, though, it stopped being funny. For me—a single, thirty-four-year-old CPA a year away from making partner at a big accounting firm—the only *real* sure things in life were an intractable caffeine addiction every tax season, and my mostly well-intentioned family giving me grief over my life choices.

Most people didn't understand that I loved my job. I loved the way the Internal Revenue Code made careful sense, and how it always gave you the right answer as long as you knew what questions to ask. Tax work was complex, but it was also neat, orderly, and consistent in a way the rest of life seldom was.

Most of all, though, I loved that I was good at what I did. It was hard to beat the high that came with knowing that very few people could do my job as well as I could.

But the night my world turned upside down, I was questioning my life choices for the first time in recent memory. It was the middle of tax season, which was always my most brutal time of year, but this year it was worse than usual. Mostly because of one absolute nightmare of a client.

The Wyatt Foundation had the biggest budget of any organization I'd ever worked with. In a show of confidence from Evelyn Anderson, the Butyl & Dowidge partner I reported to most frequently, I was handling this file solo. That was the good news. The bad news was within hours of getting the file it was obvious Wyatt was the least organized client I'd ever had.

The Wyatt Foundation was, to use a word you wouldn't find anywhere in the Internal Revenue Code, a shitshow. Its board seemed to have no idea how to run a nonprofit, and its chief financial officer seemed incapable of following simple directions. He'd been sending me new documents daily, some of which were from years I'd already told him the IRS didn't care about, and many of which were impossible to reconcile with other statements they'd sent.

I had less than three weeks to wrap everything up and get Wyatt's filing to the IRS. To say nothing of all my other files that were languishing from inattention.

I was good at working hard. But even though I was an accountant, I was still *human*. And I was nearing the breaking point.

I missed dancing around my Lakeview apartment to Taylor Swift. I missed spending time with Gracie, my temperamental cat. Above all, I missed my bed. Especially the way I used to spend at least seven hours in it every night.

I'd left my apartment at the crack of dawn that morning so I'd have a chance of getting on top of my other work before Wyatt's daily missives arrived. I had been focusing for so long on my Excel spreadsheet that when my phone buzzed with a series of texts, I nearly jumped out of my chair.

I fumbled through my briefcase until I found my phone, then reached for my glasses and slid them on. I'd taken them off hours ago; staring at my computer for too long made my vision blur. I needed to visit an optometrist, but that would have to wait until after tax season. Just like all the other forms of self-care I'd been putting off.

I smiled when I saw the texts were from my best friend, Sophie. She'd been dropping by my apartment every night the past two weeks to feed Gracie and take in my mail while I was working inhuman hours.

SOPHIE: Queen Gracie is fed and your mail is in its usual spot on the counter

SOPHIE: Also, Gracie asked me to ask you
if you are coming home soon

SOPHIE: In cat language of course

SOPHIE: She's worried you're working too
hard

I smiled. Sophie was so good to me. I glanced at the time and
saw it was already six-thirty.

Shit.

If I didn't want to be late for my monthly dinner with my family, I needed to leave the office in the next ten minutes. And I was
nowhere near finished with what I'd hoped to get done that day.

AMELIA: I'm actually meeting my family
for dinner tonight

AMELIA: Could you apologize to Gracie
for me?

SOPHIE: I mean I'm sure she'll forgive you

SOPHIE: She's a cat

SOPHIE: But I'm not a cat and I'm worried
about how late you've been working

SOPHIE: You okay?

Not really, I thought. But I wasn't going to dump how stressed
I was on Sophie. In addition to being a mom to twin toddlers, her
attorney husband had been in San Francisco the past three weeks

for depositions. She was no stranger to ridiculous demands on her time; she didn't need to hear me complain about mine.

> **AMELIA:** I'm fine. Just busy.

> **AMELIA:** Tell Gracie I hope to be home by 9:30

> **AMELIA:** Please give her scritches for me and tell her I'm sorry

> **SOPHIE:** Will you be having dinner someplace where you actually can eat something this time?

> **AMELIA:** It's an Italian restaurant this time so hopefully

I'd been a pescatarian since college, and a lactose intolerance that cropped up when I was in grad school meant I was off dairy. Ever since my brother Adam's twins were born eight years ago, though, my dietary needs were usually an afterthought at best when it came to family get-togethers. Because Adam's kids were young, only casual restaurants with a children's menu and a high level of background noise were options. And Dad liked red meat too much to take us anywhere that didn't offer it.

It was fine, though. I was the only one in our family who was single. And I didn't have kids. In the interest of being accommodating, I usually just went along with whatever the group wanted when we got together. Maybe it was the middle child in me, but making as few waves as possible had been my modus operandi for as long as I could remember. Sometimes I'd get lucky and my parents would pick an Italian restaurant with at least a few cheese-and-meat-free pasta options—like tonight. If I wasn't lucky, I'd have to wait until I got home to eat dinner.

As if on cue, my stomach chose that moment to do a comically loud rumble.

SOPHIE: Well I picked up some Chinese for the kids. They're getting fussy so I'm about to take them home, but I'll leave the leftover veggie lo mein for you in your fridge.

AMELIA: You're the literal best, Soph

AMELIA: When does Marcus get back from San Francisco?

SOPHIE: His last deposition is Thursday

SOPHIE: So he'll be back Friday

SOPHIE: In THEORY

AMELIA: You should have him on diaper duty for at least a week straight when he gets back

SOPHIE: Oh, I'm demanding a full month

I smiled at my phone, feeling grateful. Hopefully Sophie would be able to take time for herself again once Marcus was finally back home. She was so giving to others, me included. She deserved to receive occasionally, too.

> **AMELIA:** Thanks Soph
>
> **AMELIA:** You're the best
>
> **AMELIA:** When tax season is over, I'm treating you to a fancy dinner and I'm not taking no for an answer

Dinner would likely go until nine, and I didn't think I'd have the energy to go back to the office afterwards. I stuffed Wyatt's latest paperwork into my briefcase, promising myself I'd finish reviewing it at home.

The thirty-second floor was still a hive of activity as I made my way to the elevator. I tried not to let the guilt over leaving at an hour some of the partners might consider *early* wash over me.

Because if I stayed late tonight, I'd be bailing on my family. And a guilt of an entirely different kind would ruin my evening.

....

MY BUILDING'S HVAC SYSTEM RAN NONSTOP, BUT IT WAS always chilly in the lobby during the winter on account of the giant floor-to-ceiling windows. That night was no exception. Even still, it looked much colder outside. On the other side of my building's revolving glass doors, pedestrians were hunched slightly forward in the distinctive way of people trying to get to where they were going in unpleasant weather. The kind of early spring cold snap that always made me wonder why the hell my great-great-grandparents hadn't settled in California instead of Chicago when they came to the United States had rolled through two days earlier. A couple inches of snow had been packed down by foot traffic over the past few days into an icy crust on the sidewalks.

I pulled my black puffer jacket a little more tightly around my body and fished out the thin leather gloves I kept permanently stashed in its pockets. The El stop was only a few blocks away; even if it was as cold outside as it looked, I could handle it for a few blocks.

Bracing myself, I walked into the only revolving door still unlocked at that hour, and hurried outside into the brisk night air—

And was so preoccupied with guilty thoughts of the work I wasn't finishing, and of how I'd probably be late for family dinner, *again*, and of how I'd have to make it up to Sophie for bringing me lo mein despite my being a totally absent friend the past few weeks, that I didn't see the guy in the black fedora and bright blue trench coat literally sprinting down the sidewalk until he plowed into me.

"*What*—!"

The impact when we collided made me drop everything I'd been carrying. My briefcase, the gloves I'd been about to put on, the stress I'd been carrying all day like a lead ball in the pit of my stomach—it all fell to the icy sidewalk. The paperwork I'd stuffed into my briefcase just minutes ago spilled out of it on impact, landing in a puddle of icy slush.

I glared at the guy who'd just run into me.

"What the hell!" I snapped.

"Sorry." The guy's fedora was pulled down so low over his face, it covered most of it, and despite what he'd just said, he didn't *sound* sorry. He sounded distracted, and his body looked coiled for action, like he was milliseconds away from running off in the direction he'd been heading when he slammed into me.

"I doubt you're sorry," I muttered.

The guy glanced down at my feet where my things lay, and seemed to realize, for the first time, that he'd made me drop everything. The slush puddle had made quick work of the Wyatt financial reports; everything was wet now and would be impossible to read. I'd have to go back to the office and print it all out again, which I really did not have time for.

And—oh god, what if my laptop had cracked when it hit the ground? I quickly scooped up my bag and shuffled through it to make sure my MacBook was okay. Fortunately, it seemed fine.

"I *am* sorry," the guy said again. "But—look. Since you've kept me from where I was heading for nearly an entire minute now, can you do me a favor?"

The gall of this guy. He could have broken my computer! "*You're* asking *me* for a favor?" I was about to tell him exactly where he could stick his *favors*—

But then he tilted his head to the right at the same time he pushed his fedora a little farther back on his head, and I got my first real look at him.

The words died in my throat.

Maybe the stress of too many consecutive late nights in the office was finally getting to me. That must have been it. Or maybe it was just because I hadn't dated anyone casually in over a year, or anyone seriously in more than five. Whatever the reason for it, in that moment, he looked more attractive than he had any right to look, given the circumstances. He was fairly tall, probably about six foot two, but I was no slouch in the height department myself, and because of that—and because of the angle at which he'd been wearing his hat until this moment—it had initially been difficult to see much of his face. But now that I *could* see it . . .

He had high, angular cheekbones. A strong chin that sported at least three days' worth of dark blond stubble. Light-colored eyes that looked, given his fair complexion, as though they might be blue. Though most of his face was still bathed in shadow from his hat, even with its slight repositioning, so it was hard to tell.

I'd always had a thing for blond-haired, blue-eyed guys. A thing that sometimes ended up with me making decisions I'd regret later. Especially when said blond hair and blue eyes came in broad-shouldered, slim-waisted packages.

Like Mr. Fedora Asshole over here.

The fact that I could now see he was wearing a black T-shirt beneath his trench coat that said *Blame Bezos* in bright red letters, as well as a pink gingham skirt that totally clashed with his coat *and* his hat, didn't do anything to dampen my attraction. If anything, it just enhanced the dirtbag Chris Pine look he had going for him.

I closed my eyes and shook my head a little as I tried to get a grip. God, I needed a vacation. The minute tax season was over, I was booking a flight to somewhere warm and sunny.

I tore my eyes from his face. This was ridiculous. *I* was ridiculous. "I am *not* doing you a favor," I somehow managed.

"Please," he implored. The distraction in his voice was gone; in its place was a raw urgency that stunned me. "It won't take long. Please—can you start laughing? As though we are in regular conversation and I am in the process of telling you something very funny?"

I stared at him, reeling from the randomness of the request from this stranger. "I'm sorry, but . . . *what*?"

"I am trying to avoid some people." His tone was pitched low, his words coming very quickly. As though he had limited time to get them out. "I was trying to avoid them when I . . . when we . . ." He gestured expansively between us, and then to the ruined papers at my feet.

"You nearly mowed me down because you're trying to avoid some people?" This was absurd. Though that would explain his mad dash down an icy sidewalk at six-thirty on a Tuesday evening. Concern pricked at me despite my better judgment. Clearly, this guy was more than just passing strange. But what if he was also in some kind of trouble?

As if to validate my concern, he looked over his shoulder, the turn of his head frantic and jerky. When he faced me again, his eyes were bright with what looked like genuine fear. "I'm sorry, I can't explain further. But can you just like . . . laugh? That way, maybe they'll think you and I have been lost in a riveting conversation this whole time, that I am not the man they are looking for, and they will just . . . keep going." He paused, then bit his lip, considering my stunned reaction. "Or I suppose you could kiss me instead."

My jaw dropped. "*Kiss* you?" I was gobsmacked. I didn't kiss strangers. Not ever. Or, okay, not since a particularly rowdy girls' weekend back in 2015. But those had been very different circumstances. Circumstances involving colorful beads and a quantity of alcohol unbefitting a CPA on deadline.

A small part of me, though—probably the part of me that hadn't kissed anyone in about a year and hadn't had sex for what might as well have been an epoch—imagined what it would be like, kissing this bizarre stranger. He was hot, like burning, despite his odd mannerisms. The confident way he stood, his manner of speech, the bold smolder of those bright blue eyes . . .

I bet he'd kiss like the world was ending.

I bet it would be *fantastic.*

He held up his hands in front of him in defense, as though he'd interpreted my stunned silence as outrage. "Or, don't kiss me! That's also fine! You see, this is why I proposed you pretend laugh with me. While fake kissing is a time-honored way to throw pursuers off the trail—and is also fun as *hell*, let's be honest—we don't know each other. And since you seem rather angry with me, I'd assumed you would rather pretend laugh with me than pretend to kiss me."

He spoke so rapidly I could barely keep up. I had the unique sensation of listening to a record player playing music at twice its normal rate of speed. I stared at him, stupefied. Obviously, there was no chance I was going to kiss this guy, despite my moment of temptation. But laughing? When nothing was funny? That seemed almost as absurd. I took a semester of acting in college, but it had been my lowest grade at the University of Chicago. It was true what they said about accountants: most of us didn't have much of a sense of humor; fewer had any acting skills.

"I don't think I can pull off a convincing fake laugh," I admitted.

"Sure you can."

"Not when nothing's funny."

He looked confused. "There's nothing to *pull off.* You just . . . laugh."

His sincerity seemed so genuine that all at once, I knew he was telling me the truth about this bizarre situation. I didn't think I could actually help him, but what did I have to lose by trying besides a few extra precious minutes?

"Fine," I muttered. I took a deep breath and then, a moment later, I did my best attempt at a fake laugh. "Ahahaha*hahaha-haha*!" I cried out, even as I stood rigid as a board with my hands balled up into tight, anxious fists at my sides. "Oh, you are *so funny!*" I added loudly, for good measure. I sounded ridiculous. I hoped none of my coworkers could see or hear me. This was not how someone gunning for a partnership *behaved*.

As I continued fake laughing, the guy just stared at me. "You weren't kidding," he said softly, incredulous. "You really *can't* do this."

I glared at him. "I told you."

"You did," he conceded. And then a moment later, he threw his own head back—and *laughed*.

To anybody passing by, you'd think the man I was standing with had just been told the funniest joke he'd ever heard in his life. His whole body vibrated with it, his hand floating in the air as though to touch me on the shoulder, only for him to snatch it back at the last minute and clutch at his stomach.

Fake it may have been, but this man's laughter was infectious. Before I knew what was happening, I was laughing, too—at him, at the ridiculousness of this entire situation—without him even needing to prompt me. Without pretending. Everything felt light inside, in a way I seldom felt during tax season, and had never in my life felt with a stranger.

After a while, our laughter subsided. A moment of silence passed between us, punctuated only by the ubiquitous sounds of Chicago traffic. The guy looked over his shoulder, in the direction he'd originally come from. Whatever he saw this time, or didn't see, made his posture relax.

"I think they're off my trail for now." He looked at me again. "Thank you. I owe you one." And then, abruptly: "Are you an accountant, Amelia Collins?"

"How . . . how do you know my name? And what I do?" I stammered. A taxi drove by us, leaning on its horn and splattering me with a faint spray of dirty snowmelt. I ignored it and brushed a stray lock of hair out of my face as I tried to get my shit together.

Mr. Fedora Asshole shrugged. "I'm good at spotting accountants." Before I could ask him what he meant by that, one corner of his mouth quirked into something that was half smile, half smirk. I absolutely did *not* notice how full, and soft, his lips looked when he did it.

And then, laughing a little, he inclined his head meaningfully at the pile of papers from my briefcase that still lay in a soggy heap at my feet. I followed the direction of his gaze and immediately felt like a fool.

"The header on that paper says *Wyatt Foundation Tax Filings*," he pointed out, unnecessarily, as a sharp gust of wind made the ends of his trench coat flap around his legs. "The footer says *Amelia Collins*. I don't know much about . . . well. About much. But I do know that words like *tax filings* and *accountant* sort of go hand in hand. And I feel it's reasonable to assume *Amelia Collins* is you."

Damnit, I should *not* have found his voice sexy when he said all that. I couldn't help it. It was a deep voice, rich and smooth, and as sinful as silk sheets. Even when he was accusing me of something as mundane as being an accountant.

"Yeah," I admitted, even more flustered. "That's me."

He flashed me a full smile—there and then gone again, like mist at dawn. I shivered for reasons having nothing to do with the cold night air.

He cleared his throat. "I gotta go. But, since you are correct that this collision was partially my fault—"

I scoffed. "*Partially?*"

He shrugged. "If you'd not been so distracted, you probably

would have seen me coming. But since, yes, I am partly to blame . . ."

He knelt down and scooped up the papers that had fallen from my briefcase. He stood up, then handed them back to me.

They were soaked through now. Useless. I took them from him anyway, the tips of my fingers brushing up against the sides of his hands in the process. He wore no gloves; his hands were like icicles.

It must have been even colder outside than I'd realized.

"Thanks," I said, feeling a little winded.

"You're welcome." He stood up, and brushed off the front of his legs. "Now, I must be off. But do let me know if I can somehow make this up to you, later." He winked at me. "I owe you one."

It was an empty offer, of course. I'd never see him again. I floundered for something to say in response to such an awkward comment from a stranger.

Before I could come up with a reply, he shook his head. "Good luck with wherever it is you were headed in such a distracted rush, Amelia Collins."

Without another word, he turned on his heels and sprinted away.

"What a weirdo," I muttered under my breath. Not much rattled me anymore, but whatever had just happened between me and that guy . . .

Whatever that had been, it had rattled me.

But I didn't have time to think about it. I had the Brown Line to catch, a family dinner to attend, and way too much work to do to waste another second thinking about that peculiar stranger and the giddy way his laughter made me feel.

TWO

Excerpt from The Annals of Vampyric Lore,
Seventeenth Edition

"Index of Notable Vampiric Organizations," pp. 2313–14

THE COLLECTIVE

Original accounts from vampires in the court of William the Great suggest The Collective, *as it is now colloquially known,* first formed in England in the eleventh century A.D. as a social club for dilettante fledglings from powerful vampire families. While The Collective *still serves a social function for current members,* The Collective's *central mission has grown dramatically over the centuries, expanding far beyond its original scope.*

Today, the group is primarily focused on three things. First: celebrating their rarefied lineage (eligibility for membership remains limited to those who can directly trace their bloodlines to the original founding Eight). Second: creating *new vampires. And third: vigilante justice for wrongs that many in the vampire community consider trifles.*

While the vampiric community has historically turned a blind eye to most of The Collective's *antics, it has drawn more criticism in recent years. Some of its more vocal detractors have argued a group so affluent and storied ought to find better things to do with its time.*

REGINALD

I LEANED BACK IN FREDERICK'S LEATHER ARMCHAIR AND reread the The Collective's note. It was crumpled from how frequently I'd gone over it since it arrived at my home four nights ago.

I had to admit that scribbling their threat in what looked like blood but smelled like raspberry syrup was impressive. An admirable commitment to the bit—even if the bit involved wanting to kill me.

"On the one hand," Frederick began, "I'm not surprised these people are furious."

For what felt like the thousandth time in the past four days, I went back over the circumstances that had caused this predicament. "Even if I fucked up—"

"*If?*" Frederick asked, incredulous.

"Okay, fine," I conceded. "I did fuck up. I admit that. Even so, it's hard to understand why they're still this angry with me. It's been a *really* long time."

Frederick got out of his chair and began pacing his living room, hands clasped behind his back. He always did this when he was thinking. Between the two of us, Frederick had always been the more circumspect.

It was part of why he was so annoying—the man couldn't even order dinner from the South Side blood bank without agonizing over his choices for days—and why I knew I couldn't handle this situation without him.

"You're right," he finally said. "It was over a century ago. Even I didn't hold my grudge against you for that long." Frederick stopped pacing to admire a new painting his girlfriend had recently hung up behind the leather sofa. Although, calling it a *painting* was generous. Cassie called herself a *found art artist*. The framed picture Frederick was looking at had McDonald's soda straws and a bunch of other stuff glued to the canvas. *Treasures*, she called them. *Crap* was what it looked like to me.

But there'd be time to criticize Cassie's so-called art later. For now, there was preserving my life to think about.

"I'd have hoped they'd have found something better to worry about over the past hundred and fifty years," I muttered.

Frederick raised an eyebrow. "Like what?"

"Like . . . oh, Hades, I don't know." I shook my head and ran a distracted hand through my hair. "Climate change, maybe."

Frederick shot me a skeptical look.

"No, really," I continued. "Climate change is definitely more important to vampire life in the twenty-first century than a party faux pas from over one hundred years ago that *might* have resulted in slight calamity."

"Slight calamity?" Frederick asked, incredulous.

I didn't blush anymore. I couldn't; the blood stopped flowing when a person turned. But if I *could* blush, I'd probably have been doing it then. "Depending on how you view things, you could even say I'd saved those people's sorry little lives."

I turned away before I could see the face Frederick undoubtedly made at my claim, then crumpled up The Collective's letter and threw it on the floor. I wished Frederick had a fireplace I could throw it into. Watching it catch fire and disintegrate into ash . . . well. I'd never had the opportunity to throw a letter threatening my life into a fire before, but I imagined it must feel really good. But while Frederick was comfortably off, and his home was filled with the kinds of comforts usually only enjoyed by the comfortably off, he didn't have a working fireplace.

And so the stupid letter sat there like the crumpled-up wad of nasty Denny's menu it was rather than bursting into a far more satisfying ball of flames.

"Pick that up," Frederick said. He eyed the thing like it was a dog dropping. "Cassie will be home from work soon."

I snorted. "She's a slob. Why would she care?"

Frederick only glared at me. Frederick's and Cassie's different attitudes towards housekeeping were one of the few bones of contention they had as far as I could tell—though I supposed it was one thing for someone to criticize their *own* human girlfriend for leaving her dirty socks on the kitchen table and something else entirely for your friend to do it.

Especially when you were as utterly smitten with your girlfriend as Frederick was with Cassie. He didn't talk about their future plans often, but I knew he wanted to propose soon.

Bewildering.

I couldn't relate to wanting to become that close to another person. Especially when said person was human, and therefore mortal. I hadn't been able to relate to that sort of feeling in centuries. Not since . . .

Well.

Not *since*.

Love was a good look on my old friend, though. He hardly even brooded anymore. Since Cassie came into his life, sometimes he even *smiled*. I would never tell them this, but I was rooting for them. Even if I didn't really understand what they had.

I held my tongue and capitulated, picking up my death threat and stuffing it into my pocket so I wouldn't have to look at it.

"Thank you," Frederick sniffed.

"Of course. Guess I'll be off, then." I needed to go home and think through how I was going to approach this mess.

"Before you go . . ." Frederick placed a hand on my arm. He looked worried. "Do you think that woman guessed you aren't human?"

I thought back to my encounter with Amelia Collins. Dark blond hair, bright eyes. Tall. Absolutely furious with me. Under different circumstances, she'd have been just my type. I'd known it was a mistake to tell Frederick about her even as the encounter had practically poured out of me the minute I got to his apartment.

The problem was, I'd always had a thing for accountants. Their organized minds were such a delicious contrast to the intentionally erratic way I lived. But there was no time to think about what Amelia Collins might look like when she was laughing for real, or how that warm little hand of hers I'd briefly touched would feel like entwined with my own. I'd never see her again.

More importantly, she was *human*. I had sworn off fucking with anything mortal during the Carter Administration. Though perhaps it would be all right for me to hire her to help me with my taxes, once my current situation was resolved. My finances were a mess. One of the unexpected perks to living forever and having obvious advantages over humans was that money seemed to always find me, no matter how hard I tried to dodge it. I needed an accountant who was good at their job to help me figure out what was going on.

I bet she was good at her job.

I bet she was good at lots of things, even if fake laughing wasn't one of them.

Frederick cleared his throat. He was waiting for an answer. "She . . . didn't have time to notice me," I lied. "I apologized for bumping into her like the gentleman I am, and immediately flew here."

Frederick didn't need to know I was lying. Fortunately, he seemed to take me at face value. He simply nodded, then took a small step back to eye what I was wearing. "You need to start borrowing my clothes. You stick out like a sore thumb dressed like this."

I looked down at my outfit. This T-shirt and pink skirt combo had been my favorite ever since I found it at the consignment store a month ago. Frederick had a point, as much as I didn't like it, but what was the point of living forever if you had to blend in? But even I had to acknowledge that standing out too much right then might get me into trouble.

"I'll miss my band T-shirts," I said, wistfully.

"I know."

"And Old Fuzzy."

Frederick gave a sympathetic nod. Which was nice of him to do; I knew he loathed how I dressed. "Once you no longer need to blend into your surroundings quite so much, you can go back to dressing like a stolen car."

I was looking forward to that.

Hopefully, I'd live long enough to see it.

"Here," he said, pressing something thin and rectangular into my hands. "Cassie wanted me to give you this."

I vaguely recognized it as one of those flowery journal things the chain bookstore downtown sold near the registers. It said *My First Bullet Journal* across the cover in flowing pink script.

"Why did Cassie want me to have a bullet journal?" I asked. Reasonably, I thought.

Frederick put a hand on my shoulder. I stared at it mistrustfully. "You've been under a lot of strain," he said gently. "I also know you don't want to talk with Dr. Leicenster about it—"

"That man is a quack," I cut in.

"A point upon which reasonable minds can differ," he countered. "Cassie—*we*—just think that if you're going through something this difficult, and you don't want to seek professional help, at least you can journal about it and see if organizing your thoughts helps."

I didn't see how writing about my feelings would make me feel better. But I also wasn't in the mood to argue about it. I was tired, I was rattled, and I was hungry.

I just wanted to go home.

"I'll think about it," I lied. The first Little Free Library I saw on my way home would be getting a new donation. "Tell Cassie I said thanks."

THREE

Excerpt from R.C.'s bullet journal,
written in black ballpoint pen

Mission statement: ~~To live each day with courage, compassion, and curiosity. To become a better version of myself each day and inspire others in my path to do the same.~~ (Got to figure out better mission statement, the one that came with this journal is stupid)

Feelings: Stressed. Anxious. Distracted.

Roles I play in my life: Friend, enemy, "frenemy," vampire, amateur glockenspielist

Today's goals:

1. blend in (via F's boring outfits)
2. avoid getting murdered
3. try "Bullet Journaling" (most ideas Cassie thinks are good are actually <u>bad</u>, but what the heck. Nothing to lose by trying).

Tomorrow's goals: Same goals as today. Also: take out the trash.

AMELIA

IT TOOK ME A LOT LONGER THAN I WANTED TO GET MY strange interaction with Mr. Fedora Asshole out of my head.

I thought about him all the way to the El, despite telling myself to shake it off. But what if he *was* in some kind of danger? He didn't seem delusional, despite his other peculiarities. And I didn't think he had made any of it up; it was far too weird a story for any person's imagination to have conjured it out of thin air.

I couldn't seem to stop thinking about him—or, if I was being honest with myself, his striking blue eyes, or the way his broad shoulders filled out that ridiculous shirt he was wearing—until I finally made it to Italian Village, the restaurant in River North my family had picked for this month's get-together.

I opened the door to the restaurant and was greeted with the pleasant aroma of roasting garlic. My mouth watered.

I was nearly thirty minutes late. Mom would likely have something passive-aggressive to say about that. Probably something about how I was going to make myself sick if I kept working so hard.

While Mom and Dad sort of understood my brother Sam's interest in being a lawyer, the kind of practical application of math skills I used in my career made as much sense to them as being a jackalope hunter would. They didn't exactly disapprove. They just didn't understand why a person would want to *do* it, least of all someone who was related to them. Especially if it meant having to work inhuman hours several months out of every year.

Hopefully Mom's comments tonight would not get any worse than passive-aggressive.

Either way, if the delicious aroma that greeted me when I stepped inside the restaurant was anything to go by, at least dinner would be good.

Italian Village was relatively new and had been getting good buzz on social media among people who knew the Chicago food scene. So it was a lot more crowded than I'd have otherwise expected in this part of the city on a Tuesday. The host guided me through the restaurant to a table for ten near the back, where my parents, my brothers Sam and Adam and their respective spouses, my eighteen-month-old nephew Aiden, and my twin eight-year-old nieces Ashley and Hannah were already seated.

Adam's cell phone rested on the table in front of his kids, who were staring at whatever was playing, transfixed. My brother must have won the argument he always had with his wife, Jess, over whether they should let their children have screen time during dinners out.

"Sorry I'm late," I said, squeezing between the backs of Mom's and Dad's chairs and the wall behind them as I made my way to the last empty seat at the end of the table. I almost mentioned the strange interaction I'd had with that guy outside my office to explain why I was late, then decided against it. How would I even describe whatever that was? I barely understood it myself. Easier to fall on the old standby excuse. They were expecting it anyway. "Work is just . . . you know. *Wild* these days."

"We know," Sam said, giving me a small smile. "Glad you could still make it."

Sam was a second-year associate at a law firm in the Loop. Like me, he worked very long hours. Unlike me, he still managed to make our monthly family dinners on time. His husband, Scott, likely had something to do with that, though. Scott was an English professor, and with his fastidious attention to detail and legendary calendaring skills, he was the opposite of every absent-minded professor stereotype I had ever heard. And being the daughter of a retired history professor and a retired high school English teacher, I'd heard just about all of them. I suspected Scott actually kept Sam's calendar for him, with little beeps going off on Sam's phone anytime my brother needed to be somewhere.

I loved spending time with Sam and his husband. Even though their busy work schedules and mine rarely lined up, we always had fun when we did manage to find time to hang out.

Fortunately, Mom didn't seem upset with me for being late. She was fully engrossed in conversation with Scott, seated on her other side, and hadn't even noticed I'd arrived. Mom had a master's degree in nineteenth-century English literature, which she'd used to teach language arts to high school kids for thirty years, and had been a voracious reader all her life. The first time Sam brought Scott home, I hadn't even thought Mom could look so happy. Sam liked to joke that of the three of her kids, she liked Scott the best.

Honestly, he may have been right.

"Glad you could join us, Ame." Dad sat at the head of the table, directly opposite from my nieces. His voice was deep and booming and carried easily over the din of the restaurant. "Tax season keeping you busy, huh?"

It was, verbatim, the same question he'd asked every March and April in the seven years since I'd become a CPA. From anybody else, the repetitive and unimaginative questioning would feel dismissive of my career, and grating. I mean, it was still a *little* grating and dismissive, even from Dad. But I knew he wasn't doing it because he disapproved of my job. He just quite literally didn't know what else to say about my career.

You couldn't get much farther away from early twentieth-century European history than filing tax returns on behalf of nonprofit foundations.

"Yep," I said. "Super busy."

"Good girl." Dad smiled at me, then turned his attention back to the wine menu he'd been studying when I arrived. "In the mood for some Chardonnay? I ordered a bottle for the table."

I wasn't normally much of a drinker. Especially not on a work night. But suddenly, the idea of drinking something with dinner to blur the edges of the day sounded marvelous. "Sure," I said.

"Me too." Adam was making silly faces at Aiden, who was no longer interested in the iPhone and looked about thirty seconds away from a total toddler meltdown.

"Me three," Mom said. She smiled at Dad before turning to the rest of the group. "Also, now that you're all here, I wanted to see whether you'd gotten Gretchen's invitation."

Sam looked up from his menu. "What invitation?"

"Gretchen's getting married in May!" Mom was beaming. "Your father and I got ours today. Aunt Sue said you're all invited."

I fought to stifle a groan.

Lord.

Not *another* cousin getting married.

Suddenly, the wine Dad ordered couldn't arrive soon enough. Because now I knew exactly how the rest of tonight's dinner was going to go. Mom and Dad wouldn't be gently harping on me about working too hard like I'd worried.

They'd be gently harping on me about being single, instead.

The less of what I knew was coming next that I had to sit through completely sober, the better.

"We got our invitation yesterday," Jess said. "The girls are looking forward to seeing their cousins again." If that was actually true, Ashley and Hannah showed no sign of it. They seemed completely oblivious to this entire conversation, having moved on from Adam's cell phone to a copy of *American Girl* magazine that sat spread out on the table before them.

The waiter blessedly chose that moment to appear at the table with the bottle of Chardonnay. I made eye contact with him and motioned for him to place it directly in front of me. He gave me what I thought was a nod of understanding before putting the wine right by my plate. Though that might have just been my imagination.

"Wine, anyone?" I chirped. But nobody was listening to me.

"I'm so happy for Gretchen," Mom sighed. And then she leaned over to me and added, in a sympathetic half whisper, "You know how bad Gretchen's last breakup was."

I didn't know how bad Gretchen's last breakup was. Other than the fact that back when she was a junior in high school, Gretchen used to sneak out at night to see the nineteen-year-old boyfriend her parents didn't know about, I knew nothing about her dating history at all. Mom had three siblings; Dad had four. Several of my aunts and uncles had been married multiple times. Our extended family was far too large to keep close track of everyone's lives.

Gretchen had always seemed nice enough, but I hardly knew her. In fact, the only times I'd seen her since our grandmother's funeral five years ago had been at other cousins' weddings.

Of which, in the past five years, there had been more than I could count on two hands.

"Oh, yes," I said, in a voice I hoped sounded at least passably sympathetic. "That breakup. Terrible."

"She'd been single for nearly two years before she met Josh." Mom shook her head, *tsking* under her breath. "And you know that Gretchen is almost thirty-five. Aunt Sue had begun to suspect Gretchen had given up. It's so good to see someone who'd given up on romance find love, don't you think?"

She gave me a knowing look that was all too familiar.

My stomach lurched.

So I guess we *were* doing this, then.

It wasn't that I had anything against dating, or the institution of marriage. Or even weddings. Four months ago, I'd attended a bachelorette party in Nashville for one of my old grad school classmates that had featured an endless stream of bars and a drag show at the Ryman that had by itself been worth the cost of the plane fare.

Weddings celebrations could be fun. Love was worth celebrating.

But that wedding trip to Nashville was so much different than this upcoming wedding would be. No one had implied there was something wrong with me for being single, or suggested I needed to do anything to change that. Half of the girls on that trip had been single, too. Or at least, I think they'd been single. In either case, I certainly hadn't been the only one tucking dollar bills into those male strippers' G-strings.

I wasn't close enough to Gretchen to be included in any raucous parties she might be planning as part of the lead-up to her wedding. All I had to look forward to were little needling comments from Mom and her sisters about how I worked too hard and should date more, and a general feeling of being under a spotlight of loneliness.

I liked my life. I loved my career, my cat, my apartment. I loved my friends. And most of the time, I was completely fine with being single, since the last relationship I'd been in ended with more tears than I ever wanted to cry in a one-week span ever again.

Matt had been a CPA, like me. He had thick dark hair, wore these ridiculous librarian glasses that *worked* for him, and made love the same way he did everything: thoroughly, and with frequent references to the Internal Revenue Code. He was almost unconscionably hot—which was part of why I'd started dating him in the first place—but our relationship left a lot to be desired. So did Matt, I came to find out, both as a person and as a boyfriend. I was devastated when I found out he'd been cheating on me with another woman, who worked at his accounting firm— even if I knew I never wanted to listen to someone talk about step-up basis while I was on the cusp of orgasm ever again.

Regardless, ever since Matt, I'd found all the satisfaction I needed out of life between my career, my friends, and my trusty vibrator.

I couldn't tell Mom that last part, of course. I just wished she, and the rest of my family, would accept that I didn't need to be in a romantic relationship to feel complete. My own personal history suggested I was better off on my own.

I didn't say any of this to Mom, who was still pretending she was only talking about Gretchen's sad dating history and looking at me expectantly for a reaction.

I went along with it, and pretended not to realize where we were heading. What was the point? I'd been putting up with this in the lead-up to every cousin's wedding for years. Ever since things with Matt went to shit.

"Single for nearly two years," I parroted. "Poor Gretchen. Absolutely awful." I'd been functionally single for at least twice that long, but who was counting.

"Awful!" Aiden cried. He'd apparently lost interest in Adam's cell phone and was now trying hard to engage with the adults in conversation.

Mom ignored him. "Your invitation should be for you and a plus one, dear," she continued, oblivious to my mounting irritation, her voice still just above a whisper in my ear. "I double-checked with Aunt Sue. So you can definitely bring along a date. I think that would be very nice."

Mom knew full well I wasn't seeing anyone. She also knew I'd never been one for casual dating. Aunt Sue may have said I could bring a plus-one, but everyone in this family knew I'd be showing up alone.

The same way I showed up for almost every family event alone.

"That's great," I said sarcastically, and probably a bit too loudly. I grabbed for the bottle of wine again. "If I can bring a plus-one, that means I'll be able to bring my boyfriend."

I'd never really experienced a record scratch moment before, where conversations and ambient noise and even time itself seems to grind to a screeching halt. I was experiencing it now, though. No sooner were the words out of my mouth than Adam and Jess abruptly stopped talking. Sam was staring at me, his eyes wide as saucers. Even Aiden wasn't looking at his dad's phone anymore. Following the adults' leads, he'd turned his guileless blue gaze on me.

And Mom . . .

Mom was *beaming*.

It took me longer than it should have to realize that somehow, for reasons that escaped me, my family had taken my flippant comment at face value. Was I really so bad at sarcasm that not one person in my family had picked up on it?

"You're *dating* someone?" Mom sounded like Christmas had come in March. I barely heard her over the spinning of the wheels in my mind.

I opened my mouth to correct her. To say that, no—I was still just as single as ever—

And closed it again as one of the most ridiculous ideas I'd ever had began taking shape in my mind.

Maybe I really *was* working too hard and it was getting to me. Perhaps the wine I had only taken a few sips of with dinner had gone too quickly to my head on an empty stomach.

Either way, maybe—just maybe—letting them think I was seeing someone would get them off my back about being single for a little while. At least until after we were on the other side of Gretchen's wedding, and Mom's dating-related comments would go back to being occasional annoyances.

The next words out of my mouth shocked me even as I said them.

"Yes. I'm seeing someone." My voice sounded like it was coming from somewhere outside myself. I thought fleetingly of the interaction I'd had with Mr. Fedora Asshole. It had been so difficult for me to pretend at anything even as it had come as second nature to him. *If only he could see me now,* I thought, feeling a little unhinged. "I'm *so* glad I'll get to bring him to the wedding," I added, as my family continued to stare at me in surprised silence. "He'll be thrilled."

With that, I sank a little lower in my seat and poured myself another glass of Chardonnay with shaking hands. I'd already had more wine than strictly necessary for a family dinner on a Tuesday night. But if I was making questionable decisions, why not go all in?

"Is he hot?" Jess whispered conspiratorially in my ear.

Every single part of me that was capable of panicking was doing it then. "Um. Yeah?" Because in that dizzy moment, it felt like the right thing to say. "He's . . . yeah. He's definitely hot."

I didn't sound convincing even to myself, but Jess grinned at me anyway. After a quick glance at Adam to make sure he wasn't looking, she held up her hand for a fist bump.

Instead of bumping my fist with hers, I pretended not to see it and slunk down farther into my seat.

"I can't wait to meet him," Mom said, dreamily.

That made two of us.

I did my best to smile back at Mom, even as I was screaming inside.

FOUR

**Excerpt from The Annals of Vampyric Lore,
Seventeenth Edition**

"Index of Notable Historical Events," p. 1193

The arson that has since become widely known as The Incident is believed to have occurred on the evening of October 22, 1872, at a party held at the Sevastopol estate of Count Wyatt Contesque. While accounts from the party's survivors provide an inconsistent picture of events, most agree on three points:

- One: The Incident *did, in fact, occur, and was the nastiest arson-related vampire murder any person present had ever witnessed.*
- Two: *The morning after* The Incident, *several items believed to belong to Mr. Reginald Cleaves (see:* Index of Notorious Vampires, *pp.* 1123–24) *and a bombastic note believed to have been written by same were found on the premises.*

- *Three: Due to a lack of any other clues, many believe Reginald Cleaves was the arsonist.*

No formal legal action has been taken against Cleaves to date because most in the vampiric legal community agree the evidence against him is circumstantial at best. Furthermore, a small, if vocal, minority of survivor accounts insist the whole affair had been nothing but a product of the Count's vivid imagination after he'd consumed blood spiked with hallucinogens.

Despite this, Cleaves's name remains linked with The Incident *in popular imagination. The Collective (See: The Collective, infra., 982–83) remains committed to bringing him to justice as retribution for the murder of their sires (colloquially known as "The Founding Eight"), many of whom attended Count Wyatt Contesque's party and were among the number counted as missing.*

For a list of Vampires believed to have perished in The Incident, *please refer to Appendix IX.*

REGINALD

I KNEW SOMETHING WAS WRONG THE MINUTE I GOT HOME.

I didn't know how they'd gotten in. They *shouldn't* have been able to get in. The prohibition against vampire breaking and entering was as ingrained in our DNA as our desire for blood. It meant we couldn't enter someone's home without express permission from the people who lived there.

Or at least, that's what it *should* have meant.

I'd always been uncannily prescient, even when human. The

last time the hairs on the back of my neck had prickled hot like this had been seconds before The Collective's sires had turned me, and most of the other people in my village, into the vampires we ultimately became, changing the trajectory of my existence forever.

I flipped on my kitchen light and turned slowly in a circle, trying to take everything in. But even though all my synapses were firing, every instinct screaming at me to *run*, no one was there. And nothing seemed out of place. There was the pot I used to warm my meals from the North Shore blood bank, soaking in the sink where I'd left it hours ago. There was my glockenspiel in its usual spot on the bookshelf, my one remaining tie to the human man I'd once been.

And there was my most prized possession: a framed oil painting of Edward Cullen on the wall above the sink, sparkly and magnificent as he gazed moodily into the middle distance.

(I didn't care what Frederick thought about *Twilight*. I fucking loved Edward Cullen. To be able to read minds? *Epic*. Not for the first time, I wondered if the Berkeley stoner who sold me the painting fifteen years ago actually believed it when she'd said the painting's sparkles were magic.)

I grabbed the serrated knife from my knife block and clutched it in both hands. It was an admittedly frivolous purchase when I got it, given that I didn't need to slice my food, but I was glad I had it as I crept forward into the hallway, flicking on light switches as I went. I tried tapping into the rage that fueled many of the bigger mistakes I'd made in my first century as a vampire to keep my fear at bay, but it was difficult.

I'd changed a lot since those early years.

I liked to think I was a reasonably intelligent person, but despite my build, I wasn't an especially strong one. My only reliable natural defense were my fangs, but those obviously wouldn't be much help against the idiots chasing me. They were vampires, too. A nice pointy wooden stake would have been great just then, but I tended not to keep them around for obvious, not-a-fan-of-suicide reasons.

It wasn't until I went into my bedroom and switched on the light that I found what it was they'd done.

My blood turned even colder in my veins than it already was at the sight of the three-foot-tall cardboard cutout of Count von Count from *Sesame Street*, standing beside the head of my bed, looking as comfortable in his surroundings as if he lived there. He was purple and Muppety, with wide unseeing eyes and a permanent grin splitting his face. He stood with one three-finger hand extended in front of him, as though he'd been in the middle of counting something important when they'd captured his likeness.

For all I knew, he had been.

I hadn't seen *Sesame Street* since the late 1970s. Did Count von Count still get airtime? Not that I cared. I knew enough about the modern world to recognize a Muppet when I saw one, but certainly didn't follow their careers.

The bigger question was: What was he *doing* in here?

I searched my bedroom for something that might explain this. But all I found that hadn't been there that morning was the cardboard Count and my own growing sense of panic.

When I turned to face my closet, I saw the note.

They'd attached it to my closet door by means of a wooden arrow shot straight through it. It had only four words, scrawled in big blocky red capital letters with what looked like blood for ink:

WE WILL BE BACK

Oh, shit.

With difficulty, I removed the note and the arrow from the door. It left a horrible gouge in the wood. While I had to admire these weirdos' commitment to the bit, my landlord was going to kill me.

But there would be time enough to worry about security deposits later. If I was lucky.

I'd thought I'd been hiding from The Collective successfully.

Apparently, I'd been wrong. Wearing Frederick's normalcore clothes and only going out when necessary clearly wasn't enough.

Hades, this was annoying.

I needed to think up something else to throw them off my trail.

The only question was: What?

In the meantime, if they'd found my apartment, I needed to find a new place to stay. And fast.

FIVE

Minutes from March board meeting of The Collective

- Present: Guinevere, Patricia Benicio Hewitt, Giuseppe, Alexandria, Philippa, Gregorio, John, Miss Pennywhistle, Maurice J. Pettigrew
- Absent: George
- Called to order: 9:15 PM
- Memorial Hymns sung to The Founding Eight: Led by Alexandria

OLD BUSINESS:

- <u>Saint Margaret's annual bake sale</u>: A smashing success! Number of frightened human children: up 57% from last year. Number of humans exsanguinated: up 25% from last year. Recruitment: half dozen new familiars welcomed into fold. (Round of applause was given for Miss

Pennywhistle, for all her hard work in making this year's event so successful.)

- <u>The Search for Reginald Cleaves</u>: We have learned the man responsible for the deaths of our sires now lives in Chicago, Illinois. We have relocated to a house just west of the city to monitor his movements.

- Cleaves is, unfortunately, aware of our intentions and now hides in plain sight by wearing more modest attire than his usual. We believe this is due largely to Giuseppe's cardboard Muppet stunt, taken without board approval. While using The Count *appears to have successfully communicated our fury regarding the* <u>Count</u> Wyatt Contesque INCIDENT, *the implementation was as subtle as a vampire at sunrise. Giuseppe was reprimanded for acting without board approval and was admonished not to do something so silly again.*

- As no one else in the vampire community is committed to bringing the ungrateful monster responsible for THE INCIDENT to justice, it is up to us to remain vigilant. No person who would so callously end the lives not just of our sires, but of his own, should be allowed to escape justice.

NEW BUSINESS:

- <u>New castle floodlights</u>: discussion tabled until April, when the human contractor responsible for project can be present. Reminder: He works for us. NO ONE EAT HIM.
- Meeting adjourned: 10:15 PM
- April meeting will begin at 9:15 PM. George to provide refreshments.

AMELIA

SHORTLY AFTER MY IMPROMPTU *I'M DATING SOMEONE* RE-
veal, my nephew Aiden had a meltdown to rival Chernobyl. Everybody's attention immediately shifted away from me towards
trying to get the shrieking toddler to calm down.

I wasn't used to feeling gratitude towards a small child. But
my nephew *really* did me a solid when he refused to be com-
forted by cat videos on YouTube. Adam and Jess looked absolutely
wrecked by the time we left the restaurant, and I felt bad for
them, but I was so relieved to no longer be the focus of attention
that I was mostly just glad for myself.

My reprieve didn't last long, though. I had texts from Sam
and Mom before I even made it to the train station.

> **SAM:** Congratulations on the dude
>
> **SAM:** Happy for you. And trying hard not
> to be hurt that you didn't tell me before
> tonight.
>
> **SAM:** 🖤

> **MOM:** Your father and I are so happy
> you'll be bringing someone to the
> wedding, hon.
>
> **MOM:** You've been single for so long.
> We've been worried.
>
> **MOM:** We can't wait to meet the lucky
> young man. What's his name?

That was a good question, honestly. And one I hadn't the foggiest idea how to answer.

It was nearly ten by the time I got home to my Lakeview apartment, almost fifteen hours after I'd left for work that morning. My head ached from the combined effects of too much wine at dinner, the mess I'd just created for myself, and exhaustion.

When I walked inside, a little of the anxiety I'd been carrying all day melted away.

I let my briefcase slip from my shoulder and placed it on the floor beside the black stool where my calico cat, Gracie, perched like a furry judgmental owl. My home was my sanctuary, with every book and knickknack in its place, the thermostat and water pressure at just the right settings, and all the stressors that made up the rest of my life kept firmly on the other side of the closed door.

As I slid off my coat and pulled a hanger from the closet, I noticed Gracie glaring at me sanctimoniously. Gracie had an uncannily strong drunk detector for a nine-year-old cat, and her *you stayed out past curfew* face was something to behold. It told me she knew I'd had too much to drink on a Tuesday night and lied to my family about having a boyfriend. It also told me I should have been home to play with her hours ago.

"*Meow,*" Gracie lectured.

I couldn't even be mad. "I deserve that," I agreed.

"*Meow,*" Gracie said again, with feeling.

Okay, *that* was a bridge too far. "Look. I've had a really rough day." Part of me knew it was ridiculous to get into an argument with a cat. The rest of me needed Gracie to *understand*.

Instead of understanding, Gracie chose to jump onto the kitchen counter where Sophie put my mail.

Right there, on top of the spring issue of the University of Chicago alumni magazine and the new issue of *Cat Fanciers* was the wedding invitation Mom had said was coming.

I looked helplessly at Gracie, who seemed to have given up on judging my life choices in favor of bathing her right front paw.

"I don't want to open it," I told her.

Instead of backing me up, Gracie signaled this conversation was over by jumping off the counter and sauntering over to my living room couch. One downside to having a nonhuman roommate was when I needed someone to validate me, I was usually out of luck.

"Fine," I muttered. I supposed there was no point in putting off the inevitable. At least Gretchen had sent this to my apartment. My cousin Sarah had sent her invitation to my office. That tacitly pitying implication that I spent more of my life at work than I did *not* at work had just added insult to injury.

I took a deep breath and slid my finger beneath the envelope's seal.

Purple calligraphy slanted gracefully across the front of the ivory inner envelope:

Amelia Collins, Plus One

I had to admit that the invitation looked very nice. I didn't realize Shutterfly carried such formal-looking card stock.

Mr. and Mrs. Alex Madden
and Mr. and Mrs. Francis Whitlock
Do hereby request the honor of your presence at the
marriage of their children

GRETCHEN ELIZABETH
and
JOSHUA COLE

on Saturday, May 14, at 5 in the evening
at Twin Meadows Country Club, Chicago, Illinois.
Reception immediately to follow.

Another family wedding at Twin Meadows, then. Half my uncles belonged to it, so it had become a family wedding default.

I peeked inside the envelope again and saw two additional off-white three-by-five cards. One of them was an invitation to an engagement dinner at Aunt Sue's house that Sunday.

Crap.

That was *soon*.

The other card was an invitation to a couples' getaway to our families' cabins in Wisconsin the following weekend. My great-grandfather had owned several acres in Door County, and when he died, my grandfather built cabins on it, deeding one to each of his four children. My family had spent two weeks up there every summer when I was a kid; as far as I knew, my aunts had done the same thing with their children.

All my associations with the place involved hiking, fishing, s'mores, and mosquito bites. I'd always loved our family trips up there, but it seemed an odd place to hold a pre-wedding getaway celebration. But then, I wouldn't know anything about that.

Two truly terrifying thoughts occurred to me.

First: Would my family expect me to bring my nonexistent boyfriend to these events?

And then: Would I be able to find someone in time?

Either way, I probably needed to reply to Mom's and Sam's texts. I was still on the fence about whether I was actually going through with this charade, but I had to tell Sam the truth about what was going on. We'd told each other everything since childhood. I was bad at lying to anyone; it was impossible for me to lie to Sam.

> **AMELIA:** Sam, please keep this a secret until I decide what I'm going to do
>
> **AMELIA:** But when I said I was taking someone to the wedding at first I was totally just being sarcastic
>
> **AMELIA:** It wasn't until everyone BELIEVED me that I decided this could maybe be a way to get mom and dad off my back about dating somebody

His reply was immediate.

> **SAM:** Wow. Okay.
>
> **SAM:** I'll let you handle it 🩶
>
> **SAM:** I won't breathe a word to anyone. Just keep me posted on what you decide.

> **AMELIA:** Of course
>
> **AMELIA:** Thank you
>
> **AMELIA:** Love you 🩶

AMELIA: Let me know the next time you
and Scott have time for a movie night

SAM: Will do

SAM: Also, sorry to be a nag, but I got
worried when you didn't reply right away

SAM: Were you careful walking home?

I rolled my eyes.

AMELIA: Are we doing this again?

SAM: Since when is it a crime for me to
worry about my sister?

Until a few months ago, Sam had expressed what I'd always thought of as a regular, brotherly amount of concern for my safety. The past few months, though, he'd become bizarrely nervous. Last week he'd even started encouraging me to carry a sharp wooden stick in my purse if I planned to be out at night.

That's the point where I'd decided he was being ridiculous.

SAM: You don't know who could be out
there, Ame

SAM: There could be murderers,
muggers, thieves following you home

SAM: Even, you know

SAM: Vampires

I burst out laughing.

AMELIA: Thieves?

AMELIA: Vampires?????

AMELIA: You're playing too much
Baldur's Gate 3

> **SAM:** Hey, I've been playing it an entirely
> normal amount

> **SAM:** You should try it once tax season's
> over

> **SAM:** But that's beside the point

> **SAM:** You never know who or what might
> be out there, is all I'm saying

I chuckled, shaking my head.
At least he was a caring brother.

AMELIA: I was careful coming home
tonight. Okay?

> **SAM:** Liar

AMELIA: Probably

AMELIA: But you don't need to worry
about me, okay? I've lived in Chicago all
my life. It's not like I'm wandering around

**with my purse unzipped on the El or
anything.**

AMELIA: Anyway I need to think of what
to say to mom about the boyfriend I made
up so I better go

AMELIA: Love you

There. That was the easier of the two conversations over with.

I pulled up Mom's texts again and chewed on my lower lip, thinking.

Was I really going to pretend I was seeing someone and bringing them to this wedding? Could I even *pull off* a lie of this caliber?

If I knew that my family's little comments about my nonexistent love life would be limited to the day of the wedding, I could probably shrug it all off and not let it get to me. But Mom in particular became especially nudgy in the weeks leading up to a family wedding. Before Sam's, Mom had dropped names of her friends' single sons just about every time I saw her. At my cousin Sarah's, Mom had gone so far as to introduce me to three different men at the event itself.

To say nothing about the awkward comments about showing up to a series of family wedding events alone, again, that I'd get from Aunt Sue.

I didn't need this in my life right now.

Especially since all of it came with the strong implication that my life was incomplete the way it was. Which offended me more than I could say. I had a cat I adored like a daughter, good friends, and a career I enjoyed. Even if my family didn't understand what I saw in it.

So what if my Herculean workload left me with zero time to date? I was okay with it. I didn't begrudge people like my brothers—or Gretchen—their right to get married if they wanted to. Why was it such a big deal that I didn't want any of that for myself?

Maybe finding some random guy to pose as my fake boyfriend at these events would buy me a few more months of peace.

I stared at the lettering on the inner envelope again, and read the way it was addressed to *Amelia Collins, Plus One*, over and over again.

Fuck it.

I decided I had nothing to lose.

This might have been the most bananapants idea I'd ever had in my life. It was definitely more than a bit childish. But who knew? Maybe it would turn out to be one of the best ideas I'd ever had, too.

I supposed time would tell.

I replied to my mother.

AMELIA: Looking forward to you all meeting him too, Mom!

I set my phone down on the couch beside me so that I wouldn't see what, if anything, Mom wrote in response.

I counted slowly to ten, then got up and walked into my kitchen. I found the bottle of wine from when Sam and Scott came over for dinner a couple weeks ago. It was still half full, which was convenient.

I took a swig directly from the bottle. Because why not? There was no one there to judge me for it other than Gracie, and she was fast asleep.

Thus bolstered by liquid courage, I texted Sophie.

AMELIA: Hi Soph

AMELIA: I did something that was either a
genius move or else really stupid

AMELIA: Not sure which

AMELIA: Can we talk? I need your help.

SIX

**A letter, hastily scrawled in red ink
on a crumpled sheet of paper**

Freddie—

Your clothes are as boring as a church service but you
really did me a solid tonight. For a sec I thought they
might've spotted me but your stuff was the perfect
disguise.

Gonna take you up on your offer to borrow more of
your things if it's all right with you. Not sure when. You'll
know I've been by when your clothes are gone. I'm annoyed
I won't get to dress "like a stolen car" as you like to put it
but I guess I can go back to dressing the way I like after
this is over.

Anyway. Thanks again. (See? I AM capable of gratitude.
Sometimes.)

—R

AMELIA

GOSSAMER'S WASN'T A GREAT COFFEE SHOP. THE GENERIC food was likely pre-made in some large industrial kitchen somewhere, the drinks all had silly names, and the prices were more appropriate for Manhattan than Chicago.

It was halfway between my apartment and Soph's, though, which made it convenient for both of us. And the relatively low noise level made it good for both getting work done and catching up.

By the time I got there, Sophie was already at the table in the back that we'd long considered ours, wearing a red-and-white checked dress that looked adorable on her slender frame. Between the two of us, Sophie had always been the more fashionable one. That hadn't changed even after she'd had her twins and decided to stay home with them.

She had a steaming drink in front of her. My usual Americano, which this wannabe hipster coffee shop called *We Are Vivacious* for reasons passing understanding, waited for me at my seat. When Sophie saw me approaching, she broke out into a broad, knowing smile that made me regret saying anything to her about this half-baked plan in the first place.

"You got your hair done," I said. "It looks great."

"It does," Sophie agreed, tossing some of her long, black locks over her shoulder. "But let's not get sidetracked. Complimenting me on how great I look isn't why we're here."

I winced. "I almost didn't come," I admitted, flopping down into the chair across from hers. "After ten minutes on Tinder, I realized this was a terrible mistake."

"Oh my god, I'd have killed you if you'd bailed." She leaned in closer, so giddy with delight her dark brown eyes danced with it. "I got a babysitter for this and everything."

My heart ached over how little time Sophie took for herself. "When's the last time you got a babysitter?" I asked. She didn't do it often, even when Marcus was away for weeks. When I gave her her birthday present next month I would *make* her get a babysitter for those art classes.

Sophie ignored my question and pointed to a man sitting on the other side of the coffee shop. Deflecting, the way she always did, whenever I got on her about not prioritizing her needs.

"What about that guy?" she asked.

I snorted. "I told you to wait to start scoping candidates until I got here."

"But you just said you weren't having any luck on dating apps. And remind me again of when you need to present a fake boyfriend to your family?"

"The engagement dinner is on Sunday."

"That's in four days." Sophie held up four fingers in front of my face as if I hadn't heard her. "There's no time to waste. And if you're striking out on dating apps . . ." She shrugged. "You can't blame me for being proactive, is all I'm saying. And you should at least *take a look* at that guy over there before saying no."

I sighed. Sophie was right. Resigned, I looked in the direction she was pointing.

The guy looked roughly my age. His dirty-blond hair was a mess, like he'd just rolled out of bed and hadn't bothered combing it, but the rest of him looked all right. More than all right, actually. Especially the way that long-sleeved green Henley he wore clung to his broad chest and shoulders. And the thick-rimmed glasses perched on the end of his nose shouldn't have worked. But somehow, they really, *really* did.

His attention was split between a journal he'd occasionally jot notes in and the magazine in his hands. The magazine had dragons on the cover. It reminded me of the books my nerdier guy friends in college used to study before meeting up for role-playing games.

I tried to get a read on him. Was he an especially handsome tabletop gaming enthusiast? Was he a sexy librarian? But getting reads on people from their appearance had never been my strong suit. Especially in cases like these, where the longer I looked, the more flustered I got.

"What do you think?" Sophie asked.

I turned to face her, feeling a little dazed. "Absolutely not." It was debatable whether I'd be able to pull off this scheme. There was no way I'd manage it with someone I found attractive.

Sophie stared at me. "What's wrong with him? He's cute!"

She was right about that. I floundered for a response. "He's reading a magazine with dragons on it," I said, lamely.

"So?" Sophie said. "Nerds are cool again. Nerds are *hot*."

I doubted whether either of those statements were actually true, but let it slide. I looked back over at his table again and saw he was now holding the magazine upside down and peering at it with intense focus.

I saw this for the lifeline it was.

"He's reading his magazine upside down," I said.

"That's even better."

I stared at Sophie. "How is that even better?"

"It shows he has a sense of humor."

"I think it just means he's weird."

"Well, okay, fair," Sophie conceded. "But that makes him a strong candidate for this, because honestly?" Sophie tapped the table with an index finger. "Showing up with someone a bit off-kilter could be the perfect way to show your family you aren't necessarily better off with a man." She paused, then added, "And besides, only someone who's at least a *little* weird would be willing to go along with this in the first place."

She had a point. "You don't think this is a terrible idea that I absolutely should not be considering? Because I think it might be."

"No. It's one of your better ideas." Sophie leveled me with the same *stop bullshitting me* stare she'd been using on me since middle school. "You thought it was a great idea yourself when you called me at eleven last night."

I took a long sip from my Americano, just so I could hide my sheepish expression from my best friend.

"I had a momentary lapse of judgment," I muttered. Which was true. I'd consumed nearly an entire bottle of wine over the course of the evening and had been listening to Taylor Swift's *Midnights* on repeat when I'd called her. My critical thinking skills hadn't been their sharpest. Though even in the cold light of day, the impetus for my coming up with the plan in the first place still rankled. "I just don't understand why anyone in my family cares that I'm single."

"It's obnoxious," Sophie agreed. "Which is why I think your idea is brilliant."

I hesitated. "You really think it's brilliant?"

"I do," Sophie said. "You deserve to be left alone, and you are too nonconfrontational to be able to handle the tell-off certain of your family members deserve."

I sighed. My therapist would probably encourage me to either tell my family to stop it, or to just accept that this was how they were and learn to tune it out. I'd been too busy with work to see my therapist in months, though. "This fake date plan does seem like the simplest solution," I conceded.

"Yes," Sophie agreed. "This plan is a win-win. Especially for me. The idea of good, angelic, perfect-grades, always-does-everything-right Amelia showing up at a family gathering with a handsome rando she picked up from Tinder or the El or a coffee shop is going to power me on amusement value alone through the middle of next year."

I smiled in spite of myself. "I'm glad my mistakes are amusing to you."

"Oh, they are." Sophie grinned.

"Also, I don't *always* do everything right."

She snorted. "Right. When's the last time you got a parking ticket?"

My cheeks heated. "I've never gotten a parking ticket."

"What's the lowest grade you got in college?"

Now she was just trolling me. Sophie knew full well I'd been valedictorian in high school and in college. I decided not to dignify her question with a response.

But Sophie pressed on, relentless as a Peloton instructor. "And when's the last time you told off your parents?"

I swallowed. "I've never done that, either."

"Wait, really?"

"Really." I shook my head. "I never did the teenage rebellion thing. I just did as I was told. What was expected of me."

Sophie shook her head. "Ame. This idea isn't just perfect. It's about twenty years overdue." She set down her mug and leaned forward, arms folded on the table in front of her. "I bet if you take Mr. Dungeons & Dragons over there to your cousin's wedding, your great aunt Brunhilda will never give you grief again about being single."

I laughed. "I don't have a great aunt Brunhilda."

"Cousin Brunhilda, then," Sophie said with a dismissive wave of her hand.

I shook my head, amused, and then snuck another look at the guy reading his magazine just as he was setting it down.

His blue eyes met mine.

All at once, and with a dizzy sensation I usually associated with roller coasters or giving presentations in front of a large crowd, I recognized him.

It was Mr. Fedora Asshole from the night before.

It had been dark when he'd run into me, and his hat had cast most of his face in shadow. He'd traded the strange outfit from earlier for the more conventional clothing he wore right now. But there was no question that this was the same man.

It was clear he recognized me, too. His eyes widened in surprise, and those full lips of his quirked up at one corner. After another moment, his eyes flitted away again.

He began writing furiously in his journal.

He'd told me he owed me one for helping him. He probably hadn't meant it, but the fact that he'd offered might make him more inclined to say yes to this.

If I asked him to help me.

Sophie cleared her throat.

Shit. I was staring at him. I quickly whipped my head around to face her.

"So since you're definitely doing this—" she began.

"I have decided no such thing."

"—let's set up some criteria for Mr. Pretend," Sophie continued, as if I hadn't interrupted her. "To help you decide who to pick from among your *dozens* of options."

I ignored the jibe. Because lists were good. Carefully considered criteria helped people make well-reasoned decisions. The only problem was, I had no idea where to start.

"What do you think should be on the list?" I asked, feeling more foolish than I'd ever felt before.

"I'm so happy you asked." Sophie pulled out a yellow legal pad from her bag and wrote CRITERIA FOR FAKE BOY-FRIEND in large capital letters at the top. "Let's start easy. I assume you don't want to take someone to this wedding who's been convicted for a violent crime they actually committed."

I blinked at her. "Correct."

"*Not . . . a . . . violent . . . felon,*" Sophie said, jotting it down. "Got it. Next question. How old should he be?"

I thought about that. "Maybe mid-to-late thirties? If he's too young and impressionable, it could get weird. But if he's too much older than me, that could be weird, too."

"That makes sense," she agreed. "Also, someone who's too young and still believes in love or whatever might fall in love with you."

I snorted. Sophie had been married for almost ten years and was as in love with her husband today as she was when they met in college. She definitely still *believed in love or whatever.* Her willingness to play along with my cynical attitude just went to show what a good friend she was.

"No one is going to fall in love with me," I said.

"You don't know that," Sophie countered. "These fake dating schemes lead to real love all the time."

"You don't know what you're talking about."

"I do," she said. "I've read about it."

I raised an eyebrow. "Where?"

"Novels."

"Novels?" I laughed.

"Look," she said, growing serious. "It doesn't matter what literally dozens of books I have read about the subject have to say. I'm just saying it's a risk. I mean . . . look at you."

"What do you mean, look at me?" I asked. We'd been friends for a very long time, and I knew she thought my never-seen-sunlight complexion, the near-perpetual bags under my eyes, and the nondescript brownish-blondish shade of my hair made me irresistible. My reflection in the mirror and my dating history begged to differ.

"You know what I mean," Sophie said. "And either way, Mr. Dungeons & Dragons looks like he fits the old-enough-but-not-too-old requirement." She chanced a glance at me. "He also doesn't look like a violent felon."

I snorted. "I mean, I'm not sure you can tell just by looking at someone if they're a violent felon, but—"

"He's also really cute."

My heart skipped a beat. He was. And those *lips*?

Who was I kidding? He was *more* than cute.

I wrinkled my nose anyway to mask my agreement. "I still don't see it."

"Sure, Jan," she deadpanned. "I mean, Marcus and I have been together forever, but if he weren't around, I would not kick Mr. Dungeons & Dragons out of bed for eating crackers."

I turned around to face him again as I pretended to consider what she was saying.

"I suppose . . ." I began, then trailed off. "I suppose if I'm actually going to go through with this, not thinking he's cute would be a plus."

"Probably," Sophie agreed. "You falling for whoever you tap for this role would be just as inconvenient as him falling for you."

I rolled my eyes. "There is no danger of my falling for anyone." Because there wasn't. I hadn't really, truly fallen for anyone in over five years. My experience with Matt had likely cured me of ever falling for anyone again.

"Sure," Sophie said again, clearly not believing me. Then she tore off the list she'd started and handed it to me. "I gotta go home, unfortunately. The sitter can only stay until eight. But keep listing criteria for your fake date. That will make it easier for you to pick someone."

Again, I couldn't disagree with list-making. If I was going through with this nonsense plan, it made sense to go about it in an organized way.

"Okay," I agreed. "I will."

Sophie gave me an affectionate peck on the forehead. "Okay, hon. I'll see you later. And if you do end up asking out Mister Tall, Strange, and Handsome, let me know how it goes."

"*If* I ask him out," I said, placing extra emphasis on the *if*, "I promise you will be the first to know."

But even as Sophie walked away, I realized that given that I only had a few days to find somebody, it might as well be him. He fit all the criteria Sophie and I had just come up with.

And he'd said he owed me one.

True, he did seem a bit strange. He looked normal enough here, but last night had been a different story. Then again, I was strange, too, wasn't I? Wasn't everyone a bit odd, in some way or another?

And if he ended up being *completely* bizarre . . .

Well. It wasn't like we would ever see each other again after Gretchen's wedding.

I gathered up the list I'd made with Sophie and slipped it inside my briefcase.

I was going over to that man's table and giving him my ridiculous proposal.

Just as soon as I worked up the nerve to do it.

SEVEN

*Excerpt from R.C.'s bullet journal, written in blue ink,
with multiple crossed-out words*

Mission statement: ~~To live each day with courage, compassion, and curiosity. To become a better version of myself each day and inspire others in my path to do the same.~~

Feelings:

1. Distracted. (I came to this coffee shop to try and bullet journal my way back to executive functioning, or whatever that dumb bullet journaling site called it, but Amelia Collins and her friend are inexplicably HERE? And STARING at me?)

2. Confused. (How in this city of millions have A.C. and I crossed paths TWICE in 24 HOURS?! ~~And why is she checking me out?)~~

To-do list:

1. *Ignore A.C.*
2. *Focus on decoy magazine I nicked from gangly-looking teen on my way here (The Collective won't be looking for someone wearing boring Frederick-clothes and reading a magazine about dragons and their dungeons) and on bullet journal.*
3. *Okay, she looks like she's trying to decide whether to come talk to me. She looks nervous. I see none of the fierce determination I saw in her the other night. (Hades, she's pretty. I've been so distracted by everything else I'd forgotten just how pretty she is.)*
4. *Okay okay yeah, she actually IS coming over to talk to me, shit, SHIT, more soon*

AMELIA

WHEN I GOT TO THE GUY'S TABLE, I DUG MY FINGERNAILS into the meat of my palm, willing the pinch to ground me.

He hastily slammed shut the notebook he'd been writing in and set it to the side. Then he fixed me with those startling bright blue eyes. "Um. Hello?"

I hesitated, teeth worrying at my bottom lip. "I need a favor." I hated how small and nervous I sounded. Too late to back out now, though. I pulled out the chair across from his and sat down.

His eyes widened in surprise. "You need a favor?"

I gathered my courage as he continued to gaze at me. Up close, I couldn't even lie to myself and pretend he was unattractive. I reminded myself that that didn't matter. All that mattered was that he said yes.

"I do," I confirmed.

He leaned back in his chair and folded his arms across his chest. "I don't usually do favors for people."

His voice dripped with condescension. I stared at him, astounded that someone reading a literal dragon magazine could sound so cocky.

"You know what? Forget it." I'd come up with some other way—some *grown-up* way—to deal with this situation. I didn't need to resort to pranking my family. I was an adult. I was an *accountant*. This was beneath me.

I pushed back from my chair and stood to leave.

"Wait," he said. It sounded almost like pleading. "I didn't finish."

"Was something going to come after telling me you don't do favors for people?"

He shook his head. "No, what I said was I didn't *usually* do favors for people. But I did disrupt your evening last night, and I did say I'd make it up to you." He shrugged. "I didn't think you'd take me up on that since I didn't think I'd see you again. But since here you are . . . I'd be willing to consider it. Depending on what the favor is, of course."

He motioned for me to join him. I hesitated. What sort of person had a default no-favors policy? But I was without options.

"Thank you," I said, taking the chair I'd just vacated.

"You're welcome. So . . . what do you need, Amelia Collins?"

I could do this. I took a deep breath, squared my shoulders, and said, "I need someone to pretend to be my boyfriend at a family wedding."

He stared at me. A group of noisy teenagers filed past our

table and made their way over to the counter. We paid them no mind.

"I'm sorry, but . . . *what?*"

"I know this sounds bonkers—"

"It does," he agreed. "Very deeply bonkers."

"I swear this will all make sense after I've explained." I paused, considering. "It'll *maybe* make sense," I amended.

"I am all ears." The corner of his mouth quirked up into an amused half smile. Damn it, his lips were *extremely* distracting. It occurred to me that I didn't know his name. I hadn't put *know his name* on the list of fake date criteria I'd just made, but it suddenly felt like important information to have.

"Actually, could you tell me your name first?"

He raised an eyebrow. "Why?"

"You know my name, but I've just been thinking of you as *Mr. Fedora Asshole.*" That earned a surprised laugh from him. Dammit, did even his laugh have to be attractive? "It puts us on unequal footing."

His half smile slid into a smirk. "So you think about me, do you?"

I'd always thought *blushed to the roots of her hair* was just a figure of speech. Turns out I'd been wrong. If my *shoes* could blush, they'd have been doing it. "Not at all," I lied. "I mean, except for last night, when you nearly killed me when you mowed me down on the sidewalk."

"You have an exceptional flair for the dramatic for an accountant."

"I have a completely average flair for the dramatic for an accountant," I said, feeling a little unhinged. Talking to this man felt like trying to walk in a straight line on a listing ship. "Which is to say, I don't have one. And you're certainly one to talk. Last night you were wearing a fedora and a trench coat when it was, like, twenty degrees outside. You were dressed like you . . . like you . . ." I trailed off, flailing for the right words.

He winced. "Like I wanted to be seen?"

"Yes," I said. "Exactly like that. You seem dramatic as hell if I'm being honest."

"Ordinarily that observation would please me," he said, looking very displeased. "But given present circumstances, I'm not thrilled that my best attempts at blending into the background didn't work."

I had no idea what *that* meant. It didn't matter. We were getting off topic here. We were wasting time.

"Listen," I said. "Are you going to tell me your name or not?"

"Oh," he said, as if just remembering I was there. "Sure. Reginald."

"Reginald?" That was . . . certainly an unusual name for someone my age. "Is that actually your name?"

"Why would I give you a fake name?"

I shrugged. "You seem the type."

He snorted. "Fair. But Reginald is my actual name."

"And your last name?"

He sighed. "My last name is Cleaves. My full name is Reginald Cleaves. So. Now that you know who I am, will you explain to me why you need me to pretend to be your boyfriend?"

Right. That. "Reginald," I began. "Actually, is it all right if I call you Reggie?"

"Why?"

"It's less of a mouthful than *Reginald*."

He shrugged. "Suit yourself."

"Okay. Reggie," I tried again. How could I explain the situation to him in a way that didn't make me sound like a petulant teenager? Maybe that was impossible. "So, my family gives me a lot of passive-aggressive grief about being single. It kicks up several notches every time another cousin gets married. And I just found out my cousin Gretchen is getting married soon. I just thought . . ." I trailed off, racking my brain for a way to put what I was intending into words. "I thought that if I showed up to the wedding with a person I present as a boyfriend, they'll back off."

Reggie's smirk was back. Honestly, I couldn't blame him. I'd be smirking too if our positions were reversed. "And when you saw me here, minding my own business, you thought I'd be good in this role."

"Yes."

"Why?" He folded his arms on the table and leaned towards me. "We don't know each other, but I think I've already demonstrated that I'm not exactly a good, reliable person. Not only do I run into innocent accountants on sidewalks, I also read magazines upside down. *On purpose.*"

He gestured to his discarded magazine with such a self-deprecating twinkle in his eye that I couldn't help the small smile that twitched at the corners of my lips.

"I don't care about that."

"No?"

"No." I looked him right in the eye. "Are you a serial killer?"

His smile slipped. The hand resting on the table clenched into a fist. "I beg your pardon?"

"All I need from my plus-one is for them to not be a violent felon or a murderer or whatever." I shrugged. "My standards aren't high. I'm just asking for a few hours of your time, not for your hand in marriage. After the wedding, you'll never see me again. As for why I'm asking you specifically—"

"You're asking me because you find me devastatingly handsome and irresistibly charming," he deadpanned. "Right?"

I flushed at his words. "Uh . . . no." I floundered, trying to work out how to say, *Aunt Sue's dinner is Sunday and I don't have time to find anyone else, and you seem just bizarre enough to agree to this plan,* and *if I show up to these events with somebody who is a little bit terrible, it might remind my parents that there are worse things than me staying single—and yes, I do find you unfairly handsome and weirdly charming, but that has* nothing *to do with it* in a way that wouldn't be offensive to him or make me sound any more pathetic than I felt.

"It's because I'm in the right place at the right time, isn't it," he said, as though he'd read my mind, not even bothering to phrase it as a question. We might have been discussing the weather.

I hesitated. Might as well admit it. "I'm out of time. I need to find someone tonight, basically. And like you said before, you'd said you owed me one."

To my surprise, Reggie leaned back in his chair and laughed, loudly enough to make the teenagers ordering their drinks at the counter turn their heads and stare at us.

"This is the best practical joke ever," he said, still laughing. "Families have needed to mind their own business about things like this for centuries. I'm in."

I gaped at him. "You don't think this plan is ludicrous?"

"Oh, I think it's beyond ludicrous," he said. "But that's why I want in. If I can help you out of this particular jam *and* do something hilarious at the same time it would be my pleasure." He sighed, fiddling with the handle of his coffee mug. And then, in a much softer tone, he added, "And I probably do owe you one."

If his voice was sexy when he was being a cocky jerk, his voice when he was trying to be conciliatory was . . .

I didn't want to think about what it was.

Fortunately for me, the next time he spoke, he was all business. "Okay, so if we're doing this—what do I need to know?"

I considered that for a moment. What *did* he need to know before we got started?

I thought of all the Tinder dates I'd been on where sex had been expected from the get-go. Might as well address that now.

"Sex won't be part of this arrangement," I said.

Reggie started coughing. Whatever he'd expected me to say, it clearly hadn't been that. Once he'd recovered, he shifted a little in his chair. "I . . . Okay. Understood."

"Sex just isn't what this is about, you see," I continued.

"No, of course not," he agreed, quickly. "I wouldn't have assumed otherwise. This will be one of those good old-fashioned platonic fake dating arrangements."

I breathed an internal sigh of relief. So that was *that* taken care of. "The only other thing I probably should tell you is there's an engagement dinner before the wedding," I said. "Could you come to that with me, too? I think at least one family event before the wedding itself needs to happen to convince everyone."

"Makes sense," he agreed, stroking his chin. "Most of your family will be paying attention to the bride at the wedding, not to me. Or to us. The impact of our little practical joke will be greater if it's a multiple-event ruse."

Damn, he was good at this. "That's what I'm thinking," I said. "But I admit I'm flying by the seat of my pants here. I haven't—"

"Thought this through?"

I bristled—both at the admonishment and at the fact that he was right.

"How did you know what I was going to say?"

He snorted. "If there's one thing I can recognize in another person, it's when they've embarked on a course of action before they've thought the whole thing through." He inclined his head towards me before adding, "It's the way I tend to operate, myself."

Somehow, that didn't surprise me. "Well, it isn't the way *I* operate at all."

"Isn't it?" He peered at me. "The two encounters I've had with you—one: rushing out the door of your office without looking where you were going, and two: asking a complete stranger to pretend to be your boyfriend to get back at your family—suggest otherwise."

"I'll—I'll have you know I'm an *accountant*," I spluttered, feeling like an idiot.

"I am well aware." There it was again—the softness in his tone that I just didn't know what to do with. Then he added, "It suits you, by the way. Your choice of profession."

I didn't know what to do with *that*, either.

"Right," I said lamely. I needed to regain some semblance of control over this conversation. "Anyway, the engagement dinner is on Sunday. It's in Winnetka and it starts at six-thirty. And although my mom says it'll be casual, we'll probably be expected to dress up a little for it." I looked at him, trying to gauge his reaction. "Are you free?"

I expected him to pull out his phone to check if he had anything scheduled. But he answered without missing a beat. "I am wide open at six-thirty next Sunday and I'd be *delighted* to come with you."

I fidgeted with the handle of my coffee mug to distract myself from the way he had lingered on the word *delighted*. As if he really meant it. "Great," I said. God, what the hell was I doing? "It's a date."

"It's a date," he agreed.

"I should warn you, though," I added, "I can't promise the food will be any good. Especially if you're lactose intolerant or a pescatarian." I shook my head. "If you happen to have the bad luck of being both, like me, there probably won't be much you can eat besides dinner rolls and raw veggies."

He raised an eyebrow. "Don't worry about me. I don't usually eat at events like these anyway." He cleared his throat and looked pointedly down at his mug. "But why does your family not provide food that *you* can eat? Do they not know about your dietary limitations?"

I rolled my eyes. "Oh, they know. They just tend not to think much about me when planning these things."

He looked seriously affronted. "And yet they make you feel obligated to attend anyway?"

I shrugged. "At some point I just got used to them ignoring my polite requests for fish or bean dishes and gave up trying." When he didn't say anything in response to this, and just continued staring at me, I added, "I usually try to eat a small meal before getting together with family. It's fine."

I tried to play it off as not that big of a deal. I could tell by the intensity on Reggie's face and the tight set of his jaw that it wasn't working. I didn't like that he was reacting to this so much. It made it hard for me to keep pretending that it didn't hurt that my needs were seldom considered at family events.

And then, a moment later, he shook it off. He cleared his throat again. "Okay. So, there's the dinner on Sunday. Are there other wedding events I should attend?"

My face burned. There was no way I was inviting a stranger to join me on a couples' weekend up to Wisconsin with my family. "The engagement dinner on Sunday is the big one. But"—I looked away, tucking a loose strand of hair behind my ear—"I'll let you know if others come up."

Reggie nodded. "Fine." He held out a hand. "Your business card?"

I stared at his hand. Long-fingered and graceful. I wondered if he played the violin, or some other delicate musical instrument. He certainly had the hands for it.

It seemed entirely unfair that hands like these belonged to a man I would never see again after this wedding. I bet he could do all *kinds* of things with them.

Stop that, I chastised myself. *This is not what this is* about.

"Why do you need my business card?" I asked, tearing my gaze away from his hands with difficulty. "And why do you assume I have one with me?"

"If we're going through with this, we'll need some way to contact each other," he said. "I assume your business card has your contact info?"

Oh. Right.

"And I assume you have a business card with you," he continued, "because you're an accountant."

"Ordinarily I *would* have business cards with me," I conceded, thinking of the little metal business card holder I'd left in my office last night. "But I don't have any with me now. I . . . haven't been operating on all cylinders for a while."

He made a sympathetic noise. He pulled out his cell phone, typed in a passcode, and then slid it across the table to me. "We'll do this the old-fashioned way, then. Put your number in my phone."

I glanced at the display. A stab of something more than surprise went through me when I saw the contacts already in his phone.

Partly because there were only two of them.

Mostly because I knew who they were.

Frederick Fitzwilliam I only knew by name. Cassie Greenberg, though, I'd known for years.

She'd been my brother's best friend since they were kids. I hadn't thought much of her when we were growing up. She'd always struck me as an extremely unserious person who accidentally fell into things instead of achieving anything through deliberate effort. But she'd always been nice, and a good friend to Sam for many years.

The last I'd heard, Cassie had found a steady job as an art teacher and had actually started dating Frederick. Which . . .

Well.

Good for her, I supposed.

Regardless, it was downright weird that the only two contacts in this man's phone were my brother's best friend and her boyfriend. No parents, no siblings—just Cassie and Frederick.

"How do you know Cassie?" I asked. This situation suddenly felt like too strange a series of coincidences to *actually* be coincidental. Running into this person twice in two days was bizarre enough. But this?

"You know Cassie, too?" The surprise in his expression was too genuine to be fake. Which was oddly reassuring. If this were all an elaborate setup to rob or murder me, he probably wouldn't look and sound like I'd just shocked him witless.

"I do," I confirmed. "She's my brother's best friend."

"Your brother," he repeated. I watched as he mentally sifted through what I'd just told him. After a long moment, his eyes brightened. "Sam," he said, snapping his fingers. "Your brother is Sam. Right?"

A shiver ran down my spine. "You know Sam?"

"Only by name," he said. "I know Cassie has a best friend named Sam. And Cassie happens to be the girlfriend of my . . ." He trailed off, eyes going distant as he seemed to search for the right word to describe the person whose girlfriend she was.

I raised an eyebrow. "The girlfriend of . . ." I prompted.

"Frederick. The other contact in my phone. Frederick and I are . . ." He dragged a hand through his hair. "We go back a long way."

"I have a best friend like that," I said. "Her name is Sophie. We've known each other since middle school." When he didn't say anything in response to that, I asked, "Have you and Frederick been friends since you were kids, too?"

His face darkened a little. "No," he said. He didn't seem inclined to clarify. Which was fair enough. He didn't owe me an explanation.

"Well, now you have three contacts," I said. I typed my name and number into his phone before sliding it back.

"So I do." I handed my phone across the table to him, unable to look away from his graceful hands as he deftly added his own name and number.

"You don't talk to your parents?" I asked.

He paused, blinking. "Why do you ask?"

I shrugged. "It's just strange that you don't have anyone else in your phone besides two friends. That's all."

He looked at me for a long moment. "I don't talk to anyone in my family anymore, no."

That made me sad. My family drove me bonkers, but we were still close. I loved them and couldn't imagine a life where we never spoke. "I'm sorry," I said, meaning it.

He smiled, though it didn't reach his eyes. "It's fine," he said. "I've had plenty of time to get used to it." He then looked at the place on his arm where a wristwatch would be if he'd been wearing one. "Oh, look at the time. I'm afraid I have to go. I have an appointment."

"An appointment at eight in the evening on a Wednesday?" I asked, surprised.

He ignored my question and held out his hand. "Before I go . . . I'm not a lawyer, but I *think* we just entered into a contract. We should shake on it to, you know." He cleared his throat. "Make it official."

I stared at his hand. The idea of clasping it in mine sent an unexpected thrill through me.

Reggie'd been right. I *hadn't* thought this through. While I'd decided from the outset that sex wouldn't be part of the deal, it hadn't occurred to me that touching him in *some* way—while we were in front of my family, at least—would probably be necessary.

We needed to convince everyone we were dating, after all. And couples touched.

I had to get a grip on myself. If I couldn't handle a simple handshake in a coffee shop, how would I make it through touching him in front of my family?

I could do this.

I had to.

I took a deep breath. And then, tapping into the same inner source of courage that saw me through the CPA exam, took his outstretched hand. It dwarfed mine, his palm smooth and surprisingly cool to the touch.

I'd had no idea my hand had so many nerve endings. Somehow, I could feel the handshake all the way down to my toes.

"Good night, Amelia," he said, his voice smooth as silk. He was still holding my hand. He didn't seem inclined to let it go, even though he'd just said he needed to leave. "I look forward to *faking it* with you."

If it was possible to spontaneously burst into flames, that little double entendre would have done it for me right then and there. Reggie's grin was absolutely wicked, as if he knew exactly what his joke was doing to me.

My voice sounded like it was coming from far away when I said, before I could stop myself, "I look forward to faking it with you, too."

EIGHT

Excerpt from R.C.'s bullet journal,
written in alternating blue and red ink

Mission statement: ~~To live each day with courage, compassion,~~ ~~and curiosity. To become a better version of myself each day and~~ ~~inspire others in my path to do the same.~~ To live a life free of mission statements.

Feelings: Stressed & distracted (a little less than yesterday). Hungry (same as yesterday).

Pros of Fake Dating Amelia

1. Best idea for a prank I've heard in a century
2. Will be GREAT distraction from Current Situation
3. Cosplaying as human will (possibly?) help me avoid detection b/c nothing bad ever happens at suburban human weddings (too dull!!!!) and they'd never think to look for me in Winnetka (suburban vampire activity all in Naperville)

4. *Maybe she'll help me with my taxes*
5. ~~Maybe I'll get to hold her hand again~~
6. ~~Or even kiss her~~

Cons of Fake Dating Amelia

1. *Frederick will lose his fucking mind when he finds out, which will be ANNOYING*
2. *I think that's the only con, actually*

Questions?

1. *The coincidences are a lot. Us running into each other 2x? Cassie's BFF = Amelia's BROTHER?? Strange.*
2. *How does A. not have entire stable of men willing to help her? She's exquisitely beautiful, smart, etc. etc. etc. Makes no sense that she'd need to ask a stranger.*

To-Dos: Haven't told her I'm a vampire. Must do that ASAP (refuse to make same mistake Freddie did with Cassie). Hope she takes it better than Cassie did when F. told her. ~~Hope that part of her even thinks it's cool that I'm cool~~

AMELIA

WHEN I GOT HOME FROM GOSSAMER'S, I PULLED ON A tank top and pajama shorts, popped open a passion fruit LaCroix, and Googled *Reginald Cleaves*.

I had never fake dated anyone before. But at least insofar as Googling your date's name went before actually going out with them, I figured this part had to be more or less the same.

I scrolled through the list of results as I sipped my drink, frowning.

None of them fit the man I'd just had coffee with.

Agent Archibald **Cleaves** hosts a going away party for Tom Cruise at his North Hollywood home on **Reginald** Way—

In this video, **Reginald**, with the assistance of UC Berkeley's electron microscope, **cleaves** the atom into two disparate halves—

The vampire fugitive R.C. has been wanted for the murder of dozens of innocent partygoers for the better part of two centuries—

That last link made me do a double take.

Vampire fugitive?

The better part of *two centuries*?

I clicked on it, more out of morbid curiosity than anything else.

It brought me to an ancient GeoCities website that looked like it had been created twenty-five years ago and not updated since. The page was filled with enormous Comic Sans text that was so bright red it was nearly impossible to read. I skimmed, snorting when I got to a set of instructions halfway down the page:

The vampire fugitive R.C. has been wanted for the murder of dozens of innocent vampire partygoers for

the better part of two centuries!!!! We, The Collective, remain the only vampiric organization dedicated to bringing him to justice at any cost.

SHOULD ANY INFORMATION ABOUT THIS:

CRIMINAL
EVIL VAMPIRE MASTERMIND
TERRIBLE GUY
COME TO LIGHT

PLEASE EMAIL THE COLLECTIVE IMMEDIATELY AT THECOLLECTIVE_1876@HOTMAIL.COM

I rolled my eyes and closed out of the site.

Some people really had too much free time on their hands. I wasn't one of them, and I wasn't in the mood to fall down a rabbit hole of Internet absurdity this late at night.

Maybe I'd spelled Reginald's last name wrong. He never did spell it for me. I typed in a few different versions of it to see if that got better results.

Reginald Cleves.

Reginald Cleeves.

Reginald Cleives.

Still nothing that was on point.

A total lack of an Internet presence had to be some sort of red flag, right? Maybe he'd given me a fake name after all.

I yawned and rubbed at my eyes. It was late, and I was

exhausted. My alarm was set for six the next morning, and if I wanted to be able to function I needed to get to bed.

Figuring out the deal with Reggie could wait until morning.

....

I WOKE UP TO MY PHONE BUZZING LOUDLY ON MY NIGHT-stand. I normally silenced it before bed. But after getting home later than usual, and then spending the better part of two hours trying fruitlessly to find some sign of Reggie on the Internet, I'd skipped about half of my regular nightly rituals.

My bedside clock showed it was nearly two in the morning. No one I knew would be calling at this hour. I rolled over and burrowed under the covers, trying to ignore my phone. But instead of giving it up, when the caller got my voicemail, they called again.

And then again.

I fumbled around blindly on my nightstand. When my fingers closed around my phone, I held it up to my face so I could see who was calling before I shut it off.

It was Reggie.

I sat bolt upright in bed.

Why was *he* calling in the middle of the night?

I thought of what I was wearing—a skimpy T-shirt and pajama shorts. And that I was in my bed.

I groaned. I was being stupid.

Why did it matter that I probably looked like hell and wasn't wearing much clothing?

It didn't.

I ran a hand reflexively through my bedhead all the same before answering. "Hello?" I winced at the sound of my voice, still froggy with sleep.

"Amelia Collins." Reggie's voice was as deep and pleasant as it had been at the coffee shop. He sounded wide awake. That made one of us. "Did I catch you at a bad time?"

Was he serious? "It's nearly two in the morning. I was sleeping."

A pause. "Shit. Sorry about that. I hadn't realized."

"You didn't realize it was the middle of the night?" He had to be kidding me. I had something akin to an internal stopwatch that kept track of time almost as well as my phone did. It was impossible to believe that somehow it hadn't occurred to him that I'd be sleeping.

"I'm kind of nocturnal."

I flopped back down onto my bed, throwing an arm across my face. "Why are you calling?" And then I realized, too late, that instead of asking this question, I should have simply gotten off the phone. In my limited experience, phone calls that began in the middle of the night usually involved either a booty call or the fire department. I wasn't in the mood for either.

"It's late," he said, sounding sheepish. "I'm . . . sorry for waking you. We can talk later."

Okay, then—not a booty call. Or a four-alarm fire. "You woke me up for this," I said. "I'm busy tomorrow. If it's important enough to call in the middle of the night, let's do it now."

"Okay." He took a deep breath that was loud enough for me to hear through the phone. "When I got back home tonight, I realized we hadn't decided what to tell your family about our *relationship*." He put so much emphasis on the word *relationship*, I could all but see him making air quotes. "We should get those details sorted before Sunday."

I blinked up at the ceiling. *Crap.* He was right. Agreeing on a fake backstory for our relationship hadn't even occurred to me. It *should* have, though.

Why was I so bad at this?

"I hadn't thought of that." I told myself I probably would have, eventually. I'd just been so preoccupied with finding a fake date in the first place, I hadn't gotten that far.

He chuckled. "You really weren't lying when you said you hadn't thought this through."

"No," I admitted, and rolled over in bed. "So, what should we tell them?"

"Just some basic things," he said. "You know. Where we met, how long we've been dating." A pause. "The last time I rescued you from the clutches of an angry dragon. That sort of thing."

I could hear the grin in his voice. Despite the hour, I laughed. "Right. Basic things like that."

"I know you're busy, and you've clearly established that you're terrible both at pretending and the preparations you gotta make before you can pretend well." There was an insult in there, though his tone wasn't cruel. Also, I could hardly be mad; he was right. "But you know your family better than I do, so the details should come from you. Even though making things up is one of my favorite hobbies." He paused. "If it's part of an elaborate practical joke, so much the better."

"Why does this not surprise me about you?" I was smiling now, despite myself.

"Am I that obvious?"

I nodded, even though he couldn't see me do it. "Yeah. Sort of."

"I don't know if you mean that as a compliment but I'll take it as one." He chuckled. "Jot down a few ideas and we'll hash it out over email."

"I can do that." I took a deep breath and let it out slowly. I could do this. The sudden spike of panic that hit me when I'd realized I'd missed something crucial to this plan's success was slowly melting away. All at once it felt very much like the late hour it was. "On that note, I'm going back to sleep. Good night."

"Wait." His voice was suddenly urgent. "That's not the only reason I called. Or even the most important thing we need to talk about."

"What is it?"

A long pause. "There's something I have to tell you."

I waited for him to elaborate. When he didn't, and the only sound coming from his end of the phone was something that sounded like a song I vaguely remembered from the *Twilight* sound-track, I asked again, "What is it?"

"I . . . wasn't totally honest with you earlier, at the coffee shop," he said, haltingly. "I didn't *lie* to you, per se. But I omitted some important facts."

Alarm bells went off in my mind. "What did you omit?"

There was another long pause. Gracie, who'd been sleeping at the foot of the bed, lifted her head from where it had rested on her paws and looked at me, as though she were waiting for his answer, too.

"I . . . don't know how to tell you this," he admitted. "It might make you want to back out."

Oh, fuck. "You're seeing someone, aren't you." It wasn't that hard to imagine someone finding Reggie weirdly charming enough to date. He certainly was handsome enough to convince some-one to spend time with him.

A soft chuckle. "No, it's not that. I'm not dating anyone."

"You're *married*?"

"No," he said emphatically. "I promise that in fake dating you, I'm not fake cheating on anybody else."

"Then what is it?" My heart sped up in alarm. I thought back to the kinds of cryptic warnings Sam had been giving me lately. If Reggie had some kind of criminal record for violent behavior, that would be a deal-breaker. "Are you a violent felon?"

"A what?"

"Like, have you gone to jail for beating up women, or something?"

"Oh. No," he said. "Nothing like that."

"Are you a murderer?" And then, because it was the middle of the night and I was slightly delirious, that bizarro Comic Sans website from the vampire vigilante group popped into my mind. "I've got it. You're a vampire fugitive, aren't you."

"I . . ." He cleared his throat. A nervous laugh. "How did you know?"

I snorted. When he'd told me he was a fan of practical jokes, he hadn't been kidding. "Got it. You're a vampire fugitive." I flopped back down onto my pillow and threw an arm over my eyes. "Look. It's late, and I don't really care what your deal is. I just need to know you aren't going to hurt me. Can you promise me that?"

"I swear that I would *never* hurt you," he said, more earnestly than I'd ever heard him say anything.

"Excellent," I said. "Then we're good." Whatever the real thing was that he was too nervous to tell me, if it didn't implicate my physical safety, it didn't matter. The only requirements for this fake boyfriend role were having a pulse, not being a serial killer, and willingness to go along with my plans.

It sounded like he fit the bill.

I'd never see him again after Gretchen's wedding, anyway.

In the meantime, I needed to get back to sleep to have any hope of making it through work the next day.

"You're really okay with this?" he asked, sounding incredulous. "It . . . doesn't bother you?"

I yawned, snuggling back under my blankets. "Why would it
bother me?"

He laughed, sounding so unhinged that I knew this had to be
a giant practical joke. "It's usually a lot for people to take in. Most
people aren't keen on bringing vampires as dates to weddings."

I snorted, amused at his commitment to the bit. "*Fake* dates
to weddings," I corrected.

"Fake dates to weddings," he conceded. "Even still."

I yawned, sleep beckoning. "What can I say? I'm very understanding."

"*I'll* say," he said, that earnest tone back in his voice. "Do you
have any questions?"

I bit my lip, considering. This conversation would be amusing
if it wasn't the middle of the night. But it was the middle of the
night. I was too tired to keep doing this.

"If I have questions later, you'll be the first to know."

"Okay," he said at length. "Um. Well, I'm glad you're okay
with it. Though, of course, it's important you don't tell anyone
about what I just told you. We're big on secrecy, for reasons that
are probably obvious."

Whatever you say, big guy. "Fine," I said. I was drifting off again.

I could all but hear him weighing whether to say something
else. He must have gathered that I was falling asleep, though.
"Good night, Amelia," he said. "I'm sorry for waking you. Get
some sleep."

I closed my eyes and did just that.

NINE

**Text exchange between *Reginald* Cleaves
and *Frederick J. Fitzwilliam***

REGINALD: I need clothes for Sunday
night.

FREDERICK: I still completely disapprove
of you doing this.

REGINALD: I know

FREDERICK: Seriously, Reginald, what
were you THINKING.

REGINALD: That it's a great idea. That
maybe I'll get my taxes done for free.

FREDERICK: Also given how long this
situation with The Collective is likely to

persist don't you think you should buy at
least SOME of your own things?

REGINALD: why waste money on boring
clothes when I can just borrow your
boring clothes?

FREDERICK: my clothes are not boring

FREDERICK: Cassie bought them for me

REGINALD: they work for you

REGINALD: but you know I like to
stand out

FREDERICK: Indeed. In either case we
are away the next few days. I cannot
lend you anything beyond what I have
already lent you.

REGINALD: Going anywhere good?

FREDERICK: A little seaside village
in Maine that the brochure says
has beautiful sunsets and great beaches
for strolling.

FREDERICK: I'm finally formally proposing
to Cassie.

FREDERICK: And hope to work up the
nerve to ask for an answer re: what she'd

like to do about "the whole mortality
thing," as you put it the other day.

REGINALD: DUDE. That's amazing!
Thrilled for you, buddy

FREDERICK: I'm thrilled for me too. ☺

REGINALD: Nervous?

FREDERICK: Terrified.

REGINALD: You've got this, man

REGINALD: Also, do I have permission to
go into your apartment while you're
gone?

FREDERICK: ABSOLUTELY not.

FREDERICK: Not after what you did
to our mantel.

REGINALD: I said sorry

FREDERICK: Apology accepted.

FREDERICK: My answer remains no.

REGINALD: fine, fine, I'll just wear what I
have in my closet

FREDERICK: Just don't wear Old Fuzzy, any of those things you pilfered from the Steppenwolf Theatre props department back in the 1980s, or anything from your feather boa collection.

REGINALD: well now I am going to wear all that stuff EVEN HARDER

FREDERICK: I suppose that if you show up as yourself it's Amelia's problem, not mine.

FREDERICK: I gather, by the way, that Amelia eventually came around to the idea of taking a vampire with her to wedding events?

REGINALD: she actually seemed surprisingly okay with it right away??

FREDERICK: Really?

REGINALD: Yeah! I was surprised

REGINALD: I was expecting her to freak like Cassie did

FREDERICK: Honestly, so was I.

FREDERICK: In fact, the Annals suggest that humans react to "I am a vampire"

revelations rather poorly across the
board, with a lot of screaming and
wooden stakes and such.

REGINALD: Maybe Sam told Amelia about
you at some point? So now she thinks all
vampires are like an undead Mr. Rogers?

FREDERICK: Cassie says she made Sam
promise not to breathe a word about me
to anyone.

FREDERICK: And I am NOT like Mr.
Rogers.

REGINALD: An undead Bob Ross, then.
Either way, maybe Sam didn't think that
promise extended to family

FREDERICK: Hm. It's possible.

FREDERICK: In the meantime, how did
she take the news that there's
an unhinged vampire vigilante gang
after you?

REGINALD: She seemed fine with me
being a vampire fugitive!

FREDERICK: I can't believe this.

FREDERICK: Are you sure?

REGINALD: I think so? But she was falling asleep on the phone so maybe I read that part of it wrong

REGINALD: I'll follow up on it soon

AMELIA

WHEN I WALKED INTO MY OFFICE THE NEXT MORNING, MY assistant, Ellen, was organizing papers into neat piles on my desk.

"I'm so sorry," she said, looking up at me. "The Wyatt Foundation overnighted us another box of documents. These were waiting in the mail room when I got here this morning."

"Don't apologize." I tossed my briefcase on one of the blue fabric-covered chairs where my infrequent office guests sat during meetings and flopped down at my desk. "It is literally your job to bring me this stuff."

"I know," she said. "I'm just sorry this file will apparently outlive all of us."

Ellen turned and left, leaving me alone with a mounting headache.

I hadn't slept very well after getting off the phone with Reggie. It wasn't every day that someone I'd agreed to fake date called me in the middle of the night. Apparently when it happened, so did insomnia.

Too many consecutive sleepless nights were catching up with me.

I'd hoped to get caught up on a couple of files I'd been neglecting since getting the Wyatt assignment, but considering all these new documents, I could tell that wasn't happening.

Hopefully this batch would be responsive to my most recent requests. If they weren't, and if once again the CFO had sent me things like promotional materials a summer intern made for their Facebook page, or ticket stubs from an Exsanguination Society fundraiser, I'd need to set up an in-person meeting soon.

I was just about to get started when Evelyn Anderson, the senior partner I reported to most frequently, rapped on my door.

She never showed up unannounced like this. What was going on?

"Evelyn," I said, sitting up straighter. "Hi."

At fifty-seven, with her expensive suits and perfect hair, Evelyn looked better and more effortlessly elegant than anyone had a right to at thirty. I was suddenly acutely aware of what I was wearing: slacks dark enough to hide that they were overdue for a trip to the cleaners, and the one cardigan from the pile of clothes on my bedroom chair that wasn't covered in cat hair.

It could have been worse. But I hated how at loose ends I was. When my apartment was a mess, *I* was a mess. I felt unlike myself, and unmoored in a way that made me uncomfortable.

"How's it going?" she asked.

In my seven years at the firm, I could count the number of times Evelyn Anderson had initiated small talk with me on one hand. I cleared my throat, hoping it masked my surprise. "Oh, you know," I said, going for nonchalant. "It's going."

Evelyn leaned against the doorframe to my office, folding her lean arms across her chest. "I know the Wyatt Foundation file is a nightmare, Amelia. *And* I know how hard you're working on it."

"I appreciate that," I said, honestly.

"I was hoping you might give a presentation on the Wyatt Foundation to the partners once you're on the other side of this deadline," she said.

My heart leapt. "Really?"

Evelyn nodded. "I've been wanting the firm to devote more resources to helping nonprofits." She smiled at me. "After the excellent work you've been doing on this file, you'd be the perfect person to help me convince the other partners."

I couldn't believe what I was hearing. I was probably already a lock on partner, but having the attention of the same people who'd be voting on my partnership could only be good.

Even though the idea of spending even one more minute on this terrible file was repellant, and even though what I *really* wanted to do was tell Evelyn we needed to drop this client, I recognized this for the incredible compliment, and opportunity, it was.

"I'd love to present the file," I said, meaning it.

"Good," Evelyn said. "I'll have my admin set up a meeting with you and the partners for about six weeks from now." She smiled again. "Six weeks will put us after this filing deadline and give you a chance to recover from tax season."

"I appreciate that," I said. Six weeks would give me plenty of time to prepare.

"Excellent." Evelyn glanced at her wristwatch and pulled a face. "Oh, lord. It's already past nine. I'm late for a meeting." She glanced at me, and added, "Don't work too hard today."

I nodded in agreement, though I was already thinking through everything I had to accomplish before going home that night. "I won't," I lied.

....

TO MY PLEASANT SURPRISE, SOME OF THE FINANCIALS THE Wyatt Foundation had sent me were relevant. Even if most of them left me scratching my head.

What sort of foundation invested in Transylvanian silk mills *and* made regular charitable contributions to blood banks in Western Europe?

The more I dug into the financials I received that morning, the more concerned I became that the IRS wouldn't view a group with such a scattershot mission as deserving of 501(c)(3) status. If we wanted to keep this file, I'd definitely need to schedule an in-person meeting with their CFO to try and reconcile all of this.

I was still knee-deep in documents and halfway through my meager dinner of takeout pasta when Mom called. I stared at my phone, trying to decide whether I should answer it or whether, in the time-honored tradition of millennials everywhere, I should let it go to voicemail and text her later. I hadn't spoken to her since dinner the other night, so I was pretty sure she was calling to ask about the boyfriend whose name I still had not given her.

But Mom rarely called during the week unless it was an emergency. Grandma was in her nineties and lived alone. What if something had happened to her, and Mom was calling to tell me?

It was probably worth risking a conversation I didn't want to have about Reggie on the chance Mom was calling about something serious.

"Hi Mom," I said.

"Good evening, dear." Mom sounded breathy, the way she sometimes did after one of her yoga classes. Not nervous or worried. I breathed a small sigh of relief. Grandma was fine, then. But then I cringed; there was only one other reason why Mom might be calling. "Do you have a minute?"

"Yeah," I said. I put the phone on speaker and set it on my desk. If Mom wasn't calling because of an emergency, I could have this conversation while eating. "What's up?"

I could hear Mom's new puppy, an adorable little white dog that looked more like a jumpy cotton ball than an animal, barking in the background. Chloe was one of the cutest dogs I'd ever seen in my life. No wonder my parents doted on her. "So, I promised your father I wouldn't do this, but—"

"Then why are you doing it anyway?" I heard Dad say in the background.

"I just couldn't wait any longer to get all the details," Mom continued, laughing a little and ignoring Dad's interruption. "Tell me all about your new *boyfriend*."

I closed my eyes. It was entirely reasonable for Mom to have questions, given that it had been years since I'd last told her about a guy. I'd just hoped I'd have a little more time to think through what Reggie and I would say about our situation before this conversation happened.

How much information could I even give her, since *deciding what to tell my parents about Reggie* was on my to-do list for between now and Aunt Sue's party, and I didn't currently know anything about him at all?

I reached for one of the only details I had about him. "His name is Reginald. But I call him Reggie." I didn't give his last name; I still wasn't sure he'd told me his real last name anyway, given the complete lack of Internet footprint for a *Reginald Cleaves*. There was a red flag in there somewhere, but I didn't have the brain space or the time to think about that. "He can't wait to meet everybody," I added. That was probably true, since one of his primary stated reasons for wanting to do this was that he thought it would be funny to play a prank on strangers.

The puppy was still barking, probably wondering why her parents weren't paying attention to her. "Hold on a second, dear," Mom said. "Chloe needs her evening walkies. I just need to make sure your dad is ready to take her." Mom mumbled something I couldn't quite make out; Dad replied in the background with something that sounded a lot like *but I don't want to miss this*.

"Thanks, John," I heard Mom say. "Chloe's little doody bags are in the drawer closest to the fridge."

"How is the new puppy?" I asked, trying not to laugh at Mom's use of the word *doody*. If she'd ever said the word *shit* in her life, I hadn't been around to hear it.

"Oh, she's a little doll," Mom said happily. "Anyway, as for what we were discussing earlier . . . His name is Reginald?"

"Yes."

"Wonderful," Mom said. "What's he like?"

I hesitated. I couldn't very well say, *Well, Mom, he seems like a pretty weird guy, and I can't find a single trace of him on the Internet, but he's also kind of hot, and the other night when he asked if I wanted to fake kiss him to throw pursuers off his trail, I couldn't stop thinking about what his mouth would taste like.*

Should I build him up, somehow? My instincts said yes, but what if my parents then had overly high expectations, only to be completely horrified when Reggie showed up to the wedding in all his weird glory?

"He's . . ." I trailed off and bit my lip. I was no good at this. "What do you want to know?" I hedged.

"Oh," Mom said after a beat. She probably hadn't expected to have to work for this. "Well, let's see. Okay, for starters, what does he do for a living?"

A dozen potential answers came to me, but none felt right. I couldn't say he was an accountant. Someone who joked about being a vampire on a middle-of-the-night phone call could never pull off *accountant* in front of anyone who'd ever met one before. Same problem with lawyer, and doctor.

"He's . . . in tech?" I floundered, wincing at how unconvinced

I sounded. But then I realized it was the perfect lie. No one in my family worked in tech and my parents knew nothing about it. Even if Reggie didn't know anything about it either, the odds of someone seeing through the ruse before Gretchen's wedding were low.

Besides, his eccentricities sort of fit in with all the stereotypes I'd ever had of tech bros. For all I knew, he actually was one.

"Tech?" Mom asked. "What does he do in tech?"

Shit. "Oh," I said, laughing nervously. "I . . . wouldn't be able to describe his job very well. Besides, he wants to tell you all about it himself. On Sunday."

Unbelievably, Mom seemed to take that at face value. "Lovely. I'm looking forward to hearing all about his career."

Me, too. As soon as this call was over, I needed to email Reggie and let him know he'd have to pretend to have a job in tech for this to work.

"And where did you meet?" Mom pressed.

Miraculously, the right answer came to me right away. "I met him at the office." This was, technically, the truth. I guess we hadn't been *inside* my office when he plowed into me on the sidewalk, but this felt like semantics.

"You met him at work?" Mom sounded intrigued. I relaxed minutely. But then she asked, "I thought you just said he was in tech? Is he an accountant, too?"

"Um. No, he's . . . not an accountant." Shit. *Shit.* "He . . . doesn't actually work *with* me. We just met at the office." And then, because I apparently didn't know how to leave well enough alone, I added, "He sometimes does tech stuff for my firm, though."

"Lovely," Mom said again. Dad mumbled something in the background. I heard Chloe bark one more time, and then the *snick* of the front door closing. Walk time had begun, apparently.

"Well, I'm looking forward to meeting him on Sunday. It's so nice Aunt Sue is doing this for friends and family to celebrate Gretchen before the wedding hoopla begins in earnest."

"Yeah," I agreed perfunctorily. "Really nice."

"I better go," Mom said. "My yoga class starts up in twenty minutes. But I just wanted to tell you how happy your father and I are that you are taking someone to the wedding. We worry about you and how hard you work, and we just think it would be nice to see you happy." I squeezed my eyes shut tight, willing myself not to reply to that. "Please tell that new man of yours that your father and I cannot wait to meet him."

I almost protested, insisting that my thing with Reggie wasn't serious enough to justify calling him *that man of yours*. A knee-jerk reaction, and a vestige of all the times in my life when I'd had to fight for even a modicum of privacy over my personal life.

I fought against that instinct. Letting them think I wasn't seriously dating Reggie would defeat the entire purpose of all this.

"I'll let him know," I said, trying to sound like I meant it.

TEN

From: Amelia Collins (ame.jean.collins09@gmail.com)
To: Reginald Cleaves (rc69420@hotmail.com)
Subject: Stuff we will tell my family

Hi Reggie,

My mom called when I was at work and asked about
you. I tried to be cagey, since we haven't agreed on
our story yet, but I had to make up some things on
the fly. Sorry about that.

I jotted down a few more idea on my commute home.
This is a work in progress, so if you have feedback, let me
know! (Overall, I'm thinking we should stick to lies that
have a kernel of truth in them whenever we can. It'll
make it easier to sell the story.)

A. <u>Where we met</u>. I told Mom that we met at the office.
(Close enough to the truth, I think??)

B. <u>Your job</u>. I told her you worked in tech and that
sometimes you do work for my firm. (I hope that's
okay???)

C. <u>When we met</u>. This didn't come up during our call, but
I suspect it's only a matter of time before someone asks.
How about we'll say 6 weeks ago? Any longer, and my
family will wonder why I didn't tell them about you
sooner. Any shorter, and it will undercut our claim that
we're serious enough for me to take you to the wedding.

D. <u>Our first date</u>: This didn't come up either, but how
about we say you took me to Encanto's, which everyone
in my family knows is my favorite restaurant. Then we
went to Second City. (I enjoy Second City a lot; doing
both of these things together would be a plausible date
for me.)

What do you think? Thanks again, SO much, for doing
this. You're a lifesaver.

Amelia

....

From: Reginald Cleaves (rc69420@hotmail.com)
To: Amelia Collins (ame.jean.collins09@gmail.com)
Subject: Stuff we will tell my family

hey,

can honestly say no one has ever called me a lifesaver
before. Happy to help.

you know your family better than I do (I don't know them at all) and am happy to go along w/ w/e you want to tell them about backstory. I don't really know what "working in tech" is but am happy to pretend.

also, encanto's AND second city is a typical date for you?? your past boyfriends must have had a lot of $$$. (Are you sure we can't tell them our 1st date involved me saving you from a fire breathing dragon instead of fucking ENCANTO's?)

seriously though looks fine. also, should we exchange a few personal details so it seems like we know at least a little about each other?

some miscellany about me:

>   fave color—red

>   fave musical act from the past century—David Bowie

>   fave tv show—the original Muppet Show is the best fucking television program in history (I know less about Sesame Street but feel I should rectify that soon)

R.

ps: what are some things someone who's been dating u for 6 wks would know?

....

From: Amelia Collins (ame.jean.collins09@gmail.com)
To: Reginald Cleaves (rc69420@hotmail.com)
Subject: Stuff we will tell my family

Reggie,

Okay—your joke about the fire breathing dragon made me laugh for the first time in ages. Thank you for that.

Things someone I am dating would know about me:

    1. My favorite color is blue (any shade)

    2. My favorite dessert is a tie between pancakes and anything with chocolate

    3. My favorite way to destress is to watch YouTube videos of this woman who lives on an island close to the North Pole

    4. My dream vacation would be any place that doesn't have email

Amelia

ps: As for my past boyfriends having a lot of money, I didn't say that *Encanto's* and Second City were a typical first date; I only said they'd be a plausible one. I haven't had enough past boyfriends for there to be any trends.

(Also, what do you do for work? You know what I do, but I don't know what you do, and that's something a girlfriend would definitely know.)

....

From: Reginald Cleaves (rc69420@hotmail.com)
To: Amelia Collins (ame.jean.collins09@gmail.com)
Subject: Stuff we will tell my family

Amelia,

am between jobs at the moment.

I think I know that YouTube channel. does she have a dog & a bearded boyfriend & a shotgun she carries in case she comes across a polar bear or walrus? Fascinating channel. I like to watch it when I can't sleep. though living that close to the North Pole—can't say I see the appeal. nonstop sunlight 4 months out of every year seems like no way to live (though I think the 4-month-long nights would be passably okay)

hadn't meant to be funny with the dragon comment. But if I made you laugh that's a good thing. I'm sorry you hadn't laughed in "ages" beforehand. (That, too, seems like no way to live.)

R.

....

From: Amelia Collins (ame.jean.collins09@gmail.com)
To: Reginald Cleaves (rc69420@hotmail.com)
Subject: Stuff we will tell my family

Reggie,

You're between jobs? Does that mean you aren't
working right now? (It's totally okay if you're not
working, I just wanted to clarify.)

Regarding the island close to the North Pole, I'm sure
the second I got up there I'd agree that being in such a
cold place was more trouble than it was worth. But right
now, being thousands of miles away from my real life in a
place where none of it could catch up with me sounds
divine.

....

From: Reginald Cleaves (rc69420@hotmail.com)
To: Amelia Collins (ame.jean.collins09@gmail.com)
Subject: Stuff we will tell my family

No, I admit I haven't worked in quite some time.

And as to your last point, we agree.

R.

ELEVEN

Excerpt from R.C.'s bullet journal: Day 4; written in alternating shades of blue, red, and green ink

Mission statement: ~~To live each day with courage, compassion, and curiosity. To become a better version of myself each day and inspire others in my path to do the same.~~ To not make fool of self at dinner party.

Feelings: Anxious about tonight. Which is <u>STUPID</u>. ~~What does it matter if Amelia likes how I look (it DOESN'T matter).~~

To-do list:

1. Review "relationship details" established over email
2. Investigate online bullet journaling resources. Am finding this surprisingly fun and therapeutic (and it's been centuries since I've indulged these kinds of creative impulses). Maybe there are others out there who can swap ideas with me?

AMELIA

NOTHING IN MY CLOSET SEEMED RIGHT FOR AUNT SUE'S dinner.

I had suits, slacks, and blouses for work. Workout clothes for the gym, and jeans and T-shirts that I wore around the house and to the farmers market on the Saturdays I could manage to get out of bed early enough. I had a couple of sexy tops I got for a girls' weekend in Vegas years ago that were missing some of their sequins and didn't fit anymore, and three different bridesmaid dresses I'd worn to various weddings over the past few years that I hadn't gotten around to taking to Goodwill.

That was the sum total of my wardrobe.

None of it was appropriate for this dinner at Aunt Sue's. Mom had said it would be casual, but I had a very different definition of *casual* than most of the women in our family over a certain age. I needed something elegant, but not too elegant. Casual, but not too casual.

After about an hour of rummaging around in my closet and dresser, I gave up. It was already after two. While I might have been able to go out and buy something if I left right that second, there was no guarantee I'd find something appropriate that fit and still make it back in time.

Asking Sophie to lend me something would be faster. I pulled out my phone and texted her.

AMELIA: Hey

AMELIA: You around?

SOPHIE: For the next few hours

SOPHIE: What's up

AMELIA: The engagement dinner Aunt Sue's hosting is tonight and I have nothing to wear

AMELIA: Do you have anything I can borrow?

I had about four inches and at least fifteen pounds on her, but Sophie had, over the past few years, changed clothes sizes multiple times on her way to having twins and then afterwards. Even before she'd had kids, she'd always had a more expansive wardrobe than mine, which had always leaned heavily towards functional and practical items. She'd been my go-to for last-minute wardrobe assistance ever since high school. Even though my complexion was several shades fairer than her deep olive skin tone, she almost always had something that looked great on me.

Hopefully she'd have something that would work.

SOPHIE: Of course

SOPHIE: What are you thinking

AMELIA: Something appropriate for family

AMELIA: Also, since I'm bringing Reggie along as a test run fake date, maybe something that also says

AMELIA: I don't know

AMELIA: Maybe, hi, I am here with my
new boyfriend that I am pretending to
think is dreamy so that you will all finally
back off

                    SOPHIE: Glorious. I have just the thing.

Two hours and several arguments with Sophie later, I found myself standing barefoot in her spare bedroom wearing a several inches too-short black cocktail dress that felt like it would rip all the way down the back if I so much as breathed wrong.

"Nothing about this says *family gathering*," I muttered.

"It's perfect."

"I look like I'm getting ready to go clubbing."

Sophie raised a skeptical eyebrow. "Have you ever actually *gone* clubbing?"

"Yes," I lied. I scowled at my reflection in the mirror, turning to the left and the right so that I could see how the dress looked from every angle. I all but poured out of it. "Don't you have anything that's a little more conservative?"

"No."

"You're lying."

"Maybe. But Reggie's gonna lose it when he sees you in this dress, and that's all that matters."

I stared at her, incredulous. "The point of all this is not for the complete stranger I am fake dating at a couple of strategically agreed-upon events to *lose it* at Gretchen's engagement dinner."

In the end I lost the battle. Sophie was all too eager to see me wearing a dress that she likely wouldn't have occasion to wear again until the kids were in school, and I was out of both time and options.

And maybe—just maybe—I let her talk me into it because a small part of me was curious whether Reggie *would* react to me dressed this way.

"Wow," she said, spinning me in a circle in front of her so she could give me one final appraising look. "Your ass looks great in this."

"Thanks," I said. "And if by *great* you mean *two seconds away from bursting the seams on this dress*, I agree."

She snorted. "By the way, have you figured out the deal yet with his whole *there's something about me you should know* thing?"

I'd of course told Sophie about Reggie's late-night phone call first thing the following morning. "I'm still not totally sure what's going on," I admitted. "Though when we were emailing the other day, he admitted that he's between jobs right now. There's nothing wrong with being unemployed of course, but maybe he's embarrassed by it."

"Ah." Sophie nodded. "Yeah, that could be it. Guys can get really weird about it when they're dating someone more accomplished than they are."

I stared at her. "Reggie and I are not *actually* dating."

"Details," Sophie countered, waving a dismissive hand. "Regardless, even if he's been unemployed for ten years, it doesn't matter for your purposes."

"Not at all," I agreed. "And either way, if I find out definitively what his dark secret is, you'll be the first to know."

....

THREE HOURS LATER, I WAS OUTSIDE MY BUILDING WAITing for Reggie to show up. I'd been clear from the beginning that this was a no-sex arrangement, but it was better not to confuse the issue by asking him to meet me in my apartment.

I wasn't dressed warmly enough for being outside, though. It wasn't as frigid as it had been the past few days, but it was still cold. I tugged at the cream-colored cardigan I wore over my dress, wishing I'd thought to wear a coat instead. Maybe a hat and scarf, too.

I was just about to go back upstairs and pull out some sturdier winter gear when an Uber pulled up in front of me. And then Reggie stepped out of the car and I forgot all about being cold.

In hindsight, we should have gone over what he should wear tonight. Then again, how could I have known he wouldn't have intuited it? It was a family engagement party in the suburbs, not rocket science.

The man standing in front of me, however . . .

He clearly had not gotten the memo.

"Hi," he said, grinning broadly.

"Hi," I said, flabbergasted.

I knew from one unfortunate Internet search accident a few years ago that a *fursuit* meant something very specific, and that *fursuit* was not the correct term for what Reggie was wearing. But it was still the first word that leapt to mind as I stared at him. His coat looked like it had been pasted together from old newspaper clippings and my grandmother's mink stole. Except where Gran's coat had been light brown, Reginald's coat was neon yellow and as fluffy as Mom's little dog. It also looked at least two sizes too big for him, with the sleeves stopping at the midpoint of his fingers and the bottom hem falling below his hips. His pants were not fuzzy—he wore normal-fitting slacks, thank god—but they were a shade of muted mustard yellow that clashed so horribly with his coat it made the space between my eyebrows throb.

His face, though . . .

His face was perfect. Clear blue eyes, full lips that pulled up into a smirk that I was absolutely *not* tempted to kiss right off his face. Not a strand of his wavy blond hair was out of place. In fact, his hair looked better than I'd ever seen it. Much less *dirtbag Chris Pine* and much more *guy who is sexy and absolutely the fuck knows it*.

If you only saw him from the neck up, you'd think he'd just stepped out of a photo shoot. I couldn't decide whether the rest of him made him the worst possible person I could be taking to tonight's party, or the best.

If Reggie had any idea of the horny-tinged-with-*WTF* confusion swirling through me, he showed no sign of it. He was staring as unabashedly at me as I was at him. Though I think his reasons for gaping at me were different. His eyes were all but glued to my dress's low neckline, and to the just-this-side-of-indecent way it hugged my curves. His gaze moved up to my face and then slid down, down, down, before landing, and staying, on my ass.

How long had it been since a man had openly *stared* at me like this? Like I was someone he found desirable. Like I was something he wanted. I needed to tell him to knock it off, but I couldn't. It was wrong, he was a stranger, but it felt *incredible*, the way he was looking at me. My heartbeat ticked up, the tight confines of Sophie's bodice encasing me like a vise.

No.

No.

We were not doing this.

"What on *earth* are you wearing?" I blurted, grasping for the first thing I could think of to snap us both out of it.

His eyes found mine again. Then the asshole had the audacity to *pout*. It had to be against the law for men with lips like his to do such irresistible things with them.

"What's wrong with what I'm wearing?" he asked, frowning.

I managed a small laugh, gesturing to his coat. "You must be joking."

"I'm not joking," he said. "If I were joking, I'd say, *Three guys walk into a bar. The fourth guy ducks.*"

I bit my bottom lip, determined not to laugh. But I was grateful that he seemed as eager to defuse the rising tension between us as I was. "Seriously, though. Why are you dressed like . . . like . . ."

He stared at the sleeves of his coat as if seeing them for the first time. Then he gave me a sheepish smile. "It's cold tonight, but Frederick doesn't have any winter coats. I had to improvise with what's in my closet. Turns out this was the closest thing to *winter coat* I own."

"Hold on a second," I said. The eye headache from a few moments ago was returning. "Why doesn't Frederick have any winter coats even though he lives in Chicago? And why is *that* the only winter coat you own?"

Reggie gave a one-shoulder shrug. "We don't feel it when it gets cold, I guess. Not like you do. But I thought if I didn't wear a coat at all, I'd stand out too much." He glanced at his phone before I could ask any more questions. "We should go if we don't want to be late. And don't worry. I promise I'm wearing a nice shirt underneath this. I'll take off Old Fuzzy when we get to the party." He grinned at me. And then, almost as an afterthought, he added, "I nicknamed this coat *Old Fuzzy* back in the '60s."

And then, as though the reveal that he'd named his ugly coat decades before either of us were even *born* made perfect sense and wasn't worth further discussion, he opened the back door to the waiting Prius and motioned for me to get inside. An especially gallant gesture for somebody who I was increasingly convinced was more than just passing strange.

"Um. Thanks," I said, scooting inside the car and closing the door behind me. Sophie's dress was so tight and so short the bottom hem hiked all the way up to just below my crotch when I sat down. I winced, trying to tug it down as much as the too-tight fabric would allow.

And then Reggie was sitting beside me, and our Uber driver was taking us to our first official fake date.

TWELVE

Excerpt from the BoisterousBulleters Discord Server,
#welcome-channel, dated two days prior

REGINALD_THE_V: Hi. Am I doing this right?

REGINALD_THE_V: Okay so my name is Reginald

REGINALD_THE_V: I've been a bullet journaler for about a week and while I didn't think it would be my thing it's been REALLY helpful in processing my shit

REGINALD_THE_V: (Sorry for swearing. I hope that's okay?)

REGINALD_THE_V: anyhoo the lady at Joann Fabrics suggested I check out this group to get new ideas. I'm not great at the internet or stuff like that but happy to be here

TACOCATTUESDAY: Welcome Reginald!

BRAYDENSMOM: Welcome! And yes you're doing this exactly right

ADELINETHOMPSON: Hi Reginald!

ADELINETHOMPSON: And don't worry, we swear all the dingdang time in here

ADELINETHOMPSON: Also, because I'm curious—do you go by "Reginald_the_V" because you're the fifth Reginald in your family?

REGINALD_THE_V: thank you for the warm welcomes everyone!

REGINALD_THE_V: and uh no the "V" stands for something else

BRAYDENSMOM: Please don't tell me it stands for "VIRGIN"

LYDIASGOALS: OMG it's a MAN!!

AMELIA

MY PHONE STARTED BUZZING WITH NEW TEXTS THE MOment our Uber pulled away from the curb.

> **SOPHIE:** How did my dress go over with Reggie?
>
> **SOPHIE:** Did his eyes fall out of his head?
>
> **SOPHIE:** I want a full report later

I rolled my eyes and shoved my phone back into my purse. The last thing I needed was to dwell on Reggie's reaction to my dress when I was alone with him in the back of a car.

It had been a long time since I'd been in the backseat of a Prius. It was *definitely* smaller than I'd remembered. Old Fuzzy was bulky, and when Reggie set it beside him, the three of us took up just about all the available space.

Reggie moved incrementally closer to me, and I reflexively curled in on myself, trying to become as small as possible. It didn't work well, though. The outside of our legs still briefly pressed together as he shifted in his seat to make himself more comfortable.

Hiding his body beneath that hideous coat should have been a felony. He wore the kind of generically dressed-up blue button-down that guys our age tended to wear as a default when the situation called for nice attire, but stretched across his broad chest that shirt was somehow anything but generic. To make matters worse, he started rolling his shirtsleeves up to just above his elbows, which in my book was one of the sexiest things a man could do. His hands looked capable and strong, and dexterous in a way that made my mind veer helplessly into dangerous territory, just as it had in the coffee shop.

I dug my fingernails into my palm. This was neither the time nor the place for my mind to wander. We were about to fake date our pants off in front of my family, for crying out loud.

But the way his blue eyes flicked down the neckline of my dress again and rested on my cleavage for just a beat too long made me think our proximity was affecting him, too.

We had to snap out of this.

"Let's go over some last-minute details," I chirped, hoping my voice sounded businesslike and not as wobbly as I felt.

He sat up straighter. "Okay," he said, so eagerly I wondered if he was as desperate for distraction as I was. "Like what?"

"Well," I began. And then stopped. The earnest way he was looking at me, like I was a schoolteacher and he an eager student, made it hard to focus on what I'd been about to say. "There's . . . um. My aunt's house. For starters." I cringed inwardly. As if Aunt Sue's house mattered in the slightest.

"Oooh. What kind of house does she have?" He leaned closer, eager to hear more. His leg pressed against mine again. His thigh was firm and muscular, and . . . no. We were *not* doing this. "Is it one of those great big houses that look identical to all the other houses around them and cost a zillion dollars?"

I had to bite my lip to keep from laughing at his enthusiasm. From the twinkle in his eye, I guessed he was trying to be funny. "Yeah," I confirmed. "And it's completely devoid of character."

"Gross," he said, though he sounded both delighted and fascinated. "I've never been in one of those houses before."

I grinned. "If you've never been in one before, I'm jealous."

"How fancy will the party be?" he asked. "Will there be assigned seating? Ice sculptures? A string quartet playing something by Vivaldi?"

I laughed. I could feel the knot of anxiety that had taken up nearly permanent residence in the pit of my stomach these past few days loosening. I wondered if he was doing it on purpose. Whether he was determined to put me at as much ease as possible before an event I'd been dreading.

"There will probably be, like, nice tablecloths and napkins," I said. "Floral table arrangements. But probably no ice sculptures, no."

Reggie was quiet a moment, processing what I had said. The Sunday evening traffic out of the city was light and we were making good time. The skyscrapers that had flanked our car when we set out were slowly being replaced with townhomes and smaller brick buildings as we got farther from the city's center.

"What should I know about your parents?" he asked.

"My parents?"

"Yeah," he said. "Beyond what I already know, of course. Which is that they're overbearing and insufferably concerned with their adult daughter's love life."

I bristled at that. It was somehow different when the same critiques I made of my parents came from a stranger. "I wouldn't say they're insufferable. But they are a bit overbearing, yeah."

"Overbearing enough that you are going through this farce to get them off your back."

It wasn't a question. "Yes," I admitted.

Reggie nodded thoughtfully. "What would someone who's been dating you for six weeks know about them?"

I thought about that. "Dad's a retired history professor."

Reggie looked like his birthday had come early. "No *way*," he breathed. "An actual *history professor*?"

I'd have thought he was being sarcastic if his every feature didn't exude earnestness. I couldn't help but smile. "It's really not that exciting."

"Oh, but it is," he said, his eyes gleaming. "Do you have any idea how long I've wanted to meet an *actual* history professor? What does he study? No, no—don't tell me." He squeezed his eyes shut tight and pursed his lips as though trying very hard to guess correctly. "The bubonic plague and how rats have been unfairly blamed for it since the Middle Ages?"

I laughed. "No."

He cracked one eye open. "Am I close, at least?"

"Not even a little bit."

"Rats," he muttered, looking crestfallen. "No pun intended, of course."

I snickered. "Of course."

"Okay, so what about . . . famous Italian painters? The legacy of Alexander the Great? Oh!" He nearly jumped out of his seat with what, again, looked like genuine excitement. "What about American neutrality at the start of World War I?"

"You're getting closer with the last one," I said. "He studied central European history at the end of the nineteenth and beginning of the twentieth centuries." I paused, taking in Reggie's rapt expression. "He co-wrote a book on World War I when I was in high school."

"Unbelievable," he breathed. "Will I get to meet him tonight?"

"Unless he managed to finagle his way out of coming, yes."

His smile was so broad it nearly split his face in two. "Brilliant. I'll have to think of the perfect questions to stump him. Now," he said, rubbing his hands together, "what do I need to know about your mom that you haven't told me?"

I thought about that. What *did* he need to know about Mom? "Well, I guess you could say she's very eager to meet you."

"Naturally," he said. "What else?"

"She's impressed by accomplishments." That was true enough. "She's proud of my brother Sam for becoming a lawyer. I think she's also proud of me for becoming a CPA, though she's probably not as impressed by my job as she is by Sam's."

His eyes went very wide. "Why? Your job sounds really difficult."

I looked out the window to avoid his gaze. Hearing him ask the same question I'd been asking myself for years hurt more than it should have. "It might just be my imagination."

I didn't think it was, though. They threw a big party for Sam when he graduated from law school. Which was super valid, of course. Sam worked his ass off to get his degree while still hold-ing down his full-time job in marketing. When I passed the CPA exam, our parents got me a briefcase. No party. And no fuss.

"It may just be that they don't understand what I do," I hedged. "Dad was a history professor. Mom taught English. I guess they've just never seen the appeal in accounting." I shrugged. "Or maybe the whole numbers thing just confuses them."

"Well, *I* think what you do is incredibly impressive," Reggie said, with a vehemence that surprised me.

"Really?"

"Yes," he confirmed. "I'll admit I don't have a very solid grasp on what it is accountants do other than organizing . . . um, some-thing with financial documents and money, and . . . uh . . ." He reached up and rubbed the back of his neck. "Taxes, and stuff. But it seems hard, and also important."

He looked so hopelessly flustered as he tried to reassure and compliment me that I found myself utterly disarmed. I inched closer to him in the backseat before I'd realized it had happened.

"I really do like what I do," I said. "I just wish that was enough for my family."

"So do I," Reggie said, his voice full of sympathy. Then he brightened. "Hey, I have an idea. If your mother is so impressed by accomplishments, telling her *the truth* about me would scan-dalize her, wouldn't it?" He waggled his eyebrows. "Might be fun."

It took me a minute to realize what he was getting at. "Oh. You mean . . . tell her that you're not working?"

He stared at me in silence for a long moment, brow furrowed in confusion. "I mean . . . sure. That too, I guess."

I tried imagining telling Mom I was dating someone who was unemployed. "No, I don't think that would work." At the look on his face, I hastened to add, "There's nothing wrong with not having a job, I promise. It's only that it's been at least a decade since I've dated anybody who wasn't either working or pursuing a degree. Or both." I shook my head. "She just wouldn't believe I'd even have a way to *meet* somebody who wasn't working."

"I'm not working," he pointed out. "And you met me."

He wasn't wrong about that. "Mom just wouldn't get it," I said, as kindly as I could. "I promise the truth about you doesn't matter to me, but I think we should just stick to what I already told her. We met at the office. You work in tech."

He sighed. "Fine. If you told your mom I work in tech, I'll play along. Would it be okay if I gave that backstory a few creative flourishes, though?"

I didn't see any harm in that. "Sure."

"Good," he said. "Because *works in tech* sounds pretty boring."

I snorted. "Fair. But in my defense, I had to come up with something on the fly. Either way, though, we're probably over-thinking this. Let's just go with the flow." When he gave me only a blank look, I clarified. "Just be yourself."

"Just be myself," he repeated. "And pretend to be in love with you."

My face heated. We'd agreed to pretend we were dating. We never said anything about pretending to be *in love*.

But honestly? For this to work, he was probably right.

"Um, yeah," I said, wondering if my face was as red as it felt. "Other than that, just be yourself. It'll be fine."

"Famous last words," he warned.

It turned out he was right about that, too.

....

AUNT SUE WAS ONE OF THOSE MIDWESTERNERS WHO didn't think a house was a home unless its inside *and* its outside were decorated to match the season. Of course, March wasn't a specific season in Chicago. So other than the arbor Reggie and I walked beneath to get to the front door, which Aunt Sue had wrapped in fresh pine branches and festooned with one relatively understated large pink ribbon, it didn't look like she'd done anything to her yard at all.

Reggie was still impressed. "Wow," he said, stepping beneath the arbor. He peered at the pine branches above us. "Is that *real* pine?"

I was about to tell him that my aunt wouldn't be caught dead decorating with fake foliage when he reached up and snapped off a handful of pine needles—and popped them in his mouth.

"Gross," he muttered, shuddering a little, before spitting them out into his hand. He glared at them like they'd just hit his dog with their car.

I stared at him, incredulous. "Of course it's gross." Was this man an eight-year-old child? "Why the hell did you just try and eat them?"

"I *didn't*. I just wanted to see what they tasted like." His face was still contorted in sheer disgust. "To see if they tasted different, the way everything tastes different now."

"Different? Different from when?"

Instead of answering me, he reached out his hand.

My breath caught.

I was dimly aware he was wearing Old Fuzzy again, but my line of vision had mostly narrowed to his outstretched hand. All my thoughts swirled around the idea that I probably shouldn't let it hang out there without taking it if our ruse had any chance of working.

I'd anticipated touching him in front of other people, hadn't

I? If we were going to put on a convincing show for my family, public displays of affection would only help.

"Right," I said, mostly to myself.

I took his hand, interlacing our fingers. I still didn't know what he used to do for a living, but his grip was strong, suggesting the same way his broad shoulders and slim waist did that he worked out regularly.

His hand flexed within mine, just as cool to the touch as it had been both the night we met and the night at the coffee shop. Clearly, the man ran cold. I gave his hand an answering squeeze, and he grinned at me.

Then his eyes fell to my shoulders, and to my too-thin cardigan.

He frowned.

"It's been a very long time since I've done anything like *this*," he said, gesturing meaningfully between the two of us with his free hand. "But the last time I went on anything approximating a date on a chilly evening, the done thing was to offer the other person my coat."

He began to awkwardly shrug out of Old Fuzzy. The idea of him lending that hideous thing to me like we were characters in some Regency romance novel was so sweet and absurd I had to bite my lip to keep from laughing.

"I'm not cold," I lied. I placed my hand on his arm to keep him from giving me the jacket.

"Are you sure?"

I nodded vigorously. "Very. You can keep it. Or not," I added quickly, because the thing really was an eyesore.

Apparently satisfied that I wasn't about to freeze, he eased himself fully back into his coat. The right corner of his mouth kicked up into a half smile. He gave my hand another squeeze that could have been possessive in different circumstances, but I suspected was meant only to be reassuring. I refused to acknowledge the small rush of heat that gentle pressure sent through me.

"Shall we knock on the door?" he asked.

"Oh, we can just go on in," I said, my free hand already on the doorknob. "Aunt Sue never makes us knock."

His smile faltered. His grip on my hand tightened. "I'd feel better if we did. I'll need your aunt or uncle to explicitly invite me inside before I can join the party."

I peered at him. "Why?"

He didn't answer me right away. Eventually, he said, "One of my idiosyncrasies."

"Okay," I said, squeezing his hand reassuringly. I hadn't taken him for someone who adhered to formalities like this. It was strangely endearing. "I'll knock first."

He smiled at me in obvious relief. I absolutely did *not* notice how well his smile suited him. Or how much it lit up his entire face. "Thank you."

We can do this, I told myself as I knocked on the door and waited to be let in. *This will work.*

I refused to think about what I'd do if my family saw straight through us.

THIRTEEN

Text messages from Frederick J. Fitzwilliam
to Reginald Cleaves

FREDERICK: Sorry for my delayed response. Cassie and I are enjoying ourselves immensely while away and I have not been checking my messages.

FREDERICK: Anyway, no: I will NOT give you "kissing advice for humans"

FREDERICK: I am not that crass. Additionally, what are you THINKING.

AMELIA

THE PARTY WAS ALREADY IN FULL SWING BY THE TIME MY uncle Bill opened the door and invited us to come in.

Reggie surveyed the crowded room, still holding my hand. I

refused to think about how well our hands fit together, or just how *nice* it felt to be touching him. I noticed, with no small degree of envy, how at ease he seemed here. Like he wasn't at all nervous about how we barely knew each other but were about to try and convince a bunch of people we were dating anyway.

That made one of us.

I scanned the crowd for my immediate family and saw Sam chatting with his husband amid a throng of people I'd never seen before in my life.

When Sam saw us, he smiled, and motioned for us to join him.

"Leave it to Aunt Sue to throw a party for half of Winnetka and say it's only for close family and friends," he said, shaking his head. His gaze darted between me and Reggie. "Is this your—"

"Reasonably serious boyfriend who Amelia's been dating for exactly six weeks, no more, no less? Yes." Reggie stuck out his hand for Sam to shake. "I'm Reginald."

Sam blinked at him in confusion for a few moments, taking in Reggie's riot of a coat, the bright blue of his eyes, and his serious expression. He hesitantly clasped his outstretched hand.

Then dropped it again almost immediately.

He must have been as surprised by Reggie's perennially cold touch as I was at first.

"*Reginald,*" Sam repeated, as if trying to place the name. Then he snapped his fingers. "Of course. You're Frederick and Cassie's friend, right?"

"That's me," Reggie confirmed. "And you must be Sam."

"Yes." He glanced between Reggie and me. "Amelia, can I talk to you for a second?"

Sam pulled me to the side without Reggie before I could reply. His eyes, usually so warm and kind, were sharp as steel as they darted back and forth between the two of us.

"What's going on?" I asked, alarmed.

"He *seems* nice enough," he said, his voice low and urgent. "I know Frederick through Cassie, and he's one of the good ones. If Reginald is friends with him there's probably no reason for me to worry about this. But if your date does anything . . . *strange* . . . will you let me know?"

Unbelievable.

Was Sam seriously doing the whole overprotective brother thing right now? Here, at a family party, where the most dangerous thing that might happen to me would probably involve Aunt Sue's dairy-laden catering?

"Sam," I said, exasperated. "Please calm down."

Sam wasn't deterred. "Promise me."

I threw up my hands. "Fine," I said. "If Reggie does *something strange*, I'll let you know. But I already told you he's not my real boyfriend. After tonight, I won't see him again until Gretchen's wedding." I folded my arms across my chest. "After the wedding, I'll never see him again at all."

"Amelia."

Sam and I turned our heads in unison at the sound of Reggie's voice. Wow, he moved quietly. And fast. A moment ago, he'd been over there standing by a large potted plant. Now he held up a plate of food in one hand and a glass of white wine in the other.

"This is for you," he continued. "I don't know when the kitchen staff planned to serve these mushroom things, but when I glared at them, they handed over a plate." He smirked. "I have an excellent glare."

"Kitchen staff?" I blinked at him. "Do you mean my aunt and cousins?"

He shrugged. "Not sure. Whoever was preparing the food."

Sam muttered something under his breath I didn't quite

catch, though it sounded a bit like *I cannot believe I am going through this again.* In a louder voice he said, only to me: "I have to find Aunt Sue. My firm agreed to help her make some changes to her will and we wanted to hammer out the details before Tuesday. I'll call you soon, okay?"

Reggie and I both watched as he made his way out of the room.

"I don't think he likes me," Reggie mused.

"I'm sure that's not true," I said. "He's just going through an overprotective phase right now."

"No," Reggie said. "I think it *is* true. It's fine. I get that a lot."

His sad smile shouldn't have tugged at my heart. He was a stranger. But something about seeing that flicker of pain cross his face did something to me. I wanted to reach up and smooth away the furrows in his brow with the tips of my fingers.

"I'm sure everything will be fine with Sam," I said.

I hoped it would be, anyway. The last thing I needed was for my brother to be all weird about my fake boyfriend right before Gretchen's wedding.

....

THE WINE WAS GOOD, AND I DRANK DOWN MOST OF MY glass in a couple of swallows. I hadn't been in a particular hurry to start drinking, but now that a glass of wine had presented itself, I realized it was a passable way to calm myself down.

"Do you want a drink, too?" I asked Reggie. The sharp edges of my nerves were already starting to blur. "Something to eat?"

His eyes widened. He whipped his head around several times, as though trying to make certain no one had heard me. "Later," he murmured, voice pitched low. "There are too many other people around."

He said it so earnestly, the first hint of what sounded like actual anxiety in his voice since we'd gotten here. He was taking all this so seriously. It was sweet.

"I don't think anybody would think less of you if you got a drink." I nodded towards the kitchen, where a group of men I vaguely recognized as second cousins were taking beers from the fridge. I was amused to see that some of them were clearly underage—including Alex, a teenager I vaguely recognized as one of my youngest half cousins—but I was hardly going to rat anybody out at a family party. "See? People have already gotten started."

Reggie stared at me incredulously for a moment, then turned his head in the direction of the kitchen. When he saw my cousins, he huffed a laugh.

"I suppose they have started drinking," he said. And then added, unnecessarily, "Drinking *beer*, that is." He inclined his head a little closer to me. His breath was cool and sweet on my cheek. "Listen, Amelia . . ."

He looked like he was about to say more, but my parents chose that moment to appear at my side. Reggie immediately swallowed whatever it was he'd been about to say. He pressed his lips together into a faint smile, schooling his features into an expression of polite interest.

"Well, hello," he said, turning to them. "You must be Mr. and Mrs. Collins."

Mom was beaming. She wore a pink dress cinched at the waist with little appliqué flowers across the neckline. It flattered her. I'd have to remember to compliment her on it later, when my heart wasn't pounding so hard from nerves it felt like it was about to burst out of my chest.

"And you must be Reggie," she said. She looked from me to

him and then back again, her smile growing. "I'm so glad you were able to join us on such short notice."

Reggie plastered on a brilliant smile. "I wouldn't have missed this for the world," he said. "Work is always busy this time of year, but when Amelia told me how important this event was to her, I knew I had to make room in my schedule for it." And then, turning to Dad, he added, "Especially since Amelia told me there'd be an actual, living, breathing historian here. European history at the turn of the twentieth century, right?"

Boy, was he ever laying it on thick. Dad looked delighted. "In the flesh," he said, happily. "Though I'm retired now."

"I would love to chat with you sometime about your research. I'm a bit of a history buff myself." And then, as if only just remembering I was still there, he turned to me and added, "Assuming that's okay with you, of course."

The idea that my dad might be chatting later with my fake boyfriend was mildly terrifying. But Dad was looking at me so expectantly I couldn't help but smile. "Of course."

"The kids never showed much interest in what their old dad did for work," Dad explained.

Reggie looked sympathetic. "Their loss, I can assure you." He pulled a slip of paper from his pocket and handed it to my dad. "That's my phone number. Feel free to reach out anytime you want me to debunk any of your theories."

Dad laughed so hard I thought he might fall over. "Oh, you're on, young man. I'll call you as soon as this boring party is over."

Mom shot him a withering look. "*John.*"

Dad made a point of fiddling with his drink. "Well, it *is* boring," he muttered, before slinking away.

"So, Reggie," Mom said, clearly eager to change the subject.

"You mentioned something about work a moment ago. Work is busy for you this time of year, too?"

"Yes," he confirmed. "So busy." He shook his head forlornly. "Always so much to do."

Mom made a sympathetic noise. "Our Amelia works far too hard as well, which I'm sure you know."

Reggie turned to look at me, his gaze softening into something that, if I hadn't known this was an act, I could have believed was actual concern.

"She does," he agreed. "She needs to be better at taking time for herself."

He squeezed my hand, tracing invisible patterns on the back of it with his thumb.

God, he wasn't kidding when he said he was good at pretending. My face flushed—whether it was from the unexpected gentleness of his words or the way he was caressing my hand, I didn't know.

"I'll start taking more time for myself as soon as tax season is over," I said, by rote. It was the same thing I always trotted out whenever my family gave me grief over my long hours.

Mom and Reggie exchanged a knowing look.

"I wish I could believe you, hon," Mom said, wistfully.

"I've heard this line from her so many times I've lost count," Reggie agreed, shaking his head.

I glared at him. Unbelievable. Was he actually taking Mom's side?

"Although it sounds like you work too hard, too," Mom said to him, chiding. "Amelia told us you work in tech but didn't go into details. What do you do?"

My heart sped up again. Suddenly, I regretted not pinning

this detail down with him more specifically and telling him he could get creative with the explanation. How wild did he plan to get with the ad-libbing?

I decided to intervene. "I told you, Mom. We met at the office, and—"

—at the exact same moment Reggie said, "I work at a carnival."

The room vanished. Time stopped. My stomach plunged somewhere in the vicinity of my shoes. The only things that still existed in this frozen moment of time were my mother's surprised expression, my mounting horror, and the complete stranger beside me who had just dropped the mother of all bombshells in the middle of Aunt Sue's tastefully decorated living room.

The weight of Mom's stare on me was so acute I could actually feel it. But my gaze was fixed on Reggie. His expression was carefree. Breezy. Like he hadn't just said the most ridiculous thing in the world and completely deviated from the plan.

"A carnival?" Mom asked, recovering before I did. To her credit, her voice sounded only mildly strained. "You—you own a carnival?"

"Oh, no," he said, shaking his head and chuckling. "I don't own a carnival. I just work at one."

Was this another one of his practical jokes? Like when he told me he was a vampire with complete sincerity?

I realized, once again, that I knew nothing about this man. Maybe he did work at a carnival. Obviously there was nothing wrong with working at a carnival. It just wasn't what I expected him to say, or the sort of thing someone I was dating would ever, ever say. And now that he had said it, it would make convincing my parents that we were in a relationship that much harder.

My self-preservation instinct kicked in at last. I decided to proceed as though he was joking.

"Oh, Reggie," I said, forcing a fake laugh. "You're so silly."

"I am silly," he agreed. "And you're not. Which is why I was so touched when you agreed to see my carnival with me the last time I had a night off."

If Mom's eyebrows had gone any higher, they would have disappeared into her hairline.

"And what do you do at this carnival, Reggie?" she asked. "How long have you worked there?"

She was trying so hard to engage with this foolishness. It was honestly so sweet. My heart clenched with guilt at how hard she was trying to be supportive of this man she just met, and of this relationship that wasn't real.

"Well, to be honest, I've only been a *carnie* for a couple months," he said. He said the word *carnie* with relish. Like it wasn't something he just made up on the spot to be ridiculous; like it was a job he loved. "But I do a lot of different things there. I run a couple of the games. Ring toss is my favorite, because I love it when these big brawny guys can't get the rings to go where they want them to go and lose their shit." I chanced a glance at Mom out of the corner of my eye. She was watching Reggie with the kind of rapt interest she usually reserved for deeply under-priced antiques at an estate sale. "I also help set up and take down a few of the rides, which is fine, but less rewarding on a spiritual level than watching grown men act like babies when they don't win a stuffed animal."

Mom looked at me. "Why did you tell me you met at the of-fice?" Her tone was accusatory, as though implying I was embar-rassed by my carnie boyfriend but shouldn't be. It was difficult to know exactly what she was thinking, though. By that point my brain had mostly stopped functioning.

"I . . ." I began. "It's just that . . ." I swallowed. Following this conversation felt like walking through quicksand. Why couldn't I think my way out of this?

"We did meet at the office," Reggie said, coming to my rescue. "And before I was a carnie, I worked in an office of my own for about ten years. Well," he added, chuckling, "*mostly* in an office. Sometimes I was in the field. I did computer tech support."

"Oh my goodness," Mom said, her hand fluttering to her chest. "What made you decide to give that up and become a . . . a carnie?"

Reggie turned a little, and inclined his head towards me when he answered Mom's question. "I was really good at my job. I got a bunch of promotions, raises, all that stuff." He shook his head. "But I also worked nonstop, and my heart was never in it. Not even at the beginning."

To my astonishment, Mom nodded sympathetically. "It takes so much out of you to go to a job every day when your heart isn't in it. I admire you for finding the courage to leave and follow your dreams."

He grinned at her. "Thank you."

"I hope your parents are supportive of your decision, too."

His smile slipped for such a brief moment that anybody not looking at him as intently as I was would have missed it. He recovered quickly, though, and was smiling again, broad as ever, when he answered, "My parents don't have much to say about my life anymore."

I could hear the hint of pain in his voice behind the smile. He didn't even have his parents' contact info in his phone. Given how much of a chatterbox he was about everything else, his reti-

cence about his family told me there was a story there. And one
he had no interest in telling me.

As curious as I was, he didn't owe me an explanation. He
didn't owe me anything at all.

Without thinking much about it, I clasped his hand and gave
it a gentle squeeze. To my surprise, he squeezed back. Whether
it was just reflex, or gratitude for my small show of support, I
couldn't tell.

Either way, it was time to move on from this conversation.

"We both came here straight from work, Mom," I lied. "So
we're famished. We're going to get something to eat." I nodded
towards Aunt Sue's dining room table, which had been turned
into a staging area for the buffet.

"Of course," Mom said. She smiled at us both. "Don't let me
keep you. Reginald, I look forward to chatting with you more
very soon."

After Mom left in search of other people to talk to, I breathed
a sigh of relief. "You okay?"

"Sure," he said. He was smiling again. But it didn't reach his
eyes. "I'm always okay." I wasn't sure I believed him. But he was
already looking away from me, towards the direction of the buffet
table, clearly signaling this conversation was over. "Shall we?"

He held out his arm to me in wordless invitation. I swallowed.
Right. We were doing this. With a slight nod to myself, I slid my
arm through his, refusing to acknowledge how nice it felt when
he tucked me closer to his side. Odd, too. Instead of the gesture
making me feeling warmer, his body seemed to radiate chill,
even though Aunt Sue's house was well heated.

"Hungry?" I asked him.

He cleared his throat. "I ate before I came," he said, giving me
a pointed look. "But let's get you some food."

....

WE HAD TO STAND AROUND A FEW MINUTES WAITING FOR
a large group of my teenage cousins to finish loading up before
Reggie and I managed to get to the buffet. He regarded what
Aunt Sue had put out and frowned in disapproval.

"Amelia, there's almost nothing here you can eat."

He was overstating the situation, but not by much. There was
a veggie platter with cut up celery, carrots, and broccoli that had
a little cup full of ranch dressing dip in the center that Aunt Sue
likely picked up from Costco. Dessert was a yummy-looking tray
of strawberries dipped in chocolate. I could eat all of that, though
I'd have to skip the ranch. But about three-quarters of the table
was taken up by a large silver platter piled high with little meats
and squares of cheeses, and a large crystal bowl full of Aunt Sue's
family-famous macaroni and cheese that I assumed was for the
kids. None of which I could eat without serious stomach ramifi-
cations later.

I sighed. "It's like I told you. My family isn't the most accommodating of my dietary needs."

Reggie scowled. "If they were going to insist you come, the
least they could do would be to offer a more diverse menu. How
hard would it have been to get food that contains neither animal
flesh nor dairy." He shook his head. "I assume it would not be
difficult at all, though I admit I'm not an expert on food."

I was too distracted by what seemed like his genuine irritation
to linger on the strangeness of what he'd just said. He didn't know
me. Why did he care if my family was collectively a bit of a dick
about this? And why did seeing him upset on my behalf kick up
a fluttering sensation in the pit of my stomach?

I almost explained that I'd stopped making a fuss about it because it was just easier to be accommodating, but decided getting into all of this with him would be more upsetting than it was worth.

"It's fine," I said. "I'll eat when I get home."

"It's not fine." His expression was almost pained. "They're your *family*. They should be more considerate of your needs."

There was the crux of it. "Probably," I conceded. "But, hey. The food looks like it's pretty good. There's no reason why you can't eat something."

He gave a curt shake of his head. "My diet is even more limited than yours. I can't eat anything here, either."

He gave me a knowing look that implied we shared inside information about why he couldn't eat anything here. If we did, though, that was news to me. "Oh," I said, confused. "Are you a vegan?"

He blinked at me. "No." Then he huffed a laugh. "I suppose I haven't explained all the specifics of my diet to you yet, have I." He looked like he was about to do just that, but our conversation was interrupted by a small commotion coming from the entryway.

I turned and saw my cousin Gretchen, walking into the house holding hands with a guy who I assumed must be her fiancé, Josh.

Despite everything, I had to smile. Happiness looked good on her. *She* looked good, somehow tan even though it was March in Chicago. Maybe she'd just gotten back from vacation somewhere warmer. A group of cousins, my mom, and Aunt Sue were circling her, everyone talking animatedly as Gretchen laughed and held tighter to her fiancé's hand.

I was happy for her that she seemed so happy. No part of me felt wistful, though. Did that mean something was wrong with me, that I didn't want what she had?

I didn't think so.

Maybe one day my family would agree.

....

GRETCHEN AND JOSH WERE LONG GONE BY THE TIME REG-
gie and I decided we'd made enough of an appearance at this
party to head home ourselves.

As I was making my way to the room where Aunt Sue had
stashed Old Fuzzy when we arrived, Reggie stopped me with his
hand on my arm.

"Should we do some extra convincing before we leave? Give
them a little show?" His voice was low, conspiratorial. His hand
slid down to clasp mine. I turned my head to look at him, but he
was watching the living room, where a smattering of other guests
who hadn't left yet were mingling.

Reggie's words and the slightly possessive way he was holding
my hand sent a frisson of panic down my spine.

Panic, and something else that I'd have to unpack later.

I swallowed. My throat was suddenly bone-dry. "What do you
mean, *give them a little show?*" As if the look in his eyes and his
hand in mine didn't make his meaning crystal clear.

He leaned in closer. "Kiss," he said simply, his mouth a hairsbreadth from mine. His eyes danced with mischief. "I mean, we
should kiss."

I shouldn't have been so surprised by his suggestion. After all,
the whole point of tonight was to make my family think we were
dating, wasn't it? But my body clearly hadn't gotten the memo.
My heart pounded, every nerve ending in my body suddenly cen-
tered in the places where he, where his breath, were touching
me. Standing this close, it was impossible to ignore how handsome he was. How his clothes looked so good on him that if I'd

met him in different circumstances it would've been impossible to keep from ogling him.

How charming he'd been with everyone we'd spoken with that night. Including me.

I was suddenly far too aware of my breathing. Sophie's dress, my skin, felt too small to contain me.

I gathered my nerve, and reminded myself that the only point of my bringing Reggie here had been to show everyone that I was doing just fine. There was no more to it than that.

"Let's do it," I managed.

He gave an infinitesimal nod of his head and a cocky little smirk that sent my thoughts scattering. He placed one hand at my waist, the ever-present chill of his palm cutting through the fabric of my dress like I was wearing nothing at all. He inclined his head, and—

"Wait," I spluttered, panicking again, freezing. His eyes were so blue, his lips so close to mine that if I moved even a muscle, we would be kissing. "You mean, here?"

The right corner of his mouth quirked into another amused smirk. *Unfair,* I thought feebly, unable to look away from his plush lips. "This *is* a rather central location," he murmured. His words were cool puffs of air on my upturned face. He was so dazzlingly close. "But if you have another idea, I suppose we could—"

I cut off the rest of his words with my lips.

Maybe if I had planned this better, I would have been prepared for the reality of kissing Reggie. But I hadn't planned this at all, and I was completely unprepared.

With what remained of my scattered wits, I reminded myself to keep the kiss slow and chaste. Nothing that would horrify anyone or involve tongue. But it was immediately clear that Reggie had other plans; it wasn't long before my body did, too.

He kissed with a practiced ease that threatened to completely unmake me, one broad palm finding the small of my back as he tugged me closer. I went willingly, unthinkingly, my arms wrapping around his neck when he tilted his head and traced the seam of my lips with the tip of his tongue.

It wasn't supposed to be like this. My body was not supposed to react to his proximity, his touch, his kiss. This *wasn't real*. But for my body, this kiss was as real as it got. My breath quickened as the seconds slipped past, as Reggie briefly dipped his tongue into my mouth before withdrawing again. His taste was peculiar, like metal and salt, like that time I'd accidentally bitten my tongue while eating too fast and blood pooled in my mouth. It did nothing to dispel the moment, or to distract me from the very real sensations coursing through me. I clutched at the ends of his shirt collar, thinking only of bringing him closer, not even realizing I was doing it until he returned the favor by bunching up the fabric at the front of my dress in his fist.

"Amelia," he whispered against my lips.

And then, it was over. Reggie pulled back by degrees, giving me a sheepish grin.

I was warm and flushed all over. I had no doubt that my face was as red as the strawberries I'd eaten for dessert. When I looked into his eyes, the blacks of his pupils had nearly swallowed up the brilliant blue irises, but he seemed otherwise unaffected by what we'd just done.

"Do you think they bought it?" His voice was low, with an edge of gravel in it that curled my toes. "I personally think it was a convincing performance, but you know your family better than I do."

A convincing performance.

His words were the bucket of cold water over my head I desperately needed.

I shook my head a little to reorient myself. "It was good," I said lamely. His eyes widened; too late, I realized I was answering a different question from what he'd asked. I closed my eyes and tried again. "I . . . think it was convincing."

To my relief, and horror, my mom, Aunt Sue, and my sister-in-law Jess had definitely noticed what Reggie and I had just done. They were talking amongst themselves in the living room, standing about ten feet away from us and shooting us meaningful looks every few seconds. When the older women moved away, my sister-in-law gave me a theatrical wink and a big thumbs-up.

"It was convincing," I confirmed, feeling dizzy.

"Well . . ." Reggie reached up and rubbed awkwardly at the back of his neck. His composure from moments ago showed signs of cracking. Now that he was standing a small distance away I noticed that he looked almost as dazed as I felt. His other hand still rested lightly at my waist. Was it breaking our rules if I didn't want him to pull away? "That's good."

"Yeah," I heard myself agree. "Definitely good."

If only I knew where we went from here.

FOURTEEN

Text exchange between *Reginald Cleaves* and *Amelia Collins*

REGINALD: hi Amelia

REGINALD: Oh wait

REGINALD: damnit

REGINALD: it's the middle of the night again isn't it

REGINALD: you're probably sleeping

REGINALD: no need to wake up and reply to this

REGINALD: just wanted to thank you for a lovely evening

REGINALD: definitely the nicest time I'd had in a Chicago suburb in recent memory

REGINALD: one of the nicer evenings I've had anywhere at all in quite some time if I'm being honest

REGINALD: anyway

REGINALD: you are asleep

REGINALD: sleep well

AMELIA: hey

REGINALD: Amelia

REGINALD: I'm so sorry to wake you

AMELIA: it's fine

AMELIA: i was awake

REGINALD: You were?

AMELIA: yeah

AMELIA: couldn't sleep

REGINALD: sorry to hear that

AMELIA: it's fine

AMELIA: i always have insomnia after spending time with my family

AMELIA: But I am glad you had a nice time

AMELIA: I did too 😊

AMELIA: I didn't expect to at all but I did

REGINALD: I'm so glad to hear it

AMELIA: I don't think I will ever look at petunias the same way again after that joke you told me after the party

REGINALD: That really was one of my better jokes

REGINALD: If I do say so myself

AMELIA: I haven't heard enough of your jokes yet in order to make an independent assessment of that statement's truth

AMELIA: but it was a good one

REGINALD: Well it would be my pleasure to tell you more jokes

REGINALD: if you're interested in making an independent assessment

AMELIA: 😊

REGINALD: 😊

AMELIA

I DIDN'T SLEEP WELL THAT NIGHT. PROBABLY BECAUSE AF-
ter Reggie texted me in the middle of the night, I'd felt so giddy
it took me over an hour to fall back to sleep.

Yawning, I rolled over and grabbed my phone from my night-
stand. I'd missed several texts from Mom shortly after I got home
from Aunt Sue's dinner. I'd been so carried away I hadn't even
thought to check my notifications.

> **MOM:** So nice meeting Reginald last
> night.
>
> **MOM:** He seems like a lovely young man.
>
> **MOM:** And so individualistic! A rare thing
> these days.
>
> **MOM:** Dad and I thought it would be nice
> to have the two of you over for dinner.
>
> **MOM:** Just so we could get to know him
> better.

My heart gave a hard knock against my rib cage.

Dinner with my family was *not* going to happen.

It was only six-thirty in the morning and Mom probably
wasn't up yet. Which made this the perfect time to reply to her.
When she woke up and saw my texts, I'd be at work and unable
to have the long conversation about Reggie that she probably
wanted to have and that I definitely did not.

I decided to reply to the first of Mom's texts and ignore the part where she wanted to have him over for dinner. He couldn't possibly want to come, anyway.

> **AMELIA:** I'm glad you like Reggie, Mom

> **AMELIA:** He enjoyed meeting you, too

That felt like the right thing to say, though I didn't know if it was true. He hadn't said he disliked my family; it was just that after that kiss, we didn't talk about them very much.

We didn't talk about them much before the kiss, either.

For most of the party, we sat in folding chairs at the very back of the living room apart from the others, with Reggie doing his utmost to make me laugh.

He was good at making me laugh.

Really good.

In fact, I laughed harder at Aunt Sue's party than I had in god only knew how long. Ironic, given how much I'd been dreading going in the first place.

After texting Mom, I made my way into the bathroom. I peered at myself in the mirror, hands braced on either side of the sink.

I looked every bit as rumpled and distracted as I felt.

That *kiss* last night . . .

It had been years since I'd been kissed so thoroughly and well. And it hadn't even been real. Just an act, for an audience.

What would kissing Reggie be like if we were all alone? Would he be more inhibited without people watching us—or less?

I closed my eyes, and before I could tell myself not to think about it, my mind started supplying images all on its own. His hands, capable and strong, cradling my face as he urged me up against a wall. His tongue, delving deep inside my mouth, leaving me no quarter as he crowded out everything that wasn't him.

My eyes flew open.

I should *not* be thinking about this.

"No," I said to my reflection in the mirror. My cheeks were flushed, my heart racing as hard as it had last night when he'd molded his lips to mine. "We are not doing this."

It was just an act, I told myself as I turned on the water to the shower. *It meant nothing.*

Reggie had given me no sign that he viewed our arrangement as anything but transactional.

The last thing I needed was to forget that.

....

THE DAY DRAGGED ON.

It was already six in the evening, and I was woefully behind on everything I'd hoped to accomplish that day. After my third failed attempt at reading a single balance sheet, my eyes drifted of their own accord to my window. It was another dark and dreary March evening, with light rain striking the windowpane. There wasn't much to see from way up on the thirty-second floor, so I found myself following each raindrop as it slowly made its way down the glass.

Was Reggie out in this nasty weather? What was his life like when he wasn't with me?

God.

I couldn't remember the last time I'd been this distracted.

I needed to get more sleep.

"Amelia?"

I glanced up at my assistant Ellen's voice. She was standing in the open doorway to my office. "What's up?"

She looked behind her, over her shoulder. "Were you expecting anyone tonight?"

I frowned. "No. Why?"

"There's a gentleman heading straight this way." She turned to face me. "I don't recognize him."

"What?" We rarely got visitors after business hours. "Is he a client? A delivery person?"

"I don't know," Ellen said. And then, with a sly smile and sotto voce, she added, "He is *very* handsome."

Before I could even form a response to that, Reggie appeared beside her.

I was struck mute by what I saw.

Gone was the slightly off-kilter look I'd come to associate with him. There was no sign of the too-large black fedora and trench coat from our first meeting, or of the Dungeons & Dragons manual he'd read upside down at Gossamer's. And Old Fuzzy was nowhere in sight.

He stood in the doorway to my office wearing a charcoal-gray suit that would have been perfectly appropriate in the client meetings we held in the conference room. Normally, I was physiologically incapable of finding anyone wearing a suit in my building attractive, ever. But seeing *Reggie* in a suit . . .

It was a crime, honestly, that he ever wore anything else. Even though Ellen was standing *right there*, I suddenly wanted nothing more than to run my fingertips along his collar. Pull him into a kiss like the one we'd shared the night before by the knot of his red silk tie.

"Amelia," he said brightly, stepping inside my office without waiting for an invitation. "So good to see you again."

Ellen's gaze jumped quickly between him and me, eyes wide as saucers. "You know this person?"

I nodded, feeling the telltale signs of a blush creeping up the back of my neck. "Yeah, I know him."

"I don't need to call security, then?"

Reggie jumped a little at her question. Whether it was because of the slightly threatening nature of it, or because he'd forgotten Ellen was there, I couldn't tell.

"That won't be necessary," he said. "Amelia and I are—"

"Friends!" I cut in, because I'd had no idea how he'd planned to finish that sentence. "We're friends."

Reggie beamed at me. Ellen took in the expression on his face and then gave me a knowing look.

Oh, god.

"Okayyyyy," Ellen said, drawing out the word in a singsong I'd never heard her use before. "I guess I'll be on my way."

She turned to go—winking broadly at me on her way out the door.

"She seems nice," Reggie said, once she was out of earshot.

I was hyperaware of the fact that we were now alone. I shouldn't have wanted him to crowd me up against my bookshelves full of tax manuals and continue what we'd started at my aunt's house. But lord help me, I did.

"She is nice," I confirmed. *Focus on Ellen. Think about how nice she is, what a great assistant she is.* Anything *but how incredible Reggie looks in that suit and how completely alone we are.* "But can you please tell me why you're here?" I walked around my desk until I stood directly in front of him. This close, I could all but count the faint freckles dusting the bridge of his nose. Just as I could have done last night right when he'd kissed me, if I hadn't been so distracted by the feel of his mouth on mine.

"I'm trying to avoid being at home too much these days," he said, cryptically. He walked over to one of the two chairs I kept in my office for visitors, which were more decorative than functional. The moment he sat down, it was obvious it was too small for his large frame. He fidgeted, then awkwardly crossed his legs, looking uncomfortable. "I happened to be in the neighborhood and thought I'd drop by."

I stared at him. "Why are you trying to avoid being home?"

He hesitated, as though weighing how to answer that question. For the first time since he showed up, he looked fidgety and nervous. "I'm just kidding," he said, though he didn't look, or sound, like he was joking at all. "Forget I said anything. And— you know what, fuck this chair." He awkwardly stood up and stretched his arms over his head, trying to work the kinks out. "Where the devil did you get that thing, anyway?"

"IKEA," I said. "Sorry. I don't usually get visitors."

But Reggie wasn't listening. He was walking to the far wall of my office, where I'd hung my diplomas and framed photos of my family. "Your office is very organized."

"I— Thank you," I said, caught off guard by his comment.

"It's fascinating," he continued. "Everything on this wall is hung perfectly straight and in perfect alignment with everything else." He ran a finger along the top of the framed photograph of me standing beside my two siblings on one of our childhood family trips to Wisconsin. I was about seven years old in that picture; a snowdrift taller than I was towered behind us. "You even dust them."

"I do," I admitted.

The face he pulled was so mock-judgmental and silly I nearly burst out laughing.

"But *why*?" he asked.

"I like things tidy," I said, feeling defensive.

"I get that," he said. "But there isn't a single book out of place in this room. Or a single stray sheet of paper on your desk. There's liking things tidy, and then there's this." He gestured expansively to the room we were standing in. "It feels like a mausoleum."

I snorted. "Been in a lot of mausoleums?"

"More than you might think."

"Listen," I said, starting to get annoyed. "First you don't really explain why you're here, and then you start criticizing my office?" I shook my head. *This* was why I preferred being single. "Tell me why I shouldn't ask you to leave."

His expression softened. "You're right. I'm sorry." He paused, then tapped his index finger against his lips. "The real reason I dropped by is I wondered if maybe we could get a drink."

My eyes widened. *What?*

"I can't," I said, on reflex.

"Why not?"

"I have at least four more hours of work to do before I can leave tonight."

"Exactly why you should get a drink with me," he countered. "You need a break."

"I've been doing nothing *but* taking breaks this week," I protested. "And besides, you sound like you're asking me out on a date. We don't do that." And then, for good measure, I added, "We aren't dating."

A flicker of something I didn't recognize flitted across his features. There and gone again. "I know," he said. He put his hands on my arms, which I realized I'd been crossing so tightly across my chest my shoulders ached. Reggie's palms were like ice, so cold I could feel them all the way through the thin fabric of my cardigan.

He gently uncrossed my arms for me and placed them down by my sides.

"This wouldn't be a date," he continued. "Just a chance for us to spend some time together while you unwind for an hour or two."

"How is that not a date?"

He ignored the question. "You're gonna die of overwork before fifty if you don't at least occasionally have some fun."

I stared at the stack of documents on my desk. The deadline for the Wyatt filing was getting closer every day, to say nothing of all the files I'd been neglecting because of it. And here I was, contemplating leaving the office before seven. *Again.*

I wanted to tell him all this. But then I realized he was right. I *did* need a break. Not one where I was rushing off to yet another family obligation, but one where I just took some time for myself and shut my brain off for a few hours. And maybe had a drink with a handsome someone who I was definitely, absolutely not dating for real.

"It probably would be smart for us to get to know each other better before we have to pretend to be dating at the wedding," I mused.

"Would that help you?"

I stared at him, confused. "Would what help me?"

"Would it help you leave this office before midnight if you tell yourself there's a purpose to it?"

His swift and entirely accurate read of me was unsettling. And yet somehow, it was unsurprising. "Yes," I admitted, embarrassed.

"At some point you should learn how to take breaks just for the sake of relaxing," he chided. "But I'll take it." He extended his hand towards me. "Shall we?"

I stared at his hand, remembering the way it had gently cupped my cheek when he'd kissed me. I willed myself to snap out of it. Getting a drink with him tonight was about unwinding, and about getting to know him a little bit more in advance of the wedding. Nothing more.

And the way we held hands all the way to the elevator, and then out the door of my building? Simply practice for the big event itself.

If only I could have convinced my racing heart, we'd have been in business.

FIFTEEN

Memo from George, Secretary of The Collective, to John, President of The Collective

To: John
From: George
Subject: Reginald Cleaves

Dear John,

New plan needed. R.C. saw me in the lobby of the hotel where he's been staying, recognized I was a vampire, and fled.

At our next meeting we should discuss strategies that don't involve sneaking up on him in places where he lives. All attempts to apprehend him that way have failed. He's a wily one!

George

REGINALD

TAKING AMELIA COLLINS OUT FOR A DRINK HAD BEEN A bad idea.

On the scale of bad ideas I'd had over the past three hundred years, placing my hand at the small of her back and guiding her into the seedy bar a few blocks from her office probably ranked somewhere between Mardi Gras, 1989, and that thing I did that one time in Paris.

But there I was, taking her out for a drink anyway.

I probably could have blamed my poor decision-making on having just run into someone who might have been a member of The Collective. He'd worn the same generic business-type clothes anyone staying in a hotel in the Loop might wear, so I almost hadn't spotted him for what he was.

But I knew he wasn't human the second he flashed his fangs at me on my way to the lobby to get a complimentary toothbrush and the day's edition of *USA Today*.

The man could see my fangs, too, if the way his eyes zeroed in on my mouth was any guide. Another dead giveaway. The glamour that disguised our fangs from humans and let us hide in plain sight didn't work on other vampires. I'd have said this lapse in glamour functionality would one day be my villain origin story if I didn't already have at least four of those.

In either event, once I knew he knew that I knew he was a vampire, I'd sprinted out of the hotel lobby before I could find out if it was just happy coincidence that another vampire was staying at the Marriott, or whether The Collective had tracked me down again.

I'd wandered the Loop aimlessly after that, dressed in a suit Frederick lent me a week ago. My only plan had been to go on a walk to clear my head, and to possibly find a new hotel since the Marriott was now obviously out.

But the next thing I'd known, I was in front of Amelia's building, hoping to maybe catch a glimpse of her. After that it had been the easiest thing in the world to sweet talk the security officer on duty into letting me inside.

And then . . .

Well, she'd just looked so *stressed* when I found her that I'd invited her out for a drink before I could remind myself this couldn't end well.

"It's loud in here," Amelia said right in my ear, presumably so I could hear her above the noisy music. Her warm breath against my skin, tickling the little hairs at my nape, should not have excited me as much as it did. She kept close by me, smelling like lilacs and sunlight, and looking like a dream—back when my dreams were still good. She was all buttoned-up and stern and accountanty, and Hades, I wanted to *un*button her, wanted to mess up that pristine desk of hers and lay her down on it, papers and books scattering to the floor.

Could she tell just by looking at me how badly I wanted to bury my face in her hair? To bury my teeth in her neck, too—if she would allow it?

I could all but taste the way her blood would coat my tongue. Delicious, and so pure.

The truth was, I wanted to do a lot of things with Amelia that she hadn't signed up for when we started this arrangement, and had given no indication she wanted with me now.

It didn't matter that our kiss had felt like all the good things the centuries had taken from me. Companionship, and warmth.

Closeness with another person. My role in her life was limited in duration and scope. And that was how it had to stay, unless and until she said otherwise.

"Yeah this bar *is* noisy," I agreed, loudly enough for her to hear me. Forcing myself to snap out of the haze of want her proximity seemed to bring out in me, I quipped, "I wouldn't have thought all these lawyer- and banker-types had it in them."

She laughed. I couldn't hear it over the shitty bar music, but I could see it in the way her eyes crinkled at the corners and how her shoulders relaxed. And I could feel it, when she slipped her hand in mine and gave it a gentle squeeze.

"Let's find a table," she suggested.

I wasn't sure why she'd agreed to come out with me. I'd been completely evasive in my reasons for dropping by.

And I *still* couldn't understand why she was so unconcerned about me being a vampire.

But I wasn't strong enough to look a gift horse in the mouth. Now she was leading me by the hand to a table in the back, her palm pressed against mine so warm and soft it took all my self-restraint not to moan in pleasure.

"How about here?" she asked.

I looked at the table. The floor beneath our feet was so tacky with spilt beer and devil only knew what else that my shoes stuck to it, but the table looked clean enough.

"Sure," I said-shouted. "Do you want to sit here while I . . ." I jerked my thumb over my shoulder towards the bar.

Uncertainty was written all over her face. "I don't really like beer." Another point in her column. Even when I'd been able to drink beer, I remembered it tasting like unwashed asshole. "But maybe if they have some Chardonnay?"

The bar's atmosphere suggested it didn't carry things like

Chardonnay. But then, a lot of the people there looked like they worked in fancy office buildings like Amelia's. They probably had *some* sort of wine selection.

"I'll investigate options," I said.

She smiled at me, so warm and genuine it felt like the sun emerging after a century of slumber, and Hades help me, I was lost.

AMELIA

Reggie came back carrying a bottle of white wine in one hand and two wineglasses in another. Even in this crowded bar, he moved with a kind of effortless self-confidence I didn't think I'd ever seen outside of a movie. He gave the impression of a person so comfortable in his own skin that he legitimately couldn't be bothered to care what other people thought of him.

Accountants didn't move like that. Or at least, I didn't. I think I was born worried about the impression I was making among the other babies at the hospital. My self-consciousness hadn't lessened in the years since.

I refused to dwell on how hot Reggie's self-confidence made him. Nothing good would come of *that*.

He placed everything on the table, then began to pour the wine. I watched the pale golden liquid fill the glasses, telling myself to focus on that rather than the large, capable hands doing the pouring.

"Here we are," he said, handing me a glass and saving me from the direction of my thoughts. "One for you, and a decoy one for me."

"Decoy?" I took a sip. The wine was actually pretty good.

"Decoy," Reggie confirmed. "I can't drink it."

"Why not? It's not that bad."

"Doesn't matter." He raised an eyebrow. "My . . . *diet* doesn't allow wine."

He hadn't wanted to eat anything at Aunt Sue's house, either. Given my own food issues, I had no room to judge him for whatever his were, but now I was curious. "What is your diet?" Maybe I was prying, but I'd already told him about my own food limitations, so it only seemed fair.

He leaned in and pitched his voice lower. "Don't make me say it in public, Amelia. Someone might hear me."

His reluctance to go into more detail reminded me of a conversation I'd had with Sam a few years ago about a new diet he was trying in the weeks leading up to his wedding. Sam had been mortified that I'd found out about it. Maybe Reggie, like Sam, was more private and self-conscious about his eating than I was.

I had no problem letting it go. "All right," I said. "Your diet is your business. I didn't mean to be nosy."

"Thank you," he said, sounding relieved. "I'm not sure I deserve your understanding. Not just your understanding about this, but about . . . everything." He gestured expansively to himself. "I appreciate it more than you know." Then he turned so that he was facing me fully, his eyes so soft and full of what I could easily have let myself believe was genuine affection my heart stuttered. "And I appreciate *you*, for giving it to me."

He leaned in, arms folded on the table in front of him. The look he gave me was so heated it could have sparked a flame.

I swallowed. The noisy bar was suddenly far too warm. I had to remind myself to keep breathing. "I haven't done anything," I managed.

"You're wrong." He'd seemed so distracted earlier, when we

were making our way to this bar, but now he'd found his focus. It was me. "Anyone else would have run in the opposite direction the moment I shared anything about myself at all. But you aren't running. Even if you're only staying with me as part of a ruse, I'm grateful."

My eyes fell to my hands, to the wineglass in front of me, on anything and everything but him. I could feel him looking at me no matter where I turned my attention, the warmth of his gaze as much a gentle caress as his hands had given last night when he'd kissed me.

I didn't want him to keep looking at me like that. Not here. Not now.

I also wanted him to never stop.

How did a conversation about food become *this* in the blink of an eye? We were spiraling, the situation slipping out of my control way too fast.

I had to snap us out of it.

"So," I began, staring intently at my wineglass. "Can we go through the people you're likely to meet at the wedding?"

Reggie chuckled, the sound warm and inviting. If he recognized this for the diversion it was, he had the grace not to say anything. "Right," he said. He cleared his throat. "That's the reason why you agreed to come out with me tonight. So, yes. Sure. Why don't you—" He cut off abruptly, eyes caught on something just beyond my right shoulder.

"What is it?"

He inclined his head in the direction he was looking. I turned to see what had gotten his attention and my stomach dropped.

My cousin Gretchen, wearing what might have been the prettiest green dress I'd ever seen, was making her way over to us.

"Shit," I said, my panic mounting. She lived in the suburbs.

What was she doing downtown? "She's going to ask us all sorts of questions. She'll assume—"

I turned to face Reggie. Pretending to be my boyfriend right now would be going above and beyond. But I didn't see any other way around it. Not without either being rude to Gretchen or telling her the truth.

He must have guessed what I'd been about to ask him. "I've got this," he assured me. Without another word, he grabbed my hand that was closest to him and pressed a lingering kiss to my palm.

It was a simple gesture, his breath cool against my skin and the touch of his lips almost achingly gentle. Compared to the spine-melting kiss we'd shared at Aunt Sue's it was positively chaste. On some level, I was aware of that—but my racing heart didn't get the memo. He held my hand like it was something precious, and looked into my eyes as though there were nowhere he'd rather be. My breath caught as I met his gaze, and at what I could almost believe was real adoration reflected there.

I was barely aware of it when Gretchen pulled out one of the extra seats at our table and sat down. Reggie seemed not to notice her, either. He wasn't kissing my hand anymore, but he was still holding it, rubbing gentle circles on the back of it with his thumb. His touch was grounding. Exhilarating.

"Hey!" Gretchen greeted us.

I cleared my throat, hoping I wasn't blushing *too* deeply, and willed myself to get it together. Gretchen was watching both of us with a knowing expression.

"Nice to see you," I said, wincing at how breathy I sounded.

"Nice to see you, too," Gretchen said. "How wild is it that we ran into each other here? I'm so exhausted right now I almost didn't even come out with my coworkers tonight." She took a long sip from a beer that I could tell was some kind of IPA from the way I could smell its hops from where I was sitting. Setting her glass back down again, she added, "I'm sorry I didn't get a chance to catch up with you at Mom's party."

"Oh my god, don't worry about it," I said. "You had, like, a million people to entertain."

She nodded. "Yeah. You know how my mom can be. *I'm just going to invite close friends and family,* she told me." Gretchen shook her head wearily before taking another long pull from her glass. "Amelia—she invited my friends from *high school.*"

I shuddered. I couldn't even imagine being *ooh*ed and *ahh*ed over by people I hadn't seen in twenty years. "That really sucks. I'm sorry."

Gretchen shook her head. "Thanks. It was a bit stressful, but it's fine. I know Mom's intentions were good." Her gaze shifted to Reggie, who'd been watching our conversation with rapt attention. "I didn't get a chance to chat with you, either. It seems like you and my cousin are close?"

Gretchen kicked me under the table, in a way I one hundred percent interpreted as *my mom* totally *told me y'all made out at my party.*

Reggie, noticing this, slid an arm around me and pulled me and my chair over. On instinct, I slipped my arm beneath his suit jacket and wrapped it around his waist. The shirt he wore was so soft; it was only sheer force of will that prevented me from burrowing further into his side and breathing him in.

"We're definitely close," Reggie said. He pressed a kiss to the top of my head, letting his lips linger. I closed my eyes reflexively, leaning into his touch before realizing I was doing it. "We've been dating six weeks."

Gretchen gave me a knowing look. "I knew Josh was the one after six weeks."

Oh, god. My face was on fire. Reggie's hold on me tightened. "Is that so?" he asked, sounding genuinely interested.

"Yeah," Gretchen said. "If it's right, you just know. You know?"

He peered down at me, his eyes giving nothing away. "Actually, Gretchen—it's possible that maybe I do."

Oh, he was good. *Too* good. If I hadn't known better, I would have thought he actually meant it.

Gretchen stood from her chair. "Well, I better get back to my coworkers. They took me out tonight to celebrate. It would be rude of me to ditch them." Before turning to leave, she said, "I'll see you both at the couples' trip to Wisconsin, though, right?"

My heart thundered inside my rib cage.

Reggie looked at me, a question in his eyes.

Oh, *no.*

No, no, no, no, *no.*

"See you then!" I chirped at Gretchen, before Reggie had a chance to ask any questions.

It wasn't until she'd made it back to her friends at the other side of the bar that I risked a glance at Reggie. He was watching me carefully, clearly waiting for me to explain what Gretchen had meant.

"So, there's a family get-together in Wisconsin this coming weekend," I explained. "Sort of like a destination celebration for the happy couple, I guess? I'm not sure why Gretchen wants to take a vacation with extended family before the wedding, but apparently, she does." I paused. "Adult family members and their partners and families are invited. If they have them, that is," I added quickly.

"I assume you didn't tell me about the trip because you weren't planning to invite me?"

His tone was matter-of-fact, not accusatory. "When I got the invitation, we didn't know each other," I said, feeling defensive anyway. "We weren't—*aren't*—actually dating."

He didn't correct me. "And you would have thought it awkward to have a stranger along with you on this trip," he said. "Posing as your boyfriend. Right?"

I hesitated. He was still practically a stranger. It *would* be awkward spending a whole weekend with him and my family. No matter how delicious that kiss last night had been, and no matter that he had turned what could've been an excruciating family event into something fun.

No matter how readily he'd been willing to go along with the farce just now in front of Gretchen, even though it hadn't been in the script, simply because I'd needed him to.

But now there was a new worry. What if spending all that time in Wisconsin with him made me want to kiss him again? The last thing I needed was an *actual* relationship. Or an unrequited messy situation. That wasn't what this was supposed to be about.

"Would you even want to come?" I asked. "This wasn't part of the deal. And I'm sure you have better things to do than hang out with my family."

"I think you overestimate how busy I am," he said. "Will your father be there?"

What did Dad have to do with this? "I mean, yeah, I assume so."

He slapped his palm down on the table, eyes alive with excitement. "That does it. I'm coming. I didn't get a chance to stump him at your aunt's party." He was about to smack the table again, but a moment before his palm struck wood, he seemed to realize that while Gretchen had invited him to come, I hadn't. "That is, of course, if you're okay with my tagging along."

Was I okay with it? Or was letting him come a terrible idea? An entire weekend in my family's cabin, where we'd sit around and play games, and meet up with Aunt Sue, Gretchen, and the rest of the family during the day for hikes and trips to town?

Notwithstanding Reggie's claims to be excited, he'd be bored out of his mind up there. Wouldn't he?

On the other hand, it *would* be a way to further convince my family that what we had was real. And it wasn't as though we'd have to share a bed. There were two twins in the room I slept in at the cabin. There'd be no need for any awkwardness at nighttime.

Reggie was still watching me expectantly when I made up my mind.

"I'm warning you," I said. "If Dad finds out you're excited to talk to him about history, you'll be his favorite person ever."

Reggie took that as the invitation it was. His smile grew. "His favorite person *ever*? Wow. In that case, I'm *absolutely* coming. It's been centuries since I was someone's favorite person."

I smiled back at him. "You are really fond of hyperbole, aren't you."

"Oh, yes," he said, earnestly. "It's my favorite word beginning with *hyper*."

God, his sense of humor was disarming.

Dangerous.

Ignoring the warning klaxon going off in my head, I said, "If you're sure, I'll text you the details."

"Marvelous." Even if I hadn't been able to see him grinning at me, I would have heard the smile in his voice. "I'm sincerely looking forward to it."

SIXTEEN

*Excerpt from R.C.'s bullet journal: written in alternating
shades of blue, red, and green ink, with smiley and frowny
face stickers scattered throughout the page and bright
red doodled hearts by every heading*

Mission statement: ~~To live each day with courage, compassion, and
curiosity. To become a better version of myself each day and
inspire others in my path to do the same.~~ To keep self under
control in Wisconsin and not let Amelia see how badly I want to
kiss her again

Feelings: Confused. A.C. only invited me to Wisconsin because she was
put on the spot but sometimes, the way she looks at me makes me
wonder whether she likes me for real. ~~I am pathetic and delusional. How could someone like her possibly want someone like me.
The idea I might have feelings for her is terrifying~~

To-do list:

1. Pilfer South Side blood bank for supplies

2. *Pack: a. Meals; b. Old Fuzzy; c. Monopoly; d. Glockenspiel*

3. *leave note on door to throw Collective off trail if they come looking for me*

AMELIA

"YOU ARE NOT TAKING ALL THAT CRAP WITH YOU TO WIS-consin."

I looked up from the briefcase I'd been packing with work files to see Sophie standing at the foot of my bed, her arms crossed tightly across her chest. She had the same look on her face she always did whenever I did something disappointing.

Like taking work on a trip that was supposed to be a vacation.

"You're as bad as Gracie," I said. Gracie, for her part, was curled up sleeping on my bed. But if she'd been awake, I was sure she'd have been licking her paw in a way that expressed maximum disapproval.

"You're not supposed to work up there," Sophie insisted. "Family togetherness, bonding in the wilderness, hooking up with your pretend boyfriend—*that's* what this vacation is about."

I glared at her. "This trip is nothing but a family obligation. It is *not* a vacation, and *not* an opportunity to hook up with anybody."

"But you'll be there with *Reggie*," she said, voice adopting a bit of a singsong when she said his name. Her eyes danced with mischief. "Are you sure you won't have better things to do with your time than taxes?"

I ignored her suggestive tone. "There's never any better thing to do with my time than taxes."

Sophie snorted. "Oh, stop it. You told me the way he looked at you the other night. He couldn't take his eyes off you. You're seriously going to waste that?"

"I never said that."

"You said that when he saw you, he shut up for the first time since you'd met him." Sophie smirked. "I bet he had a hard-on before even getting into that Uber."

"Sophie!" I dropped the file I'd been about to put in my briefcase, scattering papers everywhere. I tried to think of how to get her to stop harping on this but was coming up empty. Especially since Reggie *had* been unable to keep his eyes off me for a good portion of Gretchen's engagement party. But thinking about my possibly having given him a hard-on . . .

No.

That would lead to nothing good.

Certainly not right now, when we were about to spend five hours together in a car, and then an entire weekend at the cabin. I'd assumed my family would rent one big van and go up together, the way we used to when I was younger. But everyone had different obligations this weekend and needed to leave at different times. So it would just be me and Reggie, alone in an enclosed space for hours.

Sophie watched as I continued packing. "I think you're into him, too."

I stared at her. "I am absolutely not *into him*." I put special emphasis on the last two words, as if the mere concept were beneath me.

"Hmm."

"What he and I have is just . . . just . . ."

Sophie arched an eyebrow. "Just what?"

"It's just an *arrangement*," I finished, lamely. "It's purely *transactional*. It isn't real."

"I know. But would it be so bad if it became real?"

"Yes."

"But why?" Sophie must have sensed I was struggling with this, because all the teasing had left her voice. "He's interesting, isn't he? And funny? Also really good-looking?"

I couldn't even deny what she was saying, because he *was* all those things. But what she was suggesting was ridiculous. "I can't make this real, Soph. For one thing, he has no Internet presence at all. That's weird, right? I have a feeling that if I look too closely, I'll come across skeletons in his closet I'll regret discovering."

Sophie shrugged. "So he has a few red flags. Who doesn't?"

"I also don't have time for a relationship." When Sophie didn't reply, only stared at me with a smirk on her face, I rolled my eyes. "Please don't tell me you think I need a boyfriend, too, Soph. I don't think I could handle it if you did."

"Not at all." Sophie sat down next to me on the bed and put a hand on my knee. She gave it a squeeze. "If you want to stay single for the rest of your life, I support you. But I also don't understand why you're fighting your attraction to this guy as hard as you are."

"I'm not attracted to him," I said. I wasn't. I mean, sure, he was *attractive*. And yes, I found myself revisiting funny things he'd said or kind things he'd done at odd moments. Like when I was taking a shower, or riding the El to work, or trying to focus on this damn Wyatt filing.

But none of that meant I was *attracted* to him. Did it?

Sophie gave me a knowing look. "Just think about it, okay? While you're up there, if the opportunity presents itself to turn this arrangement into something real, don't think your way out of what could be either a good thing or, at the very least, a short-term good time."

A *short-term good time*.

Was I even capable of something like that?

The sad thing was, I didn't think so.

I needed to change the subject, and fast. I reached across the bed to where Gracie was still curled up and dozing, oblivious to this conversation, and stroked her fur. "Be a good girl for Auntie Sophie while I'm away, Gracie," I cooed.

Sophie recognized my lame diversion tactic for what it was. "You're going to be the end of me," she said. "Can you at least promise me you'll *try* to have fun on this trip?"

That was easy enough. "Yes. I promise."

"And maybe pack some sexy underwear?"

"*Sophie.*" I laughed, to deflect from the fact that I didn't own any. "Absolutely not."

Sophie sighed. "Can't blame me for trying."

....

AT NINE THE NEXT MORNING, REGGIE WAS WAITING FOR me outside the hotel he said he was staying in while his apartment was being renovated with two large duffel bags slung over his shoulders. A not-small part of me had hoped he'd be wearing Old Fuzzy, or some other hideous thing, so that the next few hours alone in a car with this man who could get my heart racing with just a glance would be less distracting.

But as luck would, or wouldn't, have it, he looked fantastic. It couldn't have been more than twenty-five degrees outside, but jeans and a long-sleeved green Henley were all that separated him from the elements. And all that separated my eyes from the muscles I knew lay beneath them.

"No coat?" I asked when he climbed into the passenger seat beside me. He smelled good, like leather and mint. I resisted the urge to reach out and touch his shirt to see if it was as soft as it looked, but only just.

"It's in my bag," he said, jerking a thumb towards the back-seat, where he'd tossed it. "I brought some other key winter wear as well."

"Such as?"

He held up his hand and began counting off items on his fingers. "Long johns, knee socks, a knit cap with Santa on the front that has reindeer-themed earflaps, and gloves." He paused. "Oh! And a pink feather boa I found at Goodwill a week ago."

I stared at him. "A feather boa? That's key winter wear?"

He shrugged. "Probably not. But it's fun, and you said there isn't much to do in Wisconsin, so I thought maybe I would bring the fun with me."

I laughed. "I did say that, didn't I."

He jerked his thumb towards the backseat again. "You did. In that vein, I also packed a one-thousand-piece jigsaw puzzle fea-turing cats in outer space that we can do if we get bored."

An image of me and Reggie, sitting around a small coffee table with my nieces as we did a puzzle together flashed unbid-den in my mind. It nearly bowled me over with its unexpected sweetness.

"I also brought my glockenspiel." He looked at me hopefully. "I hope you like music."

I thought of what I'd taken with me on this trip: a small roller bag with a few changes of clothes, my laptop, and a briefcase full of work. Much less fun than what Reggie was bringing. I sighed; there was nothing to be done for it.

"Go ahead and fasten your seat belt and we'll be off," I said.

Reggie stared at me a moment, as though I'd just said something to him in a language he didn't understand. Then he burst out laughing.

"You're hilarious," he said between cackles. Then he added, in an uncannily good impression of me, "*Go ahead and fasten your seat belt!*"

He'd lost me. "What's so funny about wearing a seat belt?"

He shook his head, still giggling. "For you? Nothing. You *should* wear one. Car accidents can be deadly. But for me? *Everything* is funny about it." He sighed, then reached behind him and drew the seat belt across his torso. "Okay, I am *wearing my seat belt* now. Shall we be off? Oh, and I hope it's all right if you do all the driving. I never learned how."

It was good that Reggie periodically tempered his hotness with downright bizarre behavior. It made it more likely that I'd be able to focus on work on this trip. I chanced another glance at him out of the corner of my eye as I pulled away from the curb; he was examining the holster that attached the seat belt to the car with such intense interest it was like he'd never seen one before.

"I'm fine driving," I agreed. I wasn't sure I wanted him driving my car, anyway. "By the way, is there anything specific you'd like to do on this trip?"

I expected him to reply with some variation on the outdoor activities theme, because that was largely what there was to do up there. "Avoid getting stuck in the blizzard that they expect to hit sometime between now and tonight," he said instead.

I almost choked on my tongue. "*What?*"

He looked at me, incredulous. "Amelia, you're someone who plans for every eventuality. Are you telling me you haven't checked the weather forecast?"

I opened and closed my mouth several times, trying to make words form. Ordinarily, before any big trip I would check the weather multiple times.

I hadn't this time, though. I'd been too distracted.

"No. I mean . . . yes." I shook my head and tried again. "Yes, I mean to tell you that, no, I haven't checked the weather."

"You should probably do it now," he said, mildly.

One hand still on the steering wheel, I pulled my phone from my purse. And saw a long string of texts from Dad.

DAD: Looks like a storm coming

DAD: Not too concerned. Looks like it
won't hit until tomorrow

DAD: Be careful on the drive up though
just in case. We'll see you tonight

DAD: Tell your young man I'm bringing
the WWI documentary I told him about

I flushed at the reference to *my young man* but was relieved to hear Dad thought everything would be fine.

"My dad is the most weather-obsessed person I know, and he's not worried," I said. "If he looked at the forecast and thought it was safe to drive, I'm sure it's fine."

Reggie shrugged. "If that's what the history professor thinks, that's good enough for me."

I couldn't help but laugh at that. "He's bringing a World War I documentary along on the trip. He wanted me to let you know."

"Marvelous," Reggie said, grinning. "I can't wait to tell him what a jackoff Franz Ferdinand was."

....

IT STARTED SNOWING WHEN WE WERE ABOUT THIRTY MIN-utes away from the cabin. Just flurries, and nothing that interfered with my driving. But Reggie frowned, looking up at the sky through the passenger-side window.

He rummaged around in his bag for his phone. From my peripheral vision, I could see him grimacing when he pulled up the weather app.

"Um. Amelia?" He dragged a hand through his hair. "When did your father say the blizzard was supposed to start?"

He sounded uneasy. My stomach dropped. "Tomorrow."

"Well, I've got good news and bad news," he said, sounding like all he actually had was bad news. "Which would you like first?"

I gripped the steering wheel tighter. "Can I have the good news first?"

"Certainly." The snow was coming down a little heavier than it had been just moments earlier. "The good news is we won't have to wait until tomorrow to build a snowman."

I gritted my teeth. This was not happening. "When will we be able to build one?"

"If the meteorologists who live inside my phone are to be believed—and I have no reason to think they are untrustworthy—probably in a few hours," he replied. "By tomorrow we'll be able to build a snow *army*."

....

DAD: Hey hon

DAD: I just checked the weather forecast and it's worse than I thought

DAD: I don't think we're going to be able to make it up

DAD: Sam and Adam and the kids haven't left yet either

DAD: I'm encouraging them to stay home

DAD: Mom is on the phone with Aunt Sue and it looks like they're all staying home too.

I closed my eyes and rested my forehead on the steering wheel, forcing myself to breathe in and out. I counted to ten before replying to Dad's texts.

> **AMELIA:** Glad you checked the weather.

> **AMELIA:** Yes, you probably should stay home.

> **AMELIA:** Will Gretchen still be coming?

DAD: She and Josh apparently left Chicago an hour ago but are turning around.

This was fine.

Everything was going to be *fine*.

DAD: I guess that cold front moved down
from Canada more quickly than they
expected, huh?

I was going to be snowed in at my family's cabin, *alone*, with
my uncomfortably attractive fake boyfriend.

But it was *totally* fine.

DAD: You two going to be okay up there
all alone?

AMELIA: Yep. Don't worry about us.

AMELIA: We're at the cabin now

As I texted my dad, Reggie was walking around the house,
surveying the landscaping. The temperature had to have been in
the single digits out there but the goofball was walking around
without a jacket.

He had to be freezing.

Why didn't he get Old Fuzzy out of his bag?

DAD: Glad to hear it hon

DAD: Well I'd been looking forward to a
nice long weekend with the family

DAD: And I know mom was looking forward
to spending more time with Reginald

AMELIA: I know Dad

DAD: We'll just have to get together once
we're all back in Chicago .

AMELIA: Of course

AMELIA: Love you. Say hi to Mom for me.

I put my phone back into my purse and stepped out of the car.
My feet sank into the several inches of snow that had fallen in
what was probably just the past hour. Ignoring the icy wet that
was seeping into my sneakers and soaking my socks, I made my
way to where Reggie was exploring the yard with the enthusiasm
of a golden retriever puppy.

"This is fantastic," he said, with wide-eyed wonder. "Who
cares for the plants while you're away? I've never seen such sound
winterization techniques."

It was hard for me to see this yard with even a fraction of the
appreciation he had for it. When I was young, I was always excited about the exploring I could do here that I couldn't back in
Chicago. But I'd never given much thought to the cabin's landscaping.

"I'm not sure who takes care of the yard," I admitted. "My
parents handle that. I just come up here once a year." I paused,
trying to work up the courage to let him know what Dad had just
texted. "They're not coming, by the way."

His eyebrows shot up his forehead. "Your parents aren't coming?"

I shook my head. "Nope. No one is. The roads are unsafe,
apparently. It'll just be the two of us until the snowplows come."

Reggie stared at me wide-eyed, the panic that had been gripping me since realizing we'd be here alone hitting him, too. "I see," he said.

"I'm heading inside," I said, pointing to my shoes. "My feet are freezing."

I shouldered my purse and made my way to the front door, deciding I'd come back out again for my suitcase once I had proper boots on. I expected him to follow close behind, but when I got to the door and made to open it, I noticed he was still standing by the snow-covered hydrangea bushes.

He swallowed. "Do I have your permission to come inside?"

I stared at him. "Of course. I haven't made you feel unwelcome here, have I?" Suddenly, I felt bad. Had my panicking about us being alone here made him feel awkward?

"It's not that," he said. "I need explicit permission before entering someone else's home, remember?" He paused. "Like at your Aunt Sue's party."

I'd forgotten all about that. Honestly, his insistence on being explicitly invited into people's private spaces was weirdly charming. "Oh, right. Well, you're welcome to come inside."

"Thank you," he said, seeming more at ease. "I'll join you shortly, after I've walked around the house a bit more."

"Of course. Whenever you're ready." I couldn't imagine wanting to spend time outside in this weather. Especially dressed the way he was, in nothing but a long-sleeved shirt, jeans, and tennis shoes. How were his toes not freezing off? "I'll just go find some hot cocoa in the pantry."

If there was one constant on these trips, it was the packets of cheap grocery store hot cocoa that no one ever seemed to remember buying but that were somehow always on hand.

I'd need all the strength hot cocoa could give me to face whatever came next.

....

WHOEVER MY PARENTS HAD COME IN TO CLEAN THE house before this weekend had blessedly turned the thermostat up to seventy-two after leaving. The minute I got inside, I reveled in the relative warmth, sighing as the chill in my bones melted away.

A quick search of the kitchen yielded three boxes of Swiss Miss cocoa packets that looked like they'd been purchased sometime in the past five years, a couple cans of dubious store-brand soup, and a box of bouillon cubes that had expired in 2012. That was all we'd have on hand until one of us made a grocery run.

Assuming, of course, that a grocery run was even possible. The only store within fifteen minutes of the cabin tended to close when the weather was bad. Even if it was open, I had no idea if we'd be able to use my car. Dad kept a snowblower in the garage that would take care of the driveway once it stopped snowing, but the roads would likely be impassable for days.

There was a snowmobile in the garage that was usually gassed up, at least. And if it wasn't running, there were several pairs of snowshoes that might work as a last resort.

Once Reggie came in, we'd have a strategy session about how to get more food. In the meantime, I needed to let Sophie know she might need to feed Gracie longer than I'd originally planned.

AMELIA: Hey Soph

AMELIA: Reg and I are stuck up in WI because of the blizzard. The rest of the gang didn't make it out of Chicago

before the storm started so it's just us up
here.

AMELIA: Hopefully I'll still make it back
home as scheduled but there's a chance
I may need you to feed Gracie a few
extra days

That settled, I made my way down the hallway to the bedroom that had been mine ever since our families built these cabins. It was like walking down decades of childhood memories and family remembrances. Most of our school pictures were at our parents' house back in Chicago, but these walls were lined with memories we'd made here in Wisconsin. Here was a picture of me, Adam, and Sam, out on my uncle Jim's fishing boat, each of us gap-toothed and smiling. And there was a picture of Adam's kids from last summer, little Aiden wearing at least as much chocolate ice cream on his face as there was left in his cone.

I was feeling all nostalgic and warm, despite the strangeness of my present circumstances, by the time I got to my bedroom at the end of the hall—and saw that the two twin beds that had been in my room for decades had been replaced with a beautiful queen-sized bed, piled high with fluffy pillows.

Two thoughts went through my mind simultaneously:

Oh, good. Those beds were uncomfortable as hell and made me feel like I was nine years old.

And: *Oh my god, there's* only one bed.

"Seriously, I need the name of your landscaper." Reggie's delighted voice bounded down the hallway. I barely heard him over the ringing in my ears and the renewed panic coursing through my bloodstream.

One bed one bed there's only one bed.

He stopped so abruptly when he got to my bedroom and saw what I was looking at that he bumped into me from behind. I braced myself with one hand against the doorframe to keep from stumbling into the room.

When I looked at him over my shoulder, he was staring at that single queen-sized bed in the center of the room, eyes wide as saucers.

He licked his lips. "There . . . appears to be only one bed." His voice was shaking. Or maybe it was just me who was shaking.

I cleared my throat in an attempt to pull myself together. "We have full run of the house," I said. "Remember? So we . . . um." I wondered if my face was as red as it felt. "We don't have to both sleep in it, or anything."

He nodded vigorously. "Right."

"Right," I repeated. "I'll just take my bedroom and you—" I'd been about to tell him he could sleep wherever he wanted, given that this place had several bedrooms. But maybe, given my undeniable attraction to him, and how very much *not* okay it would be if I gave into it, that wasn't a great idea.

"You can sleep in the kids' room," I said. "It has a bunch of toys in it and stuff, but it's very comfortable." It was also at the exact opposite end of the house, just in case I woke up in the middle of the night and forgot how terrible an idea it would be to crawl into bed with him.

He blinked at me. "The kids' room?"

"Yes," I said. "There are two twin beds in there, so you'll have two different beds to choose from. I think that'll be a lot of fun, don't you?"

I tried to tamp down the wave of . . . *something* that came over me at the look of disappointment on his face. I *shouldn't* want him to be close to me while we slept. Not if I had even an ounce of sense.

"Okay," he said. "That's . . . fine."

"Great." I nodded.

"Good," he said. "Now, if you don't mind, I'm going get my things from the car before it's covered in a foot of snow."

He left the room, and I flopped down on my bed. As if on cue, my phone buzzed with a new text.

SOPHIE: You're snowed in with your fake boyfriend??? ALONE????? Are you KIDDING ME????

I groaned.

If nothing else, this would definitely be a memorable weekend.

SEVENTEEN

Text exchange between Reginald Cleaves and Frederick J. Fitzwilliam

REGINALD: Where does Cassie get her food

REGINALD: Also what does she eat

FREDERICK: Her food?

FREDERICK: To be frank, her taste in food is disgusting. Even if I were capable of eating human food I don't think I would ever willingly put something called "Hot Cheetos" into my body.

FREDERICK: Why do you ask?

REGINALD: I need to get some human food

FREDERICK: I guessed as much. But why?

REGINALD: A human friend has dietary limitations that her family doesn't respect

REGINALD: Which is total BS if you ask me!!!!!!

REGINALD: And I just thought I'd buy her some food she can eat to show her not everyone ignores her needs

FREDERICK: Since when do you have human friends?

REGINALD: I've always had human friends

FREDERICK: Liar.

FREDERICK: This is for Amelia isn't it.

REGINALD: No

REGINALD: Absolutely not

REGINALD: Why would you even think that??

FREDERICK: Because you haven't stopped talking about the Beautiful Brilliant Accountant since the night you met her.

FREDERICK: AND because you haven't
had human friends since we used to try
and lure them into the Thames for sport.

REGINALD: Oh man, I haven't thought
about the Thames Games in AGES

FREDERICK: Reginald.

REGINALD: Fine.

REGINALD: It's for Amelia

REGINALD: So what?

FREDERICK: Are you falling for her?

REGINALD: FALLING for her?

REGINALD: Absolutely not

FREDERICK: Oh so you're just randomly
thinking about someone other than
yourself for the first time in 200 years,
then?

FREDERICK: ☹

REGINALD: I have better things to do
than to fall for a human.

REGINALD: Also since when do you know
how to use emojis

FREDERICK: 😵 🌭 🍦 ❤️ 🏝️ 🙌

> **REGINALD:** Did Cassie teach you how to use those?

> **FREDERICK:** Obviously.

> **REGINALD:** I should have known

REGINALD

"I NEED FOOD."

The man behind the grocery store's single cash register stared at me from behind owlish glasses. His yellow plastic name tag said DEREK. "We're closed."

I looked to my left, then to my right. I was the only customer, which would have implied Derek was right about the store being closed if all the fluorescent lighting hadn't still been on and the door to the store unlocked.

"There's no *Closed* sign in the window," I pointed out.

The man's stare turned into a glare. "How did you even *get* here? The roads are a mess. State police are telling everyone to stay home."

He was right about that. On my flight there, I'd lost count of all the cars I saw in ditches or stuck in snowdrifts. If I were reliant on human modes of transportation, getting there would have been impossible.

I couldn't tell Derek that, though. "I was careful," I said. True enough.

"You're a lunatic," he said. That was true enough, too. "I'm closing now, or I'll never make it home. You gotta go."

I would do no such thing. If I left this store without groceries, Amelia would have nothing to eat but powdered cocoa until the snow melted. Unacceptable.

"Please," I said. "This storm caught us off guard and there's nothing in the house." I pulled out three one-hundred-dollar bills from my wallet and laid them neatly on the counter, glad that I'd thought to bring along a little bribery money on this trip just in case. "I'm happy to prepay for what I buy with this. You can go now if you need to."

Derek stared at the money, and then at me. "I'll get fired if my boss finds out I let a customer be here when we're supposed to be closed."

"I'll never tell," I said, giving him my most winsome smile.

Derek seemed to consider that, then pushed my money back across the counter towards me. "It'll take me another fifteen minutes to close up. You have until then to get what you need, pay for it, and get gone."

"Thank you," I said, feeling genuine relief wash over me. "I'll be fast."

But the moment Derek's back was turned, I could no longer remember what Frederick said Cassie liked to eat. He'd once mentioned something about frozen imitation fish sticks, but had he said Cassie liked them or that she *didn't* like them? He'd also said Cassie enjoyed something orange and terrible called Hot Cheetos, and I thought she also liked peanut butter. But did Cassie like peanut butter *with* Hot Cheetos? Or just straight from the jar? And what were her thoughts on peanuts that weren't in butter form?

I remembered from our initial getting-to-know-you emails

that Amelia's favorite desserts were pancakes and chocolate. There seemed to be plenty of chocolate at that store, thankfully, but she couldn't live on chocolate alone until the snowplows came. I also didn't think one could buy pancakes at the grocery store.

Or was I wrong about that?

I cursed myself for not having thought beyond *get to store so Amelia won't starve* when I set out on this expedition. And for leaving my phone back at the house so I couldn't refer to Freddie's texts. But I was wasting time. With only a few minutes left, I ran through the store, grabbing the first things I could find that I thought maybe, possibly, Amelia might like.

Hopefully, the thought would count.

AMELIA

I must have been more tired from the drive than I'd realized. It felt like one minute I'd lain down on my new bed, and the next I was waking up to the sound of someone rummaging through kitchen cupboards.

When I got there, Reggie was at the kitchen table unloading three stuffed-full grocery bags.

I glanced out the window and saw my car, rapidly disappearing beneath a growing mound of snow and barely recognizable as a car anymore. From the position of the sun, nearly touching the horizon, I had to have been asleep for at least a couple of hours.

Reggie was unpacking a supremely random assortment of groceries with focused determination. Despite the blizzard he had somehow managed to get two boxes of frozen imitation fish sticks, baby carrots, Oreos, a five-pound bag of russet potatoes, four dozen eggs, and an absolutely enormous bag of Hot Cheetos while I slept.

My stomach started rumbling as if on cue. We hadn't stopped for lunch, so it had been a while since I'd last eaten. I wanted nothing to do with the nasty-looking fish sticks or the Hot Cheetos, but the rest looked fine to me.

"How did you get all that?" I asked.

Reggie looked up from the groceries, beaming. "You're awake," he said, happily. "You'd been asleep ages."

"I guess I was tired," I admitted. "But really, how did you manage to get to the store without my car?" I jerked my thumb behind me, in the direction of the window. "We've easily gotten a foot of snow already."

Reggie went back to unpacking groceries. "I flew," he said. "I didn't know if any stores would be open, but I lucked out. I got there just before they closed."

I stared at him. "You flew?"

"Yes." He set a fourth fabric grocery bag down on the kitchen table. It said *Winnetka 2014 Fourth of July Fun Run* in faded letters; he must have found Mom's fabric bag stash in the basement. And then, sounding slightly nervous, he added, "I haven't told you this yet, mostly because it hadn't come up before now, but I can fly."

He looked at me, his brow creased, as though anxiously waiting for my reaction to this information.

I burst out laughing. His sense of humor was the very definition of absurd. And yet, somehow, it hit just right every single time. I thought of the snowmobile Dad kept permanently gassed up in the garage and how, when I'd been a kid, it had felt like flying to ride on it. That must have been what he'd taken to get the groceries.

"You have the most unexpected reactions to things I tell you," Reggie said, sounding almost awed. "Every time I think I've scared you off for good . . ." He shook his head and looked down at his hands. "You surprise me."

When he looked back at me, his gaze was full of a kind of wonder that made my heart give a hard knock against my rib cage.

Desperate to avoid eye contact with him while he was looking at me like that, I walked over to one of the grocery bags and peered inside. I gasped. "Holy shit, did you buy them *entirely* out of chocolate?" It certainly looked like it. I hadn't been to the town's single grocery store often; getting provisions on our trips had usually fallen to my parents. But if memory served, it was a tiny store not much bigger than my apartment.

Reggie's smile was so soft when I looked back at him. And inviting. It took all my restraint not to reach out and trace its shape with my fingertips. "I remember you said you liked chocolate. When the first store I went to didn't have much of it, I . . . might have flown to a second one," he admitted, sounding almost shy.

Did he seriously remember I liked chocolate just from that one email exchange we had before Aunt Sue's party? I swallowed around the lump in my throat. "Going out there in that blizzard was super dangerous. You didn't have to go to all this trouble."

"What would you have eaten if I hadn't?" he asked. "I looked through these cupboards while you were sleeping. What was here wouldn't have lasted you more than a day." He averted his eyes again and gave me a one-shoulder shrug. "Getting all of this was also a bit self-serving, I'll admit. I wanted to make sure you had your favorite foods while we were stuck here. Because the truth is . . ."

He trailed off and closed his eyes, bracing one hand on the back of a kitchen chair as if needing it for support.

When he didn't seem inclined to finish his thought, I asked, "The truth is, what?"

His next words sounded almost pained, as though they were being pulled from him against his will. "The truth is, I quite like making you happy." He shook his head. "I'm frightened to think too much about what that means, because I honestly can't remember the last time I wanted to do *anything* for another person, simply for its own sake. And without having an ulterior motive." His eyes, when they met mine, were so intense I had to look away. "But for you, I would brave a blizzard just to see you smile."

With his words, something melted inside of me. Sophie's advice from yesterday—to stop fighting it if something real happened between us—floated into my mind. I was terrible at spur-of-the-moment anything, and from the beginning, nothing about my arrangement with Reggie had been planned. But would a short-term good time, as Sophie had put it, be such a terrible thing?

Or even something more?

I would brave a blizzard just to see you smile.

I might have been an accountant, but I wasn't made of stone.

So I took a deep breath, and walked around that kitchen table until I stood right in front of him.

Pressing my mouth to his was a risk, but I did it anyway, thrilling at the unexpected pleasure of kissing him without an audience. His breath was cool against my lips as his entire body went rigid with surprise. For a split second, I worried I'd crossed a line, but then his large hands reached up to cup my face, and he started kissing me back like this was something he'd been wanting for a very long time.

"Just when I thought you couldn't surprise me more than you already had," he murmured against my lips, laughing a little. He trailed one hand lazily down my side, letting it rest on my hip. I could feel his gentle touch through the denim of my jeans. Every nerve ending in my body was alight with the need to keep kissing him. "I never imagined you would want this with someone like me."

I frowned at that. I'd never taken Reggie as someone with low self-esteem. "What's wrong with kissing someone like you?" I asked.

He pressed a kiss to the tip of my nose, and to the apple of each of my cheeks. I kept my eyes open so I could see the blue of his, count the light freckles that dusted the bridge of his nose. "It's just . . . unexpected. All of this. You."

"Bad unexpected?" I asked.

He shook his head. "No." He paused, then added, "It might add some . . . complications. But this is the very opposite of bad."

What did he mean by *complications*? He kissed me again before I could ask, bolder now, his tongue darting out to trace along the seam of my lips. I opened for him on instinct and he groaned, placing one hand at either side of my waist and hoisting me onto the kitchen table as he thrust his tongue into my mouth. I thought back to the night we met, how I'd wondered whether Reggie kissed like the world was ending, and oh, it was *exactly* like that, the way he carded his fingers through my hair, tugging just shy of too hard, as he tilted his head and kissed me deeper, harder. It was like a dam had burst inside him, all the restraint I hadn't even realized he'd been using swept away with the tide, until I had to pull back, gasping for breath in his arms.

"I want to taste you," he murmured, his lips finding my jaw, my clavicle, pressing hungry, open-mouthed kisses down the side of my neck. "God, I'm so *fucking* hard, just thinking about how sweet I know you'd be."

I froze.

Suddenly, I noticed the position we were in—me, on the kitchen table, my legs spread wide. At some point I must have done that for him. At some point, he must have stepped between them. I could feel the truth of what he'd just said, of how hard he was, just from this, pressing against me.

And now he wanted to *taste* me? I'd had full-fledged relationships that hadn't included that.

This was too much. This was happening too fast.

I couldn't move this fast.

He must have realized he'd crossed a line because he pulled back immediately. "I'm . . . sorry." He squeezed his eyes shut tight and hung his head. "I just—sorry." He carded a hand through his hair, tugging on it nervously. "Just because you're okay with *kissing* a vampire . . . no. I shouldn't have assumed you were also okay with my tasting your blood."

He gave me a sheepish smile that showed his teeth.

And for the first time since I'd met him, I saw the points of what were very obviously vampire fangs.

EIGHTEEN

Excerpt from What to Expect When You Become a Vampire, *Fifteenth Edition*

Page 97: The Vampire's Glamour

One of the most surprising things for many fledgling vampires to discover is that their fangs will only be visible to humans during times of extreme distress, when they are about to feed, and when they are sexually aroused. At all other times, a vampire's involuntary glamour obscures their fangs from humans. This is widely seen as both an evolutionary advantage and an innate self-defense mechanism (after all, a human who doesn't see fangs is less likely to try and stake and/or run away from a hungry vampire).

AMELIA

THE WORLD HAD FLIPPED ON ITS AXIS.

My hands shot out to grip the edges of the table I still perched on. I clung to them like a lifeline, fingers clenching so hard my knuckles went white. If I'd had an ounce of self-preservation instinct, I would have jumped off that table right then and there and run screaming out the door, blizzard or no blizzard.

But I couldn't move. I couldn't speak. I could hardly breathe. I was too stunned to do anything but gape at him, horrified. I wasn't used to being wrong about much.

But oh, god—I'd had it *all* wrong about him.

The dark secret he'd been harboring wasn't that he was between jobs, or was unemployed.

It was that he was a vampire.

During that middle of the night phone call, when I'd laughingly asked if he were some sort of murderer, thief, or a vampire, and he answered that yes, he was a vampire . . .

I'd only been kidding, of course. But *he* hadn't been.

How was this possible?

I had to squeeze my eyes shut tight to fight off the waves of terror and revulsion running through me.

"You're . . . you're a vampire," I finally managed. "Like, an actual *vampire*."

He looked at me blankly. Which was fair. He'd probably— *reasonably!*—assumed we'd already covered this. "I mean . . . yes?"

"I'm sorry," I said. "I just . . ." I shook my head. I had to get out of there. I was breathing too fast, like I couldn't take in enough air. *Why couldn't I get my body to move?*

Reggie stared at me wide-eyed, scrutinizing my face. Whatever he saw there must have answered whatever questions he had, because his expression changed into something akin to horror. "You didn't believe me when I told you. You thought I was joking." He jumped away from me, as though terrified his touch would scald me. "Oh, *Hades*, Amelia—"

His sudden movement was all I needed for my muscles to finally unlock. I hopped off the table and sprinted to my bedroom, heart thundering in my chest.

I threw the door closed behind me and locked it, hoping that door locks worked on vampires.

....

AFTER A FEW MOMENTS OF PACING MY BEDROOM IN A panic, my wits returned enough for me to start thinking things through.

Okay, yes. I was snowed in at my family's Wisconsin cabin with a vampire. And *yes*, a few minutes ago he'd wanted to drink my blood as part of some kinky sex thing. But when I was finally able to quiet the shrieking sound in my head enough to string two coherent thoughts together, I realized that if Reggie wanted to kill or otherwise hurt me, he likely would have done it already.

I went to my door and double-checked the lock to make sure it was still in place. Regardless of how much danger I was actually in, a locked bedroom door seemed smart.

And, hell. I barely knew him. Maybe he was just waiting for the right opportunity to suck me dry.

In the meantime, I needed to research vampires and find out everything I could. I pulled my phone from the front pocket of my jeans and breathed a sigh of relief when I saw the Wi-Fi was working. When a big storm hit up there, it sometimes went out for days.

I didn't know where to start, so I typed VAMPIRE CHARAC-TERISTICS into the browser search bar and hoped for the best.

A *lot* of links popped up. There were tons of Reddit posts by people claiming to have had sex with a vampire, but I ignored those. That wasn't the sort of information I was looking for—*I* wouldn't be having sex with a vampire—and I suspected they made those stories up for clicks, anyway. It wasn't until I got to the second page of results that I found something potentially useful: a website for an organization called The Upper-Midwestern Amateur Vampire Hunter Association.

How can you tell if the STRANGE person you just met isn't just STRANGE but is also actually a VAMPIRE trying to blend into human society? A HANDY CHECKLIST:

1. Do they wear anachronistic or otherwise bizarre clothing?
2. Do they seem impervious to cold?
3. Do they recoil at the sight of sharp sticks?
4. Are they nocturnal? If so, do they have trouble remembering that not everybody else is?
5. Have you _never_ seen them eat before? Like, not _ever_?
6. Do they require explicit permission before entering someone's residence?
7. Do they have unusual magical abilities?
8. Do they have unusually prominent canine teeth?
9. Have they told you that they are a vampire?

If you can answer yes to one or more of the above questions that's not _conclusive_ proof that the person you suspect is a vampire is actually a vampire. But at a minimum, you should be on your guard, stock up on wooden stakes and garlic, and call us right away at 1-888-VAMPIRE for an informal and completely confidential consultation.

The skeptic in me rolled her eyes over the fact that there was apparently an upper-Midwestern amateur vampire hunting guild. But as I read the checklist, my innate skepticism couldn't keep my stomach from twisting itself into a tighter and tighter knot.

I didn't know about the sharp stick thing, but the rest of the list described Reggie to a tee.

I was the world's biggest idiot not to have realized immediately that when he told me he was a vampire, he'd meant it literally.

"Fuck." I buried my face in my hands, panic rising again. This was realigning my entire worldview with respect to what was real and what wasn't. I wasn't wired for this. I'd built my life and career around predictability and logic. Around things that made sense.

How was I supposed to process imaginary monsters coming to life and hanging out with me at my family's cabin?

I couldn't do this by myself.

I needed Sophie.

Hoping against hope that she was home and would pick up, I called her.

To my relief, she answered on the first ring. "Sooooo," she crooned. "How's it going up there, all alone and snowed in with your fake boyfriend? Have you kissed him yet?"

I groaned at the reminder. God, I'd let him put his tongue in my mouth. The same mouth he used to drink people's blood! If he hadn't asked if he could *taste me* and turned everything upside down, I might have slept with him, too.

Leave it to me to not even be able to *fake* date somebody without catastrophe.

I closed my eyes and shook my head. "I did kiss him," I admitted. "And then things immediately got weird."

"Weird?" Sophie said. "I love weird. Say more."

In the background, I could hear music I vaguely recognized as the theme song to *PAW Patrol*. Suddenly, I felt bad about taking up Sophie's time while her kids were still awake. "Are you sure you have time for this?" I asked.

"Marcus is handling bedtime," she said. "Hearing about your weekend will be the best thing to happen to me this month. Now spill."

"Reggie is a vampire."

I told her every sordid detail. Afterwards, I had a fleeting moment of guilt because it was obvious Reggie didn't share information about himself with everyone. But I needed Sophie's help. Badly.

"Oh my god," she said, when I was finished. "Reggie the hot man is actually Reggie the hot vampire. But not like those people on TikTok who think they're vampires but are really just weirdos addicted to the online attention. A *real* vampire." She started laughing. "I can't believe this."

I closed my eyes. "Tell me about it."

"When you called, I'd hoped it was to let me know you'd gotten some badly needed sex." She laughed again. "I'm both disappointed that that's *not* why you're calling but also more delighted than I've ever been in my life."

I sighed, then flopped down on my bed and threw an arm over my eyes. "You're handling the news that vampires are actually real very well."

"There are a lot of strange people out there," she said. "And Reggie seems stranger than most. I guess you could say I'm shocked but not surprised."

"Fair enough," I said. "Okay, so, what do I do?"

Sophie was quiet a moment. "I think it depends. Was he a good kisser? Do you *want* to get laid?"

Unbelievable. "That is not the point."

"Sure it is."

"Sophie," I said, exasperated. "I am trapped in a house *with a vampire*. Until an hour ago, I thought vampires were imaginary and hadn't thought seriously about them since all my high school friends were going through their *Twilight* phase. I am at a loss for what to do. *Help me*."

"It is definitely unexpected," Sophie admitted. "And I know you struggle a lot when unexpected things happen. But he's been so nice to you."

I bit my lip, thinking of all the little kind and thoughtful things he'd done for me since I'd met him. The way he'd been outraged on my behalf over the lack of food options at Aunt Sue's party. How he'd agreed to come along on this family Wisconsin trip in the first place, even though he didn't have to. The way he'd gone out into a literal blizzard just to make sure I'd have enough to eat while we were trapped.

"He has been very nice," I admitted.

"Before you found out he was a vampire, had he ever done something that made you frightened for your safety?"

That was easy. "Never."

Sophie hummed. "Yeah, I really don't think he wants to hurt you."

It was a relief to hear that. "You don't?"

"No," Sophie said. "He's had tons of opportunities to kill you or drink your blood in the past few days. But instead of doing either of those things now that you're trapped in Wisconsin, he chose to play tonsil hockey with you instead."

I snorted. "*Tonsil hockey*? Really?"

"But seriously," she continued, ignoring my protest, "if a vampire you were trapped with wanted to hurt you, I'd have to think you'd already be dead."

"That had occurred to me," I admitted. "But then again, I hardly know this guy. Maybe he's the sort of vampire who gets off on luring their fake dates into a false sense of security before killing them."

A long pause. "Do some vampires do that?"

"I have no idea. But it seems plausible, doesn't it?"

"Maybe," Sophie said, sounding skeptical. "Tell me this, though. How did he react when he saw how frightened you were?"

I closed my eyes and thought of his horrified expression when he realized I hadn't believed him, earlier.

"He'd thought I already knew he was a vampire," I told her. "Which is valid. He'd *tried* to tell me the truth multiple times." I'd just been too much of a linear thinker, too oblivious, to believe him. "I ran out of the room before I could find out for sure, but I think that when he realized I'd had no idea what he was, he felt really bad about it."

"That doesn't sound like someone who's trying to lure you into his coffin so he can eat you."

It didn't. "You're right." I got out of bed and started pacing again. "But even if he isn't going to kill me, what do I *do*?"

"Do you want my honest opinion?"

I braced myself. "Yes. Please."

"Once you feel calm enough to do it, talk to him," she said. "And if you like what he has to say, see if he's good at sex stuff beyond kissing."

My cheeks flamed. "Talking to him sounds reasonable," I agreed, ignoring the rest of her advice. "We're going to be stuck here for a while."

"Great," Sophie said. "Do that. Then let me know how it goes. And now that that's settled, I should go. I need to help with the kids, and I also need to let Marcus know he owes me ten dollars."

"Why does he owe you ten dollars?" I asked, though I already suspected I'd regret it.

"We made a bet on whether you two crazy kids would get it on in Wisconsin."

"I'm going to hang up now," I said, pretending to be offended. But despite myself, I was smiling.

NINETEEN

Excerpt from the BoisterousBulleters Discord Server,
#sticker-commissions channel

REGINALD_THE_V: Okay, I need some advice

REGINALD_THE_V: So, you know the girl I've been telling
you about?

REGINALD_THE_V: Well . . . I kissed her

TACOCATTUESDAY: OMG

BRAYDENSMOM: YES FIANLLY

REGINALD_THE_V: Except I think I fucked it up

REGINALD_THE_V: pushed too far too fast

TACOCATTUESDAY: uh oh what did you do

REGINALD_THE_V: and in the process told her something
I keep v. v. v. close to the chest that I *assumed* she
already knew but that she definitely did *not* know

REGINALD_THE_V: it freaked her out. and now I don't know what to do

BRAYDENSMOM: Well it's good that you are COMMUNICATINt

BRAYDENSMOM: thats a START

TACOCATTUESDAY: how far did you push things??? Like what base

TACOCATTUESDAY: like did you ask to eat her out or smthg? right after kissing her for the first time? Because if so no wonder she's spooked

REGINALD_THE_V: I mean, I didn't ask to eat her out

REGINALD_THE_V: at least not technically

REGINALD_THE_V: More like . . . I proposed blood play. Sort of?

BRAYDENSMOM: OMG 🔥 🔥 🔥

TACOCATTUESDAY: DAMN SON

LYDIASGOALS: Listen I'm as invested in this as the rest of y'all but can we please move this convo to #off-topic?

REGINALD_THE_V: oooh yes sorry sorry, won't happen again

AMELIA

I SPENT ANOTHER TWO HOURS GOING DOWN A VAMPIRE research rabbit hole. Most of what I found ranged from unhelpful to downright bizarre, but after devoting much of my career to researching niche Internal Revenue Code provisions, I was used to leaving no stone unturned.

Just when I'd finalized the questions I wanted Reggie to answer when we talked, I heard a very soft knock on my door.

I froze.

"Amelia?" Reggie's voice was more tentative than I'd ever heard it. "It's me."

What did I do? I told Sophie I'd talk to him, but now that he was here, I was freaking out again. But then, could I really just pretend he wasn't here until the snowplows came?

Probably not.

"Yeah?" My heart was racing. Could he sense that? Could he *smell* it when my blood was pumping extra hard through my veins? I shuddered at the thought, even as the idea of it fascinated me.

"Can I come in?"

I thought of the vampire self-defense tricks I'd just read about online. I could probably break off one of the legs of my desk chair and use it as a wooden stake. I sucked at fighting, but if I really had to defend myself, I could probably do it.

I bit my lip and opened the door.

Reggie looked as though he'd spent the past two hours trying to pull his hair out by the roots. His expression turned hopeful when he saw my face, as though he hadn't expected me to acknowledge his knock.

I thought back to Aunt Sue's party, and his insistence that either she or Uncle Bill invite us in. And when we'd gotten to this house, it hadn't been enough for me to open the front door for him. He'd needed my explicit permission before coming inside.

"You need an invitation before you can come in my bedroom," I said. "Right?"

"No." He shook his head. "I need express permission from an owner or primary occupant before entering someone's home. Once I'm inside, though, I can go wherever I like. But I'd feel better about coming in if you give consent first." He paused and looked at the floor. "I know you must be scared."

My heart melted a little at his kind, patient tone, even as the idea that he'd have had to stand outside this house all night if I hadn't invited him in sent a strange, powerful thrill through me. That swimmy, shifting-sands-beneath-my-feet feeling that I'd come to associate with conversations with him washed over me again.

When I didn't say anything, he cleared his throat and tried again. "May I come in, please?"

A smart person would have said no. The person I was two weeks ago certainly would have. Then again, what was one more questionable decision, considering the sheer number of them I'd been making lately?

"You can come in," I said.

He entered right away and looked between my bed and the desk chair. The only two places to sit in the room. After only a moment's hesitation, he went for the chair. He sat forward in it, elbows on his knees. I remained standing, watching him as he stared down at his hands.

"One of the very few times in my life I thought I was being

completely honest with someone, and you thought I was playing a prank." He laughed, but there was no humor in it. "I suppose it's only fitting, in a way. Given everything. *Hades*, I should have known you didn't believe me when you took it so calmly. I just thought, *well, she knows Frederick, she must already know that vampires are out there and not all of us are so bad.*"

I stared at him. "I had no idea Frederick was a vampire." More pieces of the puzzle were sliding into place. If Frederick was a vampire, that meant Sam's best friend was dating one. That might explain why Sam had been so obsessed with my nighttime safety.

"Oh, shit," Reggie said, burying his face in his hands. "I assumed you knew about Frederick." I had never seen him look this anxious or caught so flat-footed. Not even having to put on a show at a dinner party full of my family members had made him lose his composure like this. I began to wonder whether the picture Reggie presented to the world might just be a carefully cultivated façade. Right now, it seemed the mask was slipping. For the first time, I thought I was catching a glimpse of the real Reginald.

It made him seem more human, I realized with a start.

How ironic.

But because he was *not* actually human . . . "I have questions," I said.

He nodded. "I expected as much. Ask whatever you want."

I grabbed the list I'd just created from my Internet research and started at the top. "So. You drink blood."

He looked at me. Nodded again.

I recoiled at the confirmation, even though I'd already known his answer would be yes.

I checked that question off the list and moved to the next. "And do you drink *human* blood? Or do you drink other kinds of blood?"

"Always human blood," he said. "Only human blood. I literally can't digest anything else."

That would explain his avoidance of food at Aunt Sue's party and his vague references to his *diet* when he wouldn't drink wine with me at that bar. "Do you ever drink animal blood? I thought some vampires drank animal blood."

He snorted. "*Twilight?*"

I blushed. "Um. Yeah."

"Listen, as kickass as I've always found Edward Cullen, an entire family of celibate vampires living only on animal blood . . . well." He smirked, his mask of cool indifference back in place. "None of those details apply to me."

My face went hot at the innuendo. I hid my face behind my list, focusing on the next question. Which was probably the most important one. "Since you drink human blood, can you explain how you get it?"

His eyebrows lifted in confusion. "How I get it?"

"Yes," I said. "*Where* do you get your blood from, exactly? I assume you need to kill people, but do you have criteria for who you kill, or something?"

"Oh," Reggie said, understanding. "I don't eat that way anymore, for the most part. A few years ago, I started getting takeout from blood banks." He shrugged. "I'm sure there are ethical issues involved in stealing from medical facilities, too, but it *feels* less cruel."

It certainly made me less frightened at any rate. Curiosity got the better of me before I could stop myself from asking my next question. "Does it taste the same that way?"

Reggie hesitated. "No, it doesn't. But it's fine. Though I'll admit that if I don't warm my meals to the temperature of the human body first, there's always something frustratingly missing from the experience. Drinking it cold is like having sex while wearing three condoms. Or watching Hulu with commercials." He shook his head in disgust, apparently oblivious to the way I once again felt ready to burst into flames. "I have no idea how Frederick stands drinking it straight from the fridge. Then again, I have no idea how or why he does lots of things."

"Oh," I managed, lamely. "I see."

"Can I ask you a question now?" Reggie asked.

My eyes widened. "Me?"

"I'm sure you have other questions for me, but before we get to them, I have to know. What did you think I meant when I told you I was a vampire?"

A reasonable thing for him to wonder. "It was the same night you'd told me you loved playing practical jokes." I shrugged. "You called me in the middle of the night to tell me some dark secret you were embarrassed about. When I asked if you were a vampire, I only meant it as a sarcastic joke. When you latched on to it, I assumed you were joking, too."

He stared at me. "Why would I joke about something like that?"

"Because there's no such *thing* as vampires." At the incredulous look on his face, I added, "At least, not in my world."

That earned me a wry grin. "Fair enough. So, what did you think my *real* dark secret was?"

"When we emailed each other details about ourselves you told me you were between jobs. I assumed your dark secret was that you were unemployed," I said, sheepishly. "In hindsight, it makes no sense. Especially since being unemployed is nothing to be embarrassed about. But at the time it made more sense than anything else."

His mouth quirked up at the corner. "And I'd been so proud of myself for being honest with you right off the bat, too."

"I'm sorry I didn't believe you," I said. "But I do *taxes* for a living. I'm just not equipped to believe that vampires are real. So I didn't. Not until . . ."

I trailed off, looking away. He remembered what had happened between us in the kitchen as well as I did.

"And my always needing to ask permission before entering someone's home? And the way I repeatedly refused to eat or drink anything when you offered?" he pressed. Though his voice was gentle, not accusatory. "None of that made you wonder if maybe I was telling the truth about what I was?"

I winced. "It should have," I admitted. "But I thought you were just being polite about entering. And that when it came to food, you just had a lot of dietary restrictions. Like me, I guess."

"I do have a lot of dietary restrictions," he quipped, smirking. "But it's because I literally *can't* eat anything except for . . ."

He had the decency not to finish that sentence. He knew I knew what he meant.

"Yeah," I said, quietly.

"I can leave," he added. "This house, I mean. If you don't want me to stay, I can go."

I looked out my bedroom window. The blizzard still raged. In the hours I'd spent researching vampires the sun had set completely. It would be impossible to see anything, even if the winds died down.

"It has to be *really* dangerous to drive in a storm like this," I said. "Even if you had a car, how would you get it out of the driveway?"

"I don't need to drive," he said. "I would just fly back to Chicago, the same way I flew to the grocery stores."

My heart thudded hard against my rib cage. When he'd told me he'd flown to the store, he'd meant that literally, too. I tried to recover quickly. "Chicago is a lot farther away than Pete's Groceries."

"I'll be fine," he said. His bright blue eyes were so earnest, the mask he liked to hide behind slipping again. "The last thing I want to do is make you uncomfortable."

"But there's a *blizzard* out there."

"Yes. But if you're frightened—"

"I'm not." All at once, I realized it was the truth. "A bit weirded out? Absolutely. Frightened?" I hesitated. "Maybe a little. But rationally, I know I shouldn't be. I mean, how many different opportunities have you had to drink my blood without my consent since we've met?"

I'd meant it as a rhetorical question, but he answered immediately. "Thirty-seven. No, wait—thirty-eight."

Wow. "Uh . . . okay, you having a ready answer to that cuts against the point I was trying to make. Which is that if you were going to hurt me, you'd have done it already."

"Even before I got most of my meals from blood donation facilities and still fed directly from the source, I was particular in choosing my victims." His eyes shone with sincerity. "Even at my most depraved, I never would've hurt someone like you."

I knew I shouldn't let myself be taken in by this show of vulnerability. I might not want him to fly in a blizzard, but if I'd wanted to keep a barrier between us before I knew what he actually was, I wanted to keep a ten-foot wall between us now.

But I wasn't made of stone. "I'm not kicking you out into a blizzard."

The tension he'd been carrying left him all at once. His shoulders relaxed, and relief flooded his features. "Okay."

"But," I continued, holding up a finger, "I'm not kissing you again. Ever. Or doing *other stuff* with you, either. It's one thing to be snowed in with a vampire. It's another to—"

"I got it," he cut in. Was that disappointment I saw in his eyes? "To be perfectly honest, kissing you was probably a mistake on my end, too."

That *shouldn't* have hurt. After all, I'd just told him the same thing. And yet a small part of me folded in on itself, anyway. Against my better judgment, I asked, "Why was it a mistake for you?"

He paused, jaw working. "It just was."

An awkward silence filled the room after that. The ticking of the bedside clock, the howling of the wind outside, served to underscore just how very alone we were.

"You'll sleep in the kids' room," I said, as if we hadn't already established where he'd be sleeping. Somehow, it felt important to reiterate that we would be staying in opposite ends of the cabin. The place wasn't huge, but we had to as stay far apart as possible until we could finally go home. "And I'll—"

"Sleep here," he finished for me. "Got it." He stood up and took a small step towards me. I wasn't a short person, but when he stood next to me like this, he practically towered over me. Everything about this man was just so *large*. "Sleep well, Amelia. I'll see you in the morning."

TWENTY

Telegram sent from Maurice J. Pettigrew, Treasurer of The Collective, to the Board of Directors

QUARRY HAS ATTACHED NOTE TO DOOR OF APARTMENT. STOP.
SAYS "GONE FISHIN'". STOP.
APARTMENT DOOR LOCKED. STOP.
SURVEILLANCE FROM OUTSIDE SUGGESTS HE IS NOT INSIDE. STOP.
COWARD IS CLEARLY TRYING TO HIDE. STOP.
TELL GROUP TO SEARCH LAKE MICHIGAN. STOP.
DO NOT SEE WHAT APPEAL "FISHING" HAS FOR VAMPIRES. STOP.
BUT WE ALREADY KNEW OUR BROTHER WAS ODD. STOP.

AMELIA

KISSING YOU WAS PROBABLY A MISTAKE ON MY END, TOO.

Reggie's last words to me before he left my bedroom played on a loop in my head as I tried, to no avail, to fall asleep.

Why should him regretting kissing me keep me up half the night? I regretted kissing him, too, didn't I? Out of all possible outcomes, this was the cleanest one. It was much better that he agreed we'd made a mistake than for him to be pining away for me.

Or, worse, for me to be pining away for him.

And yet there I was, staring sleepless up at the ceiling, feeling pangs of something I refused to name, as the taste of his lips on mine lingered like a delicious mistake.

The storm outside wasn't helping. Everything that seemed terrifying about stormy winter nights when I was a child seemed possible now. Monsters lurking under the bed. Witches who would cook your bones into a stew. It was probably because I was exhausted. Or maybe it was just the fact that I was stuck here all alone with a vampire, but I was suddenly anxious, in a way I hadn't been in many years and that probably should have embarrassed me, about being alone.

"This is ridiculous." I threw off my covers and climbed out of bed. It was nearly two in the morning. If I couldn't sleep, I might as well accomplish something. I pulled the old bathrobe I kept stashed on a hook in my closet over my pajamas and shouldered my briefcase.

I set up my laptop on the kitchen table. No need to fall behind on work while I was stuck here. However long that might turn out to be.

There was an email from the Wyatt Foundation waiting for me as soon as I logged into my work account.

To: Amelia Collins (ajcollins@butyldowidge.com)
From: John Richardson (jhcr12345@countwyatt.org)

Dear Ms. Collins,

The Wyatt Foundation greatly appreciates your assistance with our tax matter and we appreciate you setting up a time to meet with us in person. As such, we will reach out very soon about when it might be convenient for me to come by. Incidentally, does your office ever hold meetings in the evenings? If not, I am sure we can make a daytime arrangement work; I just wanted to double-check, as evening usually works best with my schedule, my circadian rhythms etc.

Let me know. And once you have done that, then I will let you know. And so on and so forth.

In the meantime, I have attached another set of documents to this email for your perusal.

Very truly and sincerely yours,
J.H.C. Richardson, Esq, PhD

ps: Do you know what a "tax bracket" is? Someone on our board saw the term online but none of us know what it means.

The attached documents included a nearly indecipherable firsthand account of what I thought might have been a 1952 Tunisian fabric store opening and a medical journal piece called *Inexplicable Exsanguination: A Path Forward.* I closed my eyes, groaning. Evelyn wanted me to present on the Wyatt Foundation to the partners in a few weeks, but my sense that we should close this damn file instead was growing steadily.

I sensed it immediately when Reggie entered the kitchen. It wasn't so much that I *heard* him. Rather, there was a shift in the room's energy I could feel. His perpetually boisterous presence altered the peaceful quiet I had always associated with this cabin just by walking into a room. Even when he was silent, everything about him was always so loud.

I was starting to find that when he wasn't around, I missed the noise.

The laugh that burst out of me when I looked up from my work and saw him dispelled any lingering awkwardness between us.

He wore an ancient apron of Dad's that said *Kiss the Cook* in red letters. Beneath the words was a cartoonish pair of bright red lips, all puckered up. I could have sworn Mom made him get rid of the thing years ago. Where on earth had he *found* it?

Reggie pointed at the pile of papers I'd arranged beside my computer, hand on his hip. He looked so much like Mom when she disapproved of something we'd done as kids it was uncanny. "You're usually asleep at this hour, as you've reminded me more than once. What's all this?"

"I can't sleep," I explained. "So I'm working."

"I don't think so."

"Why not?"

"Why *not*?" He stared at me. "It's the middle of the night, for starters. And we are in a *winter wonderland*."

Was he being serious? "A winter wonderland?"

"Yes."

I shook my head. "More like a winter nightmare."

The right corner of his mouth kicked up into a half smile, cracking his stern façade. But he recovered his composure quickly. He leaned over and put his hand on my laptop as if to close it.

I glared at him. "Don't."

He chuckled. "Can I just say that you are the epitome of what's wrong with young people today?"

"I thought the official boomer position was that millennials are lazy," I quipped. "Not that we work too hard."

He rolled his eyes. "First of all, I am *not* a boomer. But no," he said, shaking his head. "The problem with young people is not that they're lazy. It's that they think they have unlimited time. So they postpone the fun parts of life thinking they can get to those later. Only at the end do they realize how badly they squandered . . . well. Everything."

Holding my gaze, he slowly lowered my monitor until my laptop was closed.

"Hey!" I protested. I tried to pry his hand off my computer but he quickly covered my hand with his to keep me from shoving him off. A wicked, delicious shiver ran down my spine at the contact. I could tell from the way the muscles in his forearm tensed that he felt it, too.

I didn't know why I found that nearly unbearably hot. But I did.

"It is the middle of the night," he said again, his voice sounding more strained. "You can do that work tomorrow."

"You have no idea how behind I am."

"I don't," he agreed. "I also don't care. If you don't take a break, you'll burn yourself out before you've even started living."

"Reggie—"

"Two hours," he said, holding up two fingers. "Take a break with me for two hours. If at the end of those two hours you still think getting back to work is more important than sleeping like a normal human, then at least you'll have done something fun first." He leaned in closer, his face nearly level with my own.

"And if, instead, you decide you're enjoying your break, you can keep taking one the rest of the time we are stuck here."

With me, he didn't say. *Take that break with me.* But the implication was there—in the way he looked hopefully into my eyes, in the way his grasp on my hand tightened almost imperceptibly. His eyes were so vivid, with a sort of starburst brightness to the blue I'd never seen in anyone else's eyes.

I really must have been the densest person alive not to realize from the jump just how *not* human he was.

They were beautiful eyes, I realized.

He was beautiful.

"I suppose it wouldn't be the end of the world if I took a small break," I conceded.

"It wouldn't." I could all but hear the grin in his voice.

"Do you have ideas in mind for what we might do?"

"Yes," he said. "Loads of ideas."

I didn't know if he was being serious. "Really?"

"Yes. But I'll narrow it down to two options." He held up one finger. "First idea: we go tromping through the snow in the snowshoes I found in the basement."

I stared at him. "You're joking."

"I'm not joking," he said. "If I were joking, I would have said something like, *it's raining cats and dogs outside, and I just stepped in a poodle.*"

I snorted. "You're ridiculous."

"I am," he agreed. "No interest in snowshoeing, then?"

"It's the middle of the night." I shook my head. "Hard pass. What's your second idea?"

He smirked. "I'll show you. But first—close your eyes."

"Close my eyes?"

"If you choose option two, it's a surprise. So yes. Close them."

Did I humor him? *Trust* him? It was true that I wasn't afraid he would hurt me. But how was I supposed to react to a vampire telling me to close my eyes?

I closed them anyway. "Can you at least give me a hint?"

"No." He closed his hand around my wrist, and . . .

I'd been honest when I'd told him I wouldn't kiss him again. But the gentle, restrained way he was touching me right now stood in such delicious contrast to the way he'd grabbed me on the kitchen table earlier that suddenly . . .

That earlier moment was all I could think about.

"You're gonna love option two," he said, guiding me out of the kitchen by the hand. "Follow me."

TWENTY-ONE

Telegram sent from Maurice J. Pettigrew, Treasurer of The Collective, to the Board of Directors

LOCATED QUARRY. STOP.

WAS NOT FISHING AT ALL! STOP.

FLED TO WISCONSIN WITH HUMAN!! STOP.

WE MADE SLIGHT DETOUR EN ROUTE TO TOUR CHEESE FACTORY ROADSIDE BILLBOARD ADVERTISED AS "BEST CHEESE CURDS IN WHOLE GOSH DARN WORLD." STOP.

HAVE LONG BEEN FASCINATED BY CHEESE. STOP.

HOW IT'S MADE. STOP.

HOW AND WHY DO CHEESE CURDS SQUEAK? STOP.

WANT TO KNOW SCIENCE BEHIND IT. STOP.

TOUR SHOULD BE QUICK. STOP.

ONCE FINISHED, WILL BRING PREY TO GROUND. STOP.

WILL BRING GIFT FROM FACTORY SHOP AS APOLOGY FOR DELAY. STOP.

AMELIA

IT WAS STRANGE, BEING LED WITH MY EYES CLOSED THROUGH a house I'd been coming to since I was a child. Even stranger when the person doing the leading was a vampire who was humming an out-of-tune rendition of *Follow the Yellow Brick Road* under his breath as he led me.

"You better not be peeking." Reggie sounded delighted with himself. "If you open your eyes, you'll spoil the surprise."

I couldn't help but laugh. "I promise I'm not peeking. Where are you taking me?"

"Just a little farther. Ah. Here we are." He dropped my wrist and placed his hands on my shoulders. Then he turned me ninety degrees so that I was facing in a different direction. "You can open your eyes now."

I did.

"You're kidding me."

"We've already established that I'm not."

I turned to stare at him. "The game closet?"

"Exactly." Reggie was beaming. "I can't believe you didn't tell me this was here."

"I haven't thought of this game closet in years," I said, honestly. "It didn't occur to me you'd be interested."

His smile slipped. "Why not?" He sounded genuinely affronted. "I love games." He opened the door, then gestured theatrically for me to go inside. "After you, my lady."

The mingled scents of old books and unopened closet were nearly enough to distract me from the powerful wave of déjà vu that came over me when I stepped inside. Playing games with my family was part of the fabric of memory whenever I thought of being here. Seeing the stacks of books and games arranged neatly on those shelves made me feel twelve again.

But I hadn't actually been twelve in more than twenty years. "I don't think I've been in here since college," I mused.

I turned to face Reggie, and my mouth went dry.

All at once I realized just how small this closet was. Reggie was so tall, and his shoulders so broad, he seemed to take up all the space in the room. Maybe it would feel like that no matter where we were. He was somehow larger than life, larger than even what his own sizable person could contain. There was something about him that displaced every molecule and atom and particle around us until all I could see was him.

He didn't seem to notice the reaction I was having to being in a confined space with him. He was looking at the shelves of games, eyeing them with an excitement that reminded me of a young child on their birthday.

"What about Settlers of Catan?" He pulled a familiar square box from the top shelf. It was an ancient edition, one my brothers and I had played so many times when we were teenagers that the cards had eventually grown sticky with the snacks we'd eat while playing. He put a hand on my shoulder. I felt our nearness and our isolation, my body thrumming with it in a way I could get lost in, if I let myself.

"I like Settlers," I said, my voice shaky, trying hard not to think about how good it felt to have his hand resting there. "I'll warn you, though—I'm competitive."

"So am I."

"No, really though," I said. "I always win. My strategy is fool-proof."

He snorted. "I never took you as one to brag."

"It's not bragging if it's telling the truth." I grabbed the box, with the idea of taking it from him—but he didn't let go.

And then we were both holding the box, our fingers nearly touching.

I paused, staring down at the game in our hands. His were so much bigger than mine, his knuckles going a bit white as his grip tightened. Those hands had cradled my face so tenderly when we'd kissed. Somehow, I knew his touch would be gentle everywhere.

All at once, and with the certainty of a thunderclap, I knew that sitting next to him while playing a board game was a *terrible* idea.

He seemed to reach the same conclusion. "Are you sure you wouldn't rather go snowshoeing?" His voice was pitched higher than usual, cracking on the word *snowshoeing*. "Settlers of Catan is . . . well. It's a bit cliché as games go, isn't it?"

Suddenly, running out into the freezing night sounded like a fabulous idea. There'd be no risk of accidental proximity. No chance we'd inexplicably end up holding hands. Going to my bedroom, alone, and trying to get a few hours of sleep would have been a better decision, but at this point I was collecting bad decisions like Girl Scout badges.

Might as well keep going.

"Okay," I agreed. "Let's do it."

....

SNOWSHOEING PROVED A LOT MORE STRENUOUS THAN I remembered. Then again, the last time I'd done it had been more than ten years ago, when I was a lot younger and more used to regular physical activity.

This was also the first time I'd ever tried it in the middle of the night with a vampire, which may have also been a factor.

"Am I doing this right?" Reggie had stopped a few yards back, kneeling in the snow to adjust the straps of his snowshoes. While I was bundled up in so many layers I was practically unrecognizable, he wore only a long-sleeved flannel shirt and a pair of blue jeans. "I feel like these aren't on properly."

I trudged through the snow to where he stood. It was so bright out there, with the moon and starlight reflecting off the snow, that the headlamps we wore were practically unnecessary. I crouched beside him and rapped once on his snowshoe closest to me. "They look fine to me."

He let out a frustrated breath. "If I'm wearing them properly, why is snowshoeing so *difficult*?"

I laughed. "It just is. Do you want to turn back?"

"No," he said quickly. "You still have eighty-seven minutes left of the two-hour break you promised me. Let's soldier on."

It was always so quiet out there. That was one of the most welcome differences between regular life in Chicago and our visits up here to Wisconsin. It was even quieter now, with the snow blanketing everything and absorbing all sound. The crunching snow beneath our feet and our labored breathing were the only noises disturbing the stillness surrounding us.

Eventually, we came to a wooden shed that my grandfather would use on hunting trips back when he still came up here regularly. "Let's take a break," Reggie said. When I made no objection, he pulled me inside of it and closed the door behind us. It was warmer in there, despite it not having any heat or electricity. The broken floorboards suggested no one had been in there for a while.

"I think this is abandoned," Reggie said, echoing my thoughts.

He sat down on the small bench inside the shed and motioned for me to join him. I did, careful to leave some space between our bodies. "If it belonged to someone, I wouldn't have been able to just walk in."

Behind the shed, someone had built what looked like a little snow family. Small footprints all around the scene suggested this was the work of some of the kids who lived around here.

"I would have liked to have met the children who made these," Reggie said suddenly, sounding wistful. "I have a lot in common with kids, you know."

That surprised me. "Really? How do you mean?"

"We both live without fear," he explained. "Though it comes from different places. Kids see the world and live each day without fear because they don't yet know what they have to lose. I see the world and live each day without fear because I know all too well there's nothing left for me to lose."

His words were tinged not just with melancholy, but with resignation as well. Gone was the giddy chatterbox who nudged me out the door when he thought I was working too hard. The man who took nothing seriously and seemed willing to try anything as long as it was fun. In his place was a man who seemed both ancient and bone weary.

It was simple reflex, putting my hand on his arm. I was driven by an instinctive need to provide comfort to someone clearly in need of it. He gave no sign that he wanted to talk about what was going through his mind, but before I could talk myself out of it, I went there anyway.

"What triggered this mood?" I asked. "Is it something I said?"

He looked horrified. "What? No! Of course not." He shook his head. "I guess I'm just . . . thinking." He cleared his throat and shifted beside me on the bench. "Are you sure you want to have this conversation? The whole point of this was to give you a well-deserved break. Not to listen to me be maudlin."

Even as he said the words, I could see in his changed expression that he *wanted* to talk about it. "It's fine," I said. "You can tell me."

He took a deep breath and let it out slowly. "Do you remember the night we met? How I said people were chasing me?"

I thought back to that night. Me, walking out of my building completely distracted and worried about being late for my family's dinner. Reggie, sprinting down the sidewalk, slamming into me and making me drop everything I'd been carrying. The way he'd asked if I could either pretend to kiss him or pretend to laugh to keep his pursuers from finding him. The way I'd thought, even as it was happening, that the entire encounter must have been some bizarre fever dream.

"Vaguely," I quipped. "*Were* people chasing you?"

"Yes."

My breath caught. "Who?"

He closed his eyes and leaned back against the wall of the shed. "The group calls itself The Collective. They're like . . . I don't know. This weird vigilante vampire cult, I guess?"

"A vigilante vampire cult?" A shiver ran down my spine. "Sounds ominous."

"Yeah," he agreed. "Each member can trace themself back through bloodlines to a group of powerful vampires who died at a party over a hundred years ago." He sighed. "Technically, I can, too. Though that's the beginning and end of what we have in common." He looked at me with a familiar gleam in his eye, and it struck me that I must be getting to know him pretty well, because I guessed he was about to deflect with humor a moment before he did it. "I'm a *far* better dancer than anyone in The Collective, for starters. My parties are better, too."

I ignored his obvious attempt at distracting me. "If you have the same . . . vampire ancestors, or whatever, does that mean you're related?"

"Depends who you ask," he said, all traces of humor gone again. "I don't personally think I owe the monsters who took everything from me and made me what I am today anything at all. My . . . *siblings* disagree." He said the word with barely concealed disdain. "Central to their weird vigilante cult thing is reverence for a group called The Founding Eight. Our sires' sires' sires, basically."

"Okay. So . . . what did you do to make them want to . . . to *vigilante* you, or whatever?"

His face shuttered. He looked away from me, at the half circle of snowmen surrounding our little lean-to.

"Like I said earlier, there was a party," he said, very quietly. "A hundred and fifty years ago, give or take a decade."

I nearly choked on my tongue. "You're . . ." I tried to gather my scattered wits. "You're one hundred and fifty years old?"

"No."

"But you just said—"

"I said this party happened one hundred and fifty years ago." He gave me a sad, sardonic smile. "I was already more than a hundred years old at the time."

In a rush, I realized that all I really knew about vampires had been the handful of things Reggie had told me and little details I'd gleaned over the years via pop culture. I supposed on some level, I already knew that vampires were immortal. I'd just never had occasion to dwell on it.

Until now.

"Oh," I said weakly.

"Anyway," he continued, as if I weren't having paradigm-shifting realizations on the bench beside him, "there was a fire. Some people died. Other people think I was responsible for it. The Collective definitely does." He sighed and stared down at his hands. "The Collective never much liked the cut of my jib, so to speak. Ever since their—*our*—sires died, The Collective has felt like they have a serious stake to grind with me."

I hesitated before asking my next question. "Reggie—*were* you responsible for the fire?"

He shook his head. "No. At least, not in the way they think."

He stood up abruptly, as though he wanted to pace as he spoke. But then he seemed to think better of it when he realized that pacing would entail tromping through feet of snow. He sat down beside me again, looking a bit sheepish.

"There isn't a lot that can kill a vampire," he continued. "While most of us are nocturnal, the whole *burning up in sunlight* thing is a myth. Driving a wooden stake through our hearts would do the job, but that would kill anybody." He gave me a wry smile. "The only things that will reliably end a vampire's life are entering somebody's home without express permission—we explode like a bomb has gone off inside us, very gross—and fire. Let's just say the night I got on The Collective's bad side I was figuratively and literally playing with fire."

The wind chose that moment to pick up dramatically, rattling our shed. The gaps in the old wooden walls let in a rush of frigid air. I shivered, leaning closer to Reggie reflexively.

Slowly—as though he wanted to give me the opportunity to move away from him if his touch was unwelcome—he wrapped an arm around me, pulling me close. I let him do it without allowing myself to think about what it meant. I felt the cold bite of the wind against the cheek that wasn't pressed against his shoulder but was almost too distracted by the unexpected warmth of his body to notice.

Once we were settled again, he continued his story. "I was not a particularly nice person in the late nineteenth century," he mused. "I stopped far short of mass murder, of course," he added hastily, shooting me a sideways glance. "But at the time of the fire, I had a well-deserved reputation as a prankster and an ass. I can understand why some people at that party thought I'd set the place on fire."

"And why was that?"

His arm tightened around me a little. He looked away. "I can't say for certain, but it's probably the signed note I left by the torches out front that said *I hate you all and am going to burn this place to the ground*."

"Are you *kidding* me?" He didn't answer. He wouldn't meet my gaze. "Reggie, that was *seriously* stupid."

"I am aware." He started cracking the knuckles of his free hand against his knee. A nervous tic. "But when I wrote that note, I was just being an asshole. I never had any intention of doing anything other than piss people off. How was I supposed to know someone else at the party was going to see that note, take inspiration from it, and think to themselves *yes, burning this place down sounds like a spiffing idea*?"

He sounded despondent. If I were a more tactful person, I probably would have been sensitive to that and not asked my next question. But I had to know. "Why exactly *did* you write that note, Reggie?"

Another sharp gust of wind rattled the shed. "This was over a century before therapy became in vogue, mind you. But I'm pretty sure that if I had been seeing a therapist back then, they would've told me I was lashing out because immortality, and everything I lost to become immortal, was more than I could handle."

My heart clenched. I hadn't thought about what it must be like to live forever. But now that I *was* thinking about it, I thought I understood what he meant. Being frozen in time at age thirty-five had some obvious advantages, but how would it feel still being thirty-five, while friends and family continued to age and eventually died?

"Everybody dies in the end," he said, as if reading my thoughts. His voice was barely above a whisper. "Everybody who isn't a vampire . . . they die. Even vampires start to go a bit strange after five hundred years or so." He looked at the ground. "I've done some things I'm not proud of—played a lot of practical jokes, and worse—because . . ." He trailed off, and glanced at me out of the corner of his eye. "Probably because I was afraid to get too close to anybody. Because getting close to people only leads to eventual pain."

His words from earlier in the day came rushing back to me. *To be perfectly honest, kissing you was probably a mistake on my end, too.*

Was this what he'd meant by that?

"So," I said, trying to make sense of everything he was telling me, "for the past hundred and fifty years or so, you were a jerk to keep people from getting close?"

He raised an eyebrow. "I don't know if you can really describe my behavior in the past tense like that."

"You haven't been a jerk to me."

He gave me a small smile. "I suppose that's true." His gaze softened. "I haven't been tempted to be an asshole to you even once."

I didn't know what to do with the look he was giving me. It was too much, too warm. I couldn't look away. "Does that mean that you don't like me enough to worry about losing me?"

Even as I said the words, I knew it wasn't true. An expression I didn't recognize crossed his face. "No," he said. He gathered me even closer to him. When I didn't resist, or move away, he tipped my chin up with a finger so I had to look him in the eyes. "That isn't what it means at all."

His face was so close I could all but taste his breathing. Kissing him would have been the easiest thing in the world. Easier than *not* kissing him, honestly. A slight tilt of my head would have our lips meeting and our worlds crashing together again. He was thinking the same thing I was—I could feel it in my bones, could see it in the dilation of his eyes—but I knew he wouldn't make the first move again. My earlier admonition against future make-out sessions was clearly at the front of his mind, even as his eyes fell to my mouth.

"It's pretty out here tonight, isn't it?" I asked, desperate to break the tension simmering between us. I rested my head on his shoulder and closed my eyes. Snuggling out here wasn't kissing him, after all. *This* wasn't going to make me lose sense and want to sleep with him the way kissing him would. *This* was okay. "Let's stay out here for a little while longer before heading back inside."

He sighed. A moment later, his other arm came up to wrap around me, too.

"Of course," he murmured against the top of my head. "As long as you like."

REGINALD

Amelia must have fallen asleep.

One moment she was commenting on how beautifully the moonlight glinted off the snow in the forest. The next, her breathing had gone all deep and even, her body still and warm in my arms.

I was so entranced by the feel of her, by the fact that she hadn't so much as flinched when I told her my darkest secret, that it wasn't until she began shivering that it sank in through my thick skull that it was freezing out there.

A fierce protective surge shot through me like adrenaline.

I needed to get Amelia inside.

I gathered her up, my frozen heart breaking at how light and fragile she was. I could hurt her so easily, I realized. I never would. I cradled her against my chest, wishing my body retained some semblance of a human's warmth. It was well below freezing outside.

What if I wasn't enough to protect her from the elements?

She stirred a little when we were halfway to the house. "Don't," she murmured, head lolling against my shoulder. Her sleepy breaths were warm puffs of air against my neck. She smelled like everything I had ever wanted. *Hades*, I wanted to kiss her fully awake. I quickened my pace, hoping she was too sleepy to realize that my earlier struggles with the snowshoes had all been an act to make me seem more human. "I can walk."

Like I would really put her down before I'd gotten her back home. I wasn't sure I had it in me to set her down even once we'd gotten back inside. *Dangerous*, an internal voice was screaming. *This will only cause pain, later.*

I ignored it.

"You'd been asleep for fifteen minutes before I worked up the courage to do this," I said. And then, before I could stop my idiot mouth from saying anything else, "You're so beautiful when you're sleeping."

And then, we were at the house.

Then, her bedroom.

I carried her inside without preamble and laid her gently down on her bed. I should have turned and left the room, but I didn't. I stepped back to look at her, gorgeous and inviting, her beautiful dark blond hair curling in soft waves on her pillow.

If her eyes had been open, she'd have seen it written all over my face just how desperately I was falling for her.

There was another howling gust of wind from outside. It shook the entire house, rattling the windowpanes. The lights flickered but thankfully didn't go out. The blizzard had apparently decided it wasn't done fucking with us yet.

Amelia's eyes flew open. She tugged on my sleeve.

"Stay," she said, sounding frightened. The wind gusted again, causing the shutters on her bedroom window to creak and the eaves outside to groan. She squeezed her eyes shut again. "It's embarrassing to admit this, but winter storms terrify me at night. If I'm in my room, and you're at the other end of the cabin, it'll feel like I'm truly all alone." And then, in a much quieter voice, she added, "My bed is big enough for two."

I could almost feel my mind splitting into two clean halves.

The first wondered, *Would it* really *be so bad to stay with her in here? The bed in this room is large, and if we were wearing all our clothes . . . what would be the harm?*

The rest, in a voice that sounded suspiciously like Frederick's, threatened to stake me where I stood for even considering this.

She was human, and I'd gotten no sign from her that she wanted our arrangement to continue beyond her cousin's wedding. The potential for this to end in disaster was huge.

When I'd proposed us spending time together tonight, I'd had no ulterior motives beyond hopefully getting her to relax and make her smile.

I tried, frantically, to think this situation through. But then she tugged on my sleeve again, and looked up at me with frightened eyes, and all ability to reason left me.

"Are you sure?" I asked, quietly. I needed her to be sure.

"I don't want to sleep alone tonight," she said again. She sounded embarrassed. "I'm just not used to there being so much empty space here. I can't handle it during a storm."

"Okay," I said. "I don't sleep much at night. But I'd be happy to stay with you tonight. In here. Just, you know. To sleep." My mind was shorting out. I was babbling. If I could blush, I would definitely have been doing it then. "To keep you safe from the storm, or . . . whatever. But I'll admit I'm a bit confused. Earlier tonight you'd said our kissing was a mistake."

"This wouldn't be kissing," she said, very quickly. "It would just be—"

"Sleeping."

"Exactly."

I eyed the space on the bed beside her. There was definitely room for both of us, but what if she woke in the night, more frightened of who was sleeping beside her than the storm? Or worse: What if we ended up touching in the night as we shifted in sleep? My stomach filled with a rash of butterflies at the thought. Her head on my chest. Her legs tangled with mine beneath the covers.

No, a voice that again sounded suspiciously like Frederick's shouted.

"Would you want to create a barrier between us?" I offered, weakly. "With pillows, or something?" I thought I'd seen people do that on a television show, once. I couldn't remember how it had worked out for them in the end, but it seemed a sound strategy.

"I'm a pretty deep sleeper," she said. "I don't think a barrier is necessary."

Technically, making space for me was easy. But it didn't matter that the bed was more than large enough for both of us. The minute I lay down beside her—me on top of the blankets, her beneath them—her presence tugged at me like a magnet. The urge to roll over onto my side and look at her was overpowering.

I didn't fight it.

She lay on her back, staring up at the ceiling with an intensity that suggested she may have been trying to avoid giving in to her own temptations. Her profile was bathed in the moonlight coming in between the slats in the window blinds.

Why did someone who was so very obviously off-limits have to be so beautiful?

"Goodnight, Amelia." I was unbearably nervous, every cell in my body hyperaware of her proximity. She smiled, just a little, and my eyes fell helplessly to her lips. I'd been right, earlier, when I'd said that kissing her had been a mistake. Reaching out to trace the shape of her smile with my fingertips would surely be just as foolish.

"Goodnight," she said, pulling the covers up to her chin.

It was nearly four in the morning, and I knew she was exhausted. Sure enough, she fell asleep almost instantly.

TWENTY-TWO

*Excerpt from the BoisterousBulleters Discord Server,
#off-topic channel*

REGINALD_THE_V: hey

REGINALD_THE_V: I know it's the middle of the night and
you're all probably sleeping

REGINALD_THE_V: but I'm freaking out. i'm sleeping in A's
bed because she's afraid of the storm and she said she
only wanted to sleep but

REGINALD_THE_V: this is REALLY fucking hard

ANDIFROMAUSTRALIA: ohohoho FINALLY, I'm NEVER
awake for the good shit

ANDIFROMAUSTRALIA: when you say "this is REALLY
fucking hard" do you mean the situation is hard or that
you are hard?

REGINALD_THE_V: I meant the situation but . . . both?

ANDIFROMAUSTRALIA: YESSSSSS

AMELIA

I BLINKED MY EYES OPEN TO THE UNPLEASANT AROMA OF burnt baking soda.

I tried to sit up so I could investigate what was happening in the kitchen. But I couldn't. My face was pressed against a broad, solid chest. A heavy arm draped over my side, pulling me close.

Wait.

There was a *person in bed with me*.

I froze, the events of the previous night coming back to me in a rush.

Oh my god.

I'd asked Reggie to sleep next to me.

And he'd *agreed*.

Bright sunshine streamed in from the window. How long had we been cuddled up like this?

"Reggie?" I whispered.

He stirred without waking up, tucking me even closer to his body. We'd both slept in our clothes. Thank god for that. The fabric of his long-sleeved flannel shirt was so soft against my cheek and smelled impossibly good. The scent of laundry detergent, cool male skin, and something entirely other, something entirely *Reggie*, clung to him. I wanted to linger in it.

But no.

I couldn't give in to whatever this was.

"*Reggie*," I said again, a little louder this time. Both to wake him up and to remind my sluggish brain that I needed to get out of this bed, too, and put some distance between us. I gave his shoulder a shake. "Wake up."

He cracked open an eye.

"Amelia?" There was a moment of confusion as he struggled to focus on my face. "What—?" And then, realization hit. He jerked, and flung himself back from me as though I'd burned him. Partly, anyway; our legs still twined together beneath the covers. "Oh, *shit*. I'm sorry. I didn't realize—"

Something about this whole absurd situation—being snowed in and stuck for who knew how much longer with my vampire plus-one; telling him we absolutely could *not* kiss again, only to end up inviting him into my bed the same night and sleeping wrapped in his arms—made something inside me snap.

I started laughing. Nothing about this situation was funny, but once I got started, I couldn't stop. What began as a quiet giggle quickly became a laugh that was so hard, I was gasping.

I took some deep breaths as I tried to get myself under control. "Oh, *god*, Reggie, I can't believe that we're—"

"What's so funny?" Reggie was grinning, clearly delighted, but the corners of his eyes crinkled in confusion. He moved closer to me, his arm again wrapping around my waist. "Did I make a joke without realizing? Usually, I know it when I've been funny."

"I can't—I can't believe we're here, stuck . . . in this bed . . . You're a *vampire!*" I said between peals of laughter.

"I am," he agreed. He was beaming at me now. "And yes, we are. I made pancakes if you're hungry. I couldn't sleep. Though I may have used too much baking soda. I couldn't find a teaspoon, so I used a large measuring cup instead."

So that's what that smell was. It only made me laugh harder.

My eyes leaked with tears as I sat up and clutched my stomach. "Oh my god, I can't—"

"Do you have any idea how gorgeous you are right now?"

His words cut through my hysteria like a knife. My laughter, the ridiculousness of our situation, melted away. All that was left was our proximity, the way our legs still tangled together beneath the covers—and his bright blue eyes, boring into mine.

I swallowed. "I'm . . . I'm what?"

"I've wanted to see you like this for what feels like a century," he breathed. He sat up in bed beside me, then trailed tentative fingertips up my side, along my neck. Slowly, as though giving me the opportunity to rebuff him if I didn't want him to touch me. I *did* want, though. I shivered at his touch, at the way the space between us went suddenly breathless and hot, and made no move to stop him. "I've wanted to make you laugh like this since the night we met. You were *terrible* at pretending to laugh when I asked you to, but in hindsight I see that was a good thing. Because if I'd seen what you are like when you *truly* let go, I would have fallen to my knees. Right then and there."

Now that I wasn't laughing anymore, my breathing should have been slowing down. It wasn't. His was quickening, too. I could see it in the way his chest rose and fell, in the way his nostrils flared almost imperceptibly. If I'd been in my right mind, I probably wouldn't have inched closer to him. I certainly would have had the sense not to reach for his hand. But it felt like we resided in some liminal space here. A place where we were freed from having to worry about work and good decisions. And from the fact that most of the time, vampires like him fed on humans like me.

All the nervous anticipation coiling tight like a fist in my belly was mirrored in his expression. His eyes were fixed firmly on my face, as though not trusting what he might do if he allowed his gaze to wander.

"Can I kiss you?" His voice had gone quiet. Almost shy. "I don't want to make you—"

"Yes."

It was the wrong decision in every way. I was too busy for romantic entanglements. He was a *vampire*. But I shoved all of it to the side. I was a live wire, every nerve in my body awake in a way I had not experienced in god only knew how long. I *wanted* this. "You aren't *making me* anything."

I reached up and twined my fingers into his soft blond hair. He groaned, a broken sound, as I scraped my fingernails gently along his scalp.

When he kissed me, it was more a sweet mingling of breath, a gentle brushing of his lips against mine, than a proper kiss. He pulled back almost as soon as it began, leaving me breathless and wanting. Giving me the opportunity to end this if that was what I wanted.

"I realize that my touching you without an audience was never part of the original plan," Reggie began, his eyes never leaving my face. His lips were so soft. I *needed* them on me again. Right now. "It certainly wasn't part of mine. But ever since the night we met, all I have wanted was to touch you."

I shivered at the heat in his words. "Since the night we met?"

"Yes." His hold on me tightened as he pulled me deliberately into his lap. I straddled him, our bodies seamed together chest to chest. "Even as I walked away from you that night, all I could think about was what it would feel like to hold your hand. To kiss you." His eyes dropped to my mouth. "The reality of *that* is way better than I imagined it would be. Which just makes me wonder if the reality of touching you in other ways would be better than my imagination, too."

My heart raced at his words. His eyes fluttered closed as his nostrils flared. Could he smell it, the way my blood pumped harder through my veins? The idea of it shouldn't have excited me as much as it did.

"You've imagined touching me?" I managed.

A long pause.

He nodded.

Outside, the wind was picking up again. I barely heard it. There was only the beating of my heart, Reggie holding me so close we were breathing the same air—and me, wanting so badly for him to kiss me again it felt a little like madness.

When I spoke next, it was in a brave voice I hardly recognized. "Then do it."

His mouth was on mine before I could draw breath, devouring me in a way that left me gasping, showing none of the gentleness he had a moment ago. He kissed like a man on the verge of drowning breathes: desperate, and like he couldn't get enough. His lips pressed so hard to mine it felt bruising, his tongue tracing the seam of my lips for only a moment before plunging within.

He asked me something that sounded vaguely like *is this all right?* But I could hardly hear him over the thundering of the blood in my ears and the racing beat of my heart. I twined my arms around his broad shoulders by way of response, fingers reaching up to tangle again in his hair. This man made me reckless in a way I had never experienced before. Not with anybody.

I didn't have the words to tell him any of this, so I showed him instead.

Kissing him was like finally working out the solution to a difficult problem, euphoric both mentally and physically. I needed him shirtless so I could run my palms over his chest and feel the bunch and flex of his muscles as I touched him. I slid my hands down his body, reveling in his sharp intake of breath, pausing only when I got to the bottom hem of his flannel button-down.

I fumbled with the buttons with useless fingers. "Off," I mumbled against his lips, rendered monosyllabic with need. "I want—"

Before I could finish the thought, he yanked both the flannel and the thin T-shirt he'd been wearing beneath it over his head and tossed them over his shoulder.

Then he took each of my wrists in his hands and pinned me, arms above my head, to the mattress.

Our change in positioning seemed to unleash something within him. He kissed me again with a harsh groan, his grip on my wrists like a vise. He was everywhere, all at once, his mouth on my cheek, on my jaw, on the sensitive pulse point where neck met shoulder. I felt seconds away from bursting out of my skin, writhing beneath him as he kissed his way down my body.

What would it feel like, I wondered, to be pressed together with him flesh to flesh, with no clothes between us at all? All at once I had to know. In that moment, it was all I wanted.

I had just been about to beg him to take off my blouse and chuck it to the floor with his clothes when he released my wrists. He sat up, placing a hand on each of my shoulders.

"I need to eat something," he said, panting hard. His voice was gravel on stone. "Before we . . . *before*."

It took a moment for what he was trying to tell me to sink in. And then, all at once, it did.

He needed to *eat something*.

"Oh," I said. And then, feeling like an idiot, I asked, "Why?"

He looked away, uncomfortable. "It's just that it will be better if I do. Safer. For you."

Would he lose control during intimacy if he didn't feed now?

Would he bite me? The small part of me still capable of sense was screaming at the rest of me that his failure to elaborate further was the reddest of red flags. I wanted him too badly to care.

"Just come back quickly," I said. Begged, really. "Please."

He groaned, sounding pained. "I don't have it in me to keep you waiting long." He chuckled. "Or myself either, apparently. I stashed my supplies in the garage so they'd stay cool. I'll only be gone a few minutes. I promise."

Then he raced from the room. I heard the door to the garage creak open, then slam shut behind him.

I took the opportunity to ransack my suitcase in the hope of finding something sexy to wear when he came back. Or at least, sexier than the mismatched pink and lime-green bra and panty combo I wore beneath my clothes.

It was a lost cause. Why hadn't I followed Sophie's advice and tucked something slinky into my bag? Other than bringing along a pair of hiking boots for hikes that the feet of snow outside had now rendered impossible, the only planning ahead I'd done for this trip involved thinking through which work files I'd need to take with me.

I hadn't done any of the things I *really* should have done to get ready. Like check the weather. Or anticipate that I'd maybe want Reggie to touch me while we were here.

Frustrated, I tore off my shirt, and then my bra, hoping that the sight of my breasts would distract him from the fact that I hadn't brought anything pretty with which to dress them up. The room was cold, the air hitting my bare skin making my nipples tighten.

Then I sat back on the bed, trying to arrange the blankets around me in an enticing way. And I waited.

And waited.

And waited.

TWENTY-THREE

Telegram sent from George, Treasurer of The Collective, to The Collective's Board of Directors

CONFRONTED QUARRY OUTSIDE OF WI HOUSE WHERE HE WAS HIDING. STOP.

HE FLEW OFF BEFORE WE COULD APPREHEND. STOP.

BASED ON WIND PATTERNS BELIEVE HE IS FLYING BACK TO CHICAGO. STOP.

(WISH I COULD FLY TOO. STOP.)

(WOULD SIMPLIFY THIS WHOLE ENDEAVOR. STOP.)

(PLUS FLYING IS JUST REALLY COOL. STOP.)

AM BRINGING BACK GIFT OF FOAM "CHEESEHEAD" AS PEN-ANCE FOR LOSING QUARRY WHEN JUSTICE WAS NIGH. STOP.

AMELIA

AFTER WAITING TWENTY MINUTES FOR REGGIE TO COME back to bed, I began to worry. I scoured the cabin and the area around it, but save for a few sets of footprints in the snow about ten feet away from the front door, there was no sign of him anywhere.

By early afternoon I gave up on waiting for him to come back.

Had I seriously been stood up for sex by a vampire? After I'd *finally* listened to Sophie and decided to give into my attraction? Reggie had seemed super into the idea of sleeping together when we were in my bedroom, and I didn't think he'd faked it. But maybe he had?

God.

This was the exact opposite of what my self-esteem needed.

There was still a pint of chocolate sorbet in the freezer. Even if finishing it off in one sitting was cliché, I decided there were worse clichés to live out.

But once I had the sorbet in front of me, I thought of everything Reggie had done to get it.

I would brave a blizzard just to see you smile.

And then there was the mountainous stack of horrendous pancakes he'd left for me on the kitchen counter. He'd been right when he'd worried he'd used too much baking soda, but it didn't matter. He'd made them for me, with no idea of what he was doing, just so I'd have something special to eat for breakfast.

He'd been nothing but kind to me. And now that I was looking around the kitchen, I saw that wherever he'd gone, he'd left behind all his stuff in his hurry to get there.

Including his phone. And Old Fuzzy.

That's when the panic set in. Something was wrong.

There was only one person I could think of to talk to about this situation. It might not get me anywhere, but the more time passed, the more I knew I couldn't just sit there doing nothing.

With the half-finished pint of sorbet in one hand and my

phone in the other, I scrolled through my contacts, hoping that
I'd added Frederick at some point.

Bingo. There he was.

> **AMELIA:** Hi Frederick
>
> **AMELIA:** This is Amelia Collins
>
> **AMELIA:** Sam's sister
>
> **AMELIA:** I think we met at a party at my
> brother's house a few months ago
>
> **AMELIA:** Can you call me?

My phone started ringing immediately.

"Frederick?" My heart was in my throat.

"Am I speaking with Ms. Amelia Collins?" Frederick's manner of speech was oddly formal in such a specific way that I was
immediately able to place him. I also remembered he was a huge
Taylor Swift fan. Which, now that I knew he was a centuries-old
vampire, was equal parts fascinating and bizarre.

"This is Amelia," I confirmed. "Sorry if this is totally out of
the blue, but your friend Reggie was up here in Wisconsin with
me for a family trip. But now he's disappeared, leaving all his
stuff behind. I'm very worried." I almost added, *and I'm hurt, too.*
But I cut myself off before I could ramble any further. I didn't
know if Frederick had even known Reggie had been up here before I'd called. No need to embarrass myself beyond hope of re-
covery right off the bat.

"Hmm," Frederick said. "That is very strange. He'd told me
he planned to stay with you until the snowplows arrived."

My cheeks went warm at the implication that I was important

enough to Reggie for him to have told Frederick about me, even as the knot of dread in the pit of my stomach twisted tighter at the concern in Frederick's voice.

"You think something bad might have happened to him?" I asked.

"Possibly," he said. "What was the last thing that happened before he disappeared?"

My mind shorted out as my mouth tried to form words. How could I possibly answer that question without bursting into flames?

"Well," I began. "It was . . . He was . . ."

"Did he say anything to you about wanting to leave?" he prompted. "Or did you have a fight? I know he can be insufferable."

"No," I said quickly. "We didn't have a fight. We . . ."

Frederick was quiet as he waited for me to elaborate. When I didn't, he chuckled. "*Oh*," he said, seeming to piece together from my silence everything I hadn't told him. Was it possible to die of embarrassment? "In *that* case, yes, there's reason to be very concerned."

Oh, no. "You think so?"

"Yes," he said. "I have known him for a very long time, and I wouldn't have thought even a mob of angry torch-waving villagers could have gotten him to leave your side if you had just . . ."

I opened my mouth to clarify that we hadn't technically *just* anything but bit my tongue at the last moment. Better to just drop it and move on.

"What do you think happened to him?" I asked.

He hesitated. "Has Reginald told you anything about The Collective?"

A possibility I hadn't let myself entertain until now came

crashing in. "The vigilante vampire mob that's after him for something he didn't do?"

"That's one way of describing them." He let out a long-suffering sigh. "I *told* Reginald that if he kept behaving the way he did in the late nineteenth century there would eventually be consequences. But did he listen to me?"

He paused long enough that it felt like he was waiting for me to respond. "I'm guessing he didn't?"

"He didn't," Frederick confirmed, sounding like a disappointed parent.

"And do you think they followed him here? That that's why he disappeared?"

"I'm not certain," Frederick said. "But I believe it is entirely possible his strategy of using your fake relationship, and Wisconsin, to hide from his pursuers has stopped working."

Frederick's words were a punch in the gut. I reminded myself it made no sense to be hurt. Why did it matter that he'd had an ulterior motive for going along with this fake dating ruse? Hadn't the whole point of my suggesting it in the first place been to hide, too?

But somehow, this *felt* different. I'd never misled him about why I was doing this. Or jeopardized his safety, the way it sounded like he may have jeopardized mine.

Frederick must have picked up on something in my silence because his next words were conciliatory. "He cares about you," he said. "He'd probably stake me on the spot if he knew I was telling you this, especially since I don't think he's even admitted it to himself. But I have known Reginald for over three hundred years. Whatever his reasons for beginning this arrangement with you might have been, it is obvious to me it has become so much more."

I closed my eyes, letting Frederick's words wash over me. My emotions were a complicated tangle, with joy that Reggie cared for me jumbled up with fear over his safety—as well as some mild panic at the realization that I cared for him, too.

"I firmly believe everything will eventually work out just fine," Frederick continued, his tone gentle. "The buffoons chasing Reginald have been at it on and off for nearly one hundred and fifty years. It's taken them all this time to find him, despite the man being as inconspicuous as a fireworks display. They are delusional, ineffectual idiots." And then, as if he'd sensed the earlier direction of my thoughts, he added, "Additionally, please know that you're in no danger. You're not who they're after. Even if you were, they cannot enter your home if you don't invite them inside."

That was reassuring. "If Reggie gets in touch with you, please call me right away."

"I will," Frederick promised. "In the meantime, try not to worry."

So much easier said than done.

....

TIME SLOWED TO A CRAWL AFTER I GOT OFF THE PHONE with Frederick. I tried distracting myself by catching up on work emails, but to my immense frustration, I was way too frazzled to focus on the latest missives from the Wyatt Foundation. How was it *possible* that the last foreign return they'd filed had been for an ironworks in Milan in 1923?

I'd have to figure that out when I got back to Chicago. I didn't have the wherewithal to think about it right then.

In the meantime, I checked the weather forecast. It often took days for snowplows to dig out this part of the state, but when I saw that the forecast had temperatures rising into the fifties by the next afternoon, I breathed a huge sigh of relief. Warmer weather wouldn't melt all the snow overnight, but the major streets would likely be drivable by tomorrow.

That meant I could hopefully be out of there soon, and go to wherever Reggie might be.

I ran to my bedroom and started throwing the handful of things I'd unpacked back into my suitcase. I'd keep an eye on road conditions online and leave the second it seemed safe enough to drive.

When night fell and there was still no word on Reggie, I was so frantic for distraction that I started reading an e-book Sophie had gifted me shortly after Reggie and I entered our arrangement. It was called *The Date Who Was Fake—until He Wasn't*, by an author I still couldn't believe was *actually* named Vixxen Stampede. When Sophie sent it, I'd rolled my eyes at how obvious she was being, but right then it seemed a good alternative to anxiously pacing the cabin.

I had just gotten to the part of the book where Cynthia and Rafe, the two fake dating protagonists, had finally kissed for real, when my phone rang. I leapt for it.

"Reginald is fine," Frederick said right away when I answered. "He sent word through secure channels that The Collective found him outside your parents' cabin, but that he succeeded in giving them the slip." He cleared his throat. "He told me to tell you that, quote, *I left to lure those assholes away from you and your house and have been losing my fucking mind trying to find a pay phone to call you ever since*, end quote."

Dizzying relief swept through me. He was okay. He'd wanted to let me know why he left, but couldn't. "Did he say anything else?"

Frederick hummed his assent. "Reginald also wants you to

know that he is incredibly sorry for leaving you alone without saying goodbye, and that he only did it out of concern for your safety." A long pause. "He also said that leaving you when he did is one of the hardest things he's ever done. He placed special emphasis on the word *hardest*, but out of concern for my own sanity, I refuse to analyze why that might be."

My cheeks flamed at the double entendre. "Is he hurt?"

"He'll eventually be fine," Frederick said. "Most of the harm done to him was to his ego. There was an in-air run-in with a flock of Canada geese that he didn't say much about, but I suspect they're what kept him from reaching out sooner."

"So he really can fly, then?"

"Yes," he confirmed. "I'm surprised Reginald hasn't boasted about what an excellent flier he is. When The Collective accosted him, he simply took to the air."

Wow. It must be incredibly convenient to be able to do that. Realizing I still had almost no idea what was normal for vampires, I asked, "Can all vampires fly?"

"No," he said tersely. "I cannot fly."

"Do you have special abilities, too?"

"Yes, but . . . We're getting sidetracked."

I got the sense that special vampiric abilities were a touchy subject for him, so I let it drop. "I can't leave here until the snowplows come, but I feel like I need to *do* something, knowing he's in trouble. What else can you tell me about The Collective? Are there any online resources I can read for more information about them?"

"There's not much about them online," he said. "They aren't modern enough to know how to use the Internet well. I have heard they quite enjoy staging blood bank break-ins the morning after stadium concerts, but that's more rumor than substantiated fact. Not to mention tacky, if true." He paused, and then added, "I *can* tell you that they pose as humans most of the time. The latest I've heard is that they run a farce of a nonprofit organization that doesn't do much of anything besides hold board meetings."

My eyebrows shot up. Vampires, I knew nothing about. But nonprofits, I understood. At least when it came to their tax returns. But something about this didn't add up. "Why would vampires need a nonprofit?"

"I have no idea," Frederick admitted. "Probably to make themselves feel important. Near as I can tell, that's why they do just about everything."

"Do you know the name of the nonprofit?"

"It's probably just *The Collective,*" he said. "*The Annals of Vampyric Lore* may have something about it. I know it contains at least a few entries about them." When I didn't respond, he added, "*The Annals* is what you might get if you crossed a vampire history book with a human encyclopedia. It's wonderfully thorough."

When I got back to Chicago, I would ask for login credentials to my firm's GuideStar account so I could look The Collective up there. GuideStar allowed users to search public records for all nonprofit organizations with federal tax-exempt status. *The Collective* was probably too common a name for GuideStar to yield useful results, but it was worth checking.

I couldn't do it until I had access to the firm's account, though.

"Where can I find a copy of *The Annals?*" That didn't sound like something I'd be able to check out of my local library, but maybe the University of Chicago had it somewhere in its massive stacks. They had all kinds of weird books in their basement.

"I happen to own the complete set." The pride in Frederick's voice was unmistakable. It reminded me so much of how Dad spoke of his favorite history journals I couldn't help but smile. "Making fun of me for owning it is one of the few things Cassie and Reginald enjoy doing together."

"Could I take a peek at it when I get back to Chicago?"

"Of course," Frederick said. "But do limit yourself to the sections pertaining to The Collective. As fascinating as *I* find vampiric history, there are large sections of it that could be upsetting for a human to read. Which I'm sure you can understand."

No more needed to be said about that. "I'll stick to what I'm looking for," I promised. I glanced back at the living room couch, where Reggie had left most of his belongings. Swallowing down the lump in my throat, I said, "Reggie left his phone behind, so I don't have a way to get in touch with him. But if you talk to him—"

"I expect he will arrive this evening," Frederick said. "He didn't want to return to your cabin in case him doing so led The Collective back to you. I can pass on any message you like."

This *evening*? He'd only left the cabin that morning. The idea that Reggie could fly that fast stunned me. "Okay. When you talk with him, can you tell him that—"

I stopped. What *did* I want Frederick to tell him?

That I was relieved he was okay? That I'd been worried about him?

That being this worried about someone I'd only just met terrified me?

"I'll tell him to call you," Frederick offered. "You can take things from there."

"Yes," I agreed, heart in my throat. "Please do. And thank you."

....

I WAS JUST SETTLING DOWN TO AN EVENING GLASS OF wine and the rest of Sophie's e-book when I heard the telltale signs of a snowplow making its way down my street.

I sprang to my feet and ran to the front window. It was past eight o'clock and very dark outside, but sure enough, there was Joe McCarthy, the elderly man who'd been clearing this area since I was a kid, driving down the street in his makeshift pickup truck snowplow.

If he'd already made it to this street, the major roads should be just fine by the next morning. All I'd have to do would be use Dad's snowblower on the driveway and throw my suitcase in the car, and I could be off.

Grinning, I texted Frederick with the update.

AMELIA: I'm getting plowed!

FREDERICK: That's what she said

I stared at my phone. I didn't know Frederick well, but what little I did know made it hard to imagine him making such a crass joke.

FREDERICK: This is Reggie by the way

FREDERICK: Freddie's letting me use his phone

FREDERICK: I just got to his house. I was just about to call you.

> **FREDERICK:** I would have called you
> MUCH earlier in fact if there were even
> one fucking payphone still in operation
> between Door County and Chicago

It was like all the fear and anxiety I'd been carrying since that morning left me all at once. My whole body felt limp as a noodle as relief washed over me.

> **AMELIA:** I was so scared when you didn't
> come back

> **FREDERICK:** I'm fine I promise

> **FREDERICK:** I'm so sorry I had to leave
> without saying goodbye

> **AMELIA:** Can you call me?

> **AMELIA:** It's weird texting you and seeing
> Frederick's name

My phone rang ten seconds later.

"Hey." Reggie's voice was bright and clear. My relief grew. He really was all right. "You okay?"

I glanced at my half-drunk glass of wine. "I've been better," I admitted. And then, because I couldn't resist, I teased, "It's been a long time since I've been ghosted for sex, you know."

He groaned, so loudly and theatrically I couldn't help but laugh. "Trust me, leaving you right then was the *last* thing I wanted to do." And then, in a voice full of apology, "But I had to.

I would never have forgiven myself if something bad happened to you after I essentially led them right to your door."

His tone was so sincere I didn't doubt for a second that he meant every word of it. "It's okay," I said. "*I'm* okay, too."

Reggie let out a sigh of relief. "Amelia, I am so glad."

I paused, thinking through my next words carefully. If I regretted what had happened before he fled, if I wanted to put a stop to whatever was blossoming between us, this felt like the time to let him know. I could say we shouldn't have let ourselves get carried away. I could end this before it went any further.

I didn't regret what happened, though.

I only regretted that we didn't get to see it through.

Wanting him so much was never part of the original plan, to put it mildly. But I wanted him all the same.

"I didn't want you to leave, either," I admitted. "I *hated* that you didn't come back to bed like you said you would." And then, braving much, I asked, "Could we try it again when I get back home? This time without anyone fleeing the scene?"

The snowplow outside was getting louder. Snowplow Joe was making quick work out there. Maybe I could even leave for Chicago tonight if all the stars aligned.

Reggie chuckled. "I would love nothing more."

TWENTY-FOUR

Minutes from emergency board meeting of The Collective

- *Present: Guinevere, George, Giuseppe, Philippa, Gregorio, John, Miss Pennywhistle, Patricia Benicio Hewitt*
- *Absent: Alexandria, Maurice J. Pettigrew*
- *Called to order: 9:15 PM*
- *Memorial Hymns sung to The Founding Eight: Led by Philippa*

NEW BUSINESS:

- <u>*The Search for Reginald Cleaves*</u>: *We had him, and then lost him again just when vengeance for our ancestors appeared within reach. Devastating! One bright spot: while in Wisconsin we gleaned through context clues that R.C. now has a human paramour. This knowledge may be of use. Committee formed to think through options.*

- *Nonprofit Business: J.R. will soon meet with our accounting firm to get the "Wyatt Foundation's" tax filings in order. Giuseppe once again argued that having a nonprofit arm "is stupid," given that we are vampires. Remainder of board reminded him that the more layers of legitimacy The Collective can acquire, the more likely it is the rest of the vampiric world will finally take us seriously. Plus, our accountant says it will save us on our state tax bill and lower our marginal income tax rate (whatever that is).*
- *J.R. polled board members on what additional information to send the accountant handling our affairs.*
- *Meeting adjourned: 10:15 PM*
- *Next meeting: April 15, 9:15 PM. Philippa to provide refreshments.*

REGINALD

EVERYTHING HURT.

I liked to think of myself as every bit the flyer I'd been in my youth. But I had to face facts: I was slipping. A hundred years ago I could have made it from Amelia's cabin to Freddie's home as quickly as a car could make the trip today, but yesterday's trip had taken me nearly ten hours.

Of course, it hadn't helped that I'd suffered an injury to my right biceps from that idiot vampire's pathetic attempt at staking me outside the cabin.

That flock of Canada geese that assaulted me en route hadn't helped, either. Vicious creatures. How the hell was *I* supposed to know my flight path would intersect with their spring migration?

I closed my eyes and settled back against the pillows in Freddie's spare bedroom, unable to stop the smile from spreading across my face despite my physical injuries. My body would heal soon enough. But if Amelia hadn't forgiven me for taking off when I did, *that* pain would have lingered much longer.

I'd have to ask the bullet journal Discord ladies for suggestions on a gift I could get her to make up for what I'd done. So far, all of their relationship advice had proved remarkably sound.

A knock on the bedroom door. "Are you decent?" Freddie's voice filtered into the room from the hallway.

I sat up in bed, wincing at the ache in my side from yesterday's overexertion. "Yeah."

He opened the door and poked his head in. "How are you feeling?"

"Like I just flew hundreds of miles with an injured arm while fending off angry birds." I shrugged. "Could be worse."

Freddie hummed sympathetically. "Cassie's warming something up for you if you're hungry."

My eyes went wide. "I am hungry. But *Cassie's* warming it up for me?"

"This surprises you?"

The first time Cassie and I met, I'd just introduced her to the existence of vampirism by drinking a bag of blood directly in front of her, outing her roommate Frederick as a vampire in the process. It had admittedly been a dick move on my part, even if her reaction had been one of the funniest things to personally happen to me in decades.

"I thought the only thing Cassie hated more than me was being exposed to what we eat," I said, honestly.

"She is unlikely to chair the Reginald Cleaves Fan Club anytime soon," he acknowledged with a wry grin. "But she's coming around to the idea of what we eat. Which is good timing, given what we have planned."

His grin was so brilliant it made my chest ache. "Wow. So you're going through with it? You're going to turn her?"

He nodded. "She beat me to it and asked before I did."

When he left the room again, my mind drifted to Amelia. Again. I'd thought about her endlessly since leaving Wisconsin, no matter how hard I tried to think about anything else. For the first time in over a century, I thought I could see the appeal of getting close enough to another person to risk the pain of eventually losing them.

My mind spun with possibilities of what a future with Amelia might look like. Weekend trips to her family's cabin, preferably in the summer when there was no risk of snow. Breakfasts at her apartment, where I'd make her pancakes (with the *correct* amount of baking soda next time).

Nights in my bed, where I showed her exactly how much she meant to me.

I could never ask her to make the same choice Cassie was making and become what I was. But I could no longer lie to myself and say I didn't want her. Amelia hadn't flinched that night in the snow when I'd told her exactly who I was and what I'd done. Instead, she took me into her arms like I deserved to be there.

Her acceptance and understanding weren't anything I'd be able to forget. In this lifetime, or the next.

It was probably irrational for me to think Amelia might want to be with me beyond what we'd already agreed to. But I was nothing if not irrational. I was greedy and selfish, too. I'd take any amount of time Amelia was willing to give me and be grateful for it.

And I was just presumptuous enough to believe that maybe, just maybe, I could make her happy, too.

AMELIA

When I made it back to my apartment the following afternoon, I was greeted by Gracie, curled up on the sofa, and a note from Sophie.

> *Ame,*
>
> *Gracie and I had a lovely time while you were away. Your mail is on the kitchen counter.*
>
> *I want a FULL report on what happened in Wisconsin when you get home and no, I'm NOT talking about the snow.*
>
> *—S*

I'd wanted to see Reggie as soon as I got home, but he'd used Frederick's phone to call again while I was on the road to tell me I shouldn't come over until that night.

"I want to be sure The Collective isn't tracking me first," he'd said, sounding apologetic. "An old witch friend of Frederick's is setting up his apartment with wards. You can come over once she's finished."

So witches were real too, then? I guess nothing should have surprised me by that point.

After unpacking, I put the extra time to use by seeing what I could find about The Collective online. I had low expectations, though. Vampires were apparently very real and living among us, yet aside from a few conspiracy theories I'd seen over the years, vampires hadn't even been a blip on my radar until now.

But there had to be something online outside of conspiracy theories. It defied credibility that a gang of undead creatures could parade about without *someone* on TikTok putting visual evidence out there.

I started with Frederick's claim that they liked to stage blood bank break-ins the morning following stadium concerts, Googling first *stadium concerts worldwide since 2015* and then *blood bank break-ins worldwide since 2015*. I got two different enormous lists of hits, most of them containing links to local newspaper articles. I had zero confidence either list was complete, and didn't know what I would even do with them if they were. But it felt good to be proactive.

I desperately needed to email the Wyatt Foundation confirming our upcoming meeting. I'd gotten no work done while I was in Wisconsin, and this was time sensitive. After that was handled, I'd start cross-referencing these Internet lists and see if there was a pattern I could put together from the results.

....

"ARE YOU SURE IT'S OKAY IF I DROP BY?" I ASKED WHEN Frederick called to tell me his ward-casting friend had left.

"Please do," he insisted. "Cassie made photocopies of the sections of *The Annals* relevant to The Collective. And God's thumbs, please take Reginald with you when you go. He's been here ever since leaving Wisconsin and he's annoying me."

Frederick and Cassie's apartment wasn't hard to find. It was in an affluent part of Lincoln Park close enough to the lake that it was buffeted by winds in both winter and summer. Temperatures had mellowed after the blizzard that had hit Wisconsin, but by the time I got to Frederick's fancy brownstone, the wind chill was enough to make me pull my scarf more tightly around myself to ward off the cold.

I hesitated when I got to the third floor and stood facing their apartment. Suddenly, the idea of entering a vampire's home had me on edge. Reggie would never hurt me, and if Frederick posed a threat, Sam wouldn't be as okay with Cassie living with him as he seemed to be. Even still, now that the moment was here, I was nervous.

What if I interrupted them while they were eating or something? Reggie had made oblique references to eating, and I knew they drank blood. I'd been okay with it in theory. But seeing it in person?

I didn't think I could handle that. Not even if they drank their dinners from blood donation bags.

In the end, my desire to see Reggie won out over fear.

I knocked on the door.

Cassie opened it.

"Amelia." She smiled at me, though I couldn't tell if she was happy to see me or not. We'd never been close, and although I'd never said anything to her about it, I'd always assumed she knew I hadn't thought much of her when we were younger.

It was immediately obvious that she'd changed over the past several months. Her stance was confident, poised. For the first time since I'd known her, she looked like someone who believed in herself. I didn't know if it was from Frederick's supportive influence or from the new teaching job Sam had mentioned she'd just started. Whatever the cause, it was a good look on her.

"It's nice to see you, Cassie," I said, smiling back at her. I hoped she read the sincerity in my expression. "Is, uh . . . is Reggie here?"

She opened the door wider and motioned for me to come inside. "He's in the spare bedroom, working on his bullet journal."

"Working on his what?"

Cassie's smile grew. "His bullet journal. It's something we suggested he try when this whole mess started to process his feelings. It seems to be helping a lot. Have you ever tried bullet journaling?"

I shook my head. "I don't even know what it is."

"Oh, I think you'd like it," she said. At my skeptical look, she said, "Reginald was skeptical, too, at first. Now he's hooked. Even Frederick has decided to give it a try."

For one mad instant I thought to ask her what it was like, dating a vampire. Living with one. Loving him. I thought she might be about to volunteer this information without my asking, but then in the next minute, she was making her way into the kitchen, leaving me to find Reggie on my own.

It was just as well. This whole situation was already strange enough. I didn't think I was ready for a heart-to-heart about it with Cassie Greenberg.

The apartment was like someone had taken an antique, formal living space and splashed it with multiple coats of Disneyland. The living room featured an ornate Oriental rug, matching leather couches, and dark mahogany furniture, as well as several framed landscapes to which neon-painted beach trash seemed to have been glued. One of the couches, which looked like it must have cost thousands of dollars, had a bright green Kermit the Frog throw draped across the back.

Even before I knew Frederick was a vampire, I had a vague recollection of Sam telling me that Cassie and her boyfriend had little in common. The decorative evidence suggested that their differences went far beyond diet.

When I got to the end of the hallway, I knocked on the door to what I assumed was the spare bedroom.

"Go away," Reggie shouted from within. "I've finally got the stickers where I like them."

Stickers? "It's me."

A pause, and then the unmistakable sound of a person trying to shove a bunch of things underneath the bed. "Just a minute!" he squeaked.

When he threw open the door several awkward moments later, his hair was standing nearly on end, as though he'd spent the whole time since I'd last seen him tugging on it with anxious hands.

I hadn't even realized until that moment just how worried I'd been. Without thinking about it, I reached up and tried to gently smooth some of his hair back down again. It was a lost cause, but Reggie didn't seem to mind. His eyes slid closed in reflexive pleasure at my touch. I took in the way he was favoring his right leg, and the bandage that covered a good portion of his right forearm. "Are you all right?" I asked, alarmed.

"I am now that you're here."

"I mean it," I said. "How badly are you hurt?"

"I'm not hurt at all. I promise." I could tell from the way he wouldn't meet my eyes that he was lying. But then, if whatever was wrong with him had been serious, Frederick would have said something.

For the moment, I decided to let it go. In an echo of all the times Reggie had asked me the same question, I asked, "Can I come in?"

He grinned, all straight white teeth and boyish charm, clearly glad for the change of subject. "Please do. Let me give you a tour of the place where I've been crashing while Frederick's friend wards my apartment." He waved theatrically to the room we were standing in. "Actually, this is it."

The bedroom had a similar vibe to the rest of the apartment. Which was to say, the furniture was gorgeous and very obviously antique, while the art on the walls pushed the definition of *eyesore.*

Reggie caught me staring at the canvas that hung over the bed. It was covered in what looked a lot like soda straws. He said, by way of explanation, "Cassie loves making this shit. I guess that means Frederick loves it, too."

"How do they manage it?"

He frowned at me. "Manage what?"

I shrugged, then gestured vaguely to our surroundings. "You know. The whole *vampire-human-relationship* thing."

"Ah. That." Reggie reached up and rubbed at the back of his neck. "Honestly, even leaving that part aside, I can't think of two people who are more different. But I know they're happy, and almost disgustingly in love. So they must manage well enough." He paused, then added, "I don't think it's going to be a *vampire-human* relationship for much longer."

My mind shorted out. "You mean he's going to— She's—"

He nodded. "Frederick told me just before you came over, though I know they've been talking about him turning her for a while. Last night there was a copy of *What to Expect When You Become a Vampire* on the dining room table."

I stared at him. "That cannot be an actual book."

"It is," he said. "It's apparently the seminal work on the subject. I flipped through it last night and although I've been a vampire for centuries, even *I* picked up a few things." He shook his head ruefully. "Wish it had been around back in the 1740s when I was full of questions."

My head was spinning.

Cassie was becoming a vampire because she'd fallen in love with one.

It was too much to process.

Suddenly it was difficult to look Reggie in the eye, so I averted my gaze. I spied a strip of lacy pink ribbon sticking out from beneath the bed. I wouldn't have noticed it, given that it wasn't out of place with the rest of the apartment's eclectic decor, if I hadn't for sure heard Reggie trying to hide something in here before I came in.

"What is that?" I asked, pointing.

His eyes went wide. "Oh, it's nothing." He jostled me in his rush to get to the bed, then kicked whatever it was further beneath it.

Okay, now I was *really* curious. I bent down and, before Reggie could stop me, extracted something that looked like it was part journal, part art project made by an exuberant fifteen-year-old who'd just learned how to work a hot glue gun. It was so full of scraps and bits and bobs that the cover barely closed.

"Is this your bullet journal?" I was tempted to start leafing through the pages. But if a bullet journal was anything like a regular journal, this had Reggie's private thoughts in it. It wasn't my place to pry.

He swallowed. "How do you know about my bullet journal?"

"Cassie told me."

"Great," he muttered. He eased the thing from my hands, then set it carefully down on the bed. "Yes, it's my bullet journal. It's helped me. Emotionally, or mentally, or whatever. More than I thought it would when I started."

The vulnerability in his voice was unmistakable. "It's none of my business what you write about in here, of course," I said. "But if it's helping you process what you're going through, I think it's a good thing."

"Most of the entries aren't about The Collective."

Reggie opened the journal's cover. And then he began to slowly turn the pages, one at a time, giving me a few moments to look at each one before turning to the next one, and then the next.

The first entries were very short, the multiple cross-outs and terse lists making it obvious he'd at first been full of disdain for the entire idea of keeping a journal. That changed quickly, though. The entries soon became more vibrant, incorporating bits of fabric and markers and brightly colored stickers to track his thoughts.

"How long have you been keeping this?" I asked, marveling at the sheer attention to detail in some of the later entries. Flowers that must have taken hours to draw. Stickers that came in every color of the rainbow. "Where did you even find pipe cleaners in that shade of purple?"

"I found this website where bullet journalers share tips," he explained. "You wouldn't believe how well-resourced these people are. Not to mention how freewheeling some of them are with life advice."

I stared at him. "You chat with people online?"

"Not people," he clarified. "Bullet journalers. But yes. And to answer your other question, I started this project right before I met you, though the timing on that is just a coincidence. But let's not get sidetracked. I want to show you this page at the back. I spent a lot of time on it." He paused. "It's what I was working on when you knocked on my door."

He closed his eyes and seemed to gather his courage. Then he flipped to the last completed page. It was, in truth, a bit of an eyesore. He'd festooned it with pink and purple ribbons, and writ-

ten the passage in blue, glittery ink that reminded me of the eye
shadow I wore in seventh grade.

But when I read the words, I gasped.

*Mission statement: these are still stupid, I wish the journal didn't
include this option on every page*

Dating Amelia Collins for real: Pros and Cons

PROS:

1. *Efficiency. I can't stop thinking about her so keeping her
   with me would save time*
2. *I would always make sure she has food she can eat*
3. *She needs to laugh more. I'm good at making her
   laugh (I love making her laugh)*
4. *She makes me forget the terrible pointlessness of my
   existence (as well as all the other terrible things in
   this world) (she is so lovely)*
5. *I haven't made love to her yet and I REALLY want to. (I
   think she would enjoy it tbh)*
6. *I would devote the rest of my existence to making her
   happy and I think (???) she would enjoy that*
7. *Continued proximity to a real live historian (her dad)*

CONS:

1. *The whole immortal / not-immortal thing presents
   legitimate logistical challenges (sidenote: consult with
   Frederick re: what it's like to date a human, but don't
   tell him why I'm asking because he'll be insufferable
   for the next century if I do)*

2. I don't know if she's afraid of me or not and that also seems like it could be an impediment to a real relationship
3. I don't know if she feels the same way about me that I do about her
4. Dating her and then losing her might break what's left of my heart

As it had in Wisconsin, Reggie's playful mask had slipped just enough to show the vulnerability he hid from the rest of the world. His heart might not beat anymore, but my own heart was full enough in that moment for both of us.

I placed the journal on the bed and took his hands. I couldn't tell whether it was his that were shaking or if mine were. I rubbed my thumbs back and forth across the backs of his to try and calm us both.

"I don't do risks," I said. "Not ever. I went to college, became a CPA, and then got a job at a big accounting firm. Because I was good at that kind of work, yes. But also because it was safe." I shook my head. "I need to know a book's ending before I start it. I cannot handle surprises. Anything that isn't a predictable, sure thing terrifies me more than I can say."

His jaw worked. "I understand," he said. He started pulling away, the hurt and rejection in his eyes telling me he didn't understand at all.

So I grabbed him by the lapels of his shirt and kissed him. It was just a quick press of my lips to his, over as soon as it began.

"Will you let me finish, please?" I asked, grinning.

Reggie regarded me with a stunned expression. "By all means."

I leaned in again and pressed another featherlight kiss to the corner of his mouth. His eyes slipped closed.

"What I'm trying to say is that I want to try this, despite how out of my usual comfort zone it is." I paused and gathered my courage. He'd shown me his heart by sharing this journal entry, hadn't he? I could find it within myself to do the same. "I want to try *us*. Because I like you. A lot."

He cracked open one eye. "You'd be willing to try this even though the ending to our story would be the opposite of already written?"

I hesitated, but only for a moment. "I've never tried storytelling before. Might be fun to write our own ending, don't you think?"

He beamed at me, his hands coming up to cradle my face an instant before he leaned in and kissed me.

I'd never known that it could feel so good, being held and kissed by another person. I wound my arms around his neck to pull him closer and urge him on, though he seemed to need no encouragement. He parted his lips to deepen the kiss, sending a frisson of delicious warmth right down my spine.

I slid a hand down his broad chest. No heartbeat; only stillness. Could he tell how much my own heart was racing? Or somehow sense the rapid pulse of blood through my veins?

"I am what I am," he said a moment later, our faces still so close we were breathing the same air. "I would never, ever hurt you, but before we go any further, you should know the history books are full of examples of romantic entanglements between vampires and humans that . . . um." He trailed off and pressed another quick kiss to the corner of my mouth. As though he couldn't stop kissing me long enough to complete a full thought. "Historically, this sort of thing hasn't always ended well for the human."

I leaned back, resting my head against the wall behind me.

Reggie regarded me nervously, like he was afraid I would disappear if he let me out of his sight for an instant.

"I thought I already told you," I began, letting the corner of my mouth quirk up into the sort of half smile he was always giving me. His eyes tracked the movement of my lips. God, he was adorable. "I think history books are boring. Who needs them?"

I tried to elaborate this point by telling him about all the history documentaries I skipped out on watching as a kid, but then his mouth got in the way of more words for a while.

TWENTY-FIVE

Excerpt from What to Expect When You Become a Vampire, Fifteenth Edition

Page 163: Human Relationships—Love and Intimacy

For some considering leaving mortality behind to become a vampire, a major concern can be whether they will be able to maintain intimate relationships with humans once they have turned.

It is a question with no easy answer. Recent data from Johnson & Kettering's study suggest that most people who intentionally choose vampirism do so because they are already romantically involved with a vampire, largely due to the complications inherent in the human-vampire mortality differential. (<u>See</u>: footnote 37). That said, anecdotal data further suggest that vampires can date and have sex with humans the same way they can with anybody else, so long as they are able to fully internalize the friends not food *philosophy that we outline in chapter 2.*

Moreover, it is well documented that humans frequently find sexual relations with vampires intensely pleasurable. Addictive, even. (So, you know. There's that.)

AMELIA

WE WERE INTERRUPTED BY INSISTENT RAPPING ON THE spare bedroom door.

"Reginald."

It was Frederick.

Reggie groaned, pulling away from me. His hair was even more of a wreck now than it had been when I'd gotten there. It was so soft; I didn't think I'd ever get tired of running my hands through it.

"What is it?" he barked at the door.

"Are you canoodling in there?"

Despite the awkwardness of the situation, I nearly burst out laughing. "Canoodling?" I mouthed in Reggie's ear. "Seriously?"

"He's old-fashioned," Reggie grumbled by way of explanation. And then to Frederick, he yelled, "Go away!"

"I will not *go away,*" he retorted. "This is my home. You are obviously free to do whatever it is you like with whomever you like, but for reasons I assume you can guess, I prefer it not happen in the presence of my antiques."

Reggie glared daggers at the door. "You're seriously bringing that up now? That was nearly two hundred years ago!"

"Furniture never forgets."

Reggie looked like he was about to say something scathing in reply, but before he could do it, I put a finger to his lips. I had his full attention again immediately.

"Let's get out of here," I suggested, quietly enough that we wouldn't be overheard by the vampire standing outside the door. "I only came by in the first place to take you back home with me. And I don't really want to do this here. Do you?"

He grinned, then kissed my finger. That simple act of affection was enough to send a bolt of pure heat down my spine. Oh, I was hopeless.

"No. I don't," he confirmed. "I would love to go to your apartment." He shot a dirty look at the closed bedroom door. "Though I have to say, given some of the lovey-dovey scenarios I've overheard since staying here these past few days, Frederick is being a filthy hypocrite right now."

My cheeks flamed. I had no interest in hearing about Frederick and Cassie's sexual escapades. "Let's go to my place, then. There's privacy, and while there are no protective wards, I do have a very judgmental cat who'll keep you safe."

He pulled me into his arms and held me for a very long moment. "I need to gather up some things first. Send me your address. I'll be there soon."

On my way out of the apartment, I saw someone had left a thick manila folder on the end table by the front door. There was a Post-it note on the cover that had my name on it, underlined twice.

I flipped open the folder and saw that these were pages from *The Annals* related to The Collective. Inside, there was a note written on crisp off-white stationery, covered in neat, flowing handwriting:

Amelia—I erred on the side of over-inclusivity when making copies of The Annals. *In addition to entries pertaining to The Collective, enclosed you will also find entries pertaining*

*to Reginald. (Don't tell him—he'll kill me [figure of
speech].)*

*I do caution you to temper your enthusiasm. While I expect
these passages will give you context for The Collective's
behavior and motives, vampire historians are not as concerned
about nonprofit tax policy as one might hope. A lost
opportunity, perhaps. But as Cassie might say, "it is what it is."*

Yours in good health—FJF

I had no idea what I'd find when I read these pages. But I put
them in my bag all the same, hoping there'd be something of
value there.

....

MY APARTMENT WAS A DISASTER, BY MY STANDARDS. THERE
were dirty clothes strewn across my bed from when I'd dumped
my suitcase out earlier that day. There was a plate in my kitchen
sink from my afternoon snack. And the mail that had arrived
while I was away was still stacked, unopened, in a pile by my
front door where Sophie left it.

Reggie hadn't told me how long it would be before he came
over. And we didn't *specifically* say what we'd be doing when he
arrived. Either way, I didn't want him seeing underwear on my
bedroom floor or dirty dishes in my sink. I started shoving random things into closets and drawers for the first time in my life.
Gracie glared judgmentally when I wiped the crumbs off my
plate and put the dish away without washing it, but honestly, she
would just have to deal.

If all went as I thought it would, her mommy would be getting laid soon.

By the time I'd finished vacuuming the living room and dust-ing the handful of knickknacks on my shelves, he was there, knocking on my front door.

I opened the door to see him standing in my hallway, looking as nervous as I'd ever seen him.

He swallowed, Adam's apple bobbing in his throat. "Can I come in?"

"Of course." I stepped aside and gestured with my hand for him to enter.

"Thank you," he said. He sounded breathless. I wondered if he'd run all the way there. Or flown.

When I turned to face him, his eyes were everywhere, roam-ing over everything in my home. But he wouldn't meet my gaze.

Something was wrong.

"What is it?" I asked. "Do you think you were followed?"

He shook his head. "No. I flew. None of that lot know how to fly. I wasn't spotted."

It was surreal, listening to him talking about flying in such a matter-of-fact way. Though if I'd been able to fly for hundreds of years, maybe I'd also find it just as mundane as going for a walk.

"If you weren't followed, why are you so nervous?" I asked. "You look like you've seen a ghost." His eyes widened, and for a moment I thought maybe I'd said the wrong thing.

Before I knew what was happening, he had me crowded up against the wall that separated my living room from my bedroom. He nipped a gentle line down the column of my throat, letting his teeth lightly scrape against me as he moved.

His *real* teeth; not the ones he showed the world.

"I've wanted to touch you for so long." His mouth was every-where. On my neck, my collarbone, then moving back up to kiss along my jaw. He gave my ass a firm, possessive squeeze. *Mine*, it said. It felt so good I nearly moaned out loud. "Do you know how many times I've thought about it?"

"Tell me," I gasped. I didn't know where that bravery was coming from, but I *needed* to know. "Please."

He answered with an excruciatingly slow swipe of his tongue along the sweet, sensitive spot where my neck met my shoulder. His touch was like wildfire, and I keened, my body alight with anticipation as he mouthed at me. My knees felt seconds away from buckling. I threw my arms around his neck so that I wouldn't fall to the floor.

As though sensing my instability, he thrust his hips forward, pinning me in place between his body and the wall.

"At the coffee shop," he mumbled against my neck. His words were gentle vibrations against my heated flesh that I could feel down to my toes. "At your family's party. Every time you touched my hand, smiled, leaned over in that *tiny* fucking black dress." He shuddered against me. "By the end of the night, it was all I could do not to grab you and take you right there in front of the buffet table, your family be damned."

I huffed a breathy laugh. "Don't talk about my family right now." As hot as the idea was of Reggie losing control like that, thinking about it happening in front of my family was the last thing I wanted.

He chuckled against my shoulder. "You don't want me to talk about your dad and how I'm still upset we haven't had a chance to bond over the History Channel?"

I swatted his shoulder. He grabbed my hand and pulled it away from him, kissing its palm, the heat building between us shifting to something playful and sweet.

He leaned in, resting his forehead against mine. I didn't know much about vampire physiology, but I would have assumed that since he had no pulse, and wasn't technically alive, he wouldn't need oxygen to survive. But Reggie was breathing as heavily as I was, his chest rising and falling in time with my own.

I placed my hand flat on his chest, over the place where his heart would beat if he were human. I felt nothing beneath my palm but the fine musculature of his pectorals, the even cadence of his breathing, and the soft fabric of the plaid shirt he was wearing.

What had his human life been like, I wondered? I was coming to know the man in my arms. To care for him. But he'd had an entirely different life, once. Had he been so very different as a child? Had he had a lover, a wife—children—before his sires turned him and he became what he was today?

I flexed my hand, gathering the fabric of his shirt into my grip. Pulled him closer. I realized that I wanted to know every part of who the human Reginald Cleaves used to be, too. Not just the Reggie who was currently gazing at me like I'd hung the moon.

Hopefully, we would have time to explore his past together, later.

In the here and now, Reggie moved his hand from where it rested against the wall beside my head and covered mine with it. He squeezed gently, his bright blue eyes full of unspoken question.

Are you sure?

I'd spent my entire life avoiding risks, not putting so much as a single toe out of line. But as I looked into his eyes, and thought about what taking this leap might mean . . .

For the first time in recent memory, there was nothing I wanted more than to jump.

I didn't have to know what this meant for next week, or next month, or two years from now. I wanted this for *now*. That was enough.

I nodded. "Yes," I whispered, barely trusting my voice.

It was like a switch flipped inside him. Whereas moments ago his kisses had been gentle and restrained, now he was a man unleashed. His hands slid down my body and gripped my ass, hauling me closer to him, the chill of his touch seeping through the fabric of my clothes and down to my skin. My arms wrapped instinctively around his neck, and he held me tight, tighter, as he ravished my mouth, his tongue tracing the seam of my lips before delving inside. He smelled incredible—like the laundry detergent he must have used on his shirt, cool male skin, and his own uniquely Reggie scent. It was indescribably erotic, what we were doing. I moaned against the pleasure already rising inside me.

"I'm going to make you feel so good tonight," he promised against my lips. "Can I tell you what I plan to do?"

There was a hint of wickedness in his voice. I melted against him. "Yes." My hands slid into his hair, tugging hard on the strands of messy gold. He groaned—he liked that, I thought through my haze of lust; I'd have to file that away for later—and gripped my ass hard. "Tell me."

It took him a moment to regain composure enough to respond. "I'm going to bend you over every flat surface in this apartment like we are in one of those filthy Regency novels Frederick pretends he doesn't read," he murmured against my cheek.

I couldn't help but laugh. Even now, he was doing his utmost to disarm me. To put me at ease. But my heart was threatening to beat right out of my chest, and the way he'd begun moving against me showed me he wanted this as much as I did.

The time for jokes was over.

Risking everything, I slid my hand down his torso, not stopping until I reached the bulge at the front of his jeans.

The noise he made was so guttural it was barely human. The sound went straight between my legs, making me crave the feel of him above me, pressing me down into the mattress. I wanted to see him, to *feel* him go feral with me.

His mouth was back on my neck, kissing and licking and sucking with so much enthusiasm I would definitely have a massive bruise tomorrow. He was whimpering as he mouthed at me, his hips speeding up as I gripped him. I couldn't help but wonder whether he wanted to bite my neck and taste my blood.

A groan went through me at the thought of him sinking his teeth into me. His tongue, lapping at the puncture wounds he'd made. The pleasure of my taste driving him into an even greater frenzy.

"I better stop," he said. If he had been breathing heavily earlier, he was gasping now. "We haven't discussed . . ." He trailed off and buried his face in my neck again. "I want you—*all* of you—so badly. I just know you would taste so sweet. Like something out of my filthiest, most reprehensible wet dreams. But I . . . You . . ."

He shook himself a little, and pulled back so that he could gauge my reaction to his half confession. His eyes were wild, black pupils blown huge inside brilliant blue irises. He looked desperate. Broken.

I reached up, cupping his cheek in my free hand. He leaned into my touch, his blue eyes never leaving my face. How could I tell him what I was thinking? Slowly—so slowly—I unbuttoned his jeans.

"How connected are blood and sex for you?" I asked.

He whimpered, squeezing his eyes shut tight. His cock throbbed once, *hard*, against my palm.

"They don't have to be connected at all if you don't want them to be," he breathed. "I promise. But . . . but in order to finish, I—"

"Have you ever touched yourself, imagining drinking my blood?" The Amelia of three weeks ago could never have imagined I'd be having this conversation today. That I would be saying these things. That I would even be in this situation in the first place.

But here I was, dirty talking a vampire, trying to make him lose control. Just a little. And getting more turned on by it than anything I'd ever experienced in my life.

"Yes," he confessed. "I don't feed directly from humans anymore, but—*fuck*, yes." His face was still buried in the crook of my neck. His hips were now moving relentlessly against my hand. "So many times. Nearly every night since—*fuck*—since I met you."

We were skating dangerously close to an edge from which there would be no return. I knew that. Before we went any further, I had to know there was a safety net to catch me when I fell. "If I take you to my bedroom right now, will you want to . . ." I licked my lips without thinking about it. His eyes tracked the movement of my tongue. *Ravenous.* "Will you want to bite me?"

His answer was immediate. "Yes." He stopped his movements, his hands coming up to cup my face. Cool palms against flushed skin. "I will. If I get you in your bed, if I get you *naked*—I'll want to bite you just as badly as I'll want to fuck you."

The unadulterated lust I saw in his eyes threatened to liquefy me where I stood. "Reggie—"

"I would be so gentle with you," he murmured, fingertips caressing my chin. "You wouldn't feel a thing—and you would be in no danger. I promise. But if that's not something you want, I'll just . . ." He trailed off. Shook his head. "We can make this about you, instead. I want you however I can get you. In any way you will let me touch you."

His raw honesty cut through me like a knife.

"Okay," I said, pressing a gentle kiss to the corner of his mouth.

Wordlessly, I took his hand, and led him into my bedroom.

....

IT HAD BEEN A LONG TIME SINCE I'D HAD A MAN IN MY BED. Under normal circumstances I'd probably have been nervous about my body, worrying about whether Reggie would like what he saw when the clothes were gone.

It was hard to be nervous about anything at all, though—it was hard to even think—with the way his mouth moved hungrily against mine. It was like he was determined to worry away at all my insecurities with the tip of his tongue, until there was no room left for anything but him.

He walked me backwards through my bedroom, steering me with one hand on my hip and the other at my waist, until the backs of my knees hit my mattress.

"Lie down," he murmured. It was dark in my room, but there was enough light from the hallway, enough moonlight streaming in from my bedroom window, that I could see him clearly, broad shoulders silhouetted against the darkness. "I want to touch you."

I complied, eager for the same thing, then closed my eyes, expecting to feel the mattress dip when he got in bed with me.

Instead, I heard him kneel beside the bed. Felt his hands wrap around each of my ankles.

"What—?" I began. Then yelped as he tugged me towards the edge of the mattress.

"I want to see you let go," he explained, hands snaking beneath my skirt to tug at the edge of my underwear. "And I want it to be because of *me*. I want you to fall apart on my tongue, feel your legs quivering beside my ears as you shout my name." He drew my underwear down my legs and threw them over his shoulder. Then he shoved my skirt up to my waist. "I want to taste you. Everywhere. So badly."

"Reggie," I whimpered. I shivered as he pulled my legs over his shoulders, tilted my hips up with his hands. I was splayed open for him, naked and vulnerable, heart thundering so loudly that surely he must be able to hear it.

His mouth was just a hairsbreadth away from where I ached for him. I could feel each shaky exhalation of breath against my core. His beautiful, expressive eyes met mine. "You want this. Don't you." He closed his eyes, rubbing his cheek against the inside of my thigh. The delicious scratch of his stubble pulled a groan from me before I realized it had happened. "I can *smell* how much you want me."

I whined, wriggling in his grip. "Reggie, *please.*" I could tell he needed verbal confirmation from me that I wanted to be with him like this. But if I didn't have his mouth on me immediately, I was going to lose my mind. "I want this. I want you. *Please.*"

His mouth quirked up into a half smile. His eyes darkened. "As my lady commands."

Then his mouth was *right there*, electric, flooding me with sensations I could scarcely remember feeling before and couldn't name. He was relentless as he devoured me, sucking my clit into his mouth a moment before laving it with the achingly soft flat of his tongue. I tried to cry out but couldn't, made mindless by pleasure and pure desperate need as I lay helpless on the bed before him, held together only by the determined way he worked me and the vise grip he had on my hips. My breathing was way too fast and growing shallow, my chest heaving, my blood pounding in my veins as he teased and drew out my pleasure.

"Please," I begged again, my voice raw. I didn't even know

what I was begging for. For him to stop. For him to never stop. I wanted to come. I wanted to make *him* come so hard he would never forget it. With what was left of my sanity, I wondered: Was this something we could actually have? Despite our differences, despite what he was, could we actually be together like this, not just tonight but tomorrow night, and the night after—and have it be real? "Reggie, *please*."

My pleas seemed to spur him on, his grip on me tightening as he hauled me up even closer to his mouth. I tried to buck against his face, his clever tongue, desperate for more friction, for release. But his hold on me was too strong. He pinned me in place, keeping me right where he wanted me, preventing me from moving at all as he drove the tight coil of pleasure inside me higher, and higher.

And then—

He pushed one rough finger inside me, and then another, *so tight*, the delicious intrusion forcing every sentient thought from my head. I needed this—him—all of it. I needed it *now*.

"*Hades*," he growled against my cunt. "I cannot wait to fuck you."

His filthy words, muttered *right there*, were all I needed to hurtle headlong into orgasm. I scrabbled at the sheets, at Reggie's hair, clinging to anything I could to anchor me as the waves of bliss came again, and again, and again. Reggie coaxed me through it with his lips and tongue, holding me as he urged my body to keep going. I moaned his name, mindless, back arched like a bow above the bed, locked in pleasure that seemed to stretch on forever.

When I collapsed to the bed, boneless, he was on me in an instant.

"You are so *fucking* beautiful." His growl was visceral, animalistic. "The way you looked when you came—fuck. I nearly came too, just from that. I just—" He was tearing at my clothes in his haste to get them off me, quickly losing patience with the buttons of my blouse. They skittered to the floor as he tugged my arms out of the sleeves, and fumbled with my bra for two seconds before he had that off, too. I was too wrung out, too limp from the aftermath of what he'd given me, to help him. He didn't seem to care. Nothing was going to get in the way of what he wanted.

Which, apparently, was me—naked.

Suddenly, it was vitally important to me that I not be the only naked person in this situation. I sat up and groped for the hem of his shirt.

"Off," I mumbled. He didn't seem to notice. He gently pushed me back down onto the bed, unbuttoned my skirt, tugged it down over my hips. Taking my own clothes off was good, very good—but it wasn't enough. "It's not fair that I haven't gotten to see you yet. Take your shirt *off*, Reginald Cleaves."

At my use of his full name he stared at me, a smirk on his lips. "Impatient, are we?" But he did as I asked, lifting his shirt over his head and tossing it over his shoulder in one fluid movement.

He never broke eye contact with me, keeping his gaze trained on my face even as I let my eyes roam over his body.

"Do you like what you see?" He asked it playfully, but the intensity of his expression made clear just how much he wanted his body to please me.

And oh, it did.

Now that the barriers of clothing were gone, lying in a heap beside the bed, it was like a dam of want had broken inside of me. I moved to touch him, not even bothering to fight the impulse to do it. He was solidly built, if not overly muscular, his broad chest covered with a smattering of light brown hair I couldn't resist trailing my fingers through. His breath hitched as I experimented, tracing the defined lines of his pectoral muscles with my finger-tips, stroking down along his abdomen, and then further down still, until his stomach muscles tensed in anticipation.

Was his body much different now than it had been before he changed? I cast the thought aside as soon as it occurred to me. It didn't matter what he was like before. Because it was this Reggie who was gently pulling my hands away from his body and laying me down on the mattress. It was this Reggie who was kissing me so urgently and with such tenderness it felt like my heart was breaking.

And it was this Reggie who was kicking off his pants, then levering himself over me until we were pressed together, flesh to flesh. Hard to soft. Cool to warm.

This man was so outlandishly funny I never knew whether I wanted to hit him or to laugh. He was disarmingly kind, and so thoughtful it made my head spin. And I realized, with a sudden, all-encompassing jolt of awareness—he was mine.

If I wanted him to be.

"Amelia." He hovered over me, arms shaking with his effort to hold as still as possible. Then he shifted a little, until his tip nudged at my entrance.

His blue eyes met mine, boring into me. Needing to be sure I wanted this as badly as he did.

I nodded, and wrapped my arms around him, pulling him down into another blinding kiss.

He entered me with a single hard thrust of his hips and a loud, incoherent exhalation of pleasure. My breath stuttered, body struggling against the delicious intrusion of his body into mine. He was so big, and it had been so long since I'd done this, but the stretch of it, the completeness with which he filled me, pushed the breath from my lungs and threatened to pull me under again before we'd even begun. My hands scrabbled down his back, nails lightly scoring his flesh as I sought to anchor myself against the pleasure that was already starting to mount again. He seemed to like that, a lot, a *very* lot, hissing at the pinpricks of pleasure-pain, and then growling when I dragged my nails down his back a second time, except harder, and more forcefully.

"Amelia," he said again, voice hoarse with his fraying restraint. He still wasn't moving, was still letting my body adjust to his. But his arms were shaking badly now, and I could see in the rigid set of his jaw and the ragged way he was breathing how badly he wanted to let go.

"You don't need to hold back," I assured him. I craned my neck a little, lifted my chin so I could press my lips to his. "I want this."

His eyes drifted closed. "I will never hurt you. I swear. But towards the end, I might—" He bit off the rest of what he was about to say and buried his face in my neck. "I might lose control. Just a little. If you need me to stop—"

I tugged on his hair, lifting his head so that he had to look in my eyes. The vulnerability I saw in them nearly took my breath away. "I won't need you to stop," I assured him. "But if I do, I'll tell you. Right away. I promise."

He stared into my eyes another long moment, as if trying to find the truth of what I was saying in them. Then he closed his eyes. Nodded.

And he began to move.

"Oh," I said, the sound all but pushed out of me at the first thrust. And then, suddenly, I began to worry—irrationally, probably; and definitely about thirty minutes too late—that maybe I wouldn't be any good at sex. Reggie had been alive for hundreds of years, and he'd implied more than once that he'd had more than his fair share of sexual partners during that time. I'd had a few boyfriends, and obviously had had sex before, but compared to a lover with hundreds of years of experience, how could I possibly know what I was doing?

"Fuck," he whimpered, mouth at my ear. "You feel—so—*fucking* good." His hips were already picking up speed, his body pistoning into mine so insistently, so needfully, it obliterated all self-doubt. He grabbed both of my hands in one of his, pinning them above my head, and stared transfixed at the way my breasts bounced with his movements. The way he was looking at me—and the way it felt, my cunt clenching around him as he thrust into me again, and again, and again—

His hands dropped down to grip my ass, lifting my hips and changing the angle of our connection. Something about the new positioning opened me up to him even further, allowed him to go deeper, harder, to brush up against parts of me no one had touched before.

"Reggie," I gasped. "Oh, fuck." Something . . . something was different. I cried out again, helpless in the face of this delicious mounting pleasure, an ecstatic sort of pressure at the base of my spine that was threatening to pull me under. I felt drunk, wild, and burning hot, my body already racing towards another sharp crescendo as my hips sped up to match his movements.

Without thinking, I flung my head back onto the pillow, the angle leaving my neck completely exposed.

His hips stuttered to a stop, even as he remained fully seated inside me.

He *growled*.

"Amelia," he breathed, panting hard. His eyes were glued to my exposed neck. His hips started moving again, even faster this time. "Amelia. Amelia, *please*."

Oh, god. He was *begging*. For me.

For my blood.

"You want to bite me," I breathed, my movements matching his thrust for thrust. The edge was looming, my orgasm shimmering just out of reach. "Don't you."

He groaned, thrusts speeding up until he was fucking me at an absolutely punishing pace. And then his head dropped to my shoulder, hands fisting the sheets on either side of my head so tightly his knuckles were white. "Yes."

"Where?" I asked. I knew I was testing the limits of his fraying control. But in that moment, I didn't care. I wanted to see him unleashed, in every way. I knew he would never, ever hurt me. "Where do you want to bite me?"

"Amelia," he cried out. "Please. If you don't want me to—if you don't want it, I can't—please, don't—"

His body was taut as a bowstring as he moved above me, all muscle and sinew and bone. "Tell me." I slid my hands down his backside, then squeezed his ass, trying to pull him deeper inside. "Tell me where."

The noise he made was desperate. Broken.

"If I bit you," he breathed, "I would do it—" He abruptly stopped moving. I could feel the tension in his body and every ounce of self-control he was using in this moment to hold himself still. He gently pushed my hair away from the side of my face and gazed at my bare neck as though it held the secret to his happiness. "I would bite you right here."

He pressed two shaking fingers to my pulse point. I could all but feel the flow of blood through my veins with every beat of my heart. His eyes on me were feral. *Hungry.*

An image of him biting me, mouth suckling at the wound, flashed unbidden behind my eyelids. I cried out, body clenching around him, *hard*. I didn't know why the thought of him biting me turned me on. Maybe it was the idea that letting him do it would be the ultimate act of letting go.

"Would it feel good?" I asked. Even though I knew it would. I could *sense* it. I tensed up again, on purpose this time. Squeezing him. I watched as his eyes rolled back in his head, as he warred with what little remained of his restraint. "Would it feel good if you bit me?"

He opened his eyes and stared directly into mine. "It would feel good for both of us. My venom, it's—" He bit off the rest of what he was about to say. Shook his head. "It would make you feel good. And I'd come. Immediately." His voice was like sandpaper on stone, eyes boring into mine. "I'd come *hard*. Coming with the taste of blood in my mouth is—it's just—you have *no idea*, Amelia—"

"Then do it," I said. I reached up and drew lazy circles at the place on my neck he'd just touched. He stared at my fingertips as they moved, unable to look away. And then, because he seemed to need to hear it: "I want you to do it."

He whimpered. Squeezed his eyes shut tight.

It happened so fast I hardly saw it. One moment Reggie was above me, incoherent with need. The next, I was crying out at the unexpected pleasure of being bitten. I was making love to an animal in that moment, all vestiges of the man Reginald was most of the time lost to the creature kissing and suckling at the shallow puncture wounds he'd made in my neck. Why didn't it hurt? Why did it *feel good*, when he bit me? The pleasure from his bite raced down my spine, straight to my cunt, amplifying my need to a nearly unbearable degree. Making me insatiable. When my next orgasm crashed over me, I ran straight into the blissful release, the waves of pleasure wiping my mind of everything but him.

When I returned to myself, Reggie was groaning, fucking me so hard and so desperately I was going to have trouble walking for a week. "So beautiful, so sweet," he moaned, mouth coated red with me. He was nearing his breaking point; I could feel in the way his thrusts were becoming chaotic, frantic. I could hear it in the fevered pitch of his words. "*I knew* it. Knew you'd taste so good, I never want to leave you, want you, I—you are *mine*."

I felt, more than heard, the sound he made when he came. His hips stuttered up hard once, and again, and then his body went rigid above me, back bent in an exaggerated arc as he spilled himself. His eyes were unseeing, glassy with pleasure. I'd never seen anything more beautiful in my life.

His body felt like two hundred pounds of dead weight when he collapsed on top of me a moment later, heavy and immovable as lead. He sighed, his cool breath tickling the little hairs at the nape of my neck.

"I hope," he said, after what felt like an eternity, "that that felt even half as good for you as it did for me." He rolled off me, wincing a little as he withdrew from my body.

"I would hope the two orgasms you gave me would have given you some clue," I teased. He chuckled, then propped himself up on one elbow so he could look at the wounds he'd made on my neck. I touched them, marveling when I realized the little holes were already closing up.

"Did I hurt you?" He leaned in closer, pressing a chaste kiss to the healing skin.

I shook my head. "No. It felt . . ." I trailed off, not sure how to put how it felt into words. Then I decided to just come out with it. "It's like you said. It felt *good*. Why?"

He sighed, then gathered me into his arms. I went willingly, letting him roll us both over until my head was pillowed on his chest. His flesh was firm and cool beneath my cheek. "If our bite is painful to our victims, then it's ultimately self-defeating." He sounded almost embarrassed by the admission. He craned his neck so he could look into my eyes before continuing. "Our venom is sort of an aphrodisiac. So it can feel good for our victims, too."

When we suck them dry, he didn't say.

I shuddered at the implication that Reggie may have once used this power to subdue, and seduce, his victims. To get them to offer themselves up to him willingly. Even eagerly. Then again, I'd been the one who asked him to bite me in the first place.

"I'll never do that without your consent," he added. "I haven't been that sort of monster in many years." He leaned in close and pressed a gentle kiss to the top of my head. "We never have to do it again if you don't want to."

"I want to," I said, hurriedly. Before I could talk myself out of it. Because as ridiculous as it sounded, it was the truth. It felt *good*, having his teeth in my neck. Knowing that my blood made him feel pleasure in return. "Maybe not every day, or anything. But like—"

"Special occasions?" he suggested. "Birthdays, perhaps? Anniversaries, promotions at work?"

I stifled a laugh against his bare chest. Were we really discussing this? Joking about it? A potential future together, where we had regular sex and maybe sometimes added in a little biting to go along with it? It was as delicious a thought as it was impossible to grasp.

"Special occasions," I agreed. "That sounds good to me."

TWENTY-SIX

A note, hastily scrawled in black ink at the bottom of a
yellow lined sheet of paper

Thoughts to be transferred to bullet journal later (Will have to
make this v. quick—am at A's apartment but she's still asleep and
don't want to miss being there to curl around her body while she
sleeps & kiss her hair):

Mission Statement: To be by A's side for as long as she'll have me

Feelings: Just <u>so much happiness</u>. I cannot clearly remember
anything about my life before turning, but I know I haven't felt
this giddy, this <u>light</u>, in at least that long. It feels like I should be
<u>FRIGHTENED</u> by this. But I am anything but scared.

AMELIA

I WOKE UP THE NEXT MORNING WITH THE SUN BLAZING through my window. I groaned and made to pull my pillow over my head.

"Ow."

I froze, and grinned sheepishly when I realized my head was not resting on a pillow, but rather on Reggie's chest.

"Sorry."

"You should be sorry," he said in mock chastisement, his voice thick with sleep. He didn't look upset, though. His dirty-blond hair was an utter wreck from all the pulling on it I did last night, and the beatific smile on his face . . .

I had seen Reggie smile dozens of times by that point. His smile was a mask he wore. He smiled when he was sad, he smiled when he was anxious, or when he was playing a practical joke to deflect.

This smile, though, reached all the way to his eyes, making them crinkle at the corners. This was a *real* smile. In that moment, he looked happier, and more relaxed, than I'd ever seen him.

I tried to crane my neck so I could see out the window and gauge what time it must be from the position of the sun in the sky. Moving too much was difficult, though; Reggie seemed entirely disinterested in loosening his tight embrace.

I noticed that my blinds were not covering my window at all. I grimaced. "Shit. I must've forgotten to close the blinds before we . . . um."

Reggie pulled me closer, encouraging me to continue using his chest as a vampiric pillow. "Before we what?"

I could feel him smiling against the top of my head. I started blushing, which was ridiculous, given what we had done to each other in this bed last night, and the fact that we were stark naked in here and snuggling.

"You know what."

"I do," he agreed. "But I would very much like to hear your version of events."

His tone was light and playful, but with an undercurrent of heat that was unmistakable. The massive erection poking me in the ass was unmistakable, too.

I grinned, letting my hand slide down his torso until it rested lightly on his cock. It twitched satisfyingly against my fingertips.

"You are insatiable, aren't you?" I teased.

"Absolutely." He covered my hand with his own, encouraging me to speed up my movements. "Now, tell me all about how I gave you the best orgasms of your life last night, and about how good it felt to suck my cock."

I laughed, and pulled my hand away, swatting him playfully on the chest. "Later," I said. Truthfully, I would have loved nothing more than to spend the rest of the morning with Reggie. But I had too much to do to linger in bed. "I have important work to do."

"*I'm* important work," Reggie pouted. He tried to pull me against him again, but I was faster, and slid out of bed before he could catch me.

"You are," I agreed, laughing. "And I'll *do you* after I do my other work. I promise." I pretended to ignore his lascivious wink and pulled on a pair of jeans and a T-shirt. "But I have a meeting with this nightmare of a client this morning and I can't be late for it. Also, Frederick gave me a few potential leads that might help us track down The Collective before they can find you. I want to look into them right away in case they can help."

Reggie's demeanor grew serious at once. "A lead?" He sat up in bed, the blankets pooling around his waist. I let my eyes linger on the contours of his gorgeous body for longer than I probably should have. Did all vampires come with great abs? Or was Reggie a special case? "What is it?"

I grabbed my brush off my dresser and began running it through my tangled hair. "Two potential leads, actually. Though they may both be red herrings."

"I'm all ears."

I smiled at him. "Okay. So, first, Frederick's heard The Collective mentioned in connection with a rash of blood bank break-ins that coincide with stadium concerts around the country. Second, he told me The Collective runs some sort of nonprofit organization. I obviously have no experience handling vampires—"

"Oh, I beg to differ," Reggie cut in, waggling his eyebrows. "You handle *me* just fine."

"Um. Thank you," I said, face heating at the innuendo. "What I was about to say, though, was that while I'm new to vampires, I'm great at researching nonprofits. I may be able to triangulate where The Collective is right now based on where the most recent blood-bank-break-in-slash-stadium-concert happened. Failing that, if The Collective's nonprofit is recognized by the federal government, I might be able to find some picky state, local, or federal tax regulation that could trip them up with the IRS."

His eyes went wide. "I didn't understand a word of that. But please, keep going."

I paused, unsure how much detail I could give Reggie without boring him. When he only looked at me with rapt attention, I continued. "If The Collective has 501(c)(3) status, I'll need access to my firm's GuideStar account, but if The Collective's been sloppy about their reporting requirements . . ."

"What could happen to them?" he prompted.

"Best-case scenario? They could lose their tax-exempt status," I said. "But they could also end up owing a boatload of back taxes, depending on circumstances. If the IRS thinks their failure to comply is intentional, there could be criminal charges and jail time."

Reggie let out a low whistle. "Vampires would agree to just about anything if the alternative was facing time in a human prison. They couldn't survive the food human prisoners get. It would only be a matter of time before they attacked someone out of desperation and all hell broke loose."

I didn't doubt that was true. "I don't want to get your hopes up," I cautioned. "But let me see what I can find."

When he got out of bed and strode towards me, his expression was so reverent it took my breath away. People's eyes usually glazed over when I talked taxes. But even though I could tell Reggie wasn't following most of what I was saying, the bright gleam in his eye said he was anything but bored.

Was it possible that I'd finally found someone who thought what I did was interesting?

Having my plus-one to Gretchen's wedding be a vampire seemed like a small price to pay for that.

Reggie stood behind me, then wrapped me in his arms and held me close. He was still naked, and the chill from his bare body made me shiver a little. I didn't care. It felt wonderful, being held by him,

"You are the hardest working, most incredible and brilliant person," he murmured against the top of my head. His voice was raw, the emotion in it unmistakable. "I don't know what I did to deserve you. I'm not sure that I *do* deserve you. But I'm grateful, all the same."

I swallowed thickly. "You should hold your gratitude until I've actually done something."

I could feel him shaking his head. "You already have. But is there anything I can do to help? I feel like I shouldn't just wait around while you save my ass like this."

I leaned back against him. "You're still taking me to a family wedding in a month. That's payment enough."

He chuckled. "That's true, I am." He leaned forward and pressed a kiss to the top of my head. "Though that's no burden. I'm looking forward to it."

I craned my neck and looked up at him. "You are?"

He gave me a sly grin. "I am. Though that's mostly because I'm looking forward to finally discussing history with your dad." He paused, then added, "I want to make sure I get a chance to talk with him, in case the wedding means the end of our arrangement."

His voice had gone quiet even as his hold on me tightened, his unspoken question hanging heavy in the space between us.

Was having Reggie spend actual quality time with my dad something I could handle? More to the point: Was dating a vampire for real something I wanted?

Maybe it would be okay, for once in my life, to simply take something one step at a time. I didn't know what a future with Reggie might look like, given that I would age and die the same as any other human and he would not. And I certainly wasn't ready to do what Cassie was about to do with Frederick. It was hard to imagine I ever would be.

But maybe that was all right, too. Because what I *did* know was that the idea of never seeing Reggie again after Gretchen's wedding made me very sad. Beyond sad. When I imagined saying goodbye to him next month . . .

No.

If I knew anything at all, I knew I didn't want *that*.

Maybe that was all I needed to know for now.

I turned back to Reggie again and squeezed his hand. "Even if you and Dad don't manage to talk history at the wedding, you'll have plenty of time for it, after."

The smile he gave me in return lit up the room.

TWENTY-SEVEN

To: Amelia Collins (ajcollins@butyldowidge.com)
From: John Richardson (jhcr12345@countwyatt.org)

Dear Ms. Collins,

The Wyatt Foundation greatly appreciates your
assistance and I look forward to seeing you at nine
tomorrow morning.

I have attached another set of documents to this email
for your perusal in advance of our meeting. They deal
with the work our group did with oil refineries at the turn
of the twentieth century. I am certain they will be of
great importance to our file.

Very truly and sincerely yours,
J.H.C. Richardson, Esq, PhD

AMELIA

WHEN I GOT INTO WORK THAT MORNING EVELYN ANDER-
son was already seated at the head of the large mahogany table in
the thirty-second-floor conference room, elegant and unflappa-
ble in her wrinkle-free black pantsuit.

I was grateful she was there. I hated to admit it, but I was in
so far over my head with this file I was at risk of drowning.

"Is the Wyatt CFO still set to come in at nine?" Evelyn, the
most efficient multitasker I'd ever met, typed into her computer
as she spoke. She was probably drafting an email to a different
client as she waited for this one to arrive.

"Yes," I confirmed. I set my briefcase on the table and unpacked my laptop. "My last email from John Richardson confirmed he'd be here at nine."

"Good." Evelyn rested her elbows on the table and leaned
forward, chin in hand. "I know I'd said I wanted you to present
to the partners about this file, but after reviewing these documents and seeing what this organization is actually like, I'm having second thoughts."

She motioned to the stacks of papers her assistant set up in the
room for this meeting. As if their mere presence explained better
than words could what she was trying to say.

I'd been looking forward to proving myself to the partners by
presenting my work to them. But honestly? I was relieved. "I get
it," I said. I did. This was a terrible client and a probably unsal-
vageable file. What would I even have presented to the partners
anyway?

"When Mr. Richardson comes in, we'll talk with him one last
time about what he needs to show us to remain our client. If he

can't comply by next week, we're dropping this file," she said. "I'll tell him myself and take the heat for it if he gets upset. It's the least I can do given what you've had to put up with the past month."

I hated wasted effort more than just about anything else in the world. But Evelyn was right. From the firm's perspective, better not to sink more resources into this than we already had.

I still didn't even understand what Wyatt *did*.

"With both of us here, maybe we'll finally get somewhere," I said, trying to convey hope that I didn't feel.

Ellen popped her head into the conference room carrying a tray of coffee mugs and a thermos of coffee. "Mr. Richardson's here," she said, setting it down in the center of the table. "Should I send him in?"

"Please." Evelyn smoothed her hands down the front of her pants. "Send him in."

A few moments later, a man who looked about sixty, with graying hair and wire-rimmed spectacles perched on the end of his nose, strode into the room. He carried a large paper bag in his arms that was full nearly to bursting of what I could only assume were papers he'd brought for us.

My heart sank. This wasn't going to be the quick meeting I'd hoped it would be. Or one that would bring us closer to any sort of clarity on this file.

Mr. Richardson set his bag down, then extended his hand for me to shake. "Ms. Collins," he said, warmly. "So lovely to finally meet in person."

"Mr. Richardson." I shook his hand, the way I did with every client when greeting them. I startled, nearly gasping at how icy cold his touch was.

The only people I knew with a touch that cold were Reggie

and Frederick. Spiky tendrils of suspicion went through me, but I shoved them aside.

He was old. Maybe he had bad circulation.

"Thank you again for meeting with us," I said, still a bit unsettled as Mr. Richardson took the chair opposite mine. I began flipping through the nearest stack of papers. "As I told you, we hope that by chatting in person, we can clarify what we need from you and streamline this process."

"That would be wonderful," Mr. Richardson agreed. He hefted his giant bag onto the table and began rummaging through it. "Meeting today was an excellent idea, Ms. Collins. I apologize again for finding this process so bewildering."

"There is no need to apologize," Evelyn reassured him. "Tax filings are complicated. Making them more understandable is what we do."

She wasn't wrong that a part of our job was to make the IRS's rules easier for our clients to understand. But after the headache the Wyatt Foundation had created for me, I felt at least a *slight* apology was warranted. I watched him with dread as he started pulling things from his bag that couldn't possibly be relevant to his filing.

Like a plastic bag full of confetti. And a pamphlet from a blood donation facility south of downtown.

Wait.

A *blood donation* facility?

"I'm going to get some water," I announced, thinking quickly. "Mr. Richardson, can I get you a glass of water while I'm in the kitchen?"

Mr. Richardson paused in his rummaging. He turned his eyes to me. "No, thank you," he said, his tone even. "I don't like water."

Who didn't like water? The suspicion that had begun creeping in during our handshake grew stronger. "How about a cookie?" I pressed. "My administrative assistant brought in a batch of chocolate chip cookies she baked last night. They're delicious."

He shook his head. "I don't like cookies, either."

"Mr. Richardson," Evelyn cut in, "have you brought any financial statements or receipts from the past year? That's all we need to see from you."

"Apologies," he said. "I need to dig through all this to find what I'm looking for. Aha!" he shouted suddenly, triumphant. "Here we are."

He pulled out several sheets of paper and placed them on the table in front of Evelyn. He jabbed his finger at the stylized heading at the top of the page, which I couldn't quite make out from where I sat.

Evelyn frowned. Whatever she was reading, she wasn't happy about it. "Mr. Richardson, I don't understand. Is your organization changing its name?"

"I realize this is not what I originally retained your firm for," he said, sounding contrite. "But yes, we would like to change our name. More specifically, we would like to change the name by which the IRS recognizes us so that it matches the name we have been using informally for centuries."

For *centuries*?

Evelyn's eyes went very wide. "I beg your pardon?" she asked. "Centuries?"

Mr. Richardson blinked at her several times before giving a little giggle and shaking his head. "How silly of me to misspeak like that." He giggled again, nervously. "No organization has been around for *centuries*. What I meant to say was that we would like to change the name by which the IRS recognizes us to the name we have been going by informally for whatever length of time you wouldn't find alarming." He grinned at us, pleased with how he'd recovered from his fumble.

With a sinking feeling in the pit of my stomach, I slowly turned the papers he'd just handed Evelyn around so that the headings were easier for me to read.

At the top of the page, in enormous thirty-six-point font, were two words that had been emblazoned across my mind by that point.

The Collective

The room seemed to fall away. My blood roared in my ears.

The group that was after Reggie, and my terrible client, were the same people.

Well, I thought, my thoughts unspooling. *That explains the frigid handshake. And the request to hold these meetings in the evening.* And *the seriously bizarre stuff they've been sending me.*

I fought to stay calm so John Richardson wouldn't realize I'd figured out who and what he was. How was this situation even possible? Why would vampires even *care* about something as mundane as nonprofit organizations and taxes? I got the impression that Frederick and Reggie didn't have to worry about money. Why did The Collective?

I was distantly aware of Evelyn asking John Richardson additional questions. They probably had to do with the fact that nothing he'd just provided got us any closer to being able to file the Wyatt Foundation's tax returns, but by that point I'd mostly stopped paying attention. The clock on the conference room wall showed only a few minutes had passed since John Richardson dropped his bombshell, but in those few minutes, the beginnings of a plan to save Reggie were firming up in my mind.

"Mr. Richardson," I said. I had to act fast. "It won't take us long to file the name-change paperwork with the IRS. Once that's handled, though, we'll need to meet one more time." Evelyn shot me a bewildered look. She probably assumed we'd be closing this file after this meeting. I quickly added, "Just to tie up loose ends."

If we were going to both wrap up this file *and* deal with The Collective, one more in-person meeting was essential. But first, I needed time to do more research.

"Of course," Mr. Richardson said, smiling again. His relaxed demeanor showed he had no inkling that I was on to him. "I don't suppose an evening meeting would work for you, next time? As I've indicated before, evenings are preferable for me."

"No," Evelyn said, bluntly. "We have a strict policy not to hold meetings after business hours." This wasn't true, but from the tight set of her jaw, it was clear Evelyn was no longer having it with this file. *That* was a relief, at least.

"Daytime, then," Mr. Richardson agreed, after a beat. "I will send you some dates and times that work with my schedule."

"Wonderful," I said. My mind was racing. There were lots of things I needed to do as quickly as possible, but before I could do any of them, I needed to wrap up this meeting and get Mr. Richardson out of the building. "I think we're done for now. Mr. Richardson, may I walk you to the elevator?"

....

FREDERICK WAS PACING HIS LIVING ROOM, HANDS CLASPED behind his back, when I got to his apartment. Reggie was there, too, looking terrified. I'd texted them on my way over to explain what had happened. When he saw me, Reggie all but leapt from the leather chair he'd been sitting in and launched himself at me.

"Are you hurt? Did that asshole hurt you?"

Frederick stopped pacing and stared at him. "Expressing concern about someone else?" He shot me an amused glance. "My dear Amelia, what have you done to my terrible friend?"

I ignored him. "I'm fine," I assured Reggie. "John Richardson had no idea who I was. At the end of the meeting, I thanked him for the documents he gave us and let him know we'd have the paperwork memorializing his organization's name change filed soon." I shrugged. "He left the building without fanfare and was open to meeting one last time to wrap up loose ends."

Reggie seemed at least partially mollified. "I just can't believe we didn't see this coming."

"See what coming?" I asked. "That my awful client and the group going after you were the same people? As far as I know, my firm doesn't make a habit of representing vampires. The odds of The Collective being one of my clients had to be just about non-existent."

"Yes, but . . ." He shook his head, clearly frustrated. "You don't understand. You could have been *hurt*. And it would have been my fault."

My heart ached to see him blaming himself for this bizarre situation. "I was in no danger. John Richardson had no idea who I was, or that I had any connection to you." Thinking back to the night Reggie and I first met, I added, "You would have been really proud of how well I pretended in that meeting today."

That earned a smile from him. "I always knew you had it in you."

I blushed at the praise. "Anyway, if anyone's in any danger of something, it's their nonsense nonprofit." I looked to Frederick. "Your lead on the blood bank break-ins was helpful, but taking them down through taxes is the immediate key to getting The Collective off Reggie's back."

Frederick peered at me. "What do you mean?"

"At best, they're a walking audit risk," I explained. "I mean, they don't even know the difference between an I-9, a W-4, and a 990, for god's sake, despite me having spent the better part of the past month trying to explain it to them." I shook my head. "The IRS is on the cusp of yanking their 501(c)(3) status no matter what my firm manages to put together for them. And honestly? With what a disaster their record-keeping has been, I wouldn't be surprised if they owe a pile of back taxes so huge they'll never dig themselves out from under it."

Reggie let out a quiet moan. "You're so hot when you talk taxes," he breathed.

Frederick cleared his throat. "Focus, Reginald," he chastised.

Reggie glared at his friend. Then he sighed and reluctantly moved away from me. "Fine," he muttered.

"I'm still formulating a plan for how to take them down," I said.

"I want to be a part of it," Reggie insisted.

I patted his arm. "You will be. I promise. But in the meantime, is there anything The Collective is afraid of?" I asked. "Anyone who could talk some sense into them? Once I gain access to my firm's GuideStar account, I suspect I'll find all I need by way of research by looking up the Wyatt Foundation. Since the IRS still recognizes them as a nonprofit, they'll be in there, along with a lot of their financial data. But I'll feel better about it if it's not only me in the room for this meeting." The thought of threatening them all by myself was honestly terrifying. "Who do you know that's scary that would be willing to meet with them with me?"

"I can't think of anyone The Collective is frightened of," Frederick said. "They are essentially coddled children who have been given the gift of immortality. Even though they have become a thorn in the side of the vampiric community, people remember who they used to be and tend to treat them indulgently."

"Even when they do things like this?" That was hard to wrap my mind around.

Frederick gave Reggie a sideways glance. "How do I put this delicately?"

Reggie sighed. "Just say it."

"Reginald has not endeared himself to many over the centuries," Frederick said, carefully. "Even if people were inclined to put a stop to The Collective's nonsense, they wouldn't do it on his account."

"Okay," I said. "What about something that frightens all vampires?"

Frederick and Reggie looked at each other.

"Zelda?" Reggie suggested.

Frederick shuddered. "God's thumbs. Not her."

"Exactly." Reggie snapped his fingers. "It's pretty fair to say most of us are frightened of her, right?"

"Who is Zelda?" I asked.

"A witch who's been deeply misunderstood over the centuries," Reggie said.

Frederick scoffed. "Hardly. Her preferred nickname is *Grizelda the Terrible*," he said. "She came up with it herself. She used to keep a cauldron in her front yard to make it easier for her to cook children."

"An urban legend," Reggie protested.

Frederick leveled a stare at him. "I think you're letting your history with her cloud your judgment."

My ears perked up as a hot stab of something that felt uncomfortably like jealousy went through me. "What history?"

When Reggie answered, he spoke so reluctantly it was like the words were being pulled out of him against his will. "Zelda and I used to tag-team practical jokes on some of the more annoying members of the community." And then, with a murderous glare at Frederick, he added, "All rumors that Zelda and I were anything more than friends are rubbish."

I glanced at Frederick to check his reaction. He looked unconvinced but said nothing.

My cheeks flamed. Which was ridiculous. Even if the rumors Reggie had just alluded to *weren't* rubbish, the man was hundreds of years old. Expecting him not to have had any lovers at all before me was unreasonable.

I didn't have to like it, though.

"You think The Collective is afraid of her?" I asked Frederick, trying to steer my thoughts to safer ground.

"I can't pretend to know what goes on in their heads," he said. "But yes, probably. Most of us are."

I pondered that. "Any chance there's a passage on her in *The Annals*? Maybe there's something in there we could use to scare The Collective into leaving Reggie alone."

Frederick's face lit up. "*The Annals*?" Once again, he reminded me so much of my dad on those rare instances he got asked a question about history, it was uncanny. "You may peruse them if you'd like. I must go run a time-sensitive errand for Cassie, otherwise I'd stay here and review them with you." He glanced at Reggie. "Could you show her where I store the books?"

Reggie nodded. "Of course. Go take care of your fiancée."

Frederick's eyes were very bright. "Thank you." And then to me, he said, "I will return in a few hours. In the meantime, please do not disturb Cassie under any circumstances. She is sleeping and must rest for the next several days."

My eyebrows shot up. What sort of medical condition made someone need to sleep for days? "Is she okay?"

"She will be," Frederick said. His eyes drifted over to Reggie, as though seeking confirmation.

"She will be," Reggie agreed, reassuring. "I promise, Freddie."

"Right. Right," Frederick said, his voice so quiet it was like he was speaking to himself. And then, to me, he said, "Reginald can fill you in on the details, if you like."

The moment he left the apartment, I rounded on Reggie. "What's wrong with Cassie?"

"They got engaged last night," he explained. "As part of it, Freddie . . ." He trailed off and rubbed at the back of his neck. "He turned her. When she wakes up, Cassie will be a vampire."

My mouth fell open. Even though I'd known this was going to happen, there was nothing that could have prepared me for the reality of it.

Cassie—a person I'd known most of my life—was a vampire. I saw the way she looked at Frederick, and I wasn't so dead inside I couldn't recognize real love when I saw it on another person's face . . . but even still. The idea that Cassie had chosen this for herself to be with her lover forever was very difficult to process.

"Wow," I said. It was the understatement of the year.

"Yeah," Reggie agreed. "I don't pretend to exactly understand what it is they see in each other, but I've seen centuries worth of guys in love and guys not in love. I know what they have is the real deal."

"Sam is going to lose his goddamn mind," I said.

"Probably. But that's something for Cassie to navigate when she wakes up. It's not on you."

"Won't it be, though? Sam's my brother." Not only that, he had an incredibly black-and-white worldview. Much as I had had for most of my life. Even if I never made the same choice Cassie made, Sam would probably disapprove of my current situation if he knew how far Reggie and I had already taken things.

Reggie must have recognized how distressed I was getting, because no sooner did I think how nice it would be for him to hold me than he was out of his chair and I was in his arms.

"One step at a time," he murmured against the top of my head, before pressing a gentle kiss there for good measure. "You can worry about Sam and Cassie when it becomes an issue. There's no point in worrying about it now."

I burrowed into his chest. "Worrying about things way too far in advance is kind of my thing, though."

He chuckled. "You should work on that." He paused, then pulled back so he could look into my eyes. "Have you considered bullet journaling?"

TWENTY-EIGHT

**Excerpt from The Annals of Vampyric Lore,
Seventeenth Edition**

"Index of Notorious Witches and Vampires," pp. 1123–24

*Watson, Grizelda (b: 1625, approximate): Little is known
about Grizelda Watson's life prior to the late eighteenth century. Watson (reportedly known as* Zelda *to close friends), by
all accounts one of the most powerful witches known to
vampire-kind, first rose to prominence at that time due to her
then-unrivaled flair for the dramatic and her penchant for out-
landish practical jokes. Her infamy grew exponentially in the
last quarter of the nineteenth century, when she adopted the
nickname* Grizelda the Terrible. *She allegedly committed a
series of crimes involving arson in what is now the American
Pacific Northwest and in Chicago during the early twentieth
century.* "I like to watch things burn," *she was famously quoted
as saying.*

Watson was romantically linked with Reginald Cleaves (see: infra 2133–35) on more than one occasion, ostensibly because their public personas were similar. When asked about it, both parties consistently denied they were anything but close friends.

Watson made few public appearances in the final years of the twentieth century. In 2010, however, she was spotted in a Napa County farmers market. Subsequent sightings have confirmed that Watson now goes by the name Zelda Turret, has adopted veganism, and runs a popular hot yoga studio.

Before her disappearance from vampiric society, Watson was famously quoted as saying she "laughs hard, lives hard, and plays hard." She briefly had groupies in the final decades of the twentieth century, many of whom adopted this quote as their mantra. T-shirts bearing this slogan can still be found on Etsy.

AMELIA

AFTER FREDERICK LEFT TO GET SUPPLIES FOR CASSIE, REGgie and I paged through *The Annals* together to see if we could find anything useful about Grizelda. I could tell immediately that these books were way older than anything I'd ever seen when working in the University of Chicago Library. The lettering on the book's cover was in some kind of calligraphy that was so stylized I could barely read it.

"I can't believe Frederick has something this old just lying around," I marveled. "He gave me some excerpts the other day in case they were helpful. But those entries were so old I barely understood them."

Reggie snorted. "If you think *this* is old, you should see the clothes he used to wear before Cassie got to him."

Judging from Frederick's speech mannerisms, I found the idea that his clothes used to be very old-fashioned easy to believe.

When we finally found Grizelda's entry, we read through it together. My cheeks heated at the brief reference to Reggie being romantically linked to her, but Reggie didn't seem to be reacting to it, so I told myself to let it go.

"I hadn't realized Zelda had moved to the West Coast." Reggie sounded amused. "Good for her."

"Do you think she'd be up for helping us?"

Reggie shook his head. "If she went through all the trouble to vanish and adopt a new identity, it was probably to get away from her reputation." He bit his lip, thinking. "I suspect she wouldn't be enthusiastic about someone from her old life reaching out to ask her for help."

"Okay," I said, a bit relieved. Getting a notorious witch I didn't know to help me had been more than a little intimidating, anyway. Especially one with an ambiguous history with Reggie. But if we weren't going to ask Grizelda for help, that meant my tax expertise was the only chance we had of frightening The Collective. I was confident in my understanding of the Internal Revenue Code, but much less so in my ability to get vampires with a vendetta to back off.

But there'd be time to worry about that later. Right now, I was paging through what might have been the first history book that had ever legitimately interested me. I wanted to give it my full attention.

"I'm confused about something," I said. I flipped to the front of the volume and pointed to the date. "The cover to this thing looks ancient, and this title page says it was published in 1873. But Grizelda's entry is only a few years old."

Reggie nodded. "There's a committee that handles updating this thing." He shrugged. "They're haphazard about it, though, so some of the stuff in here is hilariously out of date. I don't think the television shows section has been updated since *M*A*S*H* went off the air, for example. But it's better than nothing."

"Fascinating," I said, meaning it. Another thought occurred to me. "Are you in the Index of Notorious Witches and Vampires?"

His eyes widened for a fraction of a second before he recovered and schooled his features. He looked down at his hands. "No."

"Are you telling me the truth?" I asked, teasing.

"Absolutely." He cleared his throat. "You know, I think we've spent enough time reading. Do you want to do *literally* anything else?"

He moved to close the book. I stuck my hand in it so that he couldn't. "If you're not in the Index, I don't see why I can't just look through it on my own for a little while."

He blinked at me. "Why would you want to?"

"It's interesting," I said, honestly. "And I'm curious about what a vampire needs to do to earn a place in there. If the lead suspect in that fire from the eighteen hundreds isn't infamous enough to be written about in here, I can't imagine what it would take to—"

"Fine," Reggie interrupted. He let out a long sigh. "Yes. I'm in there. But I don't want you to read it. It's nothing you don't already know, but somehow having my past memorialized in this . . ." He trailed off, shaking his head. "It makes me feel like I'll always be defined by things I did centuries ago. I hate it."

He looked pained. I closed the book. "Okay."

"Thank you," he said. "I meant it when I said you already know everything about me that's in there. Oh—except maybe for the part where I once had a fan club." A corner of his mouth quirked up. "Have I told you about them? *That* was pretty funny."

I couldn't tell if he was kidding about once having had a fan club or not, which itself was pretty funny. But I decided not to press it. "Okay," I said again. I leaned in closer, until our lips were nearly touching. "So. What do you want to do instead of reading this book?"

His breath caught. "We *do* have the apartment to ourselves. I could take this opportunity to thank you for everything you're doing to help me." He tilted his head and pressed a lingering kiss, and then another, to the place on my neck where he'd bitten me the night before. His intent couldn't have been clearer. The feel of his mouth on my skin sent a flash of heat straight to my core.

"Cassie's here," I pointed out. "We aren't alone." But I was already growing dizzy with want, the way he was trailing open-mouthed kisses up along the column of my throat. It had only been a few hours since we were last intimate, but the way he was mouthing at me made me want to take him back to bed with me all over again.

"She'll be asleep for days," he murmured against my skin. "We'll be quiet. She won't hear a thing."

"Won't I?"

Cassie's voice rang through the quiet apartment like a bell. Reggie and I sprang apart like naughty teenagers.

She stood at the end of the hall, just outside the bedroom she'd been sleeping in. Even at this distance, I could tell something about her was subtly different, though I'd have been hard-pressed to say what it was if I hadn't known. She looked taller, somehow. Her stance was more self-assured. It was difficult to reconcile this person with the Cassie I'd known for decades as Sam's flighty best friend.

"Cassie!" Reggie jumped from his chair, all thoughts of seducing me forgotten. He rushed to where she stood, placing a gentle hand at her elbow. "Are you all right? You shouldn't be awake right now."

"I'm all right." Her voice sounded different, too. Rougher, somehow. I didn't know if that was due to her having just woken up, or if whatever changes were happening in her body had done something to her vocal cords. "Hungry, though. It's . . . really unpleasant." Her hands shook a little; they went to her throat.

"I know. I'm sorry. Freddie went out to get something for you," Reggie assured her. "He didn't think you'd need it this soon, though. He might be a while."

Cassie nodded, and her eyes flicked to me. "Amelia. Hi." She closed her eyes, then took in a deep breath through her nose before letting it out again. Her whole body shuddered. "I think I better not be around you right now. I'm . . . not quite myself."

While lying in bed together the night before, Reggie had told me his human memories were fuzzy and insubstantial. He'd compared them to faded photographs from a different person's life. Was that because he'd last been human such a long time ago? Or did something happen to a person's mind and memories when they became a vampire?

When Cassie said she wasn't quite herself, was this what she meant? It would break Sam's heart if Cassie didn't remember their friendship anymore now that she'd turned.

"You should rest," Reggie said. "When you wake up, Freddie will be back with something for you to eat."

Cassie smiled at the mention of Frederick. At least some memories were still intact, then.

"The only thing I feel more than hunger right now is fatigue," she admitted. "Going back to bed sounds amazing. You won't think I'm rude if I leave you alone out here?"

"The only thing I think is rude about you is your art," he teased, grinning at her. She managed a watery laugh. He was trying to put her at ease. God. This man. "Now go back to sleep."

When we were alone again, Reggie sat back down in the chair next to mine, elbows on his knees. He peered at me quizzically. "What are you thinking?"

My mind was in too much of a muddle to answer that question. My thoughts were flitting from The Collective, to the choice Cassie had made, to whether I would have to make it myself one day if I wanted to be with Reggie, and then back again. My every instinct was to stop and think everything through, and not get up from that chair until every puzzle in front of me had been solved and the next ten years of my life had a nice, neat, careful plan. But I knew that wasn't possible.

Some puzzles, I was coming to realize, were only solvable in the fullness of time.

"What am I thinking?" I repeated. If I shared any of it with Reggie, he'd feel guilty. Or worse. "I'm thinking that I'd like you to hold me for a little while." That part, at least, was true.

I didn't have to ask him twice. His arms were around me as soon as the words left my mouth, his embrace steady and sure.

And then, as if reading my mind: "I don't expect anything, Amelia. I would never ask you to do anything you don't want to do." There was an unmistakable undercurrent of emotion in his words that touched my heart. "I promise."

I slid my arms around his neck, then pulled back to look into his eyes. "But what if you change your mind? What if in twenty years you don't want to be with someone who looks like she could be your mother?"

He gave me a crooked grin. "A week ago, you said you'd never see me again after Gretchen's wedding. Now we're planning our outfits for your retirement party?" I opened my mouth to reply to that, then closed it again when I realized that that was exactly what I was doing. "Amelia, I want as much of you as you are willing to share. Planning things too far into the future often amounts to little more than wasted time."

"But you might want more one day." How could he not see that? "How can you know now what you're going to want later?"

Reggie leaned in and pressed a lingering kiss to the corner of my mouth. I closed my eyes, reveling in its sweetness. "*If* I change my mind about this, we will cross that bridge when we come to it," he promised. "But I can't imagine ever feeling differently about asking you to fundamentally alter yourself at a cellular level just so I can keep you forever." He pulled back so he could look into my eyes. I wondered if he knew how much I already missed having his mouth on mine, or if he could somehow sense the rash of butterflies taking flight in my stomach at the mention of the word *forever*.

TWENTY-NINE

From: John Richardson (jhcr12345@countwyatt.org)
To: Amelia Collins (ajcollins@butyldowidge.com)
Subject: Meeting

Dear Ms. Collins,

I look forward to meeting with you one final time to get everything in order for our fillings. I have a few questions for you before we meet.

First, would it be helpful to have other members of The Wyatt Foundation/The Collective attend the meeting with me in case they are able to remember details I cannot?

Second, were the documents I sent last week regarding our organization's charitable activities in France during the first world war helpful?

Third (and I suspect you will say no to this, but it can't hurt to ask again), are you quite certain we cannot hold this meeting at night?

All best,
John Richardson

REGINALD

I FELT A BIT AT LOOSE ENDS IN AMELIA'S APARTMENT AS she finished preparing for the next day's meeting with John Richardson. She'd asked me to come over to keep her company as she worked, and so that she could bounce ideas off me as we put our plan in place. And who was I to say no?

She *was* saving my ass here.

I also strongly suspected I was falling in love with her.

Scratch that.

I strongly suspected I had *already* fallen in love with her.

For centuries, I'd made fun of men who found it impossible to deny their significant others anything they asked of them. More the fool, me.

"Thank god *The Wyatt Foundation* is a more distinctive name than *The Collective*," Amelia mused out loud from her makeshift office at her kitchen table. She'd been working for the past three hours while I puttered around her apartment and made her pancakes. It was such a domestic scene, with her working and my caring for her, it made my chest ache. "If I hadn't had a better name to search for in GuideStar, this work would have taken me days. Maybe weeks."

Her fingers flew over her keyboard, her hair piled on top of her head in a messy bun to keep it out of her face as she worked. I had no idea how she typed so fast. I also didn't know what Guide-Star was, or why exactly *The Wyatt Foundation* was a better name for our purposes than *The Collective*. But Amelia was clearly happy about it, her eyes dancing as she jotted things down on a yellow notepad beside her keyboard.

I briefly considered asking more detailed questions about what she'd said but held my tongue. I probably wouldn't have understood the answers anyway. Right now, she needed the pancakes I was attempting to make her more than she needed me slowing her down with my cluelessness about taxes. Fortunately, now that I knew it mattered how much baking soda went into the batter, this batch was going much better than the Wisconsin attempt had.

Nothing in her kitchen smelled like the Great Salt Lake had been set on fire, anyway.

"Wow," Amelia said, then let out a low whistle. "Listen to this. Unless there's some GuideStar glitch that prevented their tax returns from being uploaded, which *never* happens on this scale, it looks like neither the Wyatt Foundation nor The Collective has filed any federal tax returns in over fifty years."

That I understood. Sort of. "That sounds really bad."

Amelia nodded, her eyes bright. "It is. If the IRS finds out, these bozos will definitely lose their tax-exempt status. They will absolutely owe a Herculean amount of back taxes. And like I said the other day, some may even go to prison."

I moved to where she was sitting and wrapped my arms around her from behind. I rested my cheek against the top of her head, peeking idly at her laptop monitor in the process. The numbers on the screen were gibberish to me. The fact that something so complicated, so utterly beyond me, made intuitive sense to Amelia was possibly the hottest thing I'd ever experienced.

Mine, I thought fiercely. I tightened my hold on her, closing my eyes as I savored the sweet, tender warmth of the woman in my arms. *This brilliant woman is* mine.

For as long as she'll have me.

I shook myself a little, trying to snap out of it and focus on what she was saying. "Do you think they did it on purpose?" I managed. Her hair was so soft against my cheek, her scent driving me nearly to distraction. But now was not the moment to think about how much I wanted to take her hair out of its bun and run my fingers through it. "They'll probably tell you they didn't know what they were doing. Vampires don't keep up with the modern world too well."

"It doesn't matter if it was unintentional or not," she said, sternly.

"No?"

She turned in my arms, craning her neck a little so she could look up at me. "Failure to understand the law is not a defense to breaking it."

Well, that seemed unfair. "What if you're just a clueless vampire?"

She smiled. "I haven't specifically checked, but I'm pretty sure being a vampire isn't a defense, either. *Especially* if you're a vampire availing yourself of the same federal tax breaks us mortals get."

"Damn." I shook my head. "Are you telling me that after centuries of being complete assholes, The Collective's downfall might actually come from something as dumb as messing up on their taxes?" Thinking about it that way, the whole situation was almost funny.

"Taxes was how they got Al Capone," she said. "There's precedent."

"Good old Al Capone," I sighed, feeling suddenly wistful for the 1920s. "A bit of a dickhead, but he really did throw the best parties."

Amelia grinned at me. "Who *haven't* you met?" she teased.

"I'm pretty sure I've met everyone of consequence from the past few hundred years," I lied, pompously. She raised a suspicious eyebrow, pulling a smile out of me. Having her see right through my boasts and my bluster, and wanting to spend time with me anyway . . .

It was almost too good to be true.

"Speaking of bullshit," she said, grinning now, "can you help me figure out how to reply to this email I just got from John Richardson?"

"What I just said to you was *not* bullshit," I said, pretending outrage. I doubted I pulled it off, though. I was grinning at her from ear to ear. "But yeah, of course I can help. If you think I *can* help. What does the email say?"

She pointed at her screen, and I leaned over her shoulder to get a closer look.

"This part where he asks if others from his group should come to the meeting," I said, pointing. "Tell him no."

Amelia frowned. "You don't think if the whole group is there it would save time? Maybe they'd see reason faster this way."

I shook my head. "Tell him whatever you need to keep him from bringing anyone else to this meeting. He may not suspect anything now, but he will when you start laying out your terms. He *definitely* will when he sees me there with you." As soon as Amelia told me about her plan to confront Richardson in her offices, I'd insisted she bring me with her. *For protection*, I'd said. I'd have worried myself sick otherwise.

Fear over what might happen to Amelia welled up in me all over again at the thought of her being in the same room with more than one member of The Collective.

No.

Absolutely not.

"The last thing we need is for John Richardson to have ready backup," I clarified. Most vampires wouldn't be nearly as well-behaved in a building full of humans as Frederick and I were. If I had to guess, The Collective likely chose this John Richardson to be her interface because he was better mannered around humans than the others. *He* probably wouldn't run amok in her building and start indiscriminately snacking on CPAs. But I had no idea if the other members of The Collective would be so self-contained.

I kept all this to myself. There was no need to frighten her. Especially since the rest of The Collective wouldn't be coming.

"Okay," Amelia said. "I'll tell him we only need him to come tomorrow."

"Good," I said, satisfied.

"Any other thoughts before I type up this reply?" she asked, facing her computer again.

A thought occurred to me. "Yes. Tell him he's an idiot and an asshole."

"I'm not typing that."

"Please?" I batted my eyelashes.

She laughed. "I wish I could, believe me. But I can't. He's still technically my client."

"Can I do it, then?" I asked, pantomiming taking her laptop

away and banging on keys while she swatted playfully at my shoulder.

"How about you serve me those pancakes you made instead?" she asked, her hand on my arm. "They smell delicious."

I looked down to where she was touching me. Her soft, warm hand was pale against my dark shirt. I could feel the heat of her touch as though I were wearing nothing at all.

Was this what it would be like for us? Me taking care of Amelia by cooking for her and making her laugh whenever she needed a break? Amelia laughing at my jokes, gratefully accepting my company, and holding my hand whenever the world got to be too much?

I had to shut my eyes against the sudden blinding joy of it all.

We just had to get to the other side of tomorrow, and it could be ours.

"I'll get the pancakes," I said, when I found my voice. "I hope you like them."

THIRTY

Text messages between Reginald Cleaves and Frederick J. Fitzwilliam

REGINALD: How is Cassie?

FREDERICK: Better. She's still sleeping for large portions of the day, but she's up and around for longer stretches and eating regular meals of O positive.

FREDERICK: "What to Expect" and The Annals say she should be more or less herself again in a week

REGINALD: Glad to hear it

REGINALD: Also hey

REGINALD: I'm not asking this for any particular reason at all

REGINALD: Other than because I'm curious, and as always am extremely invested in the minutiae of your life

REGINALD: But how long were you and Cassie together before you started talking about "forever"??

REGINALD: You know, in the vampiric sense

FREDERICK: You're only asking because you're curious?

REGINALD: Yes

REGINALD: And because I care about you, my oldest friend, and want to know more about your life

FREDERICK: You are NEVER curious about my life

REGINALD: That's not true. Remember that time at that one party in Madrid when I asked about that beautiful woman you were talking to?

FREDERICK: You asked about her because you wanted to sleep with and then eat her, not because you cared about my life

REGINALD: I'm hurt

REGINALD: But okay, that's fair

                          FREDERICK: Be honest. Are you thinking
                          of asking Amelia to think about turning?

REGINALD: No!

REGINALD: Absolutely not

REGINALD: Whatever gave you that idea

                          FREDERICK: Oh you silly fool.

AMELIA

WALKING INTO MY BUILDING'S ELEVATOR WITH REGGIE ON
one side of me and Frederick on the other was among the more
surreal experiences of my life. At least, until we got off the elevator and made our way to the conference room where we'd be
meeting with John Richardson. Then that experience became
number one.

I was grateful for the awkwardness of the situation, though. It
distracted me from the nerves roiling in the pit of my stomach. I
was so anxious about this meeting I hadn't even been able to eat
breakfast, no matter how much Reggie nudged me to take a few
bites of cereal.

If all went well, we'd be getting rid of the worst client I'd ever
had *and* the weirdo vampires who'd been after Reggie for years
in one fell swoop. It was the most extreme example of killing two

birds with one stone I'd ever experienced. And it would largely be up to me to pull it off.

The pressure on me was enormous.

"Don't you think you should have dressed up more for this?" Frederick asked Reggie with obvious disdain, keeping his voice low enough that we weren't at risk of being overheard.

"No," Reggie said, at full volume. "I wanted to dress exactly as I liked for this meeting. I'm done hiding." *Exactly as he liked* turned out to be a brown gingham skirt paired with a T-shirt that said, *Don't Blame Me, I'm Todd!* and black combat boots. He honestly looked hotter in that combo than anyone had a right to look, though I wasn't certain whether that was something I should admit out loud.

"But this is a business establishment," Frederick continued, exasperated. "If you don't have any respect for yourself, at least have respect for the professionals who work here."

I unlocked the door to the conference room where our meeting would be held and let them inside. My assistant had already set out the files we'd need for this meeting, and the knot of tension I'd been carrying around all morning loosened slightly.

One less thing to worry about.

"I respect the hell out of the people who work here," Reggie said, continuing to bicker with Frederick even as they made their way into the room. "The way I dress has nothing to do with it." He pulled out a chair at one end of the table and sat down. Then he turned to me and added, sounding a lot more contrite, "I hope my appearance doesn't reflect poorly on you with your employers. I'm sorry I didn't think to ask first."

"It's fine," I said, then took a seat at the head of the table. "If all goes as planned, by the end of this meeting no one will care what any of us is wearing." I looked at them both intently. "Does everyone understand their roles?"

"I think so," Reggie said. "But why don't you go over it all one more time just in case."

Frederick took the seat next to Reginald, smirking at him. "It's a simple enough plan, don't you think?" Then he leaned over and stage-whispered in his ear: "You like it when Amelia takes charge, don't you."

"No," Reggie said, glaring at him. A moment later, he quietly murmured, "Yes."

Was it possible to combust from a combination of embarrassment, affection, and desire? I forced myself to ignore the riotous blush I could feel rising up my cheeks. I needed to focus. We were in my conference room, and in just a few minutes we'd be having a very important meeting with the head of a group of vigilante vampires. And how that meeting went would be largely up to me.

I had a moment of dizzy disorientation as I wondered, for the tenth time that morning, how any of this was happening.

"I'll go over it again, just to be sure," I agreed.

Reggie beamed at me. "I'm all ears."

Frederick snorted.

"My role has a couple of parts to it," I began, ignoring him. "First, I will let John Richardson know on behalf of Butyl and Dowidge that we are closing their file. I will lay out the tax consequences of what they've failed to do, tell them how much they almost certainly owe the IRS in back taxes, and explain how much trouble they'll be in with the IRS and potentially with the Justice Department if we report them." I paused. "I will also let them know that I know exactly who and what they really are, but no one else at my firm does. And that if they go quietly and vow to leave Reggie alone forever, it will stay that way."

"After you're finished doing the hard stuff," Reggie continued, "my job will be to talk about how I had nothing whatsoever to do with The Incident, and that even if I *had* been responsible, it's been over a century, and for the love of Hades they really need to find better things to do with their time." He paused. "If that doesn't work, I'll also offer to help them find who was really responsible."

That surprised me. This offer had not been part of the plan we'd gone over last night with Frederick over pancakes (for me) and bags of O-positive (for the two of them). "Really? You'd do that?"

"I would absolutely *offer* to help them, yes. But if they take me up on it, I'd likely only go through the motions." At my quizzical expression, he added, "The person who set the fire likely had their reasons. Even though I had nothing to do with it, I'm not sad it happened. I will not rat the actual arsonist out." A pause. "Whoever they are."

I stared at him. Did Reggie actually know who did it?

Before I could ask any follow-up questions, Frederick chimed in. "My job will be to be the adult in the room, so to speak." He gave Reggie a meaningful look. "My being here will let them know you two are not acting alone. That you do have support from within the broader vampire community."

"Good," I said. I took a deep breath, then let it out slowly. This was going to work. "Any last-minute questions?"

Just then, the door to the conference room swung open and Evelyn Anderson walked in with John Richardson.

At the sight of them, white hot panic snaked through me. No one else from my firm was supposed to be here for this. Our biggest bargaining chip was that no one but me would know the truth about his organization so long as he agreed to go gently into the night with his goons.

We *couldn't* speak openly about this situation in front of Evelyn.

Frederick and Reggie looked as alarmed by this development as I felt. John Richardson was clearly caught off guard, too. He stood rooted to the spot just inside the conference room, eyes saucer-wide and locked with Reggie's, looking like he was in a state of actual shock.

Good. That part, at least, was proceeding according to plan.

"Apologies, Amelia," Evelyn said, as she took a seat at the opposite end of the table. "I know I said you could conduct this meeting, but I talked it over with the other partners. Given today's agenda, we agreed it would be best if I was present."

She gave me a meaningful look.

Today's agenda, as far as Evelyn knew, was that we'd be closing the Wyatt Foundation file and nothing more. They must have wanted that decision to come from the firm, not me.

"Thank you, Evelyn," I said. What else could I say? She was the partner. If she wanted to be here for this meeting, there was nothing I could do about it.

John Richardson continued staring at Reggie as though he'd seen a ghost. Reggie glared at him with a hatred in his eyes I'd never seen there before. As if all that kept him from lunging across the table at him was the presence of the two humans in the room.

My mind was spinning, trying to think of a way out of this mess. "Evelyn, would it be all right if I still led the meeting? I've prepared for it, and—"

"Of course. I'll just be here in case I'm needed." Evelyn

turned her attention to Frederick and Reggie. "And who might you be?"

"My name is Reginald Cleaves," Reggie replied, eyes still on Mr. Richardson. His voice managed to hide his seething hatred, but just barely. He gestured to Frederick. "This is my friend, Frederick."

"Do you have a connection to the Wyatt file?" Evelyn continued, looking confused.

"You might say that." Reggie raised an eyebrow at Mr. Richardson. "John, do you want to explain to everyone why Freddie and I are here?"

Mr. Richardson looked as though he were about to make a run for it. He hadn't moved since he entered the conference room, his body taut as a bowstring.

At length, a muscle twitched in his jaw. "I have no idea why you're here," he said. His tone was terse, but he remained calm. As if the person his organization had been hunting for years weren't sitting less than ten feet away from him. "It seems a rather foolish decision on your part."

Evelyn, suddenly thrust into the middle of a feud between centuries-old vampires and armed with nothing but the skills she brought with her as a CPA, was struggling to make sense of what was happening. She turned to me and asked, in a quiet voice, "Are Reginald and Frederick disgruntled members of the Wyatt Foundation board?"

I had to bite the inside of my cheek to keep from bursting into hysterical laughter. *If only it were that simple.* "Something like that," I managed.

"Freddie and I came because we want to talk, John," Reggie said, ignoring both of us. He stood up and started making his way slowly to where John Richardson still stood motionless by the door. "There's a lot you and your friends think you understand, but the reality is—"

Reggie didn't get a chance to finish that sentence. "I need to make a phone call," Mr. Richardson cut in abruptly. "If *you* are here, there are other people from The Collective who need to be here as well. They're angry, Reginald Cleaves." And then, leaning in closer, he added, "You have been a very naughty boy."

He fished around in his pocket for his cell phone. His hands shook. *Good*, I thought. *He's nervous.* Without another word, he stormed out of the conference room, fingers jabbing furiously at the screen.

"One of us should probably follow him," I said, trying to stem my rising panic. "You know how disgruntled board members can get." John Richardson wandering the halls of my firm meant this situation was rapidly spiraling out of control. What would happen if more members of The Collective showed up? Frederick and Reggie didn't attack humans anymore—but I had no idea what these other vampires might do.

Evelyn nodded her agreement. "Yes. I'd prefer they not be allowed to wander the building. Perhaps we should place a call to security and not allow them in?"

"I don't know if that will help," Reggie said, before shooting me a meaningful glance. "Call security just in case, Ms. Anderson, but I'll go follow John just to be on the safe side."

"Not by yourself," Frederick said. "I'm coming, too."

"He's not going to do anything stupid in a building full of hum—" Reggie cut himself off, catching the mistake he'd been about to make at the last minute. He cleared his throat and tried again. "He won't do anything stupid in a building full of *accountants*."

"May I remind you that this is not a group known for making

carefully reasoned decisions?" Frederick said. "Or a group that is used to being around this many . . . *accountants* . . . who aren't expecting them? You're not facing them alone."

"Should we call in a mediator?" Evelyn's eyes darted back and forth between Reggie and Frederick. She obviously realized she'd lost the thread of the conversation at some point, but Evelyn Anderson was not someone used to being caught flat-footed. "Mediating board member disputes typically falls outside what we offer clients, but if calling in a mediator would help—"

"It wouldn't," Frederick said bluntly, rolling up his sleeves. "This is something we should be able to resolve amongst ourselves." He looked at me. "Especially if you're there with us, Amelia."

I stared at him, eyes wide. "Me? What good will my being there do?"

Reggie nodded towards the pile of papers on the conference room table. All the hours of work I'd done to prepare for this meeting. "You more than anyone else here should be able to end this . . . board member dispute." His eyes softened. "You've worked so hard, Amelia. You've got this. You've got *them*. We need you."

"Agreed," Frederick said. "Reginald and I have certain arguments we can make, but you're the one who knows exactly how much trouble they'll be in if they don't . . . go along with what the rest of the board wants to do."

I turned back to Evelyn. She was the partner here as well as my boss. If she wanted to follow us as we went to confront The Collective, there was nothing I could do to stop her. But if she *did* come along, god only knew how messy this might get.

"I'll make sure they know any decisions made on their file come from the firm, not from me," I said, thinking quickly.

"Fine," Evelyn said. "I'll stay here. This seems like a situation where the more people in the room there are, the more explosive things could get."

"Explosive," Reggie said, snapping his fingers. "Good word."

I let out a huge internal sigh of relief. "Thank you, Evelyn."

Evelyn said something in response, but I didn't quite hear what it was. I was already halfway out the door.

"How will we know if the others have gotten inside?" I asked when we arrived at the elevator. "How will we find them?"

"If they're here, finding them will not be a problem," Frederick said, sounding worried. Only then did I realize how much his previously calm demeanor had been an act for Evelyn's benefit. "I only hope we're not too late."

THIRTY-ONE

Excerpt from security log at 131 N. LaSalle, Chicago, Illinois, recovered the following day

10:12 a.m.: Group of four oddly dressed individuals approached desk, asked to be buzzed upstairs. When I asked for some identification, leader of group waved hand and said <u>You don't need to see our identification</u>. Group was informed I saw that in a movie once and that it wouldn't work on me, but then a very peaceful feeling came over me and I realized I <u>didn't</u> need to see their identification. Buzzed group in building with no further incident.—JSP

AMELIA

FREDERICK HAD BEEN WRONG. FINDING JOHN RICHARDson was *not* easy. After spending over an hour wandering the halls of the thirty-second and thirty-first floors of my building, carefully checking each cubicle and poking our heads inside every office that wasn't locked, there was still no sign of either him or anyone else from The Collective.

"Maybe he left," I suggested, as we waited for the elevator to take us down to the thirtieth floor. "Why are we so certain he's still here?"

"Because I can't imagine he'd leave after finally finding me." Reggie's lips were pressed together in a hard, determined line. "He's here, somewhere. We just need to find him."

The firm's mail room took up the majority of the thirtieth floor. The lack of offices with doors that closed made searching this floor faster work than searching the others had been. We walked as quickly as we could, turning our heads to peer inside each cubicle as we passed.

"There's no one here," Reggie said. The anxiety in his voice was palpable.

"Let's check the mail room," I said. "That's probably where everyone is." I hoped that was true.

It wasn't until we heard cheerful voices coming from the break room at the far end of the floor that we realized where the people who worked here were.

"Happy birthday, Janice!"

"Forty looks great on you!"

"Oh my god, you got red velvet cake. That's my favorite!"

We paused when we were about twenty feet away. "Should we go in?" I whispered to Reggie and Frederick. "I don't want to be the accountant who crashes a mail room party, but maybe we could just quickly ask if they've seen anyone hanging around who shouldn't be here?"

"That would only alarm them," Frederick said. A moment later he asked, "What is *red velvet* cake, exactly?"

"I was wondering the same thing," Reggie admitted.

"Is it made with actual red velvet?"

"I'll explain later," I muttered under my breath. We didn't have time for this. "We have to keep looking for—"

"Looking for me?" John Richardson asked, from behind me.

My blood turned to ice in my veins. Holding my breath, and with my heart pounding a rapid staccato in my chest, I slowly turned until I was facing him.

Gone was every trace of the polite, bumbling CFO I'd been dealing with for the past month. In his place was someone much more ruthless. Someone determined not to leave until he got exactly what he wanted.

He snarled at me. And his fangs, hidden in plain sight when we were all in the conference room, were clearly visible now.

Which meant—if what I'd read in *The Annals* about a vampire's fangs was correct—that he was about to feed.

"I see you laid a trap for me, Ms. Collins," he hissed, his words cold puffs of air against my skin. He leaned in close, until his fangs were less than an inch away from my throat. He *tsked* at me, as though I were a misbehaving child. "Not very nice of you to lie to me, and not disclose you were in cahoots with our quarry this entire time."

"You can't do this here!" I blurted, my thoughts unspooling "This is an accounting firm!" As if that mattered in the slightest. But I was beyond reason, barely in control of what I was saying.

Reggie shoved Richardson away from me and jumped between us. "If you bite her," he growled, his face a mask of fury. "No—if you so much as *breathe* on her, I will stake you where you stand."

On some level at least, I knew I shouldn't find Reggie's fierce protectiveness as hot as I did. But I was too stunned and terrified by what was happening to care.

John Richardson chuckled darkly, raising an eyebrow at Reggie and Frederick in turn. He shot a pointed look at their empty hands. "And with what will you stake me, naughty brother? Your fingers?"

Crap.

Crap.

We'd been so busy planning what we would *say* to John Richardson that we'd never stopped to think about how we might *fight* him if it came to that.

"We didn't think this through," Frederick muttered under his breath, echoing my sentiments. "I brought no weapons."

"I won't stake you with my fingers," Reggie said, his voice ice-cold and smooth as silk. "I'll stake you with this." To my astonishment, he withdrew a two-foot-long piece of wood that looked like it might have once been part of a broom handle from within the folds of his gingham skirt. Whatever it used to be, it had since been whittled at one end to a very sharp point. "Feeling lucky, *friend*?"

John Richardson's eyes widened as he took a step away from us. A moment later, he withdrew a small stake of his own, glaring at Reggie and Frederick in turn. "As a matter of fact, I do."

Oh, *no.*

"Our other siblings will be disappointed to miss this," John Richardson continued, oblivious to my growing horror. His eyes were sharp as steel and focused only on Reggie as he spun the stake in his hand like a miniature baton.

"Don't call me your sibling," Reggie growled.

"But it's what you are."

"*Fuck* that."

Richardson continued as if Reggie hadn't spoken. "Our siblings and I have been waiting for this retribution for a very long time, Reginald. We *had* hoped we'd all be together when it happened, but you know how it goes." He sighed theatrically. "Beggars, choosers, et cetera. I messaged them before you caught up to me, but they won't be here for at least another twenty minutes due to downtown traffic." His eyes drifted to the clock hanging on the wall above my head as if to check the time. "Pity they're going to miss this. But while they'll be disappointed that I killed you when they're not here to watch, they'd be downright furious with me if I lost this opportunity because I waited to do it until they found parking."

Reggie threw up his hands. "Okay, seriously. Why the *fuck* do you think I was the one who set that fire?" He sounded stretched completely beyond his limit. "Yes, I admit I left that stupid note all those years ago. But there were *so many people* at that party who hated those assholes. Why aren't you out there harassing them?"

"You know what you were like back then," Richardson said, the only answer he seemed inclined to give. He moved closer to Reggie, his stake firmly in hand. He jerked his chin towards me and Frederick. "You can leave," he said. "This doesn't involve either of you."

Frederick scoffed. "You're mad if you think I'm leaving."

I needed to implement the next phase of our plan, right now, before John Richardson and Reggie staked each other into piles of vampire dust.

"Mr. Richardson," I began, far more loudly than was necessary. "You will leave Reginald Cleaves alone, effective immediately, or else face dire consequences with the IRS!" Even as the words left my mouth, I cringed. Suddenly this seemed like the stupidest plan in the history of the world. As threats went, it was at best about a two on the *likely to defuse an escalating vampire fight* scale. But I didn't have a wooden stake handy, and I had a very bitable neck. Tax threats were all I had.

To my shock and relief, it seemed to work. Or at least, it seemed to distract Richardson from his interest in killing Reggie. He blinked a few times, then took a step back as he turned to face me. The murderous look on his face from only moments ago was replaced with one of abject confusion.

"Excuse me?" he said.

"You heard her," Reggie spat.

"I did," he conceded. "I just don't think I understood her. Dire consequences from the IRS?" He sounded genuinely confused. *Good.* Hopefully catching him off guard would increase the odds that our ridiculous plan would work. "You're our accountant, are you not? We're paying you to represent us and keep us out of trouble. Can't you just fix whatever it is we've done wrong?"

Was he joking? "No," I said, incredulous. "The firm is closing your file."

Richardson had the audacity to look surprised. His eyes shot to Reggie, who still looked so menacing with that stake in his hand, I would have been terrified if I didn't know him like I did.

"Does this decision have anything to do with my organization's history vis-à-vis your paramour?" Richardson asked.

Unbelievable. "No," I said, stumbling a little over his use of the term *paramour.* This guy was clearly older than dirt. "Even if threatening to bite your accountant's neck the way you just did wasn't sufficient grounds by itself for a firm to close a file—which it totally is, by the way—your organization is a mess. You've consistently refused to provide us with any of the information we need to do our jobs. We don't have the capacity to work with organizations that waste our time."

"But I sent you everything you asked for," Richardson protested, sounding hurt.

"No, you didn't," I countered. "Everything you sent was so bizarre and so *not* what I needed. I honestly judge myself for not realizing you weren't human right off the bat."

"Oh." For someone who had flashed his fangs at me mere moments ago with what seemed like every intention of tearing out my throat, Richardson was being remarkably contrite. "I apologize. It was never my intention to waste your time."

Reggie snorted. Apparently, he couldn't believe what John Richardson was saying, either.

"But it's not just that you wasted our time," I continued. "Your group is decades out of compliance with IRS requirements for nonprofits. Everything I've seen from you suggests your nonprofit is a sham. And Butyl and Dowidge doesn't represent sham organizations." I paused, letting this sink in. "Even if you hadn't been trying to kill Reggie from the moment you first contacted my firm, you're still the worst client I've ever had."

As I spoke, Richardson simply stood there, processing everything. "How much trouble are we in with the IRS, exactly?"

"A lot," I said. "Though it's hard to say exactly how much. Best-case scenario, they'll dissolve your nonprofit." I shrugged. "When that happens, you'll be getting a bill for back taxes you won't be able to pay, given your nonprofit's annual budget. And the worst-case scenario . . ."

John Richardson leaned forward, hanging on my every word. *Excellent.* "What is the worst-case scenario?"

I waited a beat before answering so my next words would have maximum impact. "Worst-case scenario is the IRS finds that you intentionally withheld taxes you owed. You could face time in jail." There. The closest thing to a mic drop any accountant ever got. I leaned in closer, readying myself for the kill. "Unless, of course, you do exactly what I tell you to do."

Richardson narrowed his eyes at me. "And what might that be?"

Bingo. This was the part I'd been looking forward to the most. The part I'd practiced in a mirror the night before until I'd gotten the ferocity of my expression just right.

"What happens next is you are going to leave Reginald Cleaves alone, forever. If you do that, we will pretend we've never heard of you if the IRS ever comes knocking." I trailed off, letting my words hang in the air for dramatic effect. In the entirety of my time as an accountant, I had never once had the opportunity to do *anything* for dramatic effect. I could all but feel Reggie looking on, beaming with pride. "If you continue to harass Reggie, however, I tell the IRS everything I know."

At my threat, John Richardson's polite demeanor melted away again. "Ah. I see what you're doing." He skewered me with his glare. "This is a conspiracy. You've concocted this . . . this . . . this *blackmail scheme* to save Reginald fucking Cleaves."

"It's not a conspiracy," I said. "I'll send you the relevant code provisions that clearly demonstrate your organization sucks as soon as we're done here. If you still don't believe me after you've read them, ask Evelyn Anderson." I grinned at him. "She has no idea who you really are and would happily confirm that the IRS is going to hate you once it finds out about you."

By this point, the break room partygoers had begun drifting back to their workstations. Among them was Janice, the woman who delivered mail to the thirty-second floor. She peered at us curiously as she made her way to her cubicle, a party hat that said *Forty Is the New Thirty!* on her head.

"Should we continue this discussion somewhere more private?"

Frederick suggested, echoing my own thoughts. "I don't think we want these people to overhear us."

"We're nearly done here," John Richardson snapped. But he leaned in closer to me before speaking again, apparently thinking better of continuing this conversation at full volume. "You can't report us to the IRS if I kill you first," he threatened.

Reggie scoffed. "You're going to attack a human in front of dozens of other people?" He shook his head. "You're letting your feelings get in the way of making good decisions, Johnny boy. Besides, if you kill her, you'll be dead before you draw your next breath."

Reggie said this all so cheerfully it sent chills down my spine. For the first time, I saw a hint of darkness in his expression that made me wonder just what sort of man he'd been before I met him.

"Evelyn Anderson will just report you if I'm too dead to do it," I said, trying my best to stay calm. "Also, Reggie's right. If you kill me here, people will see. If you don't go to jail for tax evasion, you'll go to jail for murder."

"While I'd personally find you lot dying painfully of starvation in a human prison hilarious," Reggie added, "I suspect you wouldn't feel the same way."

"I've heard they even require daily direct exposure to sunlight in prisons," Frederick added, shuddering. "Painful."

John Richardson said nothing for a long moment as he processed our offer. After what felt like an hour, he cleared his throat. "And if we agree to leave Reginald Cleaves alone, you won't talk to the IRS if they come calling?"

I let out a huge internal sigh of relief. "If you back off, yes."

"Do you swear?"

"I swear it on the vows I took when I became a CPA." There

were, of course, no vows you had to take when you became a CPA. But he didn't need to know that. And either way, I was telling the truth.

As I spoke, John Richardson shrank further and further into himself. "What are we going to do?" he asked, so quietly it was clear he was asking himself this question, not us. "We have devoted ourselves to revenge for so long."

"You could always move on from something that happened over a hundred years ago and find a different obsession to occupy the rest of your immortal lives," Frederick suggested. "Your sires wouldn't want you to spend forever bent on revenge."

"How dare you presume to know what they would want?" John Richardson snarled.

"How dare *you* presume to know?" Frederick countered.

"Or," Reggie offered, "if you don't want to diversify your interests like normal people, you could always branch out into conducting a real investigation and finding the person who *actually* set that castle ablaze. In fact—" Reggie snapped his fingers. "I could help you."

John Richardson stared at him. "You would do that?"

"Why not?" Reggie shrugged. "Sounds fun."

"If you *aren't* the person responsible, why didn't you offer to help us before?"

Reggie snorted. "It wasn't until you started sending me death threats that I realized anyone still connected me with The Incident. You'll have to excuse me for not being eager to reach out to you once I realized you wanted me dead." He shook his head. "My instinct, whenever someone wants me dead, is to hide."

John Richardson cracked a weak smile at that. "Fair enough." He then turned to me. "My siblings will be here momentarily. Could we perhaps have some time to discuss the situation before making our decision?" He shook his head. "This is blackmail," he said again, frostily. "But I will impress upon the others that you have put us in a position where we have little choice but to accept your terms. Spending any amount of time in a human prison, locked up and unable to feed, would be—"

He trailed off, shuddering.

For the first time all day, it felt like I could breathe again. This was going to work. "I'll go back to my office and send you the code provisions I just referred to. Talk to your associates about what they want to do, then let me know whether I should close your file or report you to the IRS."

John Richardson consulted his phone. "They're waiting outside the building." He glanced at me. "I will leave and go speak with them right away."

"I'll go with you," Frederick said.

"That won't be necessary," John Richardson said, hastily.

Frederick placed a hand on his arm. "Your group hasn't exactly inspired much confidence in your decision-making since the nineteenth century. We need to make certain you don't double back and return to the building to do something stupid." He turned his attention to me. "I realize this wasn't part of the original plan, but I'd feel better if I saw Mr. Richardson off myself. It's time I got going, anyway. I need to check on Cassie."

I didn't miss the note of concern in his voice when he mentioned Cassie. "Of course," I said. "See him off. And then go check on your fiancée."

Frederick gave Reggie a small nod. "I'll see you back at the apartment."

Reggie and I stared at each other in silence for a long moment after they left. There was still a chance those idiots would come after him, and I didn't think I'd be able to fully relax until we'd gotten their final decision.

"Want to see if they have any red velvet cake left in the break room?" Reggie asked, surprising me. Of all the things I'd thought he might say in this moment, that wasn't even in the top hundred.

"Why?" I asked, confused. "You can't eat it."

"True," he agreed. "But I still don't understand what *red velvet cake* is. And . . ." He trailed off, grinning at me. "I like hearing you explaining things."

And then he kissed me on the cheek so sweetly I couldn't help but agree.

....

From: John Richardson (jhcr12345@countwyatt.org)
To: Amelia Collins (ajcollins@butyldowidge.com)
Subject: your demands

Dear Ms. Collins,

Regarding our discussion earlier today, we agree to your demands (mostly because we realize we have no choice). Effective immediately we will be redirecting our efforts away from our brother Reginald and towards other parties.

For now, however, we agree it best we keep a low profile for a while, on the chance the IRS tries to find us.

All best,
John Richardson

"That went about as well as it could have."

Reggie and I sat together on my living room couch, my head resting on his shoulder. An hour earlier, after depositing a very subdued John Richardson back in the conference room with Evelyn so she could finish up with him, I'd told her I would be taking the rest of the day off. The person I'd been a few weeks ago wouldn't have dreamed of even asking for an afternoon off during tax season. And yet there I had been, setting a firm boundary, and *telling* a partner I wouldn't be reachable until the next day. All because I needed a bit of time off to rest and recuperate from what I'd just accomplished.

I hadn't even needed to look at Reggie's face on the elevator ride down to the lobby to know he'd been beaming with pride.

"It did go pretty well," I agreed. "The Collective is off your back for now, maybe forever. And I got to save the day with tax law." I grinned up at him. "That *never* happens."

Reggie chuckled and pulled me closer. "You were fantastic," he murmured. "You might be the smartest, most determined person I've known in all my more than three hundred years of living." His voice was so soft, his lips gentle against the crown of my head. "The idea that you'd use your talents to help someone like me . . ."

He trailed off, sounding too overcome to finish the thought. He buried his face in my hair on a quiet sigh.

"I don't deserve you," he finally said.

It had started raining at some point after we'd arrived at my apartment. We sat in silence, the sound of raindrops pattering against the windowpanes a soothing backdrop to my swirling thoughts. It was so pleasant, just cuddling with him on my living room sofa, with no plans for the rest of the day and no idea what, if anything, would happen next.

Honestly? I could get used to this.

"You deserve me," I said. "You buy me terrible vegetarian snacks because you don't understand what humans eat but you also don't want me going hungry during a snowstorm. You force me to take time for myself, reminding me in a way I can never seem to remember that I'm worth it. You make me laugh." I grinned at him. "And you think the way I talk about taxes is sexy."

"It *is* sexy."

I laughed. "To you, maybe. No one else thinks so."

He looked horrified. "That cannot possibly be true."

"Oh, but it is." I leaned in close again and rested my forehead against his. "You like me for who, and what, I am. I may not know the specifics of what will come next if we stay together after the wedding, but for the first time in my life, I welcome some happy uncertainty."

Without warning, he tackled me, pressing me back against the couch cushions until I was lying prone beneath him. I yelped in surprise, then sighed a moment later when he settled more comfortably on top of me. His forearms came to rest on either side of my head, bracketing me, his lips less than an inch away from mine.

The look on his face was full of such unbridled joy it took my breath away.

"I meant what I said the other day, Amelia. I will never ask you to change anything about yourself just for me," he murmured. "You are perfect and brilliant, just as you are. Every day you let me be near you will be perfect, too. No matter how many days there are, in the end."

As he kissed me, my mind drifted back to the night we first met. How wild he'd seemed to me then, with his trench coat and impossible questions. How ridiculous a request it had seemed to pretend to laugh with him.

I don't know how to pretend, I'd explained.

Maybe I'd gotten a little better at pretending since then. How fittingly ironic it was that now, at Gretchen's wedding, there would be no more pretending between us at all.

EPILOGUE

**Letter from Zelda Turret, formerly Grizelda Watson,
to Reginald Cleaves**

Hey Reg,

It's been a while. How's tricks, kid?

*I wanted to let you know that those losers who chased
you around all those years somehow found their way to my
yoga retreat out here in Napa. (I'm in Napa now by the way.
Wild, right???) I don't know if they're here because they're
turning over a new leaf from the nonsense vendetta
business, or if they're here to sniff around for evidence they'll
never find (I remain eternally grateful that there was no
CSI: Sevastapol in 1872). Either way, everyone in the world
is right about how annoying they are.*

*The good news is they seem to have forgotten all about
you. The bad news is now they're my problem (though I have
a plan in place for if they get too snoopy).*

Keep it real, friend. If you ever happen to be out this way let me know and I'll show you around.

Grizzy

ps: Thank you, by the way, for keeping my name out of this mess all these years. You're a real one.

....

ONE MONTH LATER

"Reginald." Dad's voice was patient, if not a little patronizing. "It's okay. No one ever beats me at Trivial Pursuit."

Dad was dressed for Gretchen's wedding, sitting on his living room couch wearing the smug look he got whenever he won this game. Which was basically every time he played.

Reggie was dressed for the wedding, too, wearing his new charcoal-gray suit that looked just as gorgeous on him as it had when he tried it on for me last week. I still couldn't believe Frederick and I convinced him to wear a conventional suit today instead of one of his more eclectic outfits, but it meant a lot to me that he'd agreed.

He didn't seem to notice I was watching them from the doorway. What he *did* seem was outraged. He turned on my dad. "You don't understand," he said. "The answers on the back of that little card are wrong. I was *there*."

Dad stared at him. "You were in Constantinople in 1835?"

That was my cue to intervene. So far, Sam was the only person in the family who knew what Reggie really was. It was important to Reggie that it stay that way, at least until we could determine how my family would react to the truth.

I cleared my throat, and two pairs of eyes snapped to mine.

"Almost ready to go?" I asked.

Reggie seemed to come back to himself, as if my presence reminded him that while he and my dad had gotten on like a house on fire since they started spending time together, spitting facts about the nineteenth-century Ottoman Empire was not something that could ever happen.

He sat down in the chair opposite my dad, his posture relaxing slightly. "We're almost done here."

"I'd say we're entirely done here," Dad said, cheerfully.

Reggie groaned. "Fair enough." And then to my dad he added, "I apologize for my outburst. I'm a bit of a sore loser."

Dad chuckled. "Happens to the best of us. That said, even though I won this game—"

"Which was probably due at least partly to your having memorized all the answers over the past twenty years," I quipped.

Dad gave me a sly, incriminating smile, but didn't deny my accusation. "As I was saying, Reggie, even though I won, you are *very* good at the history questions." He peered at him. "You said you were in tech support for a while, but you must have also taken a lot of history courses in college."

He shook his head. "I'm self-taught."

"Self-taught? Meaning, you watch a lot of the History Channel? You read biographies?"

"Uh . . ." Reggie reached up and rubbed at the back of his neck. "Something like that. Though most of what I've seen on the History Channel is overdramatized nonsense."

Dad was positively beaming now. "That's what I've always said!"

"Like that dumb thing they put on a few years ago about Archduke Ferdinand?"

Dad scoffed. "Trash. If you want, I can recommend you a *real* documentary about Archduke Ferdinand that will change everything you thought you knew about the start of World War I."

Reggie looked delighted. He opened his mouth to say something else, and I rushed into the room in case he blurted out something that would incriminate himself and alarm Dad.

"As glad as I am that the two of you are getting along so well," I said, "we do really need to get going. Mom left twenty minutes ago. And Reggie, you said you'd help me with my makeup."

Reggie's eyes widened a little in surprise, as though he'd forgotten all about Gretchen's wedding. "You're right," he agreed. Turning back to my dad, he said, "Any chance we can continue this later? You're a fascinating conversationalist."

My dad chuckled at that, eyes twinkling. "If I had a nickel for every time someone said that to me, I'd have a nickel." And then, to me, he added, in a conspiratorial whisper, "This one's a keeper, Ame."

Something warm and lovely bloomed in my chest at his words. And at the realization that my dad approved of someone so important to me.

Later, after Dad had left to finish getting ready himself, I grabbed Reggie's arm and gave it a gentle squeeze. "Thanks for making an effort to talk to Dad about history," I said. "Ever since he retired, he hasn't had anyone to talk to about this stuff."

"I know the feeling," Reggie said, wistfully. "And it's my sincere pleasure."

....

"HOLD STILL."

"I am holding still."

Reggie gave me a skeptical look. "You keep jerking away from me."

"That's because you keep coming at my eyes with a stick with black sludge on it."

He chuckled, then set the stick in question down on my parents' downstairs bathroom counter. "Some people call this mascara. And you don't have to be so petulant." He leaned forward, lightly kissing my cheek. "You *asked* me to do this. Remember?"

"Sorry," I said. "I don't wear makeup often. I haven't had somebody apply it for me since I was in high school, and Sophie and I were getting ready for prom."

"Then how fitting it is to have your boyfriend do it for you as we get ready for your cousin's wedding."

My boyfriend. A pleasant shiver went through me. "I think it will be easier if I do this myself.."

"Maybe," he said. "But I love doing makeup."

That shouldn't have surprised me, knowing Reggie. "You do?"

He pulled out an eyebrow pencil and drew a line just above each of my eyebrows. "I do," he confirmed. "Doing stage makeup was one of my favorite pastimes in the 1970s." He set the pencil down on the counter and grinned at me. "There. Now look at yourself in the mirror and tell me that you don't look fabulous."

Fabulous was not the word I would have used to describe my appearance. My hair was so teased and sprayed I would have looked more at home in an '80s hair band than Gretchen's wedding. And he'd used more black eyeliner on me than I'd worn cumulatively my entire life.

"I look like an electrocuted raccoon," I mused. "Aunt Sue will lose her shit if I show up looking like this."

Reggie put his thumb beneath my chin, tilting it up a little so he could examine my face. "Probably," he admitted. "I'll take it down a notch. Or possibly ten notches. By the way, I deserve an award for keeping my hands above your shoulders this entire time. It's unfair that kissing you right now will ruin my work." He turned my chin again so that I had to look into his eyes. "Incidentally, do you have any idea how brilliant you are?"

It didn't matter how often he'd said it to me by that point. My face warmed at the genuine affection in his voice as though it was the first time. I reached up and tangled my fingers through his hair because I knew he liked it when I messed it all up.

"Tell me again?" I asked.

It was the only incentive he seemed to need to lean in and brush his lips against mine. "So brilliant," he said. "The *most* brilliant. There are no words."

When he pulled back to run a washcloth beneath the faucet, I stilled his hand. "We still have a little time, don't we?" I wanted to kiss him properly before we left for the wedding.

"A little," he agreed. "But not enough for me to do what I want to do to you."

He caught up my mouth in another kiss, this time with more heat behind it. "What do you want to do to me?" I asked, already breathing hard.

He sighed and rested his forehead against mine. "I want to skip the wedding and get you back to my apartment."

"To do what?" I asked, innocently.

He gave me a wicked grin, then pushed me back until I was pinned between his body and the wall.

"We don't have time for this," I laughed. Reggie kissed up the column of my throat, undeterred, inching up the skirt of my sky-blue sheath dress until it bunched at my waist. I swatted playfully at his shoulder. "You'll get my dress all wrinkled."

"I don't care. Let's take it off." He slipped a hand between us, pressing the heel of his palm against the sensitive place that in only a month's time he'd already come to know so well. He'd been insatiable ever since we got word his pursuers had gone into hiding. So had I. I writhed against him, unable to help myself. "Do we really have to go to this thing?"

His fangs were out; I could feel their faint impression against my throat. I groaned with renewed desire. He'd bitten me a few times by that point, shocking me with how much I enjoyed it.

With how much I craved it.

But we didn't have time for this now.

I pulled his hand away from my body, then laughed breathlessly at his forlorn sigh. "Yes, we have to go to the wedding. This wedding was why I asked you out in the first place."

"You asked me out to show your family you weren't single," he said. "We've already done that." He dipped his head again and began worrying at my clavicle with his tongue.

He's right, I thought, as I gave in to sensation. Not only did my family know we were a couple, but my parents *liked* him.

But we couldn't bail on Gretchen's wedding. That would be wrong, even if in the moment I couldn't remember why.

I pushed at Reggie's shoulders until he relented and took a small step back. "I promise we can do this after the reception," I managed. "We can even leave early."

Reggie pouted like a child whose candy had just been taken away. God, he was adorable. "You promise?"

"I promise," I said. I wanted this as badly as he did. "Now let's get this makeup off my face, and then head to the ceremony before anyone wonders where we are."

....

"READY?"

"I'm ready," I said, smiling up at Reggie from where he stood just outside my car. "Let's go in."

When I'd gotten the invitation to this wedding six weeks ago, I'd initially rolled my eyes at Gretchen holding it at the same country club all our cousins had used. But Reggie couldn't go inside any sort of Christian church without, apparently, bursting into flames. (*Inconvenient*, he'd said, when he told me.)

In hindsight, I was grateful for Gretchen's lack of originality.

Aunt Sue had done a great job with the decorations. She and Uncle Bill must have spent a fortune on the flowers draped over the bannisters and all the guests' chairs. The space had been so elaborately done up that if I squinted I could almost pretend I hadn't been to five other family weddings in this exact location over the past two years.

"We should sit near the back," Reggie murmured, once we were inside. "That way I can slide my hand up your leg and whisper filthy things into your ear when I get bored."

He winked lasciviously at me.

"Behave," I warned, though I was trying not to laugh. The string ensemble from the high school where my mom had taught was playing a passable version of Pachelbel's *Canon*. I willed myself to focus on the music to distract myself from how brilliantly the sunlight streaming in through the windows brought out the blue of Reggie's eyes.

"I do what I want," he countered, his eyes twinkling with amusement. "I'll behave if it suits me." But he sat beside me in one of the back rows without further comment, taking my hand in his.

People began filing into the room in greater numbers, and it wasn't long before I saw relatives I hadn't seen since the last family wedding. Several of my mom's siblings sat towards the front of the room, casting warm smiles at Aunt Sue. Sarah, the cousin who two years ago had sent her wedding invitation to my office instead of my apartment, sat a few rows back, her husband on one side of her and her father on the other.

I couldn't be sure, but Sarah looked about five months pregnant. If she was, that meant a family baby shower invitation would be coming in my near future.

Most of my relatives smiled when they saw me, a moment before their eyes slid to Reggie. If he noticed their appraising glances, he showed no sign of caring. He was busy murmuring a quiet running commentary into my ear. He had a lot to say on everyone's outfits, the flowers, and the musical missteps of those poor high school musicians who were definitely just doing their best.

"When will parachute pants *finally* come back into style?" he mused quietly, as my cousin Elaine, who I'd never seen in anything but skintight leather pants, sat directly in front of us. Today's pair was a deep shade of burgundy. "Now *that* was fashion."

As if Elaine had guessed he was talking about her, she turned around in her seat to face us. "Isn't this place gorgeous?" she asked on a sigh.

"Yes," Reggie said. But he kept his gaze on me. "It's the most beautiful thing I've ever seen."

I couldn't help but grin at him.

A few months ago, being in that country club around so much family and their judgments would have been crushing. But sitting next to Reggie made being here easy. Reggie making me laugh, sitting beside me holding my hand . . .

It made it hard to focus on anything but him, and how happy I was.

When Gretchen walked down the aisle on her father's arm some minutes later, beautiful and smiling in her wedding dress, my mind drifted to all the times Reggie had said he'd never demand forever from me. *What if later on* I'm *the one who wants forever?* I wanted to ask him now.

I glanced at Reggie out of the corner of my eye. He was still unabashedly looking back at me, not at the bride, with an intensity I would have given anything to parse.

I covered his hand that rested on my leg and gave it a gentle squeeze.

And then the ceremony began, and all opportunity for conversation ended.

....

THE CEREMONY WAS LOVELY.

Gretchen said her vows with the practiced grace her years of voice training had given her. Josh stumbled a bit over his own vows on account of the tears welling in his eyes.

It had all been very sweet. And Reggie had stayed remarkably well-behaved through most of it, aside from the two times he had, as promised, leaned over to whisper such dirty things to me my face turned red.

"It's a good thing you kept your voice down," I said as we watched people file out of the room and make their way to the ballroom. "If Dad had overheard the weird sex stuff you just proposed doing to his only daughter, he would definitely retract his good opinion of you."

"I'm not sure that's true," Reggie said, grinning. "Your dad loves me."

"He does like you reasonably well," I teased. A massive understatement. "But he has his limits."

Reggie winked at me. "Worth it, if any of what I said made you smile."

The reception was already underway by the time we got there, arm in arm. The ballroom, just like the room where the ceremony had taken place, was bedecked in flowers. Aunt Sue had really gone all out. Lilies of the valley and chrysanthemums trailed along bannisters and railings, and large topiaries were stationed on either side of the ballroom entrance. People were already mingling at the bar with wineglasses in hand as the DJ began setting up for whatever he had planned for the evening.

"Don't look now," Reggie murmured, pulling me close, "but one of your relatives is heading straight for us."

"Who?" I whispered back.

"Here you two are." My sister-in-law Jess was smiling broadly at us and holding a glass of white wine. "That was such a lovely ceremony, don't you think?"

"It was," I agreed, smiling back at her.

"And that dress!" Jess waved dramatically with her free hand. "Gorgeous! You know, I heard she went to *New York* for it."

My eyebrows shot up in surprise. "Really? Why?" There were plenty of dress boutiques in Chicago, weren't there?

Jess shrugged and took a sip from her glass. "Who knows?" she asked. "Maybe it's just a rumor."

"Sounds like the kind of thing a jealous friend might make up and spread around behind her back," Reggie mused, stroking his chin thoughtfully.

I playfully elbowed him in the ribs, but I was laughing. "How would *you* know that?"

Jess watched us with amusement. "You make such an adorable couple. Any chance you two will be next?"

Reggie's hand froze where it rested at the small of my back.

Oh, god.

Fortunately, my brother Adam appeared a moment later. "Jess," he chastised. "Leave them alone."

"I was just teasing," she insisted. She said more words to that effect, but I wasn't listening anymore. I'd been expecting this kind of nonsense from *somebody* tonight, but I hadn't prepared Reggie enough for the actual reality of it happening.

When Jess and Adam left to go find my parents a few moments later, I turned to him to apologize on behalf of my sister-in-law. He regarded me with an anxious expression I'd never seen him wear before.

"Reggie, I'm so sorry." And then, in a quieter voice, I added, "This is exactly the sort of bullshit my family does. I should have warned you."

"Dance with me?" he asked abruptly. His voice was strained.

Of course he wanted to leave where most of the guests were still mingling and get away from my family. I didn't blame him. "Sure," I said.

And then, a moment later, the Chicken Dance polka started playing.

Groans and laughter filled the ballroom. People of all ages began tugging reluctant dance partners onto the dance floor. My parents were among them, Mom laughing and trying to fend Dad off as he pulled her from her chair.

"On second thought, let's sit this one out," I said.

Reggie looked like I'd just proposed chopping off his arm. "You must be joking," he said, horrified. He was already making his way to where dancers were assembling, hand around my wrist as he attempted to bring me with him. "I never miss a good Chicken Dance."

"Are you serious?"

"As the bubonic plague." I tried to protest, but Reggie was towing me behind him with the kind of excitement I hadn't seen in another person since we'd taken my nieces to Disney World.

We stopped when we got to the far end of the dance floor, a fair distance away from most of the other dancers. If *dancers* was even the right word to describe my flailing relatives. Reggie's eyes were bright with joy.

"Dance with me?" he asked again, hopeful.

I swallowed. "I don't know how."

"You don't know how to do the Chicken Dance?" He stared at me. "Really?"

I shook my head. "I've never learned."

"But it's easy," he said. "You just flap your arms and spin around."

Behind us, my parents, Aunt Sue and Uncle Bill, and many of Gretchen's friends were already flapping their arms, spinning each other in circles, and laughing uproariously. "It does look easy," I admitted. "This probably won't surprise you, but I usually steer clear of dancing at weddings. But . . ." I trailed off and moved closer to Reggie. I looped my arms around his neck, pulling him close. "It seems like the sort of dance you could teach me."

"Oh, it is," he agreed.

Then he kissed me.

I'd seen movies that ended where the main couple kissed at someone else's wedding. Mostly at Sophie's behest. The swelling music, the romantic crescendo had always seemed overdone and cheesy. Here, though, with family I knew and people I didn't flapping their arms and laughing all around us, kissing Reggie felt like the most perfect, romantic thing to have ever happened.

"Promise you will never leave me," he said, a minute or an hour later. He'd told me recently that he didn't technically need oxygen, but he was breathing hard all the same. "I told myself I wouldn't ask anything of you that you weren't willing to give, and I meant that. But here, at this wedding, with your cousin and her husband promising to love each other forever, and your sister-in-law asking if we might be next . . ."

The music to the Chicken Dance ended. People were swaying where they stood as a waltz began playing. Reggie and I didn't move, his arms still around me as my entire world tilted sharply on its axis.

"Reggie . . ." I began, then trailed off because I had no idea how to finish my thought. *I need to think this through* and *falling for a vampire was never the plan I had for my life* were locked in fierce battle in my mind with *I always want to laugh as much as I do when I'm with you* and *I think I might be in love with you* and *yes, yes, yes.*

When I didn't reply, Reggie began fidgeting. "All I've been able to think about this whole time," he said, "this entire day, is how I never want to let you go."

"Me, too." The words were out of my mouth before I could let my brain ruin this. "Me very too."

He closed his eyes and pulled me close. Slowly, we began to sway in time with the swelling music. "Come home with me tonight," he said. "We can figure out what our *forever* looks like together."

As I let him lead me through the steps of the dance, I knew there was nothing I wanted more.

ACKNOWLEDGMENTS

The process of writing a book looks different every time. Writing my first book involved overcoming both the terror of having my words read by people I'd never met before and a lifelong case of imposter syndrome. Writing my second book involved speaking into various forms of speech recognition software and glaring at my right elbow, wishing it worked properly and without pain.

Early in the drafting process of *My Vampire Plus-One* I developed elbow tendinitis (contracted after a particularly intense bout of knitting, a passion since childhood). While writing this book I had to accept all sorts of unpleasant truths about aging and how neither Reginald nor I were twenty-eight anymore, but the most tragic realization was that I have to say goodbye forever to the way I've always written. Specifically: lounging on the couch with my arms at ergonomically disastrous angles, surrounded by half-empty cans of Diet Coke and my indulgent cats.

Now, I must work at a *desk*. In a *chair*. Sometimes life isn't fair.

At least the part where I'm surrounded by cats and Diet Cokes hasn't changed.

All of that said, writing *My Vampire Plus-One* was just plain *fun*. Reginald is one of my favorite characters I've ever written and has been since his first appearance in *My Roommate Is a Vampire*. I've heard from readers around the world that Reggie is their favorite character from my books, too, which is so gratifying. I hope you enjoyed reading about his escapades here even half as much as I enjoyed writing them.

So many people have worked behind the scenes to bring you this book. Thank you to my agent, Gaia Banks, who took me in when I needed her and gave me the confidence I needed to make this book the best it could be. I am forever grateful to my genius editor, Kristine Swartz, without whom I suspect none of my books would have endings. Mary Baker has been instrumental in making sure I make all my deadlines and keep track of who needs what and when. Thank you as well to managing editor Christine Legon and production editor Stacy Edwards for their work in making this book readable and beautiful. Thank you, too, to Roxie Vizcarra and Colleen Reinhart for creating an absolutely showstopping cover for Reggie and Amelia's story. Thank you to Tawanna Sullivan and Emilie Mills in subrights; my publicist, Yazmine Hassan; and Hannah Engler in marketing for working tirelessly to bring this story to readers. Thank you to Kim Lionetti for her help in the earliest stages of making this book a reality.

And now to my emotional support humans! Thank you to Katie Shepard, Celia Winters, and Rebecca Gardner, for being the amazingly hilarious people you are. (And thank you to Shep for not only giving me critically helpful feedback but also for demanding I start playing Baldur's Gate 3 as a reward after meeting an especially tight deadline, thereby introducing me to our newest fictional boyfriend, Astarion.) Thank you to my darling friend Heidi Harper, who read an early draft of this book and told me it was good at a time I really needed to hear it. Thank you to Thea Guanzon and Elizabeth Davis, my darling Taylor Swift somme- liers, and to Sarah Hawley, whose friendship has been a source of much-needed validation (and levity) throughout. And of course, I'd be remiss if I didn't give a huge thank-you to the Berkletes for their wit, wisdom, and friendship.

I could not have written this book without the wonderful sup- port system I have at home. Brian and Allison, you are my every- thing. I could not do any of what I do without your endless encouragement. Thank you to my parents, who claim to be proud of me regardless of whether I do lawyer things like I origi- nally trained for or write vampire rom-coms instead. And thank you to my siblings, Gabe and Erica, for being all-around wonder- ful human beings.

Finally, I want to give a special thank-you to everyone who read my first novel and wanted to know if Reggie was getting a book, too. I wouldn't be able to do any of this without you. I can't wait to write more stories for you. From the bottom of my heart, thank you.

Jenna

Keep reading for an excerpt from
Cassie and Frederick's story in . . .

MY ROOMMATE IS A VAMPIRE

Roommate Wanted to Share Spacious Third-Floor Brownstone Apartment in Lincoln Park

Hello. I seek a roommate with whom to share my apartment. It is a spacious unit by modern standards with two large bedrooms, an open sitting area, and a semiprofessional eat-in kitchen. Large windows flank the eastern side of the apartment and provide a striking view of the lake. The unit is fully furnished in a tasteful, classical style. I am seldom home after sundown, so if you work a traditional schedule, you will usually have the apartment to yourself.

Rent: $200 per month. No pets, please. Kindly direct all serious inquiries to fjfitzwilliam@gmail.com.

"THERE HAS TO BE SOMETHING WRONG WITH THIS PLACE."

"Cassie, listen, this is a really good deal—"

"*Forget* it, Sam." That last part came out more forcefully than I'd intended—though not by much. Even though I needed his help, my embarrassment over being in this situation in the first place made accepting that help difficult. Sam meant well, but his insistence on involving himself in every part of my current situation was getting on my very last nerve.

To his credit, Sam—my oldest friend, who'd long ago acclimated to how snippy I sometimes got when I was stressed—said nothing. He simply folded his arms across his chest, waiting for me to be ready to say more.

I only needed a few moments to pull myself together and start feeling badly for snapping at him. "Sorry," I muttered under my breath. "I know you're only trying to help."

"It's all right," he said, sympathetic. "You have a lot going on. But it's okay to believe that things can get better."

I had no reason to believe that things could get better, but now wasn't the time to get into it. I simply sighed and turned my attention back to the Craigslist ad on my laptop.

"Anything that sounds too good to be true usually is."

Sam peered over my shoulder at my screen. "Not always. And you have to admit this apartment sounds great."

It did sound great. He was right about that. But . . .

"It's only two hundred a month, Sam."

"So? That's a great price."

I stared at him. "Yeah, if this were 1978. If someone's only asking for two hundred a month today there are probably dead bodies in the basement."

"You don't know that." Sam dragged a hand through his shaggy, dirty-blond hair. Messing with his hair was Sam's most obvious *I'm-bullshitting-you* tell. He'd had it since at least sixth grade, when he'd tried convincing our teacher I hadn't been the one who'd drawn bright pink flowers all over the wall of the girl's bathroom. He hadn't fooled Mrs. Baker then—I *had* drawn that aggressively neon meadow landscape—and he wasn't fooling me now.

How would he ever make it as a lawyer with such a terrible poker face?

"Maybe this person's just not home a lot and only wants a roommate for safety reasons, not income," Sam suggested. "Maybe they're an idiot and don't know what they *could* be charging."

I was still skeptical. I'd been scouring Craigslist and Facebook since my landlord taped an eviction notice to my front door two weeks ago for nonpayment of rent. There'd been nothing available this close to the Loop for less than a thousand a month. In Lincoln Park, the going rate was closer to fifteen hundred.

Two hundred wasn't just a little below market rate. It wasn't even in the same universe as market rate.

"There are also no pictures with this ad," I pointed out. "That's another red flag. I should ignore this one and keep looking." Because yes, my landlord was taking me to court next week if I didn't move out first, and *yes*, living in an apartment this cheap would really help me get on top of my shit, and maybe even keep me from ending up in this exact situation again in a few months. But I'd lived in the Chicago area for more than ten years. No deal in Lincoln Park *this* good came without a huge catch.

"Cassie." Sam's tone was quiet, patient—and more than a little patronizing. I reminded myself he was only trying to help in his very *Sam* way and bit my tongue. "This apartment is in a great location. You can easily afford it. It's close enough to the El that you'll be able to get to your jobs quickly. And if the windows are as big as this ad says they are, I bet there's tons of natural light."

My eyes widened. I hadn't thought of the lighting in the

apartment when I'd read the ad. But if it did have huge, lake-facing windows, Sam was probably right.

"Maybe I'd be able to create from home again," I mused. I hadn't lived somewhere with good enough lighting to work on my projects in almost two years. I missed it more than I liked to admit.

Sam smiled, looking relieved. "Exactly."

"Okay," I conceded. "I'm at least willing to ask for more information."

Sam reached up and put his hand on my shoulder. His warm, steady touch calmed me, just as it had every time I'd needed it to since we were kids. The knot of anxiety that had taken up what felt like permanent residence in the pit of my stomach these past two weeks began to loosen.

For the first time in ages, it felt like I could breathe again.

"We'll see the apartment and meet the roommate first, of course," he said very quickly. "I can even help you negotiate a month-to-month lease if you want. That way, if it's really awful, you can leave without breaking another lease."

Which would mean I wouldn't have to worry about getting hauled back into court by yet another angry landlord. Honestly, that would be a decent compromise. If this person turned out to be an axe murderer or a libertarian or some other awful thing, a month-to-month lease would let me leave quickly with no strings attached.

"You'd do that for me?" I asked. Not for the first time, I felt badly about how short I'd been with him lately.

"What else am I gonna do with my law degree?"

"For starters, you could use it to make tons of money at your firm instead of using it to help perennial fuckups like me."

"I'm making tons of money at my firm either way," he said,

grinning. "But since you won't let me loan you any of that money—"

"I won't," I agreed. It had been my choice to get an impractical graduate degree and end up hopelessly in student loan debt with few job prospects for my troubles. I wasn't about to make that anyone else's problem.

Sam sighed. "You won't. Right. We've been over that. Repeatedly." He shook his head and added, in a more wistful tone, "I wish you could just move in with us, Cassie. Or with Amelia. That would solve everything."

I bit my lip and pretended to study the Craigslist ad intensely to avoid having to look at him.

In truth, a large part of me was relieved that Sam and his new husband Scott had just bought a tiny lakefront condo that barely accommodated them and their two cats. While living with them would save me the stress and the hassle of what I was going through now, Sam and Scott had just gotten married two months ago. Not only would my living with them hinder their ability to have sex wherever and whenever they felt like it, the way I understood newlyweds tended to, it would also be an awkward reminder of just how long it had been since I'd last been in a relationship.

As well as a constant reminder of what a colossal failure every *other* aspect of my life was.

And, of course, living with Amelia was out of the question. Sam didn't understand that his straitlaced, perfect sister had always looked down on me and thought I was a total loser. But it was the truth.

Honestly, my finding a place to live that was neither Sam and Scott's new sofa nor Amelia's loft in Lakeview was best for all of us.

"I'll be fine," I said, trying to sound like I believed it. My stomach clenched a little at the look of concern that crossed Sam's face. "No, really—I'll be okay. I always am, aren't I?"

Sam smiled and tousled my too-short hair, which was his way of teasing me. Normally I didn't mind, but I'd cut my hair pretty dramatically on a whim a couple weeks ago because I was frustrated and needed an outlet that didn't require an internet connection. It was yet another of my not-great recent decisions. My thick, curly blond hair tended to stick up in odd places if not cut by a professional. In that moment, as Sam continued to mess with my hair, I probably looked like a Muppet who'd recently stuck her finger in a light socket.

"Stop that," I said, laughing as I shrugged away from him. But my mood was better now—which was probably exactly why Sam had done it.

He put his hand on my shoulder. "If you ever change your mind about the loan . . ."

He trailed off without finishing his sentence.

"If I change my mind about a loan, you'll be the first to know," I said. But we both knew I never would.

....

I WAITED UNTIL I WAS AT MY AFTERNOON GIG AT THE PUB-lic library to reach out to the person with the two-hundred-dollar room for rent.

Of all the part-time, not-art-related gigs I'd managed to string together since getting my MFA, this one was my favorite. Not because I loved all aspects of the work, because I didn't. While it was great being around books, I worked exclusively in the children's section. I alternated between sitting behind the check-out counter, shelving books about dinosaurs and warrior cats and dragons, and answering questions from frantic parents with tan-truming preschoolers in tow.

I'd always gotten along well with older kids. And I liked tiny humans as an abstract concept, understanding—in theory, at least—why a person might intentionally add one to their life. But while Sam and I definitely thought of his spoiled kitties as his children, nobody in my life had an actual *human* child yet. Dealing with little kids twenty hours a week in a public-facing service position was a rough introduction.

Working at the library was still my favorite part-time job, though, because of all the downtime that came with it. I didn't have nearly as much free time during my shifts at Gossamer's, the coffee shop near my soon-to-be-former apartment—which was the *worst* aspect of that particular job.

"Slow afternoon today," my manager Marcie quipped from her chair beside me. Marcie was a pleasant woman in her late fifties and effectively ran the children's section. It was our little inside joke to comment on how slow it was when we worked to-gether in the afternoon, because *every* afternoon was slow here. Between the hours of one and four, most of our patrons were ei-ther napping or still in school.

It was two o'clock. Only one kid had wandered through in the past ninety minutes. Not only was that nothing noteworthy, it was par for the course.

"It *is* slow today," I agreed, grinning at her. With that, I turned to face the circulation desk computer.

Normally, library downtime was for researching potential new employers and applying for jobs. I wasn't picky. I'd apply for just about anything—even if it had nothing to do with art—if it promised better pay and more regular hours than my current cobbled-together situation.

Sometimes, I used the time to think through future art projects. I didn't have good lighting in my current apartment, which made drawing and painting the images that formed the base of my works difficult. And while I couldn't finish my projects at the library, as my paints were too messy and the final steps involved incorporating discarded objects into my work, the circulation desk was big and well-lit enough for me to at least make preliminary sketches with a pencil.

Today, though, I needed to use my downtime to reply to that red flag of a Craigslist ad. I could have replied earlier, but I didn't—partly because I was still skeptical, but mostly because a few weeks ago I'd gotten rid of Wi-Fi to save money.

I pulled up the listing on the computer. It hadn't changed in the time since I last saw it. The oddly formal style was the same. The absurd rent amount was also the same and set off as many alarm bells now as it did when I first saw it.

But my financial situation also hadn't changed. Jobs in my field were still as hard to come by. And asking Sam for help—or my accountant parents, who loved me too much to admit to my face what a disappointment I was—was just as unthinkable as ever.

And my landlord was still planning to evict me next week. Which, to be fair, I couldn't even blame him for. He'd put up with a lot of late rent payments and art-related welding mishaps these past ten months. If I were him I'd probably evict me, too.

Before I could talk myself out of doing it, and with Sam's worried voice ringing in my ears, I opened my email. I scrolled through my inbox—an ad for a two-for-one sale at Shoe Pavilion; a headline from the *Chicago Tribune* about a bizarre string of local blood bank break-ins—and then started typing.

From: Cassie Greenberg [csgreenberg@gmail.com]
To: fjfitzwilliam@gmail.com
Subject: Your apartment listing

Hi,

I saw your ad on Craigslist looking for a roommate. My
lease is up soon and your place sounds perfect. I'm a
32-year-old art teacher and have lived in Chicago for
ten years. I'm a nonsmoker, no pets. You said in your ad
that you aren't home much at night. As for me, I'm
almost never home during the day, so this arrangement
would work out well for both of us, I think.

I'm guessing you've gotten a lot of inquiries about your
apartment given the location, price, and everything else.
But just in case the room is still available, I've included a
list of references. I hope to hear from you soon.

Cassie Greenberg

A pang of guilt shot through me over how much I'd fudged
some of the important details.

For one thing, I'd just told this complete stranger that I was an
art teacher. *Technically*, that was the truth. It's what I'd studied to be
in college, and it isn't that I didn't *want* to teach. But in my junior
year of college I fell in love with applied arts and design beyond all
hope of reason, and then in my senior year I took a course where we
studied Robert Rauschenberg and his method of combining paint-
ings with sculpture work. And that was it for me. Immediately after
graduation I threw myself into an MFA in applied arts and design.

I loved every second of it.

Until, of course, I graduated. That's when I learned, in a hurry, that my artistic vision and my skill set were too niche to appeal to most school districts hiring art teachers. University art departments were more open-minded, but getting anything more stable than a temporary adjunct position at a university was like winning the lottery. I sometimes made extra cash at art shows when someone who, like me, saw a kind of ironic beauty in rusted-out Coke cans worked into seaside landscapes and bought one of my pieces. But that didn't happen often. So yes: while technically I was an art teacher, most of my income since getting my MFA had come from low-paying, part-time jobs like this one.

None of this made me sound like an appealing potential tenant. Neither did the fact that my *references* weren't former landlords—none of whom would have good things to say about me—but just Sam, Scott, and my mom. Even if I was a disappointment to my parents, they wouldn't want their only child to become homeless.

After a few moments of angsting about it, I decided it didn't matter if I'd told a few white lies. I closed my eyes and hit *send*. What was the worst that could happen? This person—a perfect stranger—would find out I'd stretched the truth and wouldn't let me move in?

I wasn't sure I wanted the apartment anyway.

I had less than ten minutes to worry about it before I got a reply.

From: Frederick J. Fitzwilliam [fjfitzwilliam@gmail.com]
To: Cassie Greenberg [csgreenberg@gmail.com]
Subject: Your apartment listing

Dear Miss Greenberg,

Thank you for your kind message expressing interest in my extra room. As mentioned in the advertisement

the room is appointed in a modern but tasteful style. I
believe, and have been told by others, that it is also
quite spacious insofar as spare rooms are concerned.
To answer your unasked question: the room remains
entirely available, should you remain interested in it.
Do let me know at your earliest convenience whether
you would like to move in and I will have the
necessary paperwork drawn up for your signature.

Yours in good health,
Frederick J. Fitzwilliam

I stared at that name at the end of the email.

Frederick J. Fitzwilliam?

What kind of name was that?

I read the email again, trying to make sense of it as Marcie
pulled out her phone for her daily Facebook scrolling.

So, the person listing the apartment was a guy. Or, at least,
someone with a traditionally male name. That didn't faze me. If
I moved in with him, Frederick wouldn't be the first guy I'd lived
with since moving out of my parents' house.

What did faze me, though, was . . . everything else. The
email was so strangely worded and so formal, I had to wonder exactly how old this person was. And then there was the
weird assumption that I might be willing to move in sight un-
seen.

I tried to ignore these misgivings, reminding myself that all I
really cared about was that the apartment was in decent shape
and that he wasn't an axe murderer.

I needed to see the place, and meet Frederick J. Fitzwilliam
in person, before making up my mind.

From: Cassie Greenberg [csgreenberg@gmail.com]
To: Frederick J. Fitzwilliam [fjfitzwilliam@gmail.com]
Subject: Your apartment listing

Hi Frederick,

I'm super glad it's still available. The description sounds great and I'd like to come see it. I'm free tomorrow around noon if that works for you. Also, could you send me a few pictures? There weren't any with the Craigslist ad, and I'd like to see some before stopping by. Thanks!—Cassie

Once again, I had to wait only a few minutes before receiving a reply.

From: Frederick J. Fitzwilliam [fjfitzwilliam@gmail.com]
To: Cassie Greenberg [csgreenberg@gmail.com]
Subject: Your apartment listing

Hello again, Miss Greenberg,

You are welcome to visit the apartment. It makes perfect sense that you would wish to see it before making your decision. I am afraid I will be indisposed tomorrow during the noon hour. Might you be free sometime after sundown? I am typically at my best during the evening hours.

Per your request, I have attached photographs of two rooms that you would likely use with frequency should you move in. The first is of my spare bedroom as it is currently decorated. (You may, of course, change the decor however you wish should you decide to live here.) The second photograph is of the kitchen. (I thought I had included both photographs when I placed the advertisement on Craigslist. Perhaps I did it incorrectly?)

Yours in good health,
Frederick J. Fitzwilliam

After reading through Frederick's email I clicked on the pictures he sent me, and . . .

Whoa.

Whoa.

Okay.

I didn't know what this dude's deal was, but he *clearly* did not live in the same socioeconomic sphere as me. It was also possible we didn't live in the same century.

This kitchen wasn't just different from every other kitchen in every other place I'd ever lived.

It looked like it belonged to an entirely different era.

Nothing in it looked like it had been made within the last fifty years. The fridge was oddly shaped, sort of oval at the top and much smaller than most fridges I'd ever seen. It wasn't silver, or black, or cream—the only colors I'd ever associated with fridges—but rather a very unusual shade of powder blue.

It perfectly matched the oven beside it.

I vaguely remembered seeing appliances like these in an old colorized episode of *I Love Lucy* I saw when I was a kid. I got an odd, disoriented feeling when I tried to reconcile the idea that an ancient kitchen like this existed in a modern apartment.

So, I decided to stop trying and moved on to the picture of the bedroom. It was big, just like the Craigslist ad said. Somehow, it looked even more old-fashioned than the kitchen. The dresser was gorgeous, made of a dark wood I couldn't identify, with ornate curlicue carvings along the top and on the handles. It looked like something you might find at an antique show. The large, floral, probably homemade quilt covering the bed did, too.

As for the bed itself, it was an honest-to-god four-poster bed complete with a lacy white canopy hanging above it. The mattress was thick and looked sumptuous and comfortable.

I thought of all the shitty, secondhand furniture in my soon-to-be-former apartment. If I moved in here I could dump it all at a consignment shop.

These pictures, and the emails, suggested that while Frederick might be a lot older than me, he probably wouldn't steal all my stuff the day after I moved in.

I could handle an awkward roommate who was maybe in his seventies as long as he wasn't going to rob or kill me.

Then again, you could only tell so much from tone in an email.

From: Cassie Greenberg [csgreenberg@gmail.com]
To: Frederick J. Fitzwilliam [fjfitzwilliam@gmail.com]
Subject: Your apartment listing

Frederick,

Okay, those pictures are amazing. Your place looks great! I definitely want to see it, but I can't come by in the evening tomorrow until around 8. Is that too late? Let me know, and thanks.—Cassie

His next reply came in less than a minute.

From: Frederick J. Fitzwilliam [fjfitzwilliam@gmail.com]
To: Cassie Greenberg [csgreenberg@gmail.com]
Subject: Your apartment listing

Dear Miss Greenberg,

Eight o'clock tomorrow evening works perfectly with my
schedule. I will make sure to tidy up so that all looks as it
should when you arrive.

Yours in good health,
Frederick J. Fitzwilliam

Author photo by Gabriel Prusak

By day, **Jenna Levine** works to increase access to afford-able housing in the American South. By night, she writes humorous romance novels where everyone gets a happy ending. When Jenna isn't writing she can usually be found imagining she is hiking somewhere beautiful, start-ing knitting projects she won't finish, or spending time with her family and small army of cats.

VISIT JENNA LEVINE ONLINE

JennaLevine.com
JennaLevineWrites
Jeenonamit

Ready to find
your next great read?

Let us help.

Visit prh.com/nextread

Penguin
Random
House